A WANTED WOMAN

"Your turn," he said, his tone ominous.

"My turn for what?"

"To answer questions."

She retreated. Unreasonable fury and help-lessness warred inside Cord. No. He'd not let her walk away without giving him a part of herself in return.

"What is it *you* want, Wren?" His brows slanted low across his eyes. He kept advancing, slowly but inexorably. She kept retreating.

Her back bumped up against the wall, stopping her.

He towered over her.

Don't touch her, stop now, his conscience hissed. Bent on destruction, he ignored the warning and coasted his knuckles up her ribs on both sides.

He had to have more.

"You're so fine." His hands gently cupped both sides of her face. He look pained, as if he didn't want to do this but couldn't stop. His lips touched hers. Breakingly tender, as if he feared he'd shatter her with more pressure. She wanted to scream. To melt.

Other AVON ROMANCES

Coming Soon

And Don't Miss These
ROMANTIC TREASURES
from Avon Books

REBECCA WADE

A Wanted Woman

AVON BOOKS

An Imprint of HarperCollinsPublishers

This is a work of fiction. Names, characters, places, and incidents are products of the author's imagination or are used fictitiously and are not to be construed as real. Any resemblance to actual events, locales, organizations, or persons, living or dead, is entirely coincidental.

AVON BOOKS
An Imprint of HarperCollins*Publishers*
10 East 53rd Street
New York, New York 10022-5299

Copyright © 2000 by Rebecca Wade
ISBN: 0-380-81618-0
www.avonromance.com

First Avon Books paperback printing: November 2000

Avon Trademark Reg. U.S. Pat. Off. and in Other Countries, Marca Registrada, Hecho en U.S.A.
HarperCollins® is a trademark of HarperCollins Publishers Inc.

Printed in the U.S.A.

10 9 8 7 6 5 4 3 2 1

For Mom and Dad, with love.

To Mom, for sitting beside me on the couch, reading aloud, and introducing me to the wonder of books. For always being the first to believe I could do anything I set my mind to, the first to cheer me on, the first to celebrate my accomplishments. For your optimism, for your delicious biscuit breakfasts, and for loving me so well.

To Dad, for furnishing a home to grow up in where I felt safe. For playing "tickie" tickle monster, for the countless games of badminton and Uno, for throwing softballs, for knowing how to fix things, for doing the yucky jobs without complaining. For the laughs, for always hiding an Easter egg in your pocket, and for taking care of me so well.

*Thank you both
for giving me roots and wings.*

Prologue

Dallas, Texas
1872

She loved him. In mere moments, she'd tell him how she felt, he'd respond with pleasure—maybe say he wasn't worthy—and then they'd ride off together toward the moonlit horizon. A happy ending.

Wren Bradley was standing in the shadows outside the front door of her home, lying in wait. She'd excused herself from the dinner table ten minutes before, dashed to her bedroom, crawled through her bedroom window, climbed down the trellis out back, and scurried to her current tactical position.

She inched her head to the side and peered through the dining-room window. Despite the interfering lace curtain covering the object of her affection in a webbing of white, he looked absolutely beautiful to her.

Her heart squeezed so violently with longing that she moaned. Cord Caldwell was perfect. Not in a storybook-prince way. But in a way that awakened her dearest fantasies and sent all five of her senses to thrumming. He looked exactly like what she knew him to be—a man who chased criminals into the wilds of the West, into the vast, untamed places where no other officer of the law dared follow.

In his little finger he held more adventure than she'd sampled in the whole of her life. He could give her that— excitement. And so much more. She couldn't imagine ever again having cause to weep, or cuss, or fidget with restlessness if she had him for a husband.

She watched as her parents, sister, and Cord scooted back their chairs and rose from the table.

With a gasp, she jerked away from the window. Night shadows cascaded from the second story, encompassing her completely. She could hear muted conversation drawing closer as they approached the front door via the inner hallway.

Her hands started to shake, but more with supreme anticipation than terror. Her sister Alexandra and the majority of young women in . . . well, in America had harbored crushes on Cord Caldwell. Wren had adored him, too, for years, even though Alexandra continuously told her she was too young for him.

She wasn't too young for him anymore. Two months ago she'd turned sixteen, a perfectly respectable age to marry. And if she had to categorize the relationship that had blossomed between herself and Cord this past week, she would call it strictly adult.

They'd visited in a very meaningful way at Miss Hilliard's party, danced together twice night before last, and sat next to each other at the table tonight. On each occasion she'd sensed that his emotions toward her were as tender, as special, as *mature* as hers for him.

Of course, she'd have preferred it had she been able to allow their courtship more time to develop. But he was leaving tomorrow morning on another case for her father and the Pinkerton Agency. Each time he departed, his work kept him away from her for as long as eight months. She couldn't swallow her feelings and wait that long. No. Tonight she'd distinguish herself from all the other girls who coveted him but were too afraid to tell him so.

The front door swung open. She flattened herself against the red brick of the house.

Her family murmured their good-byes, Cord's heavenly voice returned them, and then he was stepping onto the landing. The door closed behind him, cutting away the golden slice of light that had illuminated him.

He buttoned the flaps of his coat together, then ducked his head and donned his Stetson one-handed. The hat was new, a creamy beige color, and so handsome on him that for a moment she thought she might faint from acute attraction.

Cord ambled down the steps and along the walkway toward the deserted street.

Wren recognized her opportunity. Her nerves were all leaping. Her knees shaking. Her lungs squeezing her heart too tightly. Yet she managed to pool every brazen cell in her body, and force out, "Cord."

He turned and squinted in her direction. "Is someone there?" he asked.

"Yes. It's me." She stepped forward, her shoes sinking into the soft earth of her mother's flower bed.

"Wren?" he said uncertainly as he approached.

He'd known it was her, had perhaps been secretly expecting her. Joy soared. "Yes, it's me, Cord."

He stopped before her. Smiled. She could barely make out his square jawline and dark hair beneath the brim of his hat.

"What are you doing out here?" he asked.

"I wanted to talk to you."

"Me?"

"Yes, you." She laughed. He had such a delightful sense of humor.

"Okay." He slung his hands into his pockets, gazed at her encouragingly.

"Well . . ." She cleared her throat, a sound that came out a tad less elegantly than one might have hoped. "I'd have waited to speak to you, if only you weren't leaving tomorrow. You are leaving tomorrow?"

"Yes."

"Right. And I do believe that a person ought to seize her opportunities. Don't you?"

"Absolutely."

He was a *man*. A rugged, honorable, dangerous man, who made all the fellows she knew look like children. She wanted him quite desperately. Wanted him to look at her with admiration and sensuality, dearly longed to be seen in public with him and acknowledged as the woman who'd stolen his affections.

"Cord. I believe that something quite precious, something to treasure, has developed between us over the past week. Oh, for longer than that," she rushed to say when he blanched, "because we've known each other through Pa for years, of course. But in this last week, our relationship has . . . heightened. I wanted to tell you . . ." She swallowed, gathered her courage. "I wanted to tell you that I care about you a great deal. In fact, I love you. And I think I could make you fall the rest of the way in love with me, too, if given the opportunity."

He didn't move, not the flutter of an eyelash, nothing.

She hurried to fill the silence. "Please take me with you when you go tomorrow. Give us the chance we deserve."

Still, he only stared.

"I can be packed and ready to go in thirty minutes."

"I . . ." He glanced away, wiped a hand down his face. "What about the boy your father introduced me to at the dance the other night?"

"Edward? I've known him all my life. We're only friends."

"Your father wants you to marry him, I think."

"Don't worry about my father and Edward. I won't let them come between us. You're the only one I want to marry."

He stepped back half a pace. She stepped forward the same distance, felt slightly sick all of a sudden now that she could see his expression in the light from the dining-room window. He was frowning.

"It's not that you're not lovely and sweet," he said, his tone consoling. "You are."

She didn't want to be lovely and sweet. She wanted him to be mad with passion for her.

"The trails I follow are no place to take a lady," he said.

"I'm hardier than I look," she assured him. "I *want* to go with you. I can sew and cook." So she'd fibbed there, but she was getting frantic, and fear was hounding her hard. "I can make myself useful to you."

"I'm sure you can. It's not that." He resettled his hat on his head, slanting it lower. His eyes turned apologetic. "I hate to hurt your feelings, but you're too young for me, and—"

"I'm sixteen."

"—while I like you as a person, very much, my feelings toward you aren't romantic."

Oh, Lordy. Shame and humiliation burned down her throat and curdled in her stomach. She'd been so sure he liked her. The horror of standing here, of having him tell her right to her face that he didn't like her *romantically*, was worse than death. Unbidden tears leapt to her eyes at the pain of it, the stunned mortification and utter desolation. How could she have been so wrong?

"I apologize if I misled you," he said.

She wanted to hiss that he *had* misled her, to blame everything on him, in order to deflect the attention from herself. She kept her lips closed. She'd only disgrace herself more, say some other awful thing she'd forever regret. Fervently, she vowed never to make a fool of herself before this man again.

A buggy trundled down the street and came to a jangling stop in front of their house. "Cord," a woman called. Wren recognized her as Miss Hilliard. The older woman shaded her eyes from the moonlight and leaned toward them. "Cord, is that you?"

Cord looked toward the buggy, and Wren furtively dashed at her eyes.

"Yeah, it's me," he said.

"Ready?" Miss Hilliard called.

"Be there in a second."

Wren stared at the woman helplessly, so miserable she could only hate her halfheartedly. Miss Hilliard was twice her age, college-educated, and rumored to be a woman who gave "favors" to men. Of course Cord liked her better.

"Is there something I can get you?" Cord asked her softly. "Water, or a handkerchief or something. I can summon your mother."

"No." He didn't understand the depth of her love for him at all if he thought a glass of water would fix this. She rolled her lips inward and clamped them with her teeth, trying to steady herself enough to speak one last sentence. The breath she sucked in wobbled. "The only favor I'd ask, is that you not tell anyone about this." Suppressed tears too clearly accented her words, and her voice had broken at the end, but at least she'd gotten it out with some shred of dignity.

"Of course," Cord said. He waited a moment more, surveying her.

She presented him with her profile.

He turned then, and walked away. She watched him climb into the buggy. Watched Miss Hilliard press a quick kiss to his lips. Watched as they trotted down the street and disappeared around the corner.

And all the while, for every torturous second, Wren stood in her mother's flower bed, in the dark, alone. And felt, physically felt with an agony that throbbed, her heart breaking.

Chapter 1

Dallas, Texas
Autumn, 1877

The last square of chocolate just sat there, a piece of heaven on a china saucer, begging to be eaten. "I shouldn't," Wren murmured, before scooping it up and popping it into her mouth.

"Oh." She closed her eyes and chewed as slowly as humanly possible. "Bliss." Her tongue swirled along the insides of her cheeks and the roof of her mouth, glorying in the dark sweetness, prolonging the ecstasy to a degree only the most advanced connoisseurs aspired to.

Finally, unfortunately, she had to swallow. Immediately afterward she realized that the best part of her day was over. It was the exact realization she had at this time every night when the chocolate went down.

She worried, quite seriously, that if she let her parents

have their way, she'd be sitting in this same seat sixty years from now, Edward by her side, watching through rheumy eyes as her mother wheeled herself in with the daily dose of chocolate.

During these months since her graduation last spring, she'd continued living with her parents as a matter of course. It was simply what unmarried women did. However, despite that she dearly loved Mother, Pa, and the undivided attention they lavished on her as their baby, she didn't know how much longer she could stand this dreary life.

When she'd been in school, she'd had studying, friends, and social activities to divert her. Absent those things, absent a purpose, it felt as if her life had fallen into a crack between sofa cushions. Jangling just under her skin was the growing need for *more* than days spent helping Cook with chores, running meaningless errands, and working needlepoint.

Had her father not been such a difficult man to disappoint, had she not loathed the thought of hurting her mother, and had her last and only heedless bid toward following her heart not ended so disastrously—she'd have snatched at her dreams long before now. As it was, those three daunting obstacles kept her waiting and hoping.

"Wren?"

She glanced toward her parents. They sat close beside each other on their dainty beige sofa. Last time she'd looked, they'd both been reading.

Her father was still engrossed in his book, but her mother was staring at her now, her head tilted to the side, a curl of gray-blond hair brushing her shoulder. "You haven't turned a single page in an hour's time."

Wren peeked at the open book in her lap, mildly surprised to find it sitting there. "That's because this particular prose," her fingertip waved over the print, "is just so lovely."

Her father's face lifted, and he regarded her with genuine interest in his brown eyes. "In that case, why don't you read it to us?"

The letters on the page solidified into words. For the first time, she noticed that the book upon her lap was the Bible, opened to Matthew I. She stifled a groan. "No, it's nothing, really—"

"C'mon, Precious," her father goaded. "Read it to us."

She cleared her throat. "Ah . . . Zerubbabel beget Abiud, Abiud beget Eliakim, Eliakim beget Azor, Azor beget Zadok." She shot them a dry grin. "Enough?"

Her mother laughed, and her father smiled in his subdued way from under the neatly trimmed edges of his beard. "You've been sitting there all this time, admiring Jesus' genealogy?" he asked.

Wren closed the Bible and placed it in its position upon the stack of books on the round marble-topped table beside her. "You caught me."

The evening's hush seeped into the parlor, enfolding it just as it had enfolded this same room every evening for the six years they'd lived here. Before that, it had enfolded their parlor in St. Louis and before that their parlor in Raleigh. The same twin vases sat atop the fireplace mantel, a triangular corner shelf held the same artifacts from her father's journeys, and the same tall clock sat in the hall counting the seconds of her passing life.

She fidgeted. The Dallas stock company would be rehearsing at this very moment. The smell of old cigars, the sight of the dimly lit stage, even the drafts that blew across her back when she visited beckoned to her. The sooner she excused herself to her room, the sooner she could escape this house in favor of the theater.

Her mother bookmarked her page and peered at Wren with concern. "What's wrong? Of late you've been acting . . . what's the word I'm looking for?"

"Strange," her father said.

"I think I'm just tired," Wren answered.

Both sets of eyebrows drifted upward simultaneously.

Pa shook his head. "You haven't been tired since the day you were born."

"Nor have you seemed happy since finishing school," Mother said.

"I've been happy."

"Wren," her mother chided. "It's Edward, isn't it? You miss him."

"Yes," Wren said, latching on to the excuse. She missed Edward escorting her places, laughing with her family, keeping her company. She didn't *ache* for him, though, and sometimes she worried that she should. Other times, she figured that not aching had its distinct advantages.

"How long has he been gone on this latest trip?" Mother asked.

Wren shrugged.

"Three months," Pa answered.

"That's a long time, Phillip."

"The board of directors for the railroad requested Edward specifically," her father answered. "He's only been with the Dallas office for two years, but he's proven himself a good accountant in that time. The best in fact, at auditing. The directors wanted him to visit all the station clerks across the South, bring them up to his standard through instruction."

"But he'll be home soon?" Mother asked.

"I expect him any day." Pa regarded Wren. "Then

you'll be engaged, and then married, and you'll have no cause to keep acting strange."

Wren smiled, pleased that he, at least, was pleased with his plans for her. Personally, they sounded dull to her, and somehow impossible. She simply couldn't play the part of wife and mother as well as her older sister Alexandra did. That her parents expected her to caused old resentments to shift within her.

"Until then, it might help to become more involved in the community," Mother suggested. "Have you considered the garden club?"

Wren cringed inside. She could just imagine herself entertaining visions of the theater while the ladies around her discussed the relative merits of larkspur versus foxglove. "No."

"How about the quilting bee?" Pa asked.

"Yes." Mother's face lit with enthusiasm. "I hear it's a lively group that meets down at the church vestry."

Lively indeed. She needed to stop this quick. "No, thank you, though. About the only things I'm interested in these days are acting and singing."

Both her parents visibly stiffened at the oft-repeated sentiment. Her mother's forehead creased, and her father's dark eyes turned guarded. He wasn't the sort of man who lost his temper. He'd been in the military, so issuing orders in a steely-quiet voice, then watching hawkishly as they were followed, was more like him.

Wren sighed. She wasn't up for a lecture tonight, so she crossed toward them. "G' night." She kissed her mother.

"Sleep well, darling."

"G' night, Pa." She doled out his kiss.

"Good night, Precious."

She was almost to the stairs when her mother called, "I've more chocolate for tomorrow night."

Unfortunately, tomorrow night's chocolate seemed small consolation. Probably because the chocolate was so many hours away. Tomorrow afternoon, when the chocolate was nearer, she'd feel better.

She climbed the stairs, still mining with her tongue for a remnant of the sweet hiding in her gums.

Her room was the smallest on the second floor, squeezed between her parents' suite and the chamber Alexandra had occupied before her marriage. Usually she liked the cheerful yellows and pinks of her room. Tonight the pastel colors seemed childish, and the walls enclosing her felt more like a cage than a sanctuary.

The mirror above the dresser framed her reflection as she smoothed two wayward blond tufts at her forehead and straightened the chain of her locket, which had, predictably, wound itself into a knot.

She pulled her black, velvet-lined cape onto her shoulders, then doused the lamp. Beyond her window, Dallas's modest skyline rested beneath a star-studded sky. She'd spent so many nights peering at this view that she knew every detail by heart. Knew where the streets became walking paths that became fields. Knew by name each and every star she'd wished upon.

She pressed open the two halves of the window and leaned into the night breeze. A lone rider plodded along the street below before passing out of sight. She looked both ways and didn't spot a single neighbor peering at her from behind curtains. Without hesitation, she climbed onto the roof.

If her father ever found out about her evening excursions, he'd bolt her window, dismantle the trellis, and inform her with rigidly controlled anger how hugely disappointed he was in her. Risking that was the price she paid to taste excitement occasionally and be free, if only for a few hours, from her crushing sense of boredom.

Bracing her toes on the gutter, she sidestepped across the inclined shingles to the spot where the trellis filled with morning glory provided a makeshift ladder into the back garden.

This was the trickiest part. She stepped one foot off the gutter into the void of black air and sent it questing for the trellis. Occasionally, she had nightmares about her parents waking one morning to find her sprawled in the grass beneath a crowd of gawking morning glory, wearing a cape and an expression of deathly surprise.

But next to the chocolate, her trips to the theater were her greatest pleasure. She concentrated on finding a foothold. There were some things in life a girl simply had to risk plunging to her death to enjoy.

She climbed down the trellis, jumped the last few feet, and landed in a crouch on cool strands of grass. It was still mild out, but she could feel autumn coiling in the earth and smell its crispy scent nipping at the wind.

She hurried out the side gate, which she oiled daily to ensure silent passage, and rushed down the vacant street, a grin pulling her cheeks tight. She loved this part. Running alone through Dallas at night challenged her courage, tested her heart, and provided her with a thrilling miniature adventure.

She always followed a different route to City Hall, not only because she didn't want to attract attention, but because varying the routine kept things interesting.

Tonight she cut through the backyards of two homes, ducked beneath the walnut trees of Mr. Minor's orchard, and hastened down Commerce Street before dodging into the alley that ran along the side of City Hall.

The back entrance, which consisted of an unmarked door set in the middle of the white clapboard wall was, as usual, open. She climbed the cramped stairwell past the first-floor door, which led to the market, and past the second-floor door, which led to the Spurs Club and newspaper headquarters. She stopped where the stairs ended, at the landing christened "3" in glossy black paint. Her breath puffing, she threw back the door and entered the world of her dreams.

There it was, the smell of half-smoked cigars she'd been missing. That scent, combined with those of sawdust, glue, and kerosene, greeted her. She inhaled the fragrance as she wove behind the large pieces of scenery stored next to the stage and made her way to the last row of the gigantic room. She always sat in the last seat of the last row, where the distance mostly obscured her. For years, the director had allowed her to sit and watch. Mostly, she suspected, because she eagerly volunteered whenever they needed a hand with props or costumes.

She freed the clasp beneath her chin and slipped off her cape without taking her attention from the rehearsal playing out onstage. Dim lighting hid in the folds of the red-satin curtain, shone on the silver hair of an aging actor, and warmed the otherwise humorless face of an actress in a tight-waisted green gown. They were in the middle of rehearsing *Rip Van Winkle*.

Yearning panged sharp and urgent within her, like the hunger pains of one starving. She'd wanted to be included in the theater's magic since attending her first show at seven years of age. Her Aunt Fanny had taken both her and Alexandra to a performance that night. Wren had worn her best white dress with a blue-satin sash. She'd sat

in a straight-backed chair just like this one and been swept
into an unforgettable world of drama and imagination.

The same overwhelming awe she'd experienced then
still pricked her skin and snagged her emotion every
time. There was nothing like it on earth. The hush when
the lights went down, the tragedy, the music, the beauty
of the words, the thunderous applause. It had the power
to transport, an ability she'd craved especially when she
was sixteen and inconsolable with lovesickness and private embarrassment. Her clandestine trips to the theater
had started then, and continued ever since.

Suddenly, the actors stopped mid-scene and launched
into a debate about staging.

She watched them with a mixture of envy, profound
respect, and more than a little desperation. Deeply, she
wanted to be up there with them. She liked to think she
might have been if it weren't for the fact that this company only held auditions when one of their players,
well . . . died. So she'd struggled to content herself with
semiannual music-academy recitals, monologues practiced alone in her room, and these solitary visits.

What was it about this place, about acting, that was
like a balm to her? She weighed her heart. Certainly, the
theater presented her with an escape from her routine life.

No, that didn't begin to do justice to its appeal for her.

On stage, the parts of her personality that some viewed
as socially unsavory in a woman—her openness, her
impetuousness, her passionate nature, became strengths
instead of weaknesses. When acting, she felt vital and talented and whole. She flourished on stage, adored riding
the swells of her own creativity.

Mostly, though, in her heart of hearts, she treasured her
dream of becoming an actress because it was the one thing

in her life that belonged completely to her. It wasn't a hand-me-down aspiration of Alexandra's, it wasn't one of her father's expectations, or her mother's hopes. It was just . . . hers. Her love. If she could carve out a career in the theater despite her parents' staunch disapproval, it would mean she'd come into her own as a woman and an actress.

Unexpected emotion tightened her throat. Pathetic to feel sorry for herself, she who'd been raised by a doting family, who'd never missed a meal or a warm night's sleep. Her vision blurred nonetheless, causing the hardwood floor to float up the four feet height of the stage and mesh with the dusty skirts of the actress in the green dress.

The players picked up where they'd left off and dialogue coasted comfortingly over her.

Cord Caldwell sat at the Spurs Club bar on a stool that was just uncomfortable enough to keep him alert and just comfortable enough to tempt him to order a drink.

Not that he would, unfortunately. He never knew when he'd need his aim to be dead-on or his head to be clear. On this particular evening he was dearly hoping for the need of both.

Cord gazed at the bartender, who was filling glasses for a trio of middle-aged gentlemen. All three were nicely dressed and looked to be passing through, as he was.

In a glance, he memorized the distinguishing features of the newcomers as well as their height and manner.

He checked the clock behind the bar. The place would be open for several more hours. As he'd done the past two nights, he'd stay until it closed, waiting to see if Sackett showed.

He'd tracked Sackett here from Little Rock two days ago, then lost his trail. Old Billy Templeton, who was nursing a whiskey at the corner table shrouded in a haze of gray-ish smoke, was now his best connection to the train robber. Billy and Sackett had been childhood friends, raised in the same hometown. The agency suspected that Billy had done groundwork for the Sackett brothers in recent years.

Cord never overlooked connections like that. If Sackett was still in Dallas, and Cord's instincts said he was, then chances were decent he'd be anxious for an ally. Eventually he'd contact Billy.

"Can I get you some more food or somethin'?"

Cord lifted his gaze to the bartender. "I don't think so."

"Coffee, then?"

"Sure. Thanks."

The bartender picked up his wash rag and moved away, wiping the top of the bar with long, circular strokes.

Cord shifted on his stool. No, still damned uncomfortable. He hooked a bootheel over the stool's crosspiece and thrummed his knuckles on the bar's edge.

Patience had always been one of his strong suits, he thought wryly. But since the agency had taken away his badge three weeks ago, he'd had none. Nothing wry about that.

Until he could get his job back he was worthless.

He could taste his desperation as strongly as he was certain it was stupid to be this desperate. Jesus, he needed to bring Sackett down. His honor had been called into question, his life's work suspended, and the only person who could clear his name was the sonofabitch outlaw Lloyd Sackett.

Cord gritted his teeth and peered toward the door.

"That's enough for tonight, everyone," the director called. "See you in the morning."

Wren watched the small troupe roll their scripts and walk tiredly backstage.

Sighing, she slipped her cloak over her shoulders. The actors were sleepy and deserved rest. Still, seeing them go deflated her. It was the same sensation that drooped over her on Christmas after all the presents were opened and the meal finished.

She told herself it was time to return home. Told her legs to start walking. Instead she remained immobile, tucking her surroundings into her memory, feeling the draft swirling across her back, listening to the company's murmurs, and trying to steal a word here and there.

She waited until everyone had gone except for her and a junior actor who started making his way around the room, dousing the lamps. As she walked toward the back stairwell, a small sign caught her eye. It had been tacked to the board the troupe used for posting announcements.

Wren stopped, curiosity pricking her.

NOTICE. Markham's Traveling Troupe of Players will hold open auditions for cast members November tenth, ten in the morning, Berryhill's Hall, Austin, Texas.

She blinked. "Oh," she breathed, wonder and air leaking from her in a reverent stream. The audition was to be held in just under three weeks.

It was like God had opened the heavens to shine His light upon this plain piece of white paper with black writing. In her eyes, it had acquired a pulsing, mythical gleam.

One hand, then the other, lifted to cover her heart.

How long had it been posted? Surely she hadn't missed it before, containing as it did such glaring allure.

They must have tacked it up today. Yes. It had been ordained that she read it at exactly this moment. It had been ordained *for her*.

She could almost hear the angels humming.

Cord spotted Sackett the instant the train robber filled the door to the Spurs Club.

Everything about Sackett was chillingly familiar to Cord. The blade-thin nose, scraggly copper hair, pale eyes. Even the brown duster hanging on his wiry body.

All Cord's hunter's instincts rushed to life, firing his heartbeat. He rested his elbows on the bar and hunched forward, intent on masking his face until Sackett had walked more fully into the establishment, and farther from escape.

Cord stared at the bar's shiny wooden surface; his peripheral vision homed in on his prey.

He'd gotten him. After three damned weeks, he'd gotten him. His body twitched with the need to take action, to trap Sackett while he had the chance.

Bring him in alive. He repeated that to himself over and over, so that he'd remember it without having to think if things got heated. He needed Sackett to talk and set the record straight.

He heard the thud of Sackett's boots as he made his way to Billy.

Cord glanced up, watched Sackett lower himself into a chair, then reached slowly and subtly for his guns.

Immediately, Sackett's gaze swung to him. The outlaw sprang from his chair, his hand flying toward his weapon.

Cord was off his stool quicker, a six-shooter in either hand. "It's over, Sackett."

The outlaw froze, fingers less than an inch from his hip holster. The bar's chatter cut to silence.

"Look who's here," Sackett sneered, appearing to relax. "God damned Caldwell."

All around them, men rose smoothly to their feet, making ready to run or hide.

Cord moved toward Sackett and simultaneously angled toward the exit, intent on blocking it.

Sackett's attention sliced to the door, then back at Cord. Disgust and something akin to humor twisted his lips in the twinkling before he hauled his gun free and started blasting.

Cord swore and dived to the ground, rolling away from the hail of bullets.

Sackett dashed past him to the door, emptying his last chamber as he ducked into the hallway beyond.

With a lunge, Cord gained his feet and sprinted after him into the corridor. There was no sign of Sackett in the direction of the public stairway.

From the other end of the hall he heard a door bang closed. He stashed one gun as he ran. When he reached the untitled door, he threw it back and stepped into a narrow stairwell.

Sackett's boots clanged down the flight below. Cord raced after him, taking three steps at a time, catching himself against the walls to stay upright before barreling forward. The sound of Sackett's steps disappeared into a squeal of hinges.

Cord hurtled down the final flight, tossed aside the door, and plunged into the blackened alley beyond. He looked both ways. Nothing.

Cursing under his breath, he rushed to the alley's Main Street opening. Nothing. He swiveled and saw Sackett run from where he'd been crouching, behind the back door that was just now swinging closed.

Cord ripped free his second gun and cocked both weapons.

At the sound of the hammers clicking back, Sackett slashed to a halt.

"Get your hands were I can see them," Cord said, his voice pitched level.

Sackett groaned, raised his hands, and grudgingly turned to face him. "You gonna shoot me, Caldwell?"

Cord assessed Sackett's options as he advanced, mentally preparing for his prey to draw, or run.

"Is that what you're gonna do?" Sackett asked. "Whose gonna straighten out your little problem with the agency, if it ain't me, then?"

The taunting tone of Sackett's voice grated along the rubble of Cord's patience. "Shut up, Sackett."

"You know as well as I do. You need me—"

Suddenly, the door flew open and a trim figure in a black cape dashed out.

Cord reached instinctively to intercept her—He was yards away.

Sackett, just feet from the door, snatched the woman against him and pressed the muzzle of his gun to her head.

A feminine scream tore into the night.

Chapter 2

Ice slashed Cord's heart. "Put her down."

"Yeah?" Sackett sneered. "You'd like that, wouldn't you? Who you gonna shoot now, big detective? The girl?"

"No, still you, Sackett. I swear, if you hurt her—"

"Hurt her?" Sackett jerked the girl backward, toward Commerce Street. "Why would I hurt her? This pretty little thing and I are getting on real good." He caressed her cheek and temple with the gun's muzzle as he drew her backward. "Aren't we, honey?"

Sweat rolled into Cord's eyes. He blinked it furiously away. *God damn it.* The tips of his forefingers shifted over the triggers, yearning to pull back. To fight. There wasn't a damn thing he could do to help her, except bluff.

He lifted his right hand and leveled his Remington at Sackett's head. He couldn't get a steady shot and

23

wouldn't risk injuring the girl even if he could. "Put her down, and you keep your life."

Sackett ducked, hiding his face behind her neck and shoulders. "I'd rather hold on to her, and keep my life that way."

Cord narrowed his eyes and his aim.

"Take that gun off me!" Sackett yelled, his voice screeching. "I'll put a bullet in her brain. I swear I will!"

He wasn't going to free the girl, Cord realized with sickening clarity. He eased down the point of his gun, unwilling to agitate Sackett further.

He wished he could see her better. He couldn't make out her features except for the shine of wide, terrified eyes and a wisp of blond hair. She was gulping for air.

"Take it easy." He raised his voice to be sure she heard. "He's mean, but he's not stupid enough to hurt you." God, he hoped not. He did this job to make things right. Not for this, not to see innocent people dragged into the fray.

Sackett snorted. "Big Pinkerton detective. Real big detective." He nailed Cord with a grin. A grin of victory. A grin that sent fury roiling through Cord's stomach and screams of injustice howling through his ears. If anything happened to the girl . . . He wouldn't *let* anything happen.

Wren couldn't get any air. The man had his arm around her, trapping her, crushing her chest.

Shock had frozen her at first. Now it was fleeing hard, and there wasn't anything to soften the reality of what couldn't, *couldn't* be happening to her. The gun was digging cold and sharp into her temple. He might pull the trigger at any moment. Would it even hurt? she wondered frantically. The metal as it tore into her skull? In that quick second would she even know she was dying?

The outlaw's mouth was close to her ear, breathing strong and yelling to the man at the far end of the alley. The Pinkerton, her captor had said. He was a Pinkerton. He'd fight for her.

Her teeth rattled with the force of her trembling.

She latched her vision and her hope on the detective. He'd spoken kindly to her. He'd said to take it easy. She needed to. She couldn't breathe. Her captor was going to shoot her in the head. And kill her—She didn't want to die.

The detective had guns. He could help her. It was dark, but she could tell that he was tall and ferociously strong-looking. He'd come for her.

A figure materialized from Main Street, behind the detective. Thank God, he could help them—

The stranger raised a gun behind the detective. She tried to scream a warning, but nothing came. Lungs felt like tar.

The stranger brought his weapon down on the back of the detective's head. She watched in horror as the detective crumpled to the alley floor.

A gag constricted her throat. No! He was all she had.

The outlaw jerked her ruthlessly back.

"No!" The word was less than a breath. Nothing.

The alley yanked from view and streetlamps careened in her deadened vision.

"You say anything, you try to scream again, and I'll kill you," her captor snarled. "You understand?"

She nodded, battling for breath. She should have fought. Should have tried earlier to assist the detective. Now there was no one.

"Same outcome if you try and struggle," he warned.

A sob ripped from her lips.

He wrenched her from her feet and threw her stomach down across the front of a saddle. He was behind her and they were moving, moving away from town, from home, from anyone who could assist her.

More sobs followed the first, uncontrollable. She pressed her fist against her lips, trying to muffle their sound, lest he shoot her for them.

Jarring pain ripped through her belly. The ground flew beneath. Pounding hooves and the sound of reins slapping horseflesh echoed in her ears.

And all Wren could think, over and over, was that she couldn't die before her life had even begun.

Cord came to with his face in the dirt.

Groggily, he flattened his palms in the alleyway grime and pushed to his knees. He shook his head, trying to clear it. The lights fuzzing around the opening of the passageway spun slowly into focus.

What had happened? He tested the back of his neck with his fingertips and winced at the pain radiating down his head to his shoulders.

He'd been running after Sackett. He squinted at the door. They'd come out there. Then faced off. Then—

The girl.

God, Sackett had the girl.

He staggered to his feet and ran a hand through his hair. She needed him. He had to think straight.

A quick scan of the alley confirmed there wasn't anyone left. No sign of Sackett or Billy, who must have been the one that clobbered the back of his neck. He listened, but heard nothing except the sound of distant laughter and the squeaking of a wagon harness. There was no telling how long he'd been out.

He picked up his guns, which had fallen to the earth, and started to walk, then run, with ground-eating strides.

He could recall it clearly now, the girl being dragged toward the mouth of the alley, with her big eyes and her blond hair. His mouth went dry.

He examined the markings in the dirt where he'd last seen Sackett. He could clearly make out Sackett's footprints and the lighter imprint of the girl's toes bumping along the earth. He followed the trail to Commerce Street where the glow of a streetlamp revealed a jumble of footprints combined with hoofprints. Sackett had mounted his horse.

Cord's head was spinning.

He looked up, waited for his vision to fall into place, then returned to studying the tracks for sign of a woman's step walking away. There was no such evidence, which meant Sackett had taken the girl with him.

"Damn it to hell." He peered down the sleeping street, lit at intervals by lampposts. What had he done?

As quickly as he could manage, he followed the hoofprints of Sackett's horse. He knew the set well, had been following them for three grueling weeks. Three weeks that should have come to an end tonight.

And now this. This was worse than before. Against orders, he'd followed Sackett. In doing so, he'd endangered an innocent girl.

Four storefronts down, in front of the Union Hotel, his horse waited where he'd hidden him. The small exertion of mounting sent teeth-grinding pain spearing through his head. Grimacing against it, he set the animal into motion.

Twice, he had to slow the pace when Sackett's prints disappeared in the webbing of other, older prints. Both times he picked Sackett up again and continued.

Cord wanted to believe he'd find the girl untouched, but he remembered too well the carnage Sackett had left behind other times. Sackett was capricious. He let some live and murdered some. The bloody memories of those he'd murdered swam to the surface and whispered to him that he was too late. That she was dead. That it was his fault.

Angrily, he reached into his jacket and pulled out his compass and gloves. In the waning light of the city he confirmed the direction that his instincts had advocated. Due south.

The town passed in a mosaic of color, trading its artificial light for the silvery glow of a nearly full moon. Plenty enough for him to see with.

In his mind's eye he imagined himself finding her, throat slit. Raped. The pounding in his head intensified until it was all he heard.

His horse took eagerly to the trail, galloping with dogged, loyal determination. They swerved around an outcropping of rock and were cutting deep into the open prairie when Cord saw it. A pale swath of color.

"Whoa." A slight movement of his thighs, and the animal slowed. Cord's vision was well accustomed to darkness and trained to see things other men never would. But he couldn't identify what he'd spotted. It looked more phantom than real.

He forced down a swallow, praying to God it was the girl—unhurt. As he neared, the inky lines of a cape distinguished themselves.

It *was* her, lying in a heap on the ground. The pale color he'd seen was the pink of her gown where the cloak had fallen open. He vaulted from his horse and ran toward her, searching for a sign of movement.

There was none.

Shaking inside, he knelt beside her. Just as he reached out to touch her, she turned her head and peered up at him from beneath the ebony cover of her hood.

Relief poured through his limbs, loosening muscles he hadn't known were clenched.

She pushed to her elbows. He wasn't much given to fanciful thoughts, but under the shadow of her hood, her eyes glimmered like opals. The strand of silky hair he recalled from earlier floated on the breeze. "You," she whispered. "You were the man in the alley?"

"Yes. Are you injured?"

Her exhale swayed on the night air. "No."

Nonetheless, he pulled off his gloves and pushed away the sides of her cape. Her clothing was rumpled, but intact. Gently, he ran his hands over her shoulders, her arms, along the bodice covering her slender waist. She tensed when he passed over her stomach. "Does it hurt here?"

"No."

He pressed the pads of his fingers against her abdomen. Though she tried, she couldn't hide a wince.

"He's getting away," she said softly.

Cord glanced southward. Topping a rise in the distance, moonlit dust unfurled in Sackett's wake. *So damned close*. And as far as the moon.

He'd seen enough injuries over the years to know that one like hers could bleed internally. She needed a doctor, and if he succeeded at nothing else tonight, he'd get her one. He owed her that.

"Go after him," she urged.

He watched Sackett's dust disintegrate and scatter to the earth, knowing every disappearing fleck of it reflected the death of his hard-won chance to clear his name.

"Go," she said. "I can see on your face that you want to."

He did want to. But he wanted to see her safely home more. He peered into her hooded features. "I'm not leaving you."

"I'll be fine."

"No."

She rested a delicate hand on his arm. "I want him to pay for what he did."

Her touch burned his skin, even through the layers of his clothing. Surprisingly intimate. "He'll pay," Cord answered. "I give you my word on that. As soon as I take you home I'll start out after him."

She stilled, seeming to consider his words. Then she nodded and slid her hand away. "Who is he?"

"A train robber named Lloyd Sackett."

"Who you've been tracking."

"Yes."

She levered herself into a sitting position, which forced an almost inaudible groan from her.

"Did he throw you across his saddle?" Cord asked.

"Mm-hm. I think I'll have a permanent saddle-horn-shaped indention where my navel used to be." Her words were faint, but steady. She attempted a chuckle.

He graced her with a smile he'd patented a decade before to use on women in distress. "Take a deep breath."

She did.

"Another." She wasn't wheezing, which reassured him. He sat back on his bootheels and regarded her.

"May I tell you a small secret?" Her tone was lighter than before, friendly.

"Anything."

"I'm glad you stayed with me. I was pretending to be noble before." She drew off her hood and moonlight washed over her face.

She was a raving beauty.

Even dropped in a pile next to a scrubby bunch of switch grass, she looked like one of the china dolls his mother had kept behind glass when he was young. Her dancing eyes had a feline slant to them at the inner corners. Her cheekbones were high and defined, her nose slender, her lips surprisingly full. She'd pulled her blond hair into an upsweep, which was mussed from the ordeal, but surviving. God, she had one of those extremely rare faces, the kind that appeared to have been formed by a master sculptor. His memory stirred. Her face held a ghost of something familiar.

"What about you?" she asked. "Are you hurt?"

"No."

She eyed him skeptically. "I saw how hard he hit you."

Idiotic. He'd been so focused on Sackett, and on her, he'd been unaware of Billy's approach. "I should have heard him come up behind me."

"Impossible. I saw him. He was walking very, very quietly." She tested a smile on him. A smile that brimmed with light and humor. So broad it coaxed the apples of her cheeks to stand out and made him wonder if this particular china doll looked as good in her drawers as she did in her dress-up clothes.

That was an evil thought to have about someone who'd just been used, abused, and dumped into the prairie. Even so, his body was reacting with primal hunger to her nearness, hardening. He imagined stretching her hands over her head and lowering on top of her, right here. Testing her mouth to see if it tasted as good as it looked. Freeing her breasts and spreading her thighs—

God, he'd been on the trail too long, denied his body for too many weeks. He'd been managing the lack of a woman fine up until now. All the pent-up lust was unleashing in a torrent, hammering through him, making him feel like a rutting dog.

She tilted her head, and he experienced another flash of recognition.

"Do you know who I am?" she asked.

"You look familiar." He frowned. "Why . . . do you know who I am?"

"Cord Caldwell," she replied instantly.

Well, this was awkward. He rarely forgot faces, especially ones like hers. "When did we last meet?"

"Five years ago, in front of Number Twelve Vine Street."

That didn't make sense. Colonel Bradley and his family were the only people he knew who lived on—His gut tightened. Hell, no. Surely he wasn't this unlucky. "Wren?" he said doubtfully, hoping he was wrong.

"Yes."

"Wren Bradley?"

"I'm afraid so."

He jerked away from her as fast as if he'd touched a sizzling brand. He pushed to his feet. A moment ago, he'd thought the situation awkward. He hadn't known the half of it.

Memories of that night five years ago came crowding back. He'd stood in the Colonel's yard in the dark like an imbecile while she'd broadsided him with declarations of love. Love. Hell, even if he'd not been a man who'd sworn off ever loving any woman, she'd not have been the one for him.

If he recalled correctly, she'd even asked him to take her out on the trail. He'd been painfully embarrassed for her, and frustrated with himself because in those days he'd had no idea how to let her down gently without shattering her sweetness. And she had been sweet.

She'd also, at the time, looked about twelve years old to him. In those days, her body had been overly skinny, her breasts masked beneath yards of girlishly chaste fabric, her hairstyle a poor attempt at something much too old for her, and her mouth two times too big for her small-boned face.

His eyes narrowed. The woman before him, with her well-rounded breasts and a mouth that fit her face, bore few vestiges of the girl she'd been.

Cord wiped a hand down his cheeks and chin and tried to digest the load of crap he'd just landed himself in. The Colonel was his boss, and the man he respected most on earth. Seconds ago he'd been . . . been fantasizing about the Colonel's baby daughter, for Christ sake.

Her father called her some pet name, like pumpkin or something. Deary. No, precious. *Precious.* Goddamned precious. Who was apparently waiting for him to say something.

"I haven't seen you around lately," he said, knowing how weak that sounded even as it passed his lips.

"Whenever you've come to town I've taken pains to avoid you."

"Have you?" he asked, because he didn't know how else to respond to such honesty.

"Yes. But I want you to know that I don't blame you in the least for what happened"—she gestured from herself to him—"between us. You handled yourself with perfect respectability. It was I who was unforgivably naive back then."

"Not unforgivably."

Her expression turned dubious.

"We all do things like that when we're young," he said.

"Did you ever profess to love a woman nine years your senior on the basis of a few dances and some snippets of small talk?"

"No."

"No. I didn't think so." Her lips bowed upward in a kindly smile. "Anyway, there's no reason for you or me to be uncomfortable. I'll strive hard not to hold your rejection of me against you"—self-deprecating warmth glittered in her eyes—"if you'll try not to hold my disgrace against me."

"I never did."

Wren studied Cord from beneath her lashes. Her scare had left her feeling all jittery inside. Like someone had taken her apart, shaken everything hard, then put her back together. Maybe that's why she was having so much trouble believing *the* Cord Caldwell had been the man in the alley. The man to rescue her. The man looking at her now with such intensity.

Fate had a nasty sense of humor sometimes.

"I'll go and get my horse," he said.

"Okay."

For five years and four months, she'd dodged any and every chance of running into him. Which hadn't stopped her from thinking of him often, and wincing every time.

. . . That wasn't quite true. Occasionally she didn't wince. There had been times, late at night when drifting off to sleep, when she'd entertained the fantasy that Cord truly did care for her, but had heroically sacrificed his tender emotions to her own best interests. He'd left her at home so she'd be safe, but had pined for her since, and searched for her frantically whenever he rode through Dallas.

She supposed she could safely put that fantasy to rest after his puzzled "You look familiar" comment.

As she watched him pat his horse on the neck, she grudgingly admitted that the man had done well for himself in the past five years. He was practically a legend now. No, not practically. He *was* a legend. Everyone in these parts knew of his accomplishments with the Pinkerton Agency. He'd caught or killed every outlaw he'd ever tracked. Usually quickly, and with more brains and daring than his counterparts.

Though she'd secretly hoped he'd aged badly—gone all to fat or lost his hair—he was heaven to look at. Even more so than she remembered, if that were possible.

He walked toward her, leading his horse.

His square jaw proclaimed him to be a man who knew how to give and receive punches. He had sinfully dark eyes, calculating enough to measure a threat at a glance. And a nose that bore evidence of having been broken once or twice. She could well imagine his brown hair, a little long in front but neat over the ears, dripping with exertion. At the moment it was tousled with wind. . . .

"Whatever happened to your hat?" she asked.

"My hat?"

"You used to wear a hat."

He reached up to where a brim would have been, seemed surprised to find it missing. "Still do. Must have left it at the club in my haste." He extended his hand. "I better be getting you back."

He helped her to her feet. She walked as upright as she could with a knot of pain for a stomach.

"I'll set you in the saddle," he offered.

"I can do it." She was terrified to find out how her body might respond if he wrapped his hands around her waist. After placing her foot in the stirrup, she twisted as she rose so that she perched sidesaddle.

He climbed onto the horse's rump behind the saddle, reached around both sides of her, and picked up the reins.

She sucked in a breath. Lordy, this was intimate.

He clicked his tongue, a throaty sound that caused her to jump. His horse started forward.

The heat of his muscled chest pulsed against her back. She could feel his breath flirting with the sensitive skin at the nape of her neck.

"You comfortable?" he asked.

She jumped again, unable to help herself. "Yes."

"Stomach okay?"

"Yes. The horse can go faster if you want."

"We'll go slow."

She stared at the blunt, powerful hands holding the reins. They were different than the hands of the men she knew. They weren't the soft-skinned hands of a gentleman, nor the dirty-nailed hands of a workman. They were somewhere in the middle. Clean, but hard. The hands of an elegant savage.

As they plodded over one acre then another, she racked her brain for some figment of witty conversation. Nothing occurred to her. She already knew everything about the past five years of his life from what Pa and Alexandra had told her. Even if she hadn't, she wouldn't have asked anyway for fear he'd think her interested in him again. "Want to hear a joke?"

Silence. Then, "Okay."

"Newlyweds sat down to dinner together. The bride said, 'My best two dishes are meat loaf and apple dumplings.' The husband took a bite and replied, 'Which one is this?' " She laughed easily.

To her chagrin, she didn't hear a single peep of laughter from behind her. She glanced over her shoulder.

He grinned. Despite the shadows in his eyes, despite that he'd lost his criminal, he grinned.

A thrill of satisfaction welled in her. For the first time

since Sackett had snatched her against him, everything in the world became right again. With Cord's power surrounding her, she felt completely and unutterably safe. Not Sackett, nor any other dark force, would dare touch her now.

She knew she wasn't exactly in her right mind, realized these thoughts weren't at all wise. Still, a person who'd endured what she had tonight was allowed some leniency. She'd swear that sitting a horse with Cord Caldwell's arms around her was actually better than chocolate.

So much resolve molded Cord's lips, that the half smile he was giving her now heralded more danger than humor. Delicious, sensual danger. It was a subtle curl of a smile she was positive a thousand women had swooned for. She had once been one of them.

Abruptly, she faced his horse's ears.

The scattered points of lights that outlined Dallas were nearing, but she still had a bit of time with him left to survive. "Interested in hearing another joke?" she asked.

This time he did chuckle. The sound of it coasted over her like a caress, as if his fingertips were stroking her earlobes, her shoulder blades, the swell of her hips. "I'd be more interested to know what you were doing running out the back door of City Hall so late at night."

"I was there to watch the actors and actresses rehearsing."

"Does your father know about your outing?"

"Not yet," she said, heart sinking. "I think it would be in both our best interests if we kept this between us."

He turned the horse's head down the street that led to her neighborhood.

"You can let me off there," she said, pointing, "by old man Sawyer's house. I'll return home the way I left, and no one will be the wiser."

In truth, her plan sounded damned appealing to Cord. He'd have loved to let her off, ride after Sackett, and strike this whole incident from memory. But what he wanted, and even what she wanted, didn't qualify.

Wishes weren't worth crap. He dealt with what *was*, and the reality here was that she needed a doctor. Whatever that meant for him, it meant.

"So?" Wren asked.

"I'm taking you to the front door."

For the second time, she looked around at him.

Damn, she was beautiful. Physical awareness throbbed within him, uninvited. He could imagine the slide of her pretty little tongue between his lips, the silky way her breasts would feel naked—

His boss's daughter.

"I'm not hurt badly, if that's what's worrying you."

He shrugged.

"You don't understand," she said, an edge of distress in her voice. "It'll cost me something important to confess."

He guided his horse onto her street and toward Number Twelve, the stately brick home with the white eyebrow-looking cornices over the windows. "Even so," he said, "we tell the truth."

She turned away.

He couldn't help thinking she had no idea what it meant to pay a price. What would it cost her when her parents discovered she'd sneaked out? A new party dress? Evenings at home basking in their adoration instead of out wandering the streets of Dallas?

Wren Bradley was as pampered—and as loved—as a child could be. She, living her perfect life on this perfect street, had no idea how lucky she was.

Not that he blamed her for her luck. China dolls were

supposed to sleep in playhouses under silken sheets. They were supposed to be handled carefully. This fine woman, with her beauty and her courage and her laughter, belonged here. She was the sort of dream, tucked away in her innocence, that kept him on the job year after year.

When Cord stopped before her home, he dismounted and reached up for her. She shook her head. With a sigh, he moved away and watched her ease slowly to the ground. Disappointment apparent in her posture, she led him to the glossy black door, knocked once, and jerked the brass bellpull twice.

She shot him a look out of the corner of her eyes. "Pa's a heavy sleeper."

He nodded as a lamp lit in a room directly above. The curtain pulled back, and the Colonel's wife peered out. The woman's eyes widened, and the curtain fell back into place.

"Thank you."

He glanced at her, unsure he'd heard her right. She didn't owe him thanks. He hadn't been able to save her when he should have.

"This is probably the last chance I'll get to say it," she said. "Thank you, that is."

"It was nothing."

"It most definitely was not nothing."

He was about to disagree when a lock turned and the door swung back. The Colonel and his wife stood on the other side of the threshold wearing matching wine-colored dressing gowns.

The Colonel looked at Wren, at Cord, then back at Wren. "What's happened?"

"I went to the theater tonight," Wren answered.

"What?" her mother gasped, lifting a hand to her mouth.

Wren spilled the entire story in one fast explanation.

For a long moment afterward, her parents just stared, clearly trying to comprehend everything. Her mother's mouth worked a couple times, but nothing came out.

"Do you have anything else to say for yourself?" the Colonel asked Wren, his tone both troubled and ominously displeased.

"No."

The Colonel looked to him. "How are you involved in this, Cord?"

"I'd cornered Sackett in the alley outside City Hall when she rushed out. Sackett carried her on her stomach across his saddle. I think we need to summon a doctor, sir."

"Of course. Yes." The Colonel's brown-gray beard framed lips set in a grave line. "You feeling poorly, Wren?"

"No, Pa. I'm fine."

"Certain?"

"Certain."

Wren's mother drew her child into the warmth of their home.

"I'll fetch the doctor at once, Ruth," the Colonel told his wife.

She nodded, then the two women ascended the stairs with their arm's looped around each other's waists.

Cord knew he'd passed Wren into the rightful hands. Regardless, remorse at leaving her twisted inside him.

Phillip watched his daughter glance at Cord before disappearing around the second-story landing. Good God, he'd been asleep two minutes ago under the assumption that everything was right with the world. And now this. Wren had been running through the city alone without his knowing. Imagine the things that could have happened to her.

He'd told her—countless times—that he had her best interests at heart. He'd thought she'd come to believe that, was maturing, that he'd succeeded in grooming most of the recklessness out of her. But clearly not.

He stared at the man who'd returned her, his fear making him angry. Angry with Wren, and with Cord for disobeying the terms of his suspension and inadvertently endangering his daughter because of it.

His best operative was standing on the darkest reaches of the stair. Phillip's old detective's eyes read an edginess the younger man couldn't quite cover.

"Colonel, I'd like to go out after Sackett. If I leave now, I'll have nearly caught up with him by morning."

Phillip crossed his arms over his chest.

"Rain's coming," Cord said. "If I wait until after the storm, it'll be too late. He's gone south. I know his direction, his horse. I can bring him in if you'll give me the chance."

Ordinarily, Phillip would have sent Cord after Sackett in a heartbeat. There was no one better. No one more fervent or more dogged. No one more qualified.

Ah, but the passion was just it. At times Cord's passion for his work rendered him invincible. At others it blinded him to the truth.

Where Sackett was concerned, it blinded him.

"The head office suspended you three weeks ago." After the war, Phillip had been promoted from fieldwork to his current position of liaison to the Pinkerton Agency's largest client, the Southern Atlantic Railroad. He doubled as supervisor of the operatives roaming the West. It was in the latter capacity that he acted now.

"Yes."

"Then why are you in Dallas chasing Lloyd Sackett?"

"I'm clearing my name the only way I can."

A sense of wastefulness swirled through Phillip. His daughter refused to heed sense. And his best operative had gotten himself into this predicament. In ideal worlds daughters did as they were instructed and good men got what they deserved. "I won't allow you to go after him."

Cord held himself frightfully still.

"If the agency has suspended you, then you know as well as I do that the rules preclude me from giving you orders to the contrary."

Cord looked away, his profile sharp with loss.

It was clear to Phillip that leaving Cord to his own devices during his suspension hadn't been enough. He needed to give Cord an assignment. Something simple that would keep him out of trouble.

He considered Cord. Squinted at the point on the stairway where his daughter had disappeared.

And got an idea.

Chapter 3

When she walked from her room the following morning, Wren was greeted by the tones of her mother's voice drifting up from the lower floor. It sounded like she was explaining last night's escapade to her sister, Alexandra. Pausing at the top of the stairs, Wren listened to her mother recap her arrival home, the doctor's visit that had followed, and the doctor's assurance that though bruised, her organs were still bravely functioning.

In Wren's opinion, "bruised" seemed too pale a word for the purplish marks scarring her belly and the soreness stretching from her ribs to her hipbones.

Gingerly, she started down the stairs. One of them creaked beneath her, and her mother and sister's conversation halted. By the time she reached the bottom, Alexandra and Mother were upon her. They fussed over her some, then each took an elbow and ushered her down the hall.

Wren hid a smile. Being the youngest, she'd had to

fight and scream and turn cartwheels to garner herself notice when she'd been little. Because of that, she'd yet to outgrow enjoying it whenever they doted on her.

Alexandra steered her into the dining room when Mother continued toward the kitchen.

"I cannot *believe* what you did last night," Alexandra whispered. "Are you recovered? You slept a long time, for you."

"What time is it?"

"Nine." Alexandra shook her head. "Sneaking out of your window! Imagine. However did you climb down?"

"It'll be my secret unto death."

"The trellis?" Alexandra studied her shrewdly. "The morning glories have looked a touch battered lately."

The dining table was clear, which meant her parents had eaten their breakfast earlier. Wren took the seat at the head, and her sister pulled up a chair at her side.

She wondered if Cord had caught Lloyd Sackett yet and made him pay. She imagined those elegant savage's hands fisting and driving into Sackett's chin, sending him spinning. He deserved punishment. The memory of Sackett, hauling her into his arms, dragging her backward with a gun to her head whipped through her thoughts. With the recollection, a chill seeped into the room, gaining strength as it gusted around her. She could hear the rasp of Sackett's breath, the grating of his feet over dirt, the drum of his horse's hooves.

"You all right?" Alexandra asked.

"I'm fine."

"You're not acting quite like yourself."

"I know." Alexandra, on the other hand, was acting and appearing just like she always did, with her gleaming blond chignon and sophisticated gown.

Yet beneath her sister's familiar presence, Wren could still *hear* Sackett. His breath. The way his teeth ground together.

She tried to squelch the memories by focusing her attention on the sunlight pouring through the windows, turning a long rectangle of hardwood floor and floral rug to gold. Her gaze followed the trail of sunshine over the dish of fruit that doubled as the table's centerpiece to the heavy sideboard with its leaf carvings. Above the door leading into the kitchen a framed placard read "God Bless This Home."

Alexandra had stitched the colorful sign when she was twelve. Like everything Alexandra touched or attempted, it had turned out remarkably well.

Although Wren had eaten meals in this room for years, things seemed different this morning. Last night, God had quite obviously given her a second chance at life. This time around she intended to make the most of it, to become someone extraordinary. She felt strangely clear-headed about that, was seeing everything—her family, her dreams, this house—in a fresh, more distanced, more resolved light.

Mother poked her head in from the kitchen. "Cook would like to know how many of you are eating."

"I've already eaten," Alexandra answered.

"Just me, then," Wren said.

Mother disappeared.

"So," Alexandra said, leaning forward, "do you want to tell me what in heaven you were thinking, sneaking out like that?"

Wren bristled. She'd intuitively known some mild censure would be forthcoming from her sister. It was still hard to hear. "Alexandra . . ."

"I'm just trying to understand."

"Are you?" She met her sister's gaze directly. Alexandra had always advised and protected her. Ordinarily, Wren followed her usual younger-sister patterns and accepted whatever Alexandra had to say with a lot of nodding. Well, acquiescence wasn't worth denying her own nature anymore.

Alexandra's brow knit. "Of course I'm trying to understand. My baby sister is gallivanting around Dallas in the middle of the night alone. She's stolen by an outlaw. She's injured."

Wren pursed her lips.

"I want to know why."

"Why? Simply because I'm not allowed to visit the theater and because I love it. I had to do what I could—"

"Really, though. Deceiving everyone? Risking your neck?"

Gritting her teeth, Wren bowed her head and took her time straightening the folds of her skirt. Despite the bonds of love that came from sharing a childhood and from knowing each other so well, Wren had always felt inferior to her sister. This was partly why, this way Alexandra had of being so perfect, then lecturing her when she wasn't. They were more similar than different, the two of them, yet the most important difference sliced the air between them now.

They'd both faced forks in the paths of their lives. Alexandra had taken the one of respectability, a husband, children. She'd been trying to lead Wren in the same direction ever since. Instead, Wren had been inching down the other path for years, now that she cared to admit it. It was a foggier path, maybe disreputable, maybe lonely, but assuredly exciting. She hadn't made much progress yet, but doggone it, she intended to rectify that.

"Wren?" Alexandra prompted.

She took a breath. "Yes," she said, looking to her sister. "It was deceptive of me, and risky. But it's my neck to risk."

By the troubled look in her sister's light blue eyes, she could tell Alexandra was formulating another reprimand. Wren reached out and placed her hand over her sister's. "I've a fairly good suspicion that Mother and Pa are going to lecture me later this morning. I'd rather . . . don't take this the wrong way, but I'd prefer to be lectured just once."

"I'm not lecturing you."

Wren smiled, breaking the news gently. "You are."

"Oh." Surprise flitted across her features. "All right. I'll let up."

"Thank you." Wren squeezed her sister's fingers.

Cook bustled in from the kitchen and set a napkin, silverware, and a cup of coffee already flavored with milk at Wren's place.

"Did you hear about my adventure?" Wren asked her.

The sunlight behind Cook made the thinnest, topmost section of her frizzy red hair appear on the verge of crackling into flames. "I'm not thinkin' you should be callin' it an adventure, Missy. There's no reason to be proud of yerself that I can tell." She regarded Wren with the displeased expression she employed for every occasion.

"You're glad to see me," Wren said, attempting to melt her with a wink. "Aren't you?"

"You want sugar in yer oatmeal?" Cook responded.

"Yes, please."

"Hrmph." Cook returned to the kitchen.

Wren sipped at the deliciously hot coffee. At the back of her mind, she could still hear Sackett's voice in her ear. She sipped again, memories of last night's reality mingled with memories of the nightmares that had followed. "Do you know that I didn't even struggle against Lloyd Sackett?" she murmured. "I let him, I *let* him, pull me from the alley and put me on his horse."

"What else could you have done?" Alexandra asked.

"I could have been less passive about my own fate. I need to remedy that."

"What? By learning to box or shoot or some such?"

"That and more."

A smile tweaked the corners of Alexandra's lips and kept on growing. It relieved Wren enormously to see that smile. It meant things were fine between them again.

"I'd pay good money to see you box," Alexandra said.

"Then start saving your pennies."

"Yes, yes, yes. Fine. Now hurry up and tell me about *him*."

"Who?"

"You know very well who, Wren Bradley."

"Let's see. . . . I was lying in the field when I heard footsteps, running, I think. I looked up and there he was. Cord Caldwell."

"What did he say?"

"He asked if I was hurt. I told him no and urged him to go after the outlaw. He wouldn't leave me."

Alexandra hummed a sigh.

Cook carried in a bowl of oatmeal and a plate loaded with eggs and sausage.

"Thank you."

"Hrmph."

Wren sampled a bite of the brown-sugar-spiced oatmeal.

"Did you ride on the saddle in front of him on the way home?" Alexandra asked.

"Yes."

"With his arms around you?"

"I don't recall," Wren bluffed. "Maybe."

"And I'm president of the United States." Despite her sarcasm, Wren could tell that Alexandra—generally a hard-to-impress person—was duly impressed by her tandem ride with the Legend.

Wren forked a hefty portion of sausage into her mouth.

"In all the years I've known him, I've never met anyone else as handsome," Alexandra commented. "Except Robert, of course."

"I know. And the closer you look, the more handsome he is."

"Mornin'."

Both sisters jerked toward the hallway entrance, which framed a very real, very near Cord Caldwell.

Wren almost choked on her sausage. What on earth was he doing here? He'd said—No one had told her—Why hadn't she attended to her appearance more carefully this morning? Her green bodice and the matching skirt were fine, but she probably had little tufts of hair standing straight up from her forehead and sheet marks on her face.

He looked straight at her. "Your stomach okay?"

His magnetism curled through the air and sent goose bumps quivering along her shoulder blades and upper arms. His dark brown hair was slick with water, and his angular jaw and hard cheeks had been freshly shaven. He was wearing trail clothes similar to those he'd had on last night—snug-fitting tan trousers and a dark blue work shirt.

Lordy. It was dangerous to become so—so giddy at the sight of him. Setting aside her fork, she forced herself to chew, to swallow. "My stomach's fine, thank you."

"I'm glad." He lowered himself into the chair across from Alexandra, who was studying him raptly.

"I thought you'd gone," Wren said.

"Well, evidently I'm more handsome the closer I am, so I decided to stay close."

Wren made a point never to blush, but heat scalded her cheeks and forehead, heat that felt unmistakably like a blush. Perfect. The redness probably looked lovely coupled with the sheet marks.

"Actually," she cleared her throat, summoning her wits, "I said that the closer you look the more sand . . . strum you are."

"I see. Sandstrum." He nodded. "I'm not familiar with that term."

"Why yes," Wren replied. "We use the term *sandstrum* frequently around here."

"What does *sandstrum* mean, exactly?" he asked.

Alexandra pressed her knuckles against obviously twitching lips.

"It means," Wren searched her brain, "not offensive."

"Yes," Alexandra said gamely, "it's an adjective."

Cook marched into the room and set a cup of coffee before Cord. "Cream or sugar?"

"Neither, thank you, ma'am."

Her formidable chin dipped. "Breakfast?"

"I'd be obliged."

Cook returned to the kitchen, rump swaying.

Cord sampled his coffee. Then he set the cup, which by all accounts was too small for his hand, back into its saucer. "Sandstrum coffee."

Alexandra laughed and Wren laughed with her, despite her intention not to find him charming.

Cord shot her a grin that clearly said I-can-pull-your-drawers-down-with-my-teeth. Lazy and masculine.

Something inside Wren tugged toward him, reaching out, wanting.

Confident, attentive, irresistible. This was the Cord she remembered from the past. Which simultaneously terrified her and made her wonder what had happened to the man who'd knelt beside her last night and stared after a departing dust trail with both longing and fury.

"I thought you were going to continue after Sackett last night," Wren said.

"That was before your father invited me to stay the night, and I accepted his offer."

"And Sackett?"

"I'll still get him."

The assurance in his eyes promised her that he would. Blue eyes. Deep, liquid, midnight blue eyes rimmed with dark lashes. She'd fancied them black last night, but could see they were still the glorious blue she'd foolishly mooned over as a girl.

Cook deposited Cord's breakfast before him. He looked inquiringly at Alexandra. "Are you taking breakfast, Mrs. Todd? I'd hate to eat in front of you."

"Cook!" Alexandra called.

Cook stopped halfway through the door. Alexandra put in an order.

Once Cook served Alexandra her food, they all worked on their portions. Though as far as Wren could tell, Alexandra was using her tea and toast as props to look becoming with.

"Will you be staying long?" Alexandra asked, her pinky elevated from the handle of her cup.

"I'm afraid not," Cord answered.

"What a shame. Wren is going to be performing in a

music academy recital in a few months, and I'm sure you'd enjoy it."

Cord glanced at Wren, genuine interest in his expression.

"Wren's brilliant onstage," Alexandra said. "Once, when she was four years old, her class at Mrs. . . . what was it Wren?"

"Mrs. Lovejoy, though I'm certain Mr. Caldwell isn't interested."

"Yes, I am."

"See?" Alexandra slanted a look at her that held a glint of mischief. "Anyhow, her class at Mrs. Lovejoy's House of Dance gave a performance. During Wren's number, Wren actually elbowed aside the other ballerinas for a position closest to the audience."

Cord drained the last of his coffee. Humor flashed in the depths of his eyes. "Really? She didn't mention it last night."

"At the end of the piece," Alexandra continued, "when the music died, all the little dancers floated to the floor . . . what were you supposed to be, Wren?"

"Flowers closing for the night."

"Yes, flowers. Anyway, they were all resting on the floor, eyes closed when the curtains shut. Wren was so near the audience, she was left on our side of the curtain."

Wren leaned back in her chair. The oft-told family tale didn't strike her as funny in the least when relayed to Cord Caldwell. He already had ample cause to think her silly.

"She unfurled, so to speak," Alexandra continued, "and noticed what had happened. Everyone there expected her to burst into tears of embarrassment, except our family. Wren plucked up the sides of her tutu with her miniature hands, bowed to the crowd, and began the number all over again."

Cord chuckled.

"Mrs. Lovejoy finally had to walk onstage," Alexandra said, "grab Wren's hand, and lead her off. On the way out, Wren was still attempting to perform the steps."

Maybe Alexandra hadn't completely forgiven her after all. Her punishment methods were just more devilish than Wren had assumed. "I'm certain you're stunned to hear I could do something so childish," Wren said dryly to Cord.

"I'm not surprised to hear you were brave even then," Cord murmured. "If that's what you mean."

He could have said a thousand derogatory things about her behavior as a four-year-old. Instead he'd chosen to be as gentlemanly and soothing as a grandfather might be, which irrationally made her long to poke him with a stick.

"What's ironic," Alexandra said, "is that Mother named her Wren because as a newborn she reminded Mother of a shy bird. Little did she know."

"Thank you for sharing all my secrets, Alexandra. Don't forget to tell him about the time I caught my hair on fire."

Cord and Alexandra grinned.

Cook pulled open the kitchen door. "Mr. Caldwell, when yer finished, Colonel Bradley is wantin' to speak with you."

"I'm finished now, ma'am." He'd cleaned his plate.

"Colonel Bradley is in the study."

"If you'll excuse me," he said to Wren and Alexandra.

"Of course," they answered.

Cord rose. He allotted Wren the same fleeting eye contact he bestowed on Alexandra, then strode from the room. Much of the tension, and much of the room's excitement, left with him. It was nicer this way. Tranquil. She wished he'd left last night when he was supposed to.

"What do you imagine Pa wishes to speak to him about?" Alexandra asked.

Whatever it was, her father would no doubt want her to account for her actions directly afterward. She eyed her sister. "I don't know. But I believe I'm next."

The Colonel rested his elbows on his desk and pressed his fingertips together.

Cord sat across from him in an armchair. The soothing browns and maroons of the room contrasted sharply with his impatience. He wished the Colonel would go ahead and hand down his sentence.

"I've a proposition for you, Cord."

Whatever the proposition was, Cord would do it.

"I want you to guard Wren."

Cord stared at him, waiting for another responsibility that had to do with catching criminals.

Nothing came.

Cord didn't know how to respond. Jesus. He liked women. But he sure as hell didn't want to follow the china doll to and from her tea parties and dressmaking appointments. He'd rather go back to pushing paper in Chicago. Hell, he'd rather clean out the Colonel's barn. At least that would be hard, honest work.

He read the calm lines of the Colonel's face, trying to gauge how much leeway the older man might be willing to extend him. Not too damned much. Cord was suspended. That he'd been caught breaking the rules during that suspension further lessened his standing.

He'd never wanted to be anything other than an operative for the Pinkerton Agency. Not since, at fourteen, he'd read an article detailing how Allan Pinkerton and his men had foiled an assassination attempt on Abraham Lincoln. He'd known then that the operatives working for Pinkerton were elite and honorable men, men with the power to make things right in the world. Back then, he'd only wanted two things. To get the hell out of his parents' house. And to do work that would bring some semblance of justice and peace to his existence.

No one had been more instrumental in helping him reach his goals than Phillip Bradley. The Colonel, a long-time associate of Pinkerton's, had taken an interest in Cord back when Cord had been at Harvard, trying hard to distinguish himself. It was the Colonel he had to thank for hiring him after graduation. The Colonel had advised him through the early years of errand running and record keeping at the Chicago office. The Colonel had promoted him to his first assignment as an operative.

"Remember when you were transferred West?" the older man asked, stealing Cord's thoughts. "We needed your tracking skills here, in a land with more outlaws than longhorns and more space than sense." He smiled.

"I came out when you did," Cord said.

"Yes. And your record in the West is excellent."

It was a record Cord had earned with sweat and blood, and a record he fully intended to maintain. He curled his fingers around the arms of his chair and waited, hoping to hell that the Colonel would talk himself out of his decision and give him a real assignment. He desperately needed to be granted the chance and the trust to finish the job he'd started with Sackett.

"In time, the agency will revoke your suspension and restore you to your position because they can't afford to lose you. However"—the Colonel studied him in his intelligent way—"at the moment, I think it best for you to cool your heels until this thing blows over."

"Colonel—"

"It's too late, Cord. You're off this case."

Cord made himself nod. The Sackett brothers had been his case from the beginning. He'd gotten all of them, except one. Somewhere south of here, Lloyd Sackett was riding free and making plans. While he was trapped in this book-choked study about to hear for the first time in his eight-year career that his case had been given to another man. Anger curled within him.

The Colonel opened the file sitting on this neatly ordered desk top. "I've assigned Jackson to Sackett's case."

Cord forced another nod. "I think Sackett might have an informant inside the railroad." He swallowed. The words came hard. "You may want to pass that along to Jackson."

The Colonel waited a few heartbeats to respond. "Do you have any evidence to substantiate your informant theory?"

"No. It's a hunch."

"Somewhat like the hunch you had that left you suspended?"

The question had been voiced gently. It still stung as bitterly as a whip's lash. He'd deserved that, he supposed. "I was only trying to help Jackson."

"I know you were. I'll consider telling him of your suspicions." The Colonel made a notation on the topmost page of the file, shut it, and met Cord's gaze. "Which is where my daughter comes in. Wren has been unhappy lately. Restless, I suppose. Still, Ruth and I never dreamt she was sneaking out at night." His lips thinned and Cord sensed how completely the thought of losing his youngest daughter disturbed the Colonel, a man who'd spied for the north in the Civil War, overcoming fears that had crushed the toughest of men.

"There's few men I'd trust to watch over my daughter," the Colonel said. "You're one of them. I'd regard it as a personal favor if you would guard her until your suspension is revoked."

Cord knew he'd have to pay whatever professional penance necessary. "I'll do it."

"Thank you. It should only be for a few weeks. Wren's suitor, the son of friends of the family, will be returning from his travels shortly. Once he's returned, he'll take over the responsibility of her. I'm sure."

Cord should have been encouraged by the news. Instead, jealousy snaked through his chest. The recognition of the emotion took him aback. He'd never been jealous of women. That he should feel possessive now, of a girl he barely knew, was ridiculous. He pushed the jealousy aside, unwilling to examine it.

"With any luck, you'll be back to doing what you do best shortly," the Colonel said.

What Cord did best was hunt wanted men. He'd never before been assigned to a wanted woman . . . or, rather, a woman he wanted.

The Colonel tapped his fingertips on the edge of his desk, thoughtful. "There's one other thing. She's gotten it into her head that she wants to be an actress. Join up with a traveling production." The gaze he leveled on Cord spoke volumes. "This nonsense about acting is the root of her problems. I'd appreciate it if you'd keep her away from it."

"I'll do my best."

The Colonel nodded, pushed from his chair, and moved to the closed door. "I'm going to summon Wren."

Cord started to rise. "I'll go—"

"I'd like you to stay."

Very well. Cord vacated his chair and leaned against the bookcases, where he hoped he'd be unobtrusive.

The Colonel returned a moment later with Wren and her mother.

Wren glanced at him as she entered. She scowled, her steps slowing.

The Colonel and his wife leaned side by side on the front edge of the desk, facing their daughter.

"You want to know why I sneaked out last night," Wren said flatly to them.

Her mother nodded.

"Does poor Mr. Caldwell have to hear this?"

"I've requested that he remain," the Colonel replied. "Some of what I have to say concerns him."

Concerns him? Wren wondered. She didn't want him here, overhearing the way her parents were about to scold her. However, against her father she needed to pick her battles wisely, and already his expression was bleak. For now, she'd acquiesce to Cord's presence. "I went to the theater to watch the actors and actresses rehearsing. That's all."

"That's a great deal," Pa said, his tone serious. "How many times have you done that without us knowing?"

"Doesn't our constitution protect a person from having to incriminate themselves?"

Her mother's gray eyes dimmed. "So you've gone often."

"Yes."

"But why?"

"It's exciting, to sit there and watch. I learn from them."

"Most of those performers you admire so much live week to week in boardinghouses," Mother said. "They travel constantly in trains and coaches. They rush through meals when they can, but often miss meals entirely. Sometimes, they're not even paid for their trouble." She anxiously pushed a trailing lock of hair into her bun. "They're regarded in many communities as little better than vagabonds. All this, for the reward of walking across a dingy stage to crowds who don't appreciate them."

"That kind of life isn't worth anything compared to the rewards you'll reap when you marry Edward and become a wife and mother," her father said. "Don't you see how happy Alexandra is in her marriage?"

"Yes." Alexandra was a completely different person. Alexandra had the Midas touch. Wren loathed being compared to her.

"You're going to have to trust us to know what's best for you," Pa was saying, his words measured but foreboding. "Your mother and I have knowledge and experience you don't."

"Think how much you have to give here, in this community," Mother said. "You can extend yourself through work with the church, spend more time encouraging your friends, entertaining visiting dignitaries, making your home comfortable for your husband, raising upstanding children."

Wren held her silence.

"You deserve that," Pa said. "You deserve more than what the life of an actress can afford you."

Wren could tell from his earnest expression that he truly thought so. Why was it that every time she heard this speech her parent's sincere ideas of "better" sounded worse and worse to her? She understood and appreciated their worries. But they didn't understand or appreciate her dreams. She took a deep breath, trying to control the frustration that had been mounting in her for months. "I apologize for scaring you last night, and I'm sorry for deceiving you and sneaking out. But with all due respect, it's my right to choose what I deserve."

Her father's eyes blazed at what he viewed as impertinence.

"You appear onstage during the music-academy recitals," Mother pointed out. "Isn't that enough?"

"No." It hadn't been enough since about the age of eleven.

The problem was that for her parents, for Edward, and for most of the "polite" people she knew, the divider between academy recitals and a career as an actress was also the inflexible line of demarcation between respectability and ruin.

"You were lucky not to have been hurt before now," Pa said. "You could have been killed, walking alone through the streets at night. In my time, I saw far too many dead bodies belonging to women less careless than you."

During his years in the military, he'd witnessed awful carnage. He'd also grown accustomed to unquestioned control. Well, she was sick of it. "I'm going to learn to defend myself."

"I don't think that's wise," Pa said. "It's also unnecessary, at least for the near future. I've assigned Mr. Caldwell to watch over you as your guardian."

Her bottom lip sagged.

"He's very accomplished," Mother commented.

"Starting today, he'll be protecting you at all times," Pa said.

"D-Doesn't Mr. Caldwell have more . . . more important cases to attend to?" Wren stammered, stunned that her father would go this far, stunned that Cord would agree to it.

"Keeping you safe is important work."

"Pa! Please assure me you're not seriously contemplating this."

He frowned and kept silent.

A guardian? Tension infused Wren's body in a defensive rush, knotting her muscles. Acting as her father's henchman, Cord would be honor-bound to oppose her goals, which would make him her enemy. As if he wasn't already. As if he wasn't the last man on earth she wanted to spend time with. She spared a look at Cord. "Forgive me, I'm about to speak rudely in front of you."

He dipped his chin.

"No," she said to her parents. "I don't want him following me."

"Wren," her mother warned.

"You spoke of freedom," Wren said, "then assigned me a chaperone?" She felt awful, her injured stomach a mass of quivers and her heart racing.

Her father's shoulders pulled back. "We're afraid for you."

"I can learn to protect myself. That's what freedom means."

Her mother released a short, distraught sigh.

"You're living under our roof." Pa pitched his voice soft, but firm. "So long as you continue to do so, you'll abide by our rules. The current rule is Mr. Caldwell's protection. I'm sorry, Wren, but you brought this on yourself."

Doggone it, she hated that. The guilt he was trying to force on her because she'd dared leave the house so she could sit—*just sit*—close to that which she loved.

"The thing that no one seems to understand is that I'm an adult woman." She looked beseechingly at each parent, struggled to keep her voice calm. "I'm twenty-one years old. It's past time I started making choices for myself."

"You're under our roof," Pa repeated.

"Maybe that's just it." For a long time now, she'd been straddling two worlds. Hoping to remain her father's *Precious*, and longing for freedom. The middle ground had been adequate until now.

"I wanted . . . For some time I've wanted to keep on being your baby and I've wanted to be a woman, too. I see, suddenly, that I can't be both." Her terror last night had provided her with clarity of vision, and the determination to make what she could of her life while she still had strength and breath. "I can't have both, and of the two I choose to be a woman. I'm moving out."

Both of her parents paled. Her mother started crying, and Wren felt an answering wetness build behind her eyes. She'd never been able to bear it when her mother wept.

"You may move out when you marry Edward," Pa said, his tone as unyielding as his face. "Just as Alexandra did."

Clearly, duty, devotion, and fear had kept her here too long. Reverberations of finality and loss, for all the years she'd been their darling daughter, shifted through her. Those times were over. She didn't belong to them anymore. "I wish I could be as perfect as Alexandra. I've tried, but I can't. My decision's made. I'm going to leave."

"No," her father said. "I won't pay for that."

"I'm afraid this is the first time in my life, Pa, that you don't have the right to tell me no." Her knees were shaking. "I have some of my own money saved."

"I won't allow—"

"Phillip," her mother whispered. She pulled a handkerchief from her pocket and blotted her tears.

Wren refused to cry, but she could feel her emotions building, clogging her throat. She was trying to be strong, but in truth, hurting them this way was terrible. She wanted it to be over.

"Oh, darling," Mother said, her expression crestfallen, "it's not necessary, surely, for you to move out."

"I think it is."

"Where will you go?" she asked.

"I don't know." The memory of the notice she'd seen at the theater sprang vividly to mind. Austin. "I'd appreciate it if I could stay here a few more nights, just long enough to pack my things."

"Of course, of course," Mother soothed, her eyelashes matting together with more moisture.

"Thank you." She looked to her father.

His face was stricken.

"I love you both," Wren said.

"We love you, too," her mother replied. Her father remained silent.

Heart heavy, Wren turned to leave.

"I'm not relieving Mr. Caldwell of his responsibilities as they pertain to you," Pa said.

Slowly, she faced him once more. "I wish you would."

He shook his head, a near-miniscule motion that rejected her plea. He'd not relent.

She pulled in a breath. Her skirt swirled as she turned to Cord, who regarded her with eyes that smoldered an indigo challenge. The legendary detective with a reputation for always getting his man, and his woman, had no idea what he was in for.

Chapter 4

The next morning, Alexandra Bradley Todd found a note in her husband's jacket pocket. A pink, lilac-scented note that she hadn't written.

She stretched it between her fingers, eyes narrow.

Robert,
Thank you! Thank you! Thank you! I shall not dis-
appoint you, I promise. I shall give you my utmost
in this, our secret agreement.

There wasn't even a proper closing salutation. Not a "sincerely" or an "until we meet again" or best yet, a "not romantically yours." There was only *Theodora*, signed in swirly, flowy handwriting.

Alexandra blinked. She reread it, sure this time she'd find something in it that would show her it wasn't what it looked like. That this note could not possibly be a love note to her husband.

But she saw only the gushing thankfulness of the words, capped off with that plain Theodora.

She ought to read it still again. Surely she'd find an explanation this time. Something that would prove how innocent this was, how purely professional.

Our secret agreement. Not much professional about that.

She set aside his suit jacket. She'd been straightening their bedroom while the children washed their hands and brushed their teeth. It was an everyday kind of thing to do, she thought, dazed. To straighten their room before rushing off to begin the day.

Robert had a habit of taking off his jacket when he came home at night, of resting it over the corner chair. Alexandra brushed her fingertips over the carved wooden back of the chair. They'd purchased it on their honeymoon in Cape Cod—their honeymoon! God, the audacity of him. To rest his cheating jacket on their chair.

Slowly, she turned, looking through eyes that wouldn't quite focus and a brain that wouldn't quite think. Untold mornings, almost every morning, she picked his jacket up, smoothed the lapels, and hung it in the armoire for him.

The armoire appeared strange to her now, unfamiliar. As if she hadn't hung her gowns in it every day for years.

Often, his jacket pockets rattled with coins or papers. She always cleared them for him, then put the stuff from his pockets into the crystal dish on his side of the dresser. Her gaze bored into the crystal dish she'd always thought so pretty in its simplicity.

Where was she supposed to put illicit love notes?

She began to fold the pink piece of stationery. In half, in quarters, smaller, smaller still.

"Have you seen my silver cuff link?" Robert asked.

Her senses clanged. Like a thief, Alexandra rushed to hide the evidence of her guilt. Quickly, she stuffed the note into her skirt pocket.

He walked through the door, straightening his tie. "I can only find one." He canted his head at her. "Did I startle you?"

"Yes." She couldn't quite meet his eyes, so she looked at everything but him. "I was just . . . you know, straightening up in here. I thought you'd gone."

"Not quite yet. Just finished my eggs."

"Oh."

He bent to rummage through his drawers. She searched his movements, his face, his posture for some sign of guilt. His every motion looked at once completely normal and flagrantly unfamiliar.

She wondered how long it had been since she'd studied him objectively, like another woman might. His charcoal gray suit jacket stretched across wide shoulders on a body that was otherwise tall and spare. He had inky black hair and dark eyes rimmed with even darker lashes. From head to toe he exuded elegance, and had the manners to match. Any woman, this Theodora included, would see in him what Alexandra had originally seen. They'd think him startlingly attractive.

Fear burrowed deep inside her.

"So you haven't seen it?" he asked.

She blinked at the question, moved to the crystal dish with all his paraphernalia in it, and fished out the silver cuff link almost immediately. "Here."

"Thanks." He faced the mirror above the dresser as he worked the cuff link into place. "Do you have anything particular planned for the children today?"

"Nothing special." From behind his shoulder she caught a glimpse of her dazed expression in the mirror. She cleared her throat, backed away. "You?"

"Nothing special."

"Hm." An awkward pause followed.

He bussed her cheek. "I'll see you tonight."

"Do you . . . do you know when you'll be home?"

He didn't glance back as he passed through the doorway. "Five o'clock, as usual." He worked with her father at the Southern Atlantic Railroad offices. Robert ordinarily kept regular hours, although recently he'd been working late more often.

For long moments after he left she stood stock-still, her mind churning. Was there any chance, no matter how remote, that *her* Robert, could be having an affair, making love to someone else, loving someone else? Without her knowing?

No. Maybe she and Robert had allowed some distance to creep between them these past months. They hadn't retired to bed at the same time in a while, he hadn't been cuddling her body against the warm length of his, they hadn't made love as often. He had his work, and she had the children. . . . They'd been busy, that was all. Nothing to worry about.

She was the overachieving Bradley sister. A success at all she attempted. Things like affairs didn't happen to her. She didn't let them happen.

"Mommy!" Four-year-old Elizabeth tore around the edge of the open door. "Look at my pretty hair!" She pointed all her fingers at the pert little bun atop her head. Nanny had outdone herself today. Elizabeth's black shiny hair, so like her father's, struck startling contrast to the pink flowers pinned all the way around the base of the topknot.

"Beautiful!" Alexandra exclaimed, overly bright. She smiled, and took her daughter's hand. In the hallway, she turned to see Nanny herding three-year-old Robbie toward them. He had that adorable, pressed look about him. Every hair had been combed into place, every fold of his clothing perfectly tucked. He wore this particular look for less than two minutes at the beginning of each day.

"To the park?" Nanny asked.

"To the park."

Elizabeth and Robbie started fidgeting, half-jumping really, with excitement. Alexandra opened the door for them and watched as they spilled down the steps.

The familiar path beneath her feet, the sunshine, the sight of her children running before her, combined to ease the pall of finding Theodora's letter. This, their family, their home, a walk to the park and back, was real. Lilac-scented letters and secret agreements weren't.

Robert wasn't having an affair. No, no, no, no. Couldn't be.

Surely not.

Wren thrust a hairpin through the underside of her hat. The yellow concoction with the lavender-and-white-striped ribbons shuddered at the impact.

Since her showdown with her parents yesterday, she'd spent most of her time in her room. Some of the hours she'd passed lying in bed resting her stomach and reddening her neck with all the locket twisting she'd done.

Some of the hours filling her trunks with her belongings. All of the hours thinking. The more she'd considered her situation, the more sure she'd grown that her initial urge to travel to Austin was the right one. The audition represented her one best chance, and if there'd ever been a time to take her fate in her hands, spread her wings, and try to taste the sky—this was it.

She stuck in another hairpin, then another, before realizing she'd practically glued the hat to her head.

No matter how much her stomach still pained her, she needed to get out of this house. Her inactivity and the tension between her and her parents was more than she could stand. Besides, there were a few errands she needed to run this afternoon in preparation for her trip.

With her fingertips, she smoothed the fine wisps of hair at her forehead. Whether the hat, the purple bodice, and matching skirt she'd chosen were armor enough against Cord Caldwell remained to be seen. Somehow, she doubted it.

She scooped up her reticule and made her way downstairs. Cord was sitting in the parlor, alone, dressed formally, and writing in a small, leather-bound book. He shut it with a snap when he saw her.

Careful to turn her back so he couldn't see, she extracted from her reticule the generous allowance her parents had given her for the month. Every penny of it, she piled onto the entry table. From now on, she'd use only money she'd earned herself. The fund she'd cultivated through hours of caring for a local family's children during her school years wasn't large, but at least it belonged to her.

Without sparing a look in Cord's direction, she breezed through the front door. She had some pointed questions to ask him, but not inside the house where Cook and Mother could overhear. When she reached the street, she turned toward town.

As expected, the door closed behind her. His footfalls brought him even with her.

Mutinous excitement sizzled down the center of her chest. Pathetic. Her involuntary reaction to him chafed at her pride, made her angry with herself.

"Do you think you should go out today?" he asked.

"I always go out."

"I'm worried about your injury, that's all."

She glanced at him. He was gazing at her with eyes that glittered like sapphires in the morning sunlight.

"My stomach feels fine." She increased the pace.

She expected him to try and control her. To ask her again to return home, or attempt to overrule her proclamation that she was well.

Instead, he held his silence and walked companionably beside her, matching stride for stride. Though she kept her attention firmly forward, his image had burned into her brain.

He'd traded his work clothes for a black suit, which made her wonder whether he felt he needed to dress up in her company. The suit was single-breasted and cut simply and straight. Beneath he wore a black vest and a collared white shirt. He looked comfortable in the suit and as effortlessly in control as he had in his denim trousers.

Unable to resist, she risked another peek out of the corners of her eyes.

He dipped his head and donned his Stetson one-handed, in a gesture that looked as natural to him as breathing. The hat she recalled from years ago was faded beige now, dirt-streaked and bearing the scars of many a renegade hunt. It also looked thoroughly, inarguably wonderful on him in a dangerous sort of way.

Wren cringed inwardly.

As soon as they reached the crossroads at the end of her block, she stopped and faced him. "May I ask why you agreed to this assignment?"

He regarded her for a long moment with his measuring, all-seeing detective's eyes. "Your father requested it of me as a favor."

"And you accepted just that simply?"

"I accepted."

"What about him?" She gestured southward. "What about Lloyd Sackett? Yesterday morning you told me you were still planning to go after him."

"I was."

"What happened to change your mind? You can't want to chaperone me while Sackett goes free. He's your case, isn't he?"

"Not at the moment."

Wren searched his face. Despite his amiable tone, coldness settled in the lines of his cheeks, and she sensed suffering in him that went soul deep.

"My father . . . my father didn't take you off the case because of me, did he? Because of what happened night before last?"

"It wasn't because of you."

"Then why?" She understood her father's motives for punishing her. But Cord?

He repositioned his hat, tilting the brim even lower over his eyes. "I was suspended a few weeks ago."

"Suspended?" she asked, dumbfounded. "For what?"

"I made a bad decision."

A bad decision? What was that supposed to mean? He could have made a bad decision by bedding Allan Pinkerton's wife or a bad decision by accidentally shooting the last nosy woman who'd asked him one question too many. "What kind of a bad decision?"

"It's not for you to worry about."

She thought back over what had happened the other night. "Am I to assume that you'd tracked Lloyd Sackett to the alley alongside City Hall without permission?"

"You can assume that."

"In that case, *why* didn't you let me sneak back home instead of insisting on taking me to the door? No one had to know about your involvement."

"It wouldn't have been right to slink away after what happened."

"Right! Look at us now. My father has given you this ridiculous assignment, and he's given me a guard dog I don't want."

His gaze bored right through to her soul. "I don't regret what I did. I don't regret that you were cared for by a doctor. And I sure as hell don't regret that you're well."

"I told you I was well back then, and you didn't believe me!"

"I respected your opinion. But you were putting up a brave front, just like you're putting one up now."

Her nostrils flared on a furious inhale. "I can make my own choices, thank you very much. I'd appreciate it if you'd resign from this assignment, plead with my father, or do whatever else it is you need to do. I don't care. I just want to be left alone."

"In eight years, I've never quit an assignment. I'm not about to quit one now."

"But if you talk to him, he'll listen. If you explain to him that I don't need a guardian—"

"You heard your father as well as I did. No matter what, he still wants me to protect you. So I will."

"But if you ask—"

"No. You're stuck with me."

Mute with frustration, she curled her fingers into fists. She wanted to shake him for trapping her like this, for refusing to help. Couldn't he see what she was trying to do? How hard she was fighting for her own freedom? "Why won't you help me?"

"Because I owe your father. He needs assistance with you, and it's not in me to refuse him. Wouldn't be right."

"Maybe you didn't understand what I was saying to him yesterday," she said tightly. "I don't need anyone to protect me anymore. Not my parents, not my sister, and certainly not you." She stepped out into the street.

Cord's arm wrapped around her middle, stopping her just as a carriage careened in front of her nose. She gasped as the wind generated by its terrifyingly close passing flushed over her features.

Cord set her gently upright. "What were you were saying?" he asked, a grin curling the edges of his lips. His gaze flicked over her in that way he had. That sensual, knowing way that made her entire body rush with heat.

"Oh!" Exasperating man! This time she looked both ways before hurrying across the street. Cord fell in beside her.

They went five blocks, then turned onto Main Street with nothing but the sound of their footsteps and the growing city's ever-present scent of lumber between them.

It was one thing to spend a few minutes with Cord Caldwell while he rescued her from Sackett. That contact had provided her a chance to confront her demons about him and to show him that she'd turned out all right despite her gawky beginnings. It was quite another thing to be forced together with him for days on end.

That simply couldn't happen. Cord Caldwell had single-handedly set her independence back five years. She'd not allow him another five. Which meant that she'd have to run away when he wasn't looking and keep her destination secret. Fine. Tonight she'd flee to Austin—the sooner the better. If her evasion made him look bad with her father, doubly fine. The cad deserved it.

With a twist of her fingers, Wren extinguished the lamp. Her bedroom plunged into darkness. She stood at her open window and peered into the night.

A plump moon shed its light over the city. Everything, including the air and the sighing of the trees, had gone still. Even the stars seemed to be waiting with bated breath.

Out of the distant quiet came the rasp of Sackett's breath, the clutch of his arms dragging her back, the thunder of pounding hooves.

She shook her head to scatter her thoughts. It was late, which probably accounted for her fancifulness. She'd forced herself to wait until the stroke of midnight, in hopes that Cord and her parents would, by now, be sleeping soundly.

Her mother had come upstairs with a supper tray and a dose of chocolate earlier in the evening. They'd sat together on Wren's bed chatting quietly about any subject except the one glaring between them. Her father hadn't made an appearance. In the last day and a half they'd spoken only when they chanced to meet in the hallways. His few words to her had been rife with disillusionment, her few to him painfully stiff.

Frowning, she ran her fingertip down the painted edge of the window, feeling the tiny ridges beneath. She hated the wedge she'd driven between herself and her parents. Despite it, or maybe because of it, she especially regretted that she wouldn't be able to bid them a proper goodbye. Cord's watchfulness precluded it. She couldn't very well share an obtrusive, tearful scene with her parents, then depart undetected minutes later.

She'd leave the house now and go straight to the depot, a building cavernous enough to hide in until morning, when the train to Austin would pull away from the station with her on it.

She eased the hood of her cloak over her hair with a soundless *whoosh*. As usual, darkness completely bathed the windows of her neighbors. Their obliviousness was as trustworthy as ever.

Time to leave. She sighed, looked behind her one last time at the bedroom of her childhood. Maybe it was best this way, to make a clean, fast break from her old ways.

Before she could wallow in the regret melting through her, she hitched up the front of her skirt and lifted a foot over the sill—

"Going somewhere?"

She jumped, a gasp jutting from her lips.

"Didn't mean to startle you." Cord's disembodied voice coasted upward from somewhere below. *He* was somewhere below. Doggone him. *Doggone him!*

She jerked her leg back over the sill. Had there been something breakable near at hand, she'd have hurled it. She contented herself with a half gurgle, half growl brimming with exasperation, disappointment, humiliation. Doggone him.

How had he known what she'd attempt? Why hadn't she seen him there?

Though she squinted, she could still only just make him out. There, barely visible beneath the edge of the roof, leaning against her mother's picket fence. He'd dressed almost entirely in black. Did they teach them these things in detective school?

"On your way to the theater?" he asked, his tone casual.

"Yes," she fibbed.

She surveyed his insolent silhouette. He had to sleep at some point tonight, didn't he? She'd simply wait until then.

"Your mother and I had a talk about gardening earlier." His smile gleamed pale. He appeared to toss away a blade of grass he'd been munching. "I persuaded her that a trellis up the back wall of the house wasn't the best place to grow morning glory."

"Is that so?" she asked disinterestedly. Inwardly, her hopes sank. Without that trellis, there was no way off this roof.

"Yep. She asked me to remove the trellis, and I obliged."

"How interesting."

Again, the faint shine of his smile.

"If you'll excuse me," she said.

"Certainly."

She closed the windows, then the shutters, and bit off a curse word she saved only for the direst situations.

Her heeled shoes rapped the floor as she began to pace. So much for exiting the house via her familiar bedroom-window route. She'd have to leave by one of the downstairs doors. How could she do it?

Back and forth she strode, not even bothering to take off her cloak. Her skin began to grow warm beneath its folds.

She couldn't. There was no way she could stroll out the doors without Cord noticing unless she organized a diversion. But wouldn't a diversion raise his suspicion? Yes. She didn't see it, any way at all to leave as herself. . . .

She stopped abruptly.

That was it. She couldn't freely leave as herself, but she could—most certainly could—walk out the door as someone else.

He'd had one hell of a night's sleep.

Cord let himself onto the Bradleys' small front landing. Maybe the cold air on his face would wake him up. At the moment his senses were dull, his eyes puffy, his head achy. He'd been so worried all night that the china doll would try to sneak away again that he'd barely slept. The scraps of rest he had managed had been lousy. Finally, he'd given up, put on a pot of coffee, washed up, and made his way out here.

Wren Bradley was an obstinate little thing. If he hadn't been waiting outside last night, she'd likely have maimed herself trying to climb down a nonexistent trellis. Had she really thought she'd get away so easily? It'd have to be a cold day in hell before a predictable stunt like that would fool him.

He leaned against the rail leading down the front steps and took a sip from the cup he held. Damn fancy china cups. They held two and a half swallows and didn't keep even that much hot.

A faint rustling drifted from the house through the door he'd purposely left ajar. Probably meant Cook was up. After him, she'd been the first to rise yesterday morning.

He looked out over the dawn, which was just minutes old. He swallowed more coffee, followed by a strong inhale and a ragged exhale. Five years ago, his job hadn't made him this tired. He'd sure never been this tired in the company of a woman.

A young, beautiful, passionate woman who still, like years before, didn't seem to realize how naive and sheltered she was. As far as he was concerned, Wren would do best to stick her parents' money back into her pocket and bide her time until she married the man the Colonel had chosen for her. These acting notions of hers were worse than doomed.

Within the house, a floorboard creaked. He used his boot to tip the door all the way open. Frowning, he listened. He made out scuffling noises coming from the direction of the kitchen. The opening and closing of a cabinet door. Then Eliza, the Bradley's cook and resident housekeeper, made a quick turn from the kitchen into the hallway.

He could only see her back as she ambled the few feet to the rear door, hips swaying. She wore a hat pulled low over frizzy red hair. The same basket she'd taken to the market early yesterday swung from her elbow.

"Morning," he said.

"Hrmph." She freed the locks and let herself out.

Funny, that was the same response he'd garnered to the same greeting yesterday morning. He took another sip of the hot brew, another deep breath, and looked back in the direction of the dawn.

Thirty minutes later Cord was sitting at the dining-room table reading the *Dallas Herald* when Cook walked downstairs from the second story.

He lifted his head from the article, stared straight ahead.

Her ponderous footfalls moved past the dining room into the kitchen. He heard her root around in there for a moment. The instant she murmured, "Wherever did my basket get off to?" Cord knew.

He shot from his chair, pounded up the stairs. Ignoring the nicety of knocking, he pushed his way into Wren's room. His gaze cataloged it in a single sweeping glance. No toiletries on the dressing table, tidy bed, all of her porcelain figurines left in perfect position. Damn it. He threw open the door to the armoire and found nothing. Empty. Same with her dresser drawers.

How in the *hell* had she gotten all her trunks past him? The customary craving of the chase—the desire to hunt and find—pounded through him. He was less accustomed to the burn of insulted pride.

In the guest room he'd been given, it took him just seconds to throw his shaving kit, comb, logbook, and writing supplies into his saddlebags. His pride had been smarting since his suspension, but this was damn near *it*. The last straw. There was no way in hell he was going to let a woman best him. He still couldn't believe he'd stood there and watched her walk out the door in broad daylight.

He shrugged into his coat as the stairs blurred beneath

his feet. From the hat rack near the door, he snatched his hat.

Cook glanced up when he stopped in the kitchen doorway.

"Wren's left," he said without preamble. He didn't have the time for more.

The older woman rose from where she'd been searching at the bottom of the pantry. She planted her hands on her hips and regarded him, slightly out of breath. "Is she the one who took my basket?"

"Yes. Will you tell Colonel and Mrs. Bradley that Wren's moved out, but not to worry, that I've gone with her."

"Doesn't look to me like yer with her."

"I will be. I'll send a telegram as soon as we reach our destination."

She scrunched her lips and pushed a wiry curl of red hair off her temple. "Hrmph."

Cord ran toward the stables. Between what had happened with Sackett, this piss-poor assignment he'd been given, and Wren's disappearance—the doll was turning out to be a slew of trouble. He'd known convicted felons who'd given him less.

Where would she have gone, he asked himself, wracking his brain for ideas as he saddled his horse. Where? He flicked the girth strap through the ring and pulled hard.

He'd start at the only place he knew for a fact she went when alone.
                                                        •

Cord stood inside City Hall's vacant theater assessing a board on which all manner of announcements had been posted. Since no one had yet arrived to question, this board amounted to the sum of his leads. Not a one of them helped him any. Anxiousness crackled across his nerves.

A young man pushed through the center doorway. Cord's attention honed on him, predatory and fast. The man stumbled to a halt.

"You work here?" Cord asked.

"Yes, sir."

"Cord Caldwell, Pinkerton Agency. What was posted here?" He gestured toward an empty space on the board. Four tacks and tiny triangles of white paper attested to the piece of paper that once connected them.

The kid's Adam's apple bobbed as he approached. "Uh—"

"Quickly."

"It was a notice for an audition that'll be held in Austin. Director made me take it down, seeing as he didn't want any of the company members getting ideas and leaving."

"Austin." Cord's instincts stirred, pricking the back of his neck. "You know who Wren Bradley is?"

"I do."

"Would she have had a chance to see the notice?"

The kid pushed back his hat and was halfway through a scratch when his face lit. "Yeah. When I was turning off the lights the other night I saw her looking at the board. The notice was up then."

Cord was halfway to the door when a train's whistle shrieked into the sky. He started to run.

Cord pushed to the front of the milling line of passengers waiting to pay train fares. "Is Wren Bradley on this train?" he asked the ticket agent, angling his head toward the string of cars seconds away from leaving the depot en route to Austin.

"Sir, there's a line—"

"Pinkerton Agency," Cord interrupted, flashing the badge he kept on the inner cover of his logbook since his suspension.

"I see," the man replied with a gulp. Suddenly eager to help, he ran his finger along the column of his bookkeeping notations.

Cord waited without breathing, his grip on his logbook iron tight.

The ticketer flipped one page, then another, and another. "No sir, there's no Miss Bradley on the eight-seventy-five."

"Sure?"

"Yes, sir."

Cord stormed through the crowd, his saddlebags thumping against his back. The sunlight doused him when he reached the depot's platform.

"All aboard," the conductor called, his voice deep against the hissing of steam that plumed into the air. The last few passengers hopped onto the metal stairs of the cars.

Something wasn't right. Cord's intuition was screaming at him that she was on this train. He didn't trust the agent's information, and he didn't trust Wren. He started trotting along the side of the train, searching for her through the windows. No time. The platform had emptied of all but friends and relatives waving good-bye. He ran faster. He passed the car containing the railroad's safe. A Pinkerton operative he knew, a man named Wilkes, was leaning his weight against the wooden door on the inside, in the process of rolling the barricade closed.

"Hold it for me," Cord yelled as he sprinted past.

Wilkes's surprised expression jerked from view.

No, no, not her, not her, not her. Damn it, she was here somewhere. Close. He could feel it.

The great engine heaved, and the train lumbered forward. He increased his speed to make up for the forward motion of the vehicle.

Not her, not her, and still he ran. *Damn it, Wren—*

There she was. His feet slashed to a stop. He watched her profile pull from view, unmistakable. The lemon-and-butter-colored hair, the pretty nose. Her head was bent forward, eyes closed.

The train picked up speed. The safe car where the Pinkertons rode sped toward him. As instructed, the door had been left open. Wilkes was waiting for him at the front edge of the opening, one arm anchored within, one arm outstretched.

Cord grasped Wilkes's outstretched forearm as the door came even with him and leapt inside.

"Please, God, just let me get out of this station without being found," Wren prayed silently, eyes squeezed closed, head bowed, fingers tightly interlaced in her lap. *I'm so close, and I want this so much. Please let me escape, Lord, let me not be caught, not now in these last moments when I'm so close. And God, I pray that my parents will find it in their hearts to forgive me for this. If you'll only let this train get the rest of the way out of the station—*

"Ma'am?" The voice of the lady in the seat next to her cut into her petitions. "Care for a gingersnap?"

Wren lifted her head enough to focus on the proffered cookie.

"I packed them for the trip," the lady commented.

"No. Thank you, though."

"As you like." The lady chewed heartily.

Afraid to look out her window for fear they'd not yet cleared the station, Wren slid her gaze slowly toward the passing scenery and sneaked a peek. Fields. Fields!

She stared fully out her window at beautiful, blessed fields. Not a house in sight. Just a sandy road snaking into the distance and a family of prairie chickens racing for cover.

The relief that rushed through her was so intense, her eyes watered. She piled one hand, then the other, atop her heart.

She'd done it. She'd been so afraid he'd track her down and find her, despite the precautions she'd taken. But no.

If a tiny stab of disappointment that she'd not see Cord again penetrated the glory of her successful dash for freedom—she discounted it entirely. This is what mattered—her future. She was an independent woman who'd purchased her ticket by independent means, just like any other single lady riding this train. An important step. A truly monumental moment.

Smiling with self-satisfaction, she relaxed her hands into her lap and rested her head against the seat back. The scenery trundled past in a blur that made her suddenly, thoroughly exhausted.

Not surprisingly. She'd stayed awake all night. It had taken every spare minute she'd had to create her disguise. She'd begun by raiding Alexandra's old room, which her mother used to store all manner of items. It was also where Cord happened to be sleeping during his stay, so Wren had quaked with worry that he'd return from his vigil outside and find her. He hadn't, and she'd returned to her room, arms overflowing with an old black gown that looked like something Cook would wear, red and orange embroidery thread, and batting left over from Alexandra's triumphant decorative-pillow-making phase.

Back in her room, she'd turned her lamp extremely low so as not to arouse notice and spent the rest of the night straining her eyes.

Fortunately, the hat Cook had given her for her last birthday was identical to Cook's own preferred style. Once she'd located it in a hatbox beneath her bed, she'd carefully chosen threads by hue, frayed them and curled them using the blade of her scissors, and stitched them onto the back of her hat so that they'd look from several yards away like Cook's red hair tucked up. Then she'd donned the black gown and spent a good deal of time arranging the batting underneath so that her shape resembled Cook's girth.

Add a fairly good imitation of Cook's posture, her walk, and her distinctive "Hrmph," and *voilà!* She'd tricked Cord Caldwell good and well.

Once she'd cleared her parents' property, she'd raced to Mr. Minor's orchard and shed her disguise at the base of a pecan tree. She'd walked away wearing her own clothing, which she'd had on beneath the costume. From the depot, she'd sent her Aunt Fanny a telegram. She'd told her aunt a vague version of the truth, that she needed to take a break from Dallas and was on her way to Austin for a visit.

Her eyelids drooped. Was it any wonder she wanted to be an actress? She had skills.

And in Austin . . . she yawned, half-asleep already. In Austin she'd use them to win herself a career.

Chapter 5

$\sim\!\infty\!\infty\!\sim$

Wren stepped off the train onto the narrow, white-washed slats that served as the Austin depot's platform. The crush of people disembarking under a blistering afternoon sun carried her forward. Aunt Fanny was nowhere in sight.

She groaned. Ten hours on a train which made frequent, grinding stops had been torture. She'd never much liked long rides on trains, or stages, or horseback, for that matter. Today's trip had been no exception. The constant sitting and occasional dozing had frayed her temper.

A matronly woman with an ostrich feather on her hat shouldered into Wren, almost knocking her over the platform rail into the muddy ditch beyond. With a gasp of outrage, Wren found her footing. *Just forge ahead*, she told herself. *You've come a long way with just a tiny bit farther to go.*

A gaggle of bodies parted.

Standing ten yards away, his feet braced apart, was Cord Caldwell.

"No." Her legs ceased to work, and strangers swarmed between them, almost shielding him from view. Not quite, though. She could still see the tip of his scarred renegade hunter's hat—a sign that mocked her. That hat boasted how very, very good he was at his job. At tracking those who wished to flee.

Lordy, let her have somehow made a mistake, let him have been a figment of her overtired imagination. She looked away, looked back, absurdly hoping he'd disappeared.

He was still there. Strong, tall, unmovable, legendary. His saddle bags slung over a muscled shoulder. Shock enveloped her in numbing waves. She'd been so sure that she'd gotten away. She couldn't *believe* he'd been on her train the whole time.

How on earth had he known her destination? However he'd done it, she could read on his expression that it had been elementary for him. Her hopefulness heavied to cloying disappointment.

She was so worn-out, she didn't even have enough fight left to flee. The last of the people separating them drifted away on a wave of small talk.

She and Cord stood facing each other, like gunmen who'd marched off their paces and were waiting only for their enemy to draw. The man was devastatingly good to look at, which made her dislike him all the more in this moment. That rugged jaw, and blue eyes glinting with dark victory. How tacky of him to eye her that way. How foolish of her to respond to him so strongly. This tugging she experienced inside herself every time she saw him was impossible.

Wren reluctantly covered the distance between them. He'd defeated her, but she refused to give him the satisfaction of seeing how much.

"How was your ride?" he asked. She could almost cut his wariness toward her. Fancy him being wary when she was the obvious loser in today's battle of minds.

"My ride? Well," her lips pursed. "I sat next to a woman shedding gingersnap crumbs, in front of a teething baby, and behind a lady with a huge ostrich feather on her hat. After all that, I've the pleasure of finding you here to greet me. Need I say more?" She set her satchel on the ground and planted her hands on hips. "And your ride?"

"The usual. Chatted with some of the boys."

"Pinkerton boys?"

"Yep."

She leaned toward him and sniffed. He smelled of fragrant cigar smoke. "You chatted and you smoked. What else did you do? Play poker?"

"Maybe," he said.

"Chatted, smoked, played poker. Any jokes told?"

"Jokes were told."

"Should you be so kind as to alert me of your presence the next time we ride together by train, I'll join you in the Pinkerton car."

He used his thumb to nudge up his hat. "We'll see. Did you arrange for anyone to meet you?"

"Yes, my Aunt Fanny."

"Had it all planned out, didn't you?"

She flicked her gaze over him. "Apparently not." She took a couple breaths, struggling to corral her courage. "Are you going to try and force me onto the next train back to Dallas? Because if you are, I think it only fair to warn you that you'll have a fight on your hands the likes of which you've never seen." She blew a wisp of hair off her forehead and gestured to the ground. "I'm not against dropping to the earth and screaming."

Tense quiet hummed between them. "As tempting as that sounds, it won't be necessary."

"No?" she asked, surprised.

"I won't force you to go back."

As relieved as she was about that, she couldn't help but wonder why. In his face she saw a determination, a hardness she'd come to associate with his work. He couldn't be planning to continue his hunt for Sackett after all it had cost him. Could he? Suddenly she suspected he was planning to do exactly that. Perhaps Cord had reasons of his own for wanting out from under her father's watchful eye.

A child's sob wafted across the air on a humid gust.

Cord's vision swept to a point beyond her. "Can I count on you not to run off for two seconds?"

"I'm too tired to run at present."

He picked up her satchel, walked past her, and approached a young boy. The child was dressed in an oversize shirt, which had been tucked into a ragged pair of pants and fastened around the waist by a length of rope. He was wandering along the splintery platform sobbing, his small fingers curved into his mouth, his gaze darting.

Cord set his hand on top the boy's head, halting his motion with that single steady touch. Gently, Cord turned the child toward him and knelt.

The boy looked up at him with panicky brown eyes.

"What's the matter?"

Wren barely heard Cord's softly spoken question. She neared, stopping behind him.

The boy made an unintelligible response.

Carefully, Cord guided the boy's hands from his mouth. As if he hadn't even noticed that the fingers were coated with tears and spit, he enveloped both small hands in one of his large, square ones.

Wren's heart wrenched.

"Are you lost?" Cord asked.

The boy nodded.

"Were you with your mother?"

"Uh-hum." His lips trembled. "I was."

"Where did you see her last?"

He extracted a hand from Cord's hold and pointed with a dirty-nailed finger in the direction of the station house. "I think she left for home without me."

"No. She wouldn't do that."

"I got lots of siblings. I think she forgot me."

"Not possible." Cord stood, still holding one of the boy's hands. "I bet she's inside. I'll help you find her." Cord drew him toward the station house. He glanced back to check on Wren.

She swallowed the lump in her throat and nodded, silently assuring him that she was following.

"I didn't see her in there," the boy said, his voice shaky.

"I'm taller than you are," Cord replied. "That helps me to spot people."

"Oh." The boy turned a hopeful, worshipful expression on Cord.

Wren's emotions swelled with a possessive pride she had absolutely no right to feel.

Seeing Cord walk hand in hand with the child made her wonder what it must be like for him, to carry the hopes of so many. Cord bore the expectations of the agency, the families of the victims he served, the railroads, sometimes the nation. Did he even notice that he was doing it now?

They entered the jammed station house just as a tired, frazzled woman rushed in from a back room.

"Does your mother have brown hair?" Cord asked.

"Yes."

"Is she wearing a brown dress?"

"Yes!"

Cord caught the woman's searching gaze and motioned her over. She wove anxiously through the throng.

When the boy spotted her, he let out a yelp of delight, scrambled to her, and threw himself around her legs.

The woman bent to hug him. "Thank God you're safe. I was so worried about you."

"I's worried, too."

"Didn't I tell you to stay close?"

"Yes, ma'am."

She smoothed the tears from his cheeks with her thumbs. "Okay. From now on, we'll hold on to each other tighter. Okay? Okay. It's all better now."

He nodded.

"Thank you," she said to Cord and Wren as she straightened. "That was good of you."

"You're welcome, ma'am," Cord said.

"Is there anything I can give you?"

"No, nothing."

She smiled gratefully, inclining her head in gratitude. Her son clutched her threadbare skirt with both fists as she led him away.

Cord made Wren feel small. She'd been so immersed in her own troubles that he'd almost reached the youngster before she'd discerned his intent, or the need of it.

Side by side, they picked their way through the bodies back to the yard beyond.

"What does your aunt look like?" he asked.

Wren cleared her throat in an attempt to regain her composure. This man was the same one who'd shattered her heart. She couldn't let herself forget that. "Aunt Fanny has gray hair, likely worn in a frivolous style. Pleasantly plump. Black gown."

His attention moved over the crowd. "Rosy cheeks?"

"That's the lady."

"I'll try and cut us a path over to her. Here," Cord shuttled her up beside him, protecting her with an arm across her upper back as they started forward.

She tried to pull away, but he wouldn't let her. Oh, God help her. She closed her eyes briefly, drawing on the last of her fortitude to resist noticing how good his arm felt around her.

Beyond the depot and the hodgepodge of structures, she spotted the capitol building. Its white dome speared upward, adjacent to a Texas flag stirring in the breeze. She'd not failed entirely. Her disguise had accomplished something critical—it had gotten her here. Her feet were treading on the ground of Austin, city of her one great chance. Her audition would be held in just a little over two weeks, on November 10.

"Wren!" a feminine voice pierced the gathering.

She looked up to see Aunt Fanny, waving a frilly lavender handkerchief and holding a matching lavender parasol, both of which looked glaringly odd coupled with her staid black mourning gown.

"Aunt Fanny!" Wren rushed ahead of Cord to embrace her father's elder sister. Fanny's hug smelled of butterscotch candy and rose toilet water.

"Oh, my little bird! My dearest heart." Fanny squashed Wren's nose against her bosom and wouldn't let go. "I received the telegram you sent this morning, and of course I'm here to get you. How lovely that you've finally heeded my pleas and come for a visit. How's your father?"

"Very well," Wren murmured into a taffeta-covered breast.

"And your dear mother?"

"Also well."

"Alexandra?"

"Wonderful."

"Oh. Littlest bird." Fanny crooned the nickname she'd always favored for her, then stroked her back before releasing her.

Upon straightening Wren noticed, with a pang of dismay, that Fanny was crying. "Aunt Fanny—"

"Don't mind me." Fanny fluttered her handkerchief around the region of her eyes. "It's just that you've grown since I've seen you last. All changed."

"I saw you three months ago," Wren reminded her gently.

"You've grown, bird. I *swear*."

Wren kissed Fanny's cheek and hugged her again. Fanny had lost her husband in the war and had no children to dote upon. Understandably, she'd turned her huge capacity for loving onto her nieces.

"Aunt Fanny, I'd like to introduce you to Mr. Cord Caldwell." She pulled away enough to gesture to him.

"Oh, Mr. Caldwell. I do say." Fanny extended a dimpled hand.

Cord took it, and bestowed a kiss.

"*I do say!*" Fanny exclaimed.

"Pleased to meet you, ma'am."

"You must, must, must call me Aunt Fanny. Nothing less! I swear." She laughed her trademark laugh. A loud, hearty guffaw, the kind most people reserved for truly hilarious moments, followed by . . . Wren listened for the telltale finish . . . a gasp and a high-pitched hiccup. "And who might you be in relation to Wren?"

"I'm her . . . protector." He looked momentarily uncomfortable. "The Colonel felt she needed company."

"A protector. Imagine! Our bird doing anything dangerous enough to merit protection."

"My sentiment exactly," Wren said, her expression wry.

"However, now that I've laid eyes on Mr. Caldwell, I shall have to scold you, bird, if you *don't* attempt anything dangerous. We Bradley women must do what whatever necessary to keep such a man near at hand."

"There's nothing I'd rather do than stay near the two of you," Cord said, catching Fanny fully in the sights of his masculine charm. He had a way of looking at a woman as if she were the only one in the world.

Even Wren, who knew better, felt a flutter at the sight of his smile. His charm only made him more dangerous.

"Mr. Caldwell!" Aunt Fanny twittered, clearly won over. Laugh gasp hiccup. Her attention swung to Wren. "Where are your trunks? Do tell me you brought trunks!"

"I brought several. I assume they're being unloaded from the baggage car."

"Excellent! Once Helmut has dropped us off at home, I'll have him come straight back with the wagon to fetch them." She waved her hands toward herself like two chubby, ivory fans. "Come, come both of you." Her skirts flapped as she led them toward the line of carriages. "To think, a man in the house again. A man! There hasn't been a man in my house in nigh on fifteen—seventeen years now."

"Pa stayed there last Christmas," Wren pointed out, trying to keep up.

"I'm not talking about brothers. Or husbands of relatives, or dear friends."

"Oh." As if that left many categories.

Fanny stopped before the side door of her open-topped carriage. "This is ours, let's climb in. Yes, that's it, bird, just clamber on up there. I'm positively thrilled to have you both! Won't I be the envy of my Sunday school class." Again the belly laugh. Gasp. Hiccup.

Once they'd settled, Wren and Cord opposite Fanny with their thighs touching, her aunt turned to the long-suffering-looking Asian gentleman sitting upon the driver's seat. "I believe we're ready to go on home now, Helmut."

"Yes, Aunt Fanny."

The carriage rumbled into motion.

"What a lovely afternoon. I had Helmut fold back the top so we could enjoy a ride in the fresh air." Fanny smoothed a hand over her hair.

Wren tilted her head and tried to figure how her aunt had accomplished the style. She'd somehow wound her gray hair, white at the temples, into two unflattering lumps on either side of her head, above her ears. A loop of gray-white braid sprouted from the exact center of each lump.

"How are your talents in the performing arts coming, bird?"

"Quite well." Fanny, bless her, had always been an avid supporter of her theatrical attempts.

"You know Evangeline Wilcox, don't you?" Fanny inquired.

"No."

"Come, the elderly lady from the bakery?"

Wren did what she always did when Fanny insisted that she knew people she didn't—she pursed her lips as if she was thinking hard, and nodded.

"Ima Harrigan, then. I *swear* you know Ima."

More pursing of lips, more feigned concentrated thinking.

"Anyhow, Ima's son Johnny just married a darling girl, from, oh, let me see, Tennessee I think. That Tennessee is beautiful country, don't you believe so, Mr. Caldwell?"

"Yes, I do."

"So do I!" She laughed gaily. "Anyway, Johnny's wife attended singing and acting lessons with Mr. Miles Fenner last time she was here in Austin. Do you know of Miles Fenner?"

"Yes," Wren replied at once, her interest in the conversation rising dramatically. While he'd never performed in a starring role, Miles Fenner had played important secondary characters on stages from New York to California.

"He's here in Austin," Aunt Fanny said, "enjoying a few years off to spend time with his dear relatives, the Wileys. He's taken on a few select students and instructs them in one of the parlors at Raymond House."

Wren's mouth watered. She'd have loved to take lessons from Miles Fenner. Unfortunately, the money she had remaining after her train ticket was dwindling fast. She couldn't begin to afford what he must be charging.

"Johnny's wife's singing ability improved an astonishing amount under his tutelage," Aunt Fanny said. "Would you be interested in studying under him?"

"Of course but—"

"Then it's done. I'll see to it that you're scheduled in immediately."

"Aunt Fanny, you don't have to—"

"I want to. You must allow your old aunt a few pleasures, bird. Besides, what would your parents say if I didn't care for you as I should while you're under my roof?"

Wren knew exactly what her parents would say if they knew Aunt Fanny was encouraging her so generously. "Thank you." The words were inadequate. "I don't know how I'll ever repay you."

"Think nothing of it. Doesn't the golden shade of Wren's traveling costume remind you of daffodils, Mr. Caldwell? I grow daffodils in the spring. I can't wait for spring, can you, Mr. Caldwell?"

"No, Aunt Fanny."

"Me neither. Me neither! Ah, spring, with the whispering breezes. . . ."

Wren leaned into the comfortable seat, which caused her thigh to rub inadvertently against Cord's. Immediately, she scooted as far from him as the quarters allowed and tried hard not to notice how the skin on the outside of her leg tingled from the contact.

He was her father's henchman, that much he'd made abundantly clear. In Pa's name he'd do everything in his power to oppose her dreams. For all practical purposes he was her enemy. Despite that, almost rebelliously, her thigh continued to tingle.

Late on her second night in Austin, Wren let herself out Fanny's front door, hoping for solitude. The past day had been a busy one, filled with unpacking and numerous visits to the homes of Aunt Fanny's friends. Her aunt carried on as if Wren knew all the women intimately, when in truth her recollections of them were foggy at best.

She settled onto the swing that hung suspended from the covered porch. Soft light slanted through the window at her back, illuminating her skirts, the boards at her feet, the steps.

Though she'd rather have been sleeping, her mind was spinning too fast to allow it. She'd left home for good. She'd truly done it, and tonight the enormity of her actions were catching up with her. Nostalgia, doubt, excitement, regret, and independence had all gusted through her these past hours.

She still didn't feel quite like the person she'd been before Sackett had snatched her. Maybe because she wasn't anymore. Maybe because she'd never feel that same way, be that same woman again.

She eyed the vacant prairie extending in all directions from Fanny's property and consciously tried to relax taut shoulder muscles.

You say anything, you try to scream again and I'll kill you. Sackett's harsh whisper snaked out of the night.

Her heart thudded. Faster, faster. "Stop it," she whispered to herself. She looked behind her, toward the shadowed corners of the porch. No sign of Sackett. See. Don't be a coward, don't let him best you. It's safe.

The hitching of his breath, terrifyingly loud, panted at the back of her neck. She squeezed shut her eyes, trying to block out the feel of his arms, the ice of the gun against her temple.

Just ignore it, she told herself. *He can't hurt you.*

But he had hurt her.

She sat, trembling, her cold fingertips digging into the wooden armrest of the swing. Horse's hooves clawed the earth, deafening her, wrapping her in terror, taking her away from anyone, from Cord. Where was Cord? She needed him—

"Need help?"

She opened her eyes to see him emerge from the fields, his hands in his pockets. Unexpectedly, he smiled. That awful, beautiful smile. The smile that promised her he knew exactly what she looked like naked.

She held herself immobile while the fear flushed away. Unmistakably, Cord had the power to make her feel safe. Had she not been so grateful to see him, she'd have groaned. He was the last man on earth who had the right to make her feel that way . . . the last man she ought to allow that right.

He lowered himself onto the porch swing next to her. It dipped with his solid, secure weight. "Need help getting this thing moving?" he asked.

She smiled shakily at him.

His brow knit. "You okay?"

"Yes," she said, thinking how kind he could be at the most disarming and necessary moments. "The eye that never sleeps" really did apply to him. She'd never dreamed Pinkerton operatives took the company slogan so seriously.

Using his heels, he started to rock the swing. The motion and his protective presence lulled her. Back and forth they went.

After a time he said, "So, you want to tell me how you got those trunks out of your room?"

She smiled inwardly. It's the first time he'd mentioned

the deception she'd pulled yesterday morning. Apparently, it had been gnawing at him despite his silence. "You've been dying to know, haven't you?"

"Not dying."

She waited for him to plead with her to tell him how she'd done it. When he didn't, she found she couldn't resist revealing the full extent of her cleverness. "When you followed me on my errands the other day, I slipped into the back room at the mercantile and handed Jimmy a note and some money. He followed instructions by arriving at the house, telling Cook I'd finally hired someone to do what she's been pestering me to do for months—clean out the attic. Then Jimmy proceeded to walk down the stairs with several trunks, unquestioned. He carted them to the depot for me."

She thought she saw a small sliver of admiration light his eyes—small, but crucial to her.

"What about your train ticket?" he asked. "Your name wasn't on the books."

"No. Whether or not you arrived in time for the train's departure I knew that's the first place you'd check. I intercepted a lady outside the depot. For a small fee, she agreed to buy my ticket under her name. Amazing how far money will get you." She shrugged. "Your turn to tell your secrets."

"What secrets?" he asked.

"Namely, how did you track me?"

He explained.

It hadn't occurred to her that he'd visit the theater first when she disappeared. Thank God the notice had already been discarded. That meant he didn't know the day or the time of her audition. She very much feared her father had expressly forbidden him to let her anywhere near theaters.

Moonlit seconds slipped past. She noticed that their thighs were almost touching like they had in the carriage, and inched as far from him as the seat allowed. Their eyes met, before her gaze skittered away and she tried to move even farther from him.

If he were as honest as she, Cord would have warned her against flattening her injured midsection against the armrest. As it was, he didn't want to make her more defensive and suspicious around him than she was already.

"I think," she said slowly, staring straight ahead, "it's time we made our peace with each other, you and I."

He stuck his forearm behind his head, a makeshift pillow, and canted his face toward her. He could hardly credit it. She was raising the white flag. The light coming from inside picked out the flawless line of her cheekbone and those damned lips. All pink and wide and full. There were things he wanted to do to those lips. Things he wanted those lips to do to him. If she'd been anyone but the Colonel's daughter. . . .

But that was exactly who she was. That, and a woman smart enough to have made an ass out of him yesterday morning. Ironically, he respected her for that. Her resourcefulness had forced him to admit that she no longer belonged in the pretty and pampered box he'd mentally placed her in since she'd blurted out that she loved him at sixteen. She'd changed.

She was still pretty, and she was still delicate, but she had a core of strength running down the center of her now. A china doll as tough as she appeared to be fragile. Her contradictions fascinated him.

Five years ago, she'd stared at him with open adoration. She no longer did, and never would again. A ridiculous sense of loss flared inside him. How stupid. He squelched the feeling fast, sure as hell he didn't want her getting ideas about him again. In his time, he'd already had to tell more women than he'd ever wanted to that he didn't love them. It wasn't their fault, and he always felt bad about letting them down, but love wasn't an option he allowed himself, and hadn't been since earliest childhood.

"We can be unwilling adversaries," she said. "We're united in that neither of us wants to be tied to the other."

"Right."

"We both may have . . . things we want to accomplish in Austin without . . . certain parties finding out. I'm willing to let you do what you have to do without interfering, if you'll do the same for me."

He hid his surprise by moving not a single muscle, not even the tiniest lift of an eyebrow. Damn if the little chit wasn't blackmailing him. God, she was canny. She'd somehow deduced that he had his own purposes here, and she was right. He needed to do what he could during his stay to further his search for Sackett. Without that, he was nothing. No one.

She was offering not to alert her father to his doings, if he'd keep quiet about her audition. He set his jaw, weighing his options. "In order to keep you safe, I'm honor-bound not to let you out of my sight," he said carefully. On that, he wouldn't compromise.

"I know. I don't expect you to."

Her father had asked him to keep her away from the theater. If she won herself a part in the acting troupe, he'd have to admit to the Colonel that he'd allowed her to audition. Was that chance worth the ability to pursue Sackett while in Austin? How much was he willing to pay?

"I know my father probably asked you to bar me from the theater," Wren said, correctly figuring the cause of his hesitation. "I'm not asking him now. I'm asking you."

Could he afford to allow Wren a margin of leniency? At the heart of it, she was asking for what he'd already seen her struggle fiercely for—just enough respect and independence to make her own choices.

"Do we have a deal?" she asked, voice tense.

He hadn't gotten to be good at his job without taking necessary risks. He always made his own decisions about cases that belonged to him. Hers was no exception. And he never let outlaws go, no matter what.

"Yes," he said. "We have a deal." He still didn't trust her, and he doubted she trusted him.

Upstairs, someone extinguished a lamp, casting the two of them into an even greater blanket of solitude.

Wren rushed to her feet, he guessed because she couldn't bear sitting beside him a moment longer. He regarded her calmly as she went to stand at the rail that ran between pale columns all the way around the porch.

Her back partially turned to him, she extracted a folded handkerchief. Even in the murky light, he could see that it was stitched with elaborate swirls around the border and a curling W at the corner.

She was something. So fine. In flashes, like right now, she made him feel as if he'd been on the trail too long. As if he needed to come in from the cold to a home like this one and a woman like her.

She uncovered a dark rectangle. "Chocolate," she explained before breaking it in half. "Here, have some."

"No thanks."

"Take it." She set it on his knee and went back to the rail.

"I really shouldn't," she whispered, just before popping the chocolate into her mouth. Her eyes sank closed while she chewed.

Silently, Cord pushed from the swing and moved toward her. God. His erection strained. If she sucked this much enjoyment from chocolate, he could only imagine. . . .

She opened heavy lids. Jumped to find him so close. "What?" she brushed her fingers over her lips and chin. "Did I get some on my face?"

"Yes. On your lip. Open up, it's right. . . ."

Looking dubious, she backed away.

"Open up," he commanded.

She parted her lips on a kind of grimace and he tossed his chocolate in. Right on the center of her tongue. Perfect aim.

"Oh!" Her lips snapped shut. Then, "Oooohh," as realization and taste combined. She worked the sweet between her teeth, her eyes still regarding him cautiously.

He liked chocolate. But he'd never again eat it if he could give her his instead.

"Thank you," she said, her tone formal. "I like surprises."

"You're welcome." He leaned back, propping his hips against the rail, crossing his arms.

"Since you're in such a generous mood, I'm thinking this might be the time to make another request."

He hoped like hell the request involved her mouth and his. . . . No, he amended. A request like that would be soul-destroying to decline. He probably wouldn't survive it. "You're pushing your luck, Wren."

"I know, but since we're going to be together for the next few days, unwillingly, I wondered if you would teach me . . . In truth, I'm *asking* you if you will teach me how to protect myself."

He didn't answer. Just sat there, thinking about the idea.

"Sometimes, since Sackett, I'm afraid, and I hate that. I want to have back the confidence I had before." She paused, clearly trying to articulate what she was feeling. "I'm determined to learn to protect myself, because I don't want to be weak or helpless should anything like that happen to me again. You have knowledge I need."

He knew how much pride it had cost her to tell him that, to ask for his help. Warmth opened within his chest. He stared toward the prairie without seeing it, fighting to eradicate his softening.

"I'll—I'll offer you something in return."

"What?" he asked, illogically irritated that she didn't think him noble enough to give her anything out of simple kindness.

"No more escapes," she said.

He regarded her skeptically.

"That's right." She rushed onward, refusing to allow him a chance to say no. "Despite the current evidence to the contrary, you have to sleep sometimes, I assume. Don't you?"

"Sometimes."

"Well, so far you've gotten no sleep, and eventually you'd perish from exhaustion and I'd be left unprotected." She scoured his face with her gray gaze, scowled.

"In addition, to sweeten the deal, you can wear whatever clothing you're comfortable in. I don't expect you to continue dressing in suits when you're around me. I'm not that fancy, for heaven's sake."

"How is this bargain going to work?"

"At the end of . . . every full day . . ."

He got the impression she was making this up as she went along.

". . . during which I haven't sneaked away, you'll teach me . . . something."

"Something?"

"Yes. Shooting or hitting or kicking. Whatever it is you think I'd benefit from learning."

"I see."

While he considered, her hand rose to her locket. She started twisting it. Starlight glittered along the chain as it writhed. "So will you?"

He'd seen women die because they hadn't known how to raise a hand in their own defense. "Yes" he said, partly because he couldn't stand the sight of her distress any longer.

"Did you say yes?" She arched excitedly toward him.

He prayed she'd not give him cause to regret either of the compromises he'd made tonight. "Yes."

Wren pulled his hand to her lips and kissed his knuckles.

Longing clutched him, so tight he sucked in a breath. How long had it been since anyone had touched him like that? With true tenderness? Forever.

A need, for something he didn't have, something he didn't understand, swamped him. Crippled him. He was stunned and shamed by it because it illuminated as nothing had before the depth of his vulnerability.

Wren felt Cord's hand tense within her own.

I've overstepped, she realized. A tide of gratitude had momentarily carried her away and she'd kissed his hand. With anyone else, such a gesture would have been innocent.

His face turned to stone.

Doggone it, I should have thought before acting. Now she'd made them both uncomfortable. He likely feared she was about to profess her undying love again. The strain between them heightened.

Cord tugged slightly.

She let go, waited an awkward moment for him to speak, then retreated a few steps toward the door. She tried to pick the right words to tell him that she just did things like that occasionally. It didn't mean anything—

"I wonder, Wren. What's going to become of your relationship with your suitor if your dreams of acting are realized?"

She swallowed. "Who? Edward?"

"I don't know. He's not my suitor."

"I'll worry about Edward's reaction when the time comes."

"Is he the kind of man who'll wait?"

Her ire sparked. "Is this any of your business?"

"Everything about you is my business until your father tells me otherwise."

The steel in his tone was ominous enough to make her shiver. "I'll answer your question, but not because you have the right to ask it. Of course Edward will wait for me. He's waited all his life."

"Do you love him?"

"Now that, I'm absolutely positive, is none of your concern." How dare he! She'd thought once that she'd loved the man standing in front of her, had told him so, and he'd rejected her. Now, five years later he had the audacity to care whom she loved? No, he'd had his chance to care, back when she'd been a child.

Nowadays she was a woman with aspirations apart from him and he was a Legend of near-mythical proportions in this part of the country, a man married to his job. His gaze, as black as onyx, drilled into her, stripping the clothing from her body and leaving her bare. She didn't know whether to slap him or to sob because of how devastatingly handsome he was to her. Even now.

"You best go back in," he said.

"Believe me, I can't leave fast enough." She marched to the door, the reckless part of her not wanting to leave and hoping he'd stop her.

He didn't, of course. As she was closing the door behind her, she caught one last glimpse of him, standing alone below a sky full of her wishing stars. In a dizzying wave, she remembered all the times she'd pleaded with those same stars to answer her prayers. To grant her a dream.

Chapter 6

❝I'm going to teach you to hold the pistol with two hands. So face the target directly."

Wren nodded.

Cord eyed her posture. "Legs shoulder width apart. Don't lock them, though."

"Okay."

Concentration was already evident on her face, and he hadn't even handed her his gun yet.

All day, Wren had been trying to break free from her aunt long enough for their first lesson.

Cord knew because he'd heard almost every syllable that had passed between them throughout the day. Even when he was downstairs and they up, their voices had carried. The feminine talk should have driven him to distraction, but he'd been strangely contented listening to Wren's voice.

It was just as well they'd decided to allow each other as

109

much freedom and privacy as Cord's promise to protect her allowed. The craving he'd felt when she'd kissed his hand last night was something he never wanted to experience again. As it was, he'd lost his temper and hours of sleep over that one small contact.

It was deep into the afternoon now, and Wren appeared to be taking this hard-won lesson very seriously. Her silvery eyes were intent.

Cord handed her his six-shooter. "Repeat back to me the high points of everything I've explained so far, and we can start shooting."

She cushioned it in her left hand and used her right to point as she spoke. "This is the grip. This is the trigger. When pulled back the trigger sets off a charge in this end, the breech end of the barrel. Basically, an explosion is caused in a tube that's closed at one end. The expanding gases of the explosion force the bullet out at high speed. The bullet emerges from the muzzle end. Here."

Cord almost fell to the ground in amazement. Whoever would have thought the china doll would have a head for guns? He hid his astonishment, because he didn't want to offend her. "Good. What about the ammunition?"

"The primary designation of ammunition is caliber."

"Which refers to?"

"The diameter of the bore."

"And the bore is?"

"The empty chamber which the bullet is fired through." He started to grin. "And the caliber of this pistol?"

"This is a Remington Model 1874. Its caliber is forty-four."

"Which means?"

"Point-four-four of an inch in diameter." She matched his smile with a reserved one of her own. The curl of her lips made the apples of her cheeks stand out as they were wont to do when she was truly pleased. "How'd I do?"

"You know how you did."

"That well?" she asked.

"That well. Let's shoot." They were standing knee-deep in grass a few hundred yards behind Aunt Fanny's house, which was situated on a huge plot of land on the outskirts of the city. He'd staked a makeshift wooden target into the ground twenty yards away.

He stepped close and gently placed her fingers into the proper grip position. He was so close he could hear her breath quicken.

His own blood leapt in response. He stilled, and stared at the blend of his dark fingers against her satiny light ones. He wanted to watch those light fingers trail over his chest, his naked thighs, wrap around the thrust of his arousal.

He stepped abruptly back at the same moment she did. He cleared his throat and gestured harshly toward the target. "Extend your arms and point the gun at that, keeping the top of the weapon in a continuous line with your forearms and wrists."

"I understand."

"Now align the sights." He pointed out the upright sight at the front and the notch at the rear, careful this time to avoid touching her. "Position the top of the front post until it's level with the top of the rear sight, centered between the notch."

Her brows drew together diligently as she aimed.

Cord leaned closer, setting his head beside hers so he could see what she was seeing down the barrel of his gun. "What are you aiming at?" he asked.

"Ah, the ground," she answered, her voice thready.

"Do you have reason to shoot the ground?"

"No. Could you . . . not stand so close to me?"

"Do you want my help or not?"

She swallowed convulsively. "I do."

"Then tell me, what are you aiming at now?" Cord asked, staying stubbornly close so he could judge her aim.

"The wooden target, not that I have any more cause to shoot it than I did the ground."

"Your aim looks about right." He moved away, and visibly saw her relax. "Try for the bird's nest up and to the right." He watched her search the treetops, spot the nest, and lift the gun. "Now your aunt's parlor window."

She swiveled.

"Fine. Now the barrel out back."

The gun arced through the air.

"Now the chicken with the black spots."

She spun toward the coop and aimed.

"Good."

Wren lowered the gun.

"In addition to aiming and pulling the trigger, shooting is about awareness," he said. "You've got to learn to listen and to observe. When you're in trouble, you'll need to move quickly and spot your target even quicker."

Wren nodded solemnly. He'd never seen someone so desperate to learn. "Close your eyes."

"My eyes?"

He nodded. "Close 'em."

A frown lingering about her forehead, her lids drifted shut.

At least in this she was willing to trust him. A sharp ache twisted through his chest. "I'm going to throw things," he said. "I want you to turn toward the sound, then open your eyes and aim."

"Okay." The bronze of the sun shone in the palest strands of her hair.

He wrenched his gaze from her, picked up a stick, and threw it.

She pivoted, opened her eyes, pointed the gun.

"Well done. Now faster."

They spent several minutes on the exercise. If anyone had told him a week ago that he'd be standing in a field throwing rocks, he'd have called them a liar. And yet here he was, his reputation in shreds and Lloyd Sackett on the loose. His disgrace with the agency broiled at the back of his mind all the time.

He hoisted a rock and threw it overhanded, hard. Wren's indigo skirts flared as she swiveled. She lifted the gun, her profile focused.

"Just a few more," he murmured.

He threw two more sticks and one more rock, assessing her reactions all the while.

"Let's fire it," he decided.

She blinked at him. Rose from the day's unexpected heat blossomed along the high ridge of her cheekbones and across her nose. Unmistakable anticipation glinted in her eyes.

"Ready for that?" he asked.

"Yes."

He nodded toward the target. "Go ahead, then. The first three chambers are empty, so you'll be dry firing. Check each time the hammer falls back to see if your aim has jumped off course. If it has, you're pulling it. The idea is to keep your grip firm, but easy. And to exert no pressure in any direction accept for straight back and smooth with the trigger."

She gave herself a delicate shake before concentrating on sighting the weapon.

"I can't focus on both the sights and the target," she said.

"No, good observation. Focus only on the front sight, at the muzzle end of the barrel. Everything else will be slightly fuzzy."

"What part of the target do you want me to hit?"

He resettled his hat with his hand. "If you hit any part of it, you'll be the best student I've ever had."

"Ah. I'd like to be the best." She grew so intent, he worried she'd give herself a headache. "I want to hit the letter *O*."

The target had been the side of a packing crate once. Several letters were still visible. "Fine. Aim the top of the front post just below the *O*, then."

She dry fired three times, squeezing the trigger with exacting gentleness. "Am I ready?"

"Ready. When you fire the recoil is going to push the gun toward you. Nothing to worry about," he added when her eyes widened, "just wanted you to be prepared. Take a breath, let some of it out, then hold the rest when you shoot."

"Wish me luck."

"You don't need it."

"I hope I don't inadvertently kill a squirrel."

"You won't."

He could see she was trembling a little. She took an inordinate amount of time aiming, and he let her. Finally, looking determined enough to run the bullet to the target if she had to, she pulled the trigger. Gunfire cracked the air. Wren yelped and stumbled backward.

He caught her and righted her in one motion. The instant he'd steadied her, he removed his hand and stepped away. "What do you think?"

"Did I hit it?"

"Not that time, doll."

"Then I think I can do better."

He laughed. That she could make him do so, despite an erection, was a feat no woman had ever accomplished with him before. Laughter and torturous desire simultaneously. Strange for a single-minded man, used to experiencing one emotion at a time. "I couldn't explain what the force of shooting a gun would feel like," he said. "Some things you just have to experience to understand."

"It was . . . powerful."

"Yes."

She didn't turn to try again. She just kept studying him. In the distance he could hear the roll of carriage wheels against earth and someone somewhere beating dirt from a rug.

"Thank you, Cord. For this."

"It's nothing."

"Not to me. It means a lot that you would believe that I could learn this. And that you would take the time to teach me."

He didn't know what to say. She obviously needed someone at this point in her life to believe in her. He was an unlikely choice to do so, a man who's loyalty was first to her father. Who was nothing to her. Who had nothing to offer her. "Hit the target this time and prove me a good teacher."

Resolve settling into her expression, she turned and raised the weapon. The gun roared.

This time, wood flew.

Hot damn, she'd hit it! They looked at each other, both grinning broadly with triumph.

Cord tried to remember the last time he'd experienced such pride. It ran down the center of him, singing like a waterfall, rushing and filling all the crevices of his life that had been empty since childhood. He shook his head, marveling at her.

"I hit the *T*, didn't I?" she asked.

"Yep, you hit the *T*."

"I was still aiming for the *O*." She shrugged. "But at the moment I'm too happy to care."

"As you should be. You'll get better with practice. Like anything else, it takes time."

"Did it take you time?"

"Years. I'm still learning."

"When did you start?"

"When I was about seven, I guess."

"Who taught you?"

His father had. He remembered, in a series of knife-sharp flashes, what had happened the day he and his father had returned from their first shooting lesson. His mother sitting at the kitchen table reading a letter and sobbing. His father's devastation when he learned the letter was from his wife's lover, the man she'd promised she would never communicate with again. The screaming fight that had followed.

"You're frowning," Wren said.

Instantly, Cord cleared his expression. "My father taught me."

She lifted a hand to shade her eyes. "I bet your father brags about you to all his friends," she said.

"I wish I could say he did."

A lovely little bracket formed on either side of her lips. "How could he not brag about you?"

He wondered what it was about her that made him want to tell her things he'd never told anyone. "He wasn't pleased with the career I chose."

"What did he want you to become?"

"A doctor, like him."

"Why didn't you?"

"Because I didn't want to be like him." And because the job he did now answered something basic within him. Through his work he made things better for people. He brought order to mess. He fixed things. He got justice for those who couldn't get it for themselves.

"I guess we've more in common than the fact that we don't want to be chained to one another," she said quietly.

The realization startled him. Why hadn't he seen it before? He'd assumed her life to be perfect because of the luxury of it, when he, of all people, knew that growing up with wealth had nothing to do with contentment. They had—both of them—broken away.

"Cord, I—"

"You've got one more bullet."

She gave him a troubled look.

"Let's get back to it."

Tomorrow, after he took Wren to her first singing lesson, he'd do what he could to track Sackett. Not because of his parents, but because in his own eyes he was just deadwood until he got his purpose back.

Halfway across the country, Edward Clifton walked from the Southern Atlantic's railroad offices in Atlanta. He stopped on the sidewalk and dusted off his top hat before settling it on his head at a dapper angle.

He looked both ways along the city street, saw the well-oiled buggies, the gaily dressed ladies. He turned in the direction of his hotel, his walking stick tapping in time to his footfalls.

This business trip for the Southern Atlantic had taken him away from Dallas longer than usual. Three months, which was too long.

He'd had enough of dealing with ineptitude. More than his fill of patiently explaining the railroad's new accounting methods to clerks across the deep South.

Stopping outside his hotel, he glanced up at the gray facade with the white window trim. This was the last time he'd return here. As of today, he'd finished his work in Atlanta and had only Macon left to visit.

Burdens began to lift from his shoulders, one after the other. Just one more city, and then he could go home. Macon shouldn't take him long. A week at most.

He pushed through the hotel's front door and hurried past the talkative tones of his hostesses, the Misses Merriweather.

Once he'd gained his room, he hung his hat, propped up his cane, and sat on the edge of the skinny bed to pry off his shoes. With a contented sigh, he tugged the pillow from beneath the quilt and reclined against it.

His fingers drew as if magnetized to the inside pocket of his coat. All day long he'd felt the bulk of the little velvet box, which was far too valuable ever to leave in a hotel room unattended. Especially around two spinster sisters with designs.

The lid opened soundlessly beneath his fingers. Nestled within the dark green velvet bed a ring sparkled. A platinum ring containing the fattest diamond he'd ever seen.

He smiled.

Wren could hardly put him off any longer when she saw this. He took it out, studied it, and anticipated the look on her face when he gave it to her. The delight, the amazement, the thankfulness.

Resting the box on his belly, he squinted toward the window and the sky beyond. He'd been anxious for this a long time. All his life. It had been hard growing up under the weight of constant gratitude to the Colonel, a man who had taken his impoverished parents beneath his wing before he'd been born, before he'd had a chance to voice his objection. His mother and father had ingrained indebtedness into him just as surely as they had polite manners and habits of cleanliness. He could be excused, or ought to be, he supposed, for being born with pride. The scraping humility had always felt like a coat that didn't fit him—too tight, uncomfortable.

Not that he didn't love the Colonel. No one, but no one, worshiped the man as much as he.

His eyes narrowed as he assessed the ring, thinking of Colonel Phillip Bradley. Beneath great respect, envy spiraled. He'd disliked himself for fostering lesser emotions toward the man once. No longer. He'd matured to live in company with them, to accept them without hanging his head. Through no fault of his own, he'd had to work harder than most, be smarter. That merited resentment, which in turn fostered a healthy ambition. Because of it, he'd succeeded where others had wallowed in failure.

He angled the ring toward the window and white sparks glistened in the diamond's heart. Marrying Wren would be the final proof of how far he'd come and of how little he had to apologize for anymore. His parents could continue to grovel as long as they wished. He would sit at the Colonel's table as his son soon, as his equal. There could be no better wife for him than Wren. He wanted her with the same voracious need that had driven him to graduate the schools he'd attended with the highest marks, to climb the ranks of the Southern Atlantic with such speed.

As soon as he arrived in Dallas, he'd pay the Colonel a visit and ask for Wren's hand. He'd already chosen the words he'd say, had practiced them repeatedly. Not that he needed his request to be perfect. The Colonel had approved of the match since the womb.

Beautiful, wealthy, highborn Wren.

He could hardly wait to call her wife.

Chapter 7

Wren sat in the hallway of Raymond House Hotel, her rear positioned on a spindly antique chair, her hands folded carefully in her lap. Across the high, narrow table alongside her, sat the spindly chair's mate. Unoccupied.

Cord had chosen instead to lean against the opposite wall while they waited for Mr. Miles Fenner to finish his current lesson. Since their arrival ten minutes ago, they'd been overhearing his student's divine soprano. A soprano *so* abysmally divine that the sound of it tore Wren's instincts between strangling herself with the nearby curtain cord or simply sprinting toward the wilderness.

She caught herself twisting her locket. She dropped it and returned her gloved fingers to a polite pile in her lap. She intensely disliked the nervousness skittering around and around her belly. Never before had she been nervous singing in front of an audience.

Then again, none of those audiences had contained a renowned Broadway star.

"You worried?" Cord asked.

"A little." She tried to draw on some of his obviously overflowing store of strength. He looked magnificent. After their conversation on the swing he'd reverted to wearing his trail clothes. Today, a green-flannel shirt which emphasized the blue of his eyes. Wonderful-looking creases and worn patches marked his denim trousers and his canvas coat. He clasped his renegade hunter's hat at his side with one of those broad hands that she fully adored and had lain in bed last night thinking of for hours.

All yesterday afternoon and evening after their shooting lesson, she'd been jumpy and awkward around him. Regrettably, her near-painful awareness of him hadn't been enough to discourage her imagination. Visions of him gazing at her in that frankly sensual way, smiling at her from beneath the brim of his hat had hounded her. She'd attempted to halt them by chanting, *Edward is my suitor.* Sometimes that had worked. Most of the time it hadn't.

"How come?" he asked.

"How come what?"

"You're nervous."

"Oh." She reached for her locket. "Because that's Miles Fenner in there."

"And?"

"He's only one of the most famous supporting actors of our time."

He looked doubtful, which exasperated her.

"At one point he was with Lester Wallack's stock company in New York City. He's played alongside the likes of Rose Coughlan and Maurice Barrymore."

When he gave no response, she said, "Please tell me you know of Wallack's company."

"I've heard of it."

"Their productions are amazing. Exquisite, really."

Cord's eyes narrowed. "How old is this Fenner?"

"I'm not sure. Forty-five or so. But if anything, he's improved with age. I've seen him onstage three times—"

"That's enough about him." Cord's head clunked against the wall. He stared grouchily at the ceiling, before slanting his attention back toward her. "Tell me why all that makes you nervous."

She ran her tongue along her teeth, top to bottom, and wished for chocolate. "I suppose because I want him to think I'm good."

A frown passed over his features. He walked to her, hunkered down on his heels, his face level with hers, his hat held between his legs. "Will you listen to me for a second?"

She pulled in a breath and nodded.

"He may have seen a lot of talent in his day. But he has never seen anything like you."

There was that disarming kindness again. Appreciation rushed to her eyes, and for a moment she thought she'd cry over the simple sweetness of his words.

The door to the parlor swung open. Wren and Cord simultaneously pushed to their feet.

A statuesque woman floated from within.

Wren had always been cognizant of her own feminine attributes. And thus, she swiftly realized that the woman before her had more attributes than she did—and better. She was blonder than Wren, taller, and prettier, with a slender figure that physically should have been incapable of supporting such large and perfect breasts.

"Hello," the apparition said, her young face ideally flattered by the apple green collar of her gown.

"Hello." Wren had a similar-colored gown packed in one of her trunks at Aunt Fanny's. She most assuredly would *not* be wearing it now. She hadn't thought she could like the woman less, until the newcomer turned toward Cord. Her heart-shaped mouth parted on a delighted gasp.

Cord nodded to her.

"I'm Robin. Robin Wentworth."

Had she said Robin? *Robin*! How dare she have a bird name, too? And, for that matter, how dare she be named after the robin, which everyone knew was superior to the unremarkable brown wren.

"And you're Mr. Caldwell," Robin said before Cord could speak. "I'm certain you don't remember, but we met last year in Galveston." She gave him the exact enamored perusal that Wren knew he must receive from beautiful women countless times every week.

"How could I forget?" he said smoothly.

"I certainly didn't," she murmured. A blush tinted her cheeks, as if she'd surprised herself with the admission. She dipped her chin in farewell, then glided toward the lobby. Wren noticed that she carried a folder tied with a silvery ribbon under her arm. Robin had brought music. Wren had no music. No music!

A robust man—big of chest, of bones, of belly filled the opening to the parlor. "Well. Who do we have here? Miss . . . ah," he consulted his list, "Miss Bradley?"

The rich baritone was exactly as she remembered it from his performances. "Yes." Awe swam through her. More wrinkles than she'd have thought lined his face, and his burgundy frock coat was more sumptuous than she'd have guessed he'd wear. Otherwise, he was just as she'd envisioned.

"I know the Colonel," Mr. Fenner said. "We've mutual friends."

"Oh," she said, because nothing else came to mind.

"And who are you?" he asked Cord.

"Cord Caldwell."

Cord didn't seem inclined to explain his presence further, so Wren added, "My escort."

"Fine." Mr. Fenner pulled the door wide and motioned for her to enter. "Miss Bradley will be finished with her lesson in precisely one hour," he said to Cord. "You may fetch her then."

"I'll be here."

Just before the door closed Cord winked at her. *Wonderful*, she thought. Another thing to lie in bed at night remembering, when she should be lying in bed thinking of her audition constantly and Edward at least occasionally.

"We'll begin with our voice practice and move directly to our dramatic work afterward," Mr. Fenner said. "Did you bring music?"

"No, I didn't."

"Bring music tomorrow."

"Yes, sir."

He walked as if he were still onstage, his movements exaggerated. He stuffed his list in his inside jacket pocket and waved her to a music stand, void of papers. All the parlor's furniture had been pushed to the walls, so that the only three items that remained in the center of the red-and-gold carpet were the piano, its bench, and the music stand.

"I'm a tremendous admirer of yours," Wren said.

He sat with a flourish at the bench and canted his head toward her. The hair atop his rectangular face was unusually black and thick for a man of his age. "Thank you, that's good to hear. What have you seen me in?"

"Uncle Tom's Cabin, Among the Gypsies, Ten Nights in a Bar-Room."

"Yes. And what did you most enjoy about my performances?"

"Your stage presence, the authenticity of your dialogue, the richness of your voice."

He studied her.

She studied him as fully, thinking how odd and magnificent it was to be conversing privately with one of her idols.

"Voice," he said. "Which brings us back to your reason for coming. I presume you want to perform."

"Very much."

"For the stage or for the private enjoyment of your family?"

"For the stage."

"Those are two different things."

"Yes."

He considered her a moment more. "Let's begin then. We shall, of course, start with scales to warm up your vocal cords and lips. Sing the word 'bumblebee' at each scale. I will accompany you on the piano."

"Bumblebee?" she asked, needing to ascertain she'd heard him correctly.

"Quite so." He set his fingers on the keys and began.

"Bumblebee bumblebee bumblebee bumblebee bumblebee!"

"Breathe, Miss Bradley. Breathe. Again."

"Bumblebee bumblebee bumblebee bumblebee bumblebee!"

His lips twisted and she wondered how impressed he expected to be by "bumblebee" sung in scales. She certainly wasn't impressed with herself. She sounded strained.

"Four more times," he declared.

When she'd finished, her lips were so warm as to almost be flaming.

"Now then. We'll move on to a musical piece so that I might better evaluate your talents. A nonthreatening song, I think." His thumbed through his stack of music, then set "Amazing Grace" before her.

Her nostrils flared with her inhales as she tried to steady her heart and her nerves. The pages of music were unnecessary. Like many songs, and many plays for that matter, she already knew the words by heart.

Striking the notes at a faster tempo than she was accustomed to, he peered at her across one wide shoulder.

Wren forced herself to dive into the piece. The first line sounded awful. The second line improved, and shortly, she rose to the tune and the challenge. Her voice expanded. She used every technique she'd ever been taught and a few she'd taught herself, until the last note of the song hung in the air.

The room turned deathly silent. Wren waited, excited, trying not to smile.

"That was ghastly," Mr. Fenner said.

A pain, an awful rending pain, grated through her chest. She continued to hold his gaze, refusing to bow to the part of her that was dying. Or the vain part of her that was urging her to sob or cower or flee. He'd called her singing ghastly.

Oh, Lord. She was never going to make it, if that was true. Never going to act for an audience, or move them to tears with her songs. Never going to justify all the time she'd invested in this, or the pain she'd given her parents. The bleakness of those possibilities robbed her breath. She couldn't find words.

"Whoever told you that you had the ability to sing on the stage?" he asked.

She tried to keep her expression neutral, so that he wouldn't know how mortally he'd wounded her. It was hard. Her chest was caving in, her entire body quivering from the inside out. "My sister, my aunt—"

He was shaking his head. "Who in the *industry*?"

"Mrs. Lovejoy, my music and dance teacher."

"Well. I'm sorry to tell you this, but she deceived you." He sighed theatrically. "This is the most difficult part of my profession, but trust me, my long experience has taught me it's kindest to tell you the truth. It's not that your voice is ghastly, exactly. I shouldn't have used quite that term. It's that your tone is off, your pitch inelegant, your general sound too throaty. . . ."

He continued, and Wren listened. But she no longer heard because she couldn't, and still keep any shred of her passion alive. Nor was she any longer impressed by Mr. Miles Fenner.

As his words droned on, an emotion swept steadily beneath her—catching her, carrying her inch by inch above all the dragging doubts. It was a trait she'd cultivated through thousands of hours of practice and infinite nights of planning.

Determination.

Mr. Fenner must be wrong. The conclusion started

soft, but grew in volume and assurance. Maybe she was inexperienced, maybe unpolished, undoubtedly she had a great deal to learn. But she could *do* this. She believed it down deep.

In her memory, the notice advertising the upcoming audition pulsed with heavenly light. This thing of hers . . . This desire to perform was a precious thing. It was a dream. A dream as closely held and as dearly wanted as any dream since the beginning of time. Hers to protect.

". . . And those are just a few of the reasons why your voice isn't suited to the stage."

She saw Mr. Fenner for what he was, just a man. Fallible, egotistical, insensitive, but knowledgeable. He could teach her. And whatever she could learn from him, whatever would help her improve, she was willing to suffer for in order to gain.

She stuck out her chin, and coerced her lips into a smile. "It sounds as if we have our work cut out for us."

He scowled. "I've no wish to hurt your feelings—"

"Whoever said anything about hurt feelings, Mr. Fenner?" She sniffed. "Would you like to hear a joke?"

"A joke?"

"Yes."

"Ah—"

"What does an aspiring actress have in common with the United States of America?"

He appeared baffled.

"A good constitution," she answered. "So if you've a care for my feelings, you'll help me improve."

"Miss Bradley—"

"A dream is a dream, Mr. Fenner, and I'm quite

attached to mine. Now, I've diverted you enough. Let's return to our lesson. Shall we?"

Cord walked under a placard proclaiming the squat, brick building attached to it to be Austin's railroad offices. The bell hanging on the inside of the door pealed his arrival as he strode inside. Exactly the clerk he'd been expecting, the one with the mustache, side whiskers, and spectacles, was working behind the desk.

"Mr. Caldwell!" The man hurried to his feet and approached, stopping behind the high console that ran the length of the office. "So good to see you again."

"Likewise, James."

"How long since you were last in Austin? Six months?"

"About that."

"I heard tell of your troubles with the agency." James rolled his lips inward. His timid face softened into apologetic lines.

Damn. Just how far and fast had word spread? Ordinarily, the agency held their cards closer to the vest.

"I was sorry," James said, "very sorry, to hear about that. I'm sure things will be cleared up soon. Soon enough."

Cord nodded. Unfortunately, things hadn't been cleared up soon enough for him. It was already too late to restore his reputation fully.

"What can I do for you?" James asked.

"I'd like to look at some records."

"Records?"

"I need to know how much money was aboard each of the trains robbed, or attempted to be robbed, by the Sackett gang."

James appeared to taste the idea, swirling it around his mouth. He glanced over his shoulder at the line of cabinets containing railroad information.

Cord waited, hating that this man should hesitate to give him information he was normally invited to inspect.

James plucked his pencil from behind his ear and rolled it between his hands. He chuckled self-consciously. "Remember that time we were both on the five-eleven to Birmingham? The Dunning gang blasted apart the doors and there we were, guarding a safe that held fifty-five hundred dollars."

"I remember."

"So do I because you saved my life." Another chuckle, this one aborted too soon. "I haven't accompanied money anywhere since."

Cord nodded, mentally gauging how much time he had before Wren finished her lesson.

"Anyway." He stuck the pencil behind his ear, pulled back his narrow shoulders. "I'll collect those records you're after. It's the least I can do for you. However, it'll take me some time to hunt out all the trains the Sackett brothers attempted to rob."

Cord pulled his leather logbook from his coat pocket and extracted the page he'd written last night. "These are the ones they've hit." He passed it over.

The clerk scanned the page with appreciation. "You've included train numbers, dates, and times. Good. Very good."

"Is there anything else you need?"

James looked up. "No. I'll cross-reference this information against our accounts." He moved to the gap in the desk and swung upward the plank that rested there, clearing a space for Cord to pass. "If you'd like to take a seat in the back. . . . I'll pour you some coffee while you wait."

"Thank you, but I've got somewhere to be. I'll come back later."

"Yes. Of course. I'll have the information ready."

Cord palmed his logbook and moved to the door. Before pressing it open, he paused. "One other thing."

"Yes?"

"Where can I buy chocolate around here?"

"Chocolate, Mr. Caldwell?"

Cord nodded. "Price isn't a consideration. I want the best in the city." Damned if he'd been out of Wren's company less than half an hour, and already he missed her.

Chapter 8

Wren frowned at the tapestry of nighttime sky. Somehow the stars beyond Aunt Fanny's guest bedroom window didn't compare to her own stars at home. They were fine to wish upon. Fine. But not as responsive.

She sighed over the tiredness tugging at her. Except for her cherished daily defense lessons with Cord, she'd spent the last five days practicing the monologue she'd be performing at the audition, attending dramatic instruction with Mr. Fenner, wondering where Cord disappeared to during those lessons, and singing bumblebee. Bumblebee high, bumblebee low, bumblebee morning, noon, and night. Bumblebee until she fervently hated the insect. And still she sang it, because the audition was only one week away and she was hell-bent to improve before then.

Her throat convulsed around a swallow. She lifted the pads of her fingers and tested the region just below her jaw. This wasn't the first time in the past days she'd sung herself to within an inch of hoarseness.

Her white nightdress billowed in the midnight breeze as she swiveled. She scowled at the bed, doubtful about attempting sleep again even though her muscles were begging her to. She'd extinguished the lamp twice already tonight, only to turn from her back onto her side, from her side onto her back, tormented by thoughts of Cord and Miles Fenner and a ghastly voice which, unfortunately, she appeared to be the owner of.

She'd not even been able to sing herself to sleep as she usually did when rest eluded her. Her exhausted voice and her irritation with said voice had stolen away even that puny comfort.

No, she'd not scoot under the covers again until she was snoring standing up and could be assured of sleep.

A cup of tea laced with honey would ease the sting from her throat and help to calm her. From the closet, she snatched out a silky, ice-blue robe. She tied the sash into a bow around her waist and passed into the unlit upper hallway.

Aunt Fanny's house was arranged much like her home in Dallas. Living rooms on the first floor, sleeping rooms on the second. At this ungodly hour, the house slumbered in blankets of shadow. Some rooms hid beneath impenetrable ebony coverlets, some behind light sheets of starlight.

Just then the curtain at the end of the hall stirred as if someone was hiding behind it, waiting for her. The hair rose along the back of her neck in the instant before she heard his breath. Sackett's breath. His arms. His gun—

Wren reached for the upper banister. "Stop it." She gripped the smooth wood hard. "Just stop it, Wren."

But the recollection was clawing at her, gaining. *You say anything, you try to scream again, and I'll kill you. I'll kill you.* She bit her lip, felt the world spin as she was lifted, tossed over the front of the saddle. Splintering pain, horses' hooves.

Wren began to move, faster and faster until she was outrunning the nightmare. She stopped before the undulating curtain, thrust it aside. The window beyond was open.

"It's just the breeze," she murmured to herself. Very deliberately she shut the pane, and the curtain ceased its ghostly movement.

Wren wiped chilled hands over her face. More determined than ever, she started toward the stairs. This time she kept to the iridescent stretches, feeling far safer upon the path the moon had charted for her than in the darkness. She followed it down the last few steps and across the octagonally patterned foyer rug into the parlor. A ladder of translucent color led her toward the dining room and kitchen.

A smile arched across her lips. She might not be able to rid herself of Sackett's memory just yet, but walking on moonlight? *That* she could do. Her slippered feet moved across the carpeting. She glanced at the sofa as she passed—Pure, unexpected terror bolted through her. She shrieked and skittered to the side.

The body on the sofa shifted. She was on the verge of screaming when she recognized him. Cord, leaning up on his elbow, gazing at her through heavy-lidded eyes.

"You scared me." She piled her hands on her racing heart.

He was stretched out on the sofa, his brown hair mussed with sleep, a lone, wrinkled sheet slanted low across his waist. She didn't see another stitch of clothing on him. His upper body was bare, unyielding muscles mounding his shoulders, upper arms, chest. Defined ridges crossed his belly. His earthy masculinity—oh, Lordy—his sensuality had never been so blunt.

This was a terrible time for her to see him like this. They'd finally established an uneasy companionship. She didn't want anything to rattle the fragility or safe distance of their current relationship.

"Excuse me for frightening you," he said, his voice scratchy.

"No, *excuse me*," she whispered, hopelessly fascinated by his appearance. "I'm so sorry to wake you. I had no idea you were sleeping here."

His other elbow rose to brace him. The sheet moved atop his legs.

Liquid warmth swirled through her abdomen . . . and lower. Oh, Lordy. "I—I was just on my way to the kitchen." Wren realized her hands were still resting on her heart. She buried one in her robe's pocket, used the other to twist her locket.

His chin dipped in a slow nod. "For a minute there I'd thought you'd come for me." The sound of his voice reminded her of the time she'd secretly swigged her father's port. Hot, smooth, dark. It had the same effect on her as the port, blazing down the center of her.

"No." She gestured weakly toward the kitchen. "I—I thought you slept in Aunt Fanny's other guest bedroom."

"The other bedroom's Helmut's. He's particular about his things and doesn't like to share."

"Oh." He was gazing at her so intensely she could barely breathe. "Are you comfortable out here?" Lordy, how inane that sounded.

"A little less so since your arrival," he replied dryly.

"Again, I apologize for interrupting you."

"It's not that."

She wasn't sure, in that case, why he was uncomfortable. Jerkily, she took a half step toward the dining room. "I'll be very quiet so that you can go back to sleep."

He swung his legs to the floor.

She licked her lips, pure longing, pure anticipation leaping inside her, keeping her rooted to the spot.

She thought she saw him hide a smile in the instant before he stood, his eyes never leaving hers. The sheet dropped to the floor with a soft *whoosh*.

For an agonized moment Wren stared at his face and wondered if he was completely nude. Either way, doggone it, she couldn't stand *not* to look. Brazenly, she lowered her gaze, half-thrilled and half-terrified by what she'd find.

She found drawers. Soft, cotton ones that rested low on his hips, held by little more than a white tie in the front. Fold creases marred the fabric that pooled slightly at his bare feet.

Nothing in her fondest girlish fantasies of him had prepared her for this.

He reached for the navy blue shirt he'd worn earlier. His muscles rippled as he shrugged into it. He left it unbuttoned and it fell open, exposing the center of his chest and stomach. He seemed perfectly at ease with his state of undress. Not caring, no, practically inviting her to look her fill.

She admired him fervently, wished she could stand unclothed before him with the same confidence and ease. The idea of doing so caused the heat between her legs to throb.

She tugged on the looped ends of her bow, tightening the tie at her waist. She'd simply keep pretending to be as comfortable as he, even though it was getting more difficult every day, as this uninvited attraction to him had intensified.

"What were you wanting in the kitchen?" he asked.

"A cup of tea with honey. For my throat."

"I'll join you."

"Okay." She tried to act as if she was accustomed to having tea in the middle of the night with half-naked legendary men. In the kitchen, Cord fed wood to the stove while she lit the lamp on the small pine table and set the kettle to boil.

"Your throat hurting you?" he asked.

"Only a bit." She opened a cupboard and reached for the tin of tea.

"There's chocolate behind there," he said as she was about to nudge the cabinet door closed.

She froze. "Chocolate? Where?"

"Behind the maple syrup and the cinnamon."

Wren rooted past those items. Sure enough, she spotted a neat, foil-wrapped slab. She carried the items to the table and they settled into chairs opposite each other. "How did you know?" she asked with wonder, unwrapping the sweet.

"I'm a detective."

"*Finally*"—she braved a small smile—"an assignment worthy of your talents." She broke off two rows of chocolate and handed one to him.

Wren revolved her portion, studying its texture, color, and general perfection. "I shouldn't," she said, before snapping it in two and popping half into her mouth. Blissfully, she chewed and swallowed. She opened her eyes to find Cord watching her intently. Chocolate melted down the insides of her cheeks.

Because she felt a sudden need for another shot of bolstering chocolate, she tossed back the second half. It ran over her taste buds, sinfully smooth. So rich she had to knead it a couple of times with her tongue before it eased down her throat.

Cord leaned toward her, his elbows on the table, his shirt gaping open.

Chocolate. She needed more chocolate.

"You've got a crumb," he said, touching his finger to her bottom lip and causing her skin to burn at the spot.

Remembering their game, she parted her lips. He set his entire section on her tongue. Her mouth closed, but she couldn't bring herself to work her jaws, so immersed was she in the intoxicating spell of his gaze.

The screech of the kettle shattered the moment. She rose, chewing his chocolate, and shakily poured hot water. This was exactly why she had to consciously steel herself every time they were alone together. Because otherwise she found herself craving things from him she'd craved when she was a silly sixteen-year-old, hopelessly infatuated with him. The last time, she'd paid for her cravings with humiliation and a heart that had taken years to heal. She wanted to be, had to be, smarter now.

"Here." She returned to the table, set two cups between them, and reached to break off another row of chocolate. "Have some more—"

"No."

She glanced up, hands stilled.

"Thank you, though."

"You don't like chocolate?"

"You can save mine for next time."

She was tempted to question his sanity, but decided she'd been rude enough already, invading his privacy and stuffing her mouth with sweets in front of him. She carefully wrapped the chocolate, then set about filling Fanny's silver tea ball and dunking it into her water. From the pot on the table, she added copious amounts of honey. "I sang quite a lot today," she explained.

"Bumblebees," he said.

"You heard?"

"I heard."

"Yes. Well, I was practicing."

He nodded solemnly, as if he, a man who lived by facts and logic, understood her dreams of the theater. She felt pathetically grateful to him for that. Which didn't say much. Was she really so desperate for an ally that she'd imagine Cord to be one even for an instant?

"Does your stomach still pain you?" he asked, a serious look on his face.

She forced her dark thoughts away. "No. Even the bruises have almost completely faded."

"Good."

Quiet stretched. Wren sipped her tea twice and wished he'd at least dip his tea into his cup of water. "You don't like tea?" she asked at last.

"I'm more of a coffee man."

She smiled faintly above the steaming rim of her cup. "I suppose you're going to point to a drip on my bottom lip, then pour all your water down my throat."

"Do you want it?" He nudged his cup toward her.

"No, it's yours."

"I don't care. I'd give you anything of mine, if you wanted it."

She blinked at him while fear and excitement lifted her stomach into a dizzying flip.

Cord's forehead wrinkled. He looked at the table.

Did he have any idea how attractive he was? With that square jaw and those shrewd, bottomless, heart-stopping eyes? She wondered if he'd ever felt affectionately, or passionately, about any of the hordes of women who fell asleep dreaming of him. "Have you ever been in love?" she whispered.

He looked up. A grin, wary and disbelieving, spread across his lips. Leaning back in his chair, he combed his fingers through his hair, then locked his hands behind his head. His shirt pulled open even wider. "Conversations with you are never dull."

"Dull? No, I hope not. So have you?"

"No."

"Never even the tiniest bit in love?"

"No."

"How can that be? I happen to know that there have been quite a . . ." No need to feed his conceit. "Well, a *few* women over the years, who've been half in love with you." *Including me*.

He winked at her and dropped his hands. "You'll have to introduce me to these few women."

She'd rather stick splinters beneath her fingernails. Why had she started this conversation, anyway? She didn't want him to look right at her and tell her he didn't love anyone. Nor did she want him to look right at her and tell her he did. She grabbed her cup. "My point is that there's certainly enough interest on the side of the female population."

"Thanks for the reassurance."

The pungent tea slicked along her raw throat. She told herself to let the subject go, but couldn't seem to. "How is it that you plan to marry without ever loving anyone?"

"Who said anything about planning to marry?"

She set down her cup. "Everyone marries eventually."

"Not me."

For some terrible reason, his admission caused disappointment to sink into her heart, like a stone sinking to the bottom of a lake. "Why not you?"

He didn't answer.

"Please tell me." Her necklace twisted so high it nipped her neck. "I'd like to know," she said more softly. "I have a curious nature."

"And a talkative one."

"Is it because of your parents?" she asked. "Was their marriage unhappy?"

"How'd you know about my parents?"

"I just guessed. The expression on your face the first day we practiced shooting. . . ."

He shifted, looked to the door as if to make sure he could run for it if he needed to. "Unhappy is too weak a word for their marriage."

"Why was it so bad?"

He stared at the door as if he could see through it, down the tunnel of time, to a household so miserable he'd forsworn marriage because of it.

She wanted to shake his parents and demand to know what they'd done to him, what scars their carelessness had left on their child, who'd deserved better. Whatever the answer was, she could tell by the rigid lines of his profile that he wasn't going to tell her about it tonight. "Not all marriages are like that," she said, when he didn't answer her.

"I know." His gaze cut to her face. "It's fine for most people. Just not for me."

"I'm sorry to hear that."

"Don't be. It's how I want it."

She sipped her tea, profoundly sad that this man, full of so many kindnesses and such charm, should go through his days without a son who looked like him to crawl upon his shoulders, or a woman who loved him to hold him at night and curl her toes around his.

Ridiculously, Wren felt sorry for herself, too.

It's how I want it, he'd said.

Loving him would be a doomed endeavor for all those women, like she'd once been, who dared hope. She slid her fingertip round and round the lip of her cup. "If not marriage, then what is it you want?"

"In the future?"

"Yes."

"I think a lot about buying a plot of land here in Texas one day. Getting some peace and quiet to go with it."

She smiled softly, thinking what a handsome rancher he'd make and how in her opinion he'd already earned the right, tenfold, to some peace and quiet after his years of catching outlaws. What violence he must have seen, what unrest. "What about now? What do you want now?"

"My job back."

Lately, she'd worried about that. Cord wanted to catch Sackett, so much he'd struck a deal not to interfere with her audition. So much, that she feared he'd endanger himself. Too much for his own good. "Anxious to be rid of me?" She'd intended the question to come out light, but it sounded hollow.

"Anxious to be useful again."

"I hope I won't hold you much longer, Cord. I don't want to be a millstone around your neck."

"You haven't held me from anything." His brow darkened. "My suspension is my fault and no one else's."

He did that often, she'd noticed. Took all the blame.

She collected her cup and chocolate. He reached to help her, but she swept the remaining items from the table before he could. Their conversations had gotten darned depressing ever since the chocolate. One should always begin and end with chocolate, to keep things sweet and simple.

Best to take her sorry emotions and her weary body to bed and be done with the day. She turned to find him standing alongside the table, looking somewhat lost and somewhat angry and somewhat dangerous.

A thrill skidded through her. Heart knocking, she slipped past him. In the parlor, his tousled sheet lay in a heap on the floor. His boots and folded clothing rested beside it. His leather book on the table. His renegade's hat. His things, all so very male. She smelled him, the scent of maroon leather and soap, in the second before she felt his breath coast along the shell of her ear.

Chapter 9

"**Y**our turn," he said, his tone ominous.

She swirled. "My turn for what?"

"To answer questions."

She retreated. Unreasonable fury and helplessness warred inside Cord. She'd asked him questions, he'd answered them, and now she had the gall to be mad at him for it. No. He'd not let her walk away without giving him a part of herself in return.

These last days he'd been unable to get her out of his mind. Did she have to make it worse by looking at him with transparent lust one minute, then turning her back on him the next? His fingers itched for her. "What is it *you* want, Wren?" His brows slanted low across his eyes. He kept advancing, slowly but inexorably. She kept retreating.

"Me?" The word trembled.

"You." It was time she paid the piper.

Her back bumped up against the wall, stopping her.

He set his bare feet on either side of her slippered ones. He towered over her.

Alarm bells clanged in his head, distant. For once he didn't soften his perusal of her into something polite. He gazed at her like he wanted to, hard and blatant. Unapologetic.

She shivered sensually in reaction. "You know I want to win a part in the audition."

"What else?"

"That's all."

"And in the future?"

"I just told you. Acting is all there is for me."

Don't touch her, stop now, his conscience hissed. Bent on destruction, he ignored the warning and coasted his knuckles up her ribs on both sides. His body betrayed him with a need that fisted in his gut. He had to have more.

Wren nearly died, waiting for him to touch her again. If he'd only take his gaze off of her, just for a moment, she could find her sanity. But he didn't, so she couldn't. This was wrong. Too dangerous. Too dangerous! And then one of his knuckles, softer than butterfly wings, drifted up her neck.

She sucked in air.

"Easy," he breathed. His finger caressed her cheek. "Easy."

She tilted her head back and curled her fingers into Aunt Fanny's wallpaper. Her heart sang with its pounding. She couldn't move, couldn't force herself to make him stop—didn't want to.

"You're so fine." His hands gently cupped both sides of her face. The harshness of seconds ago had vanished. He looked pained, as if he didn't want to do this but couldn't stop. His lips touched hers. Breakingly tender, as if he feared he'd shatter her with more pressure. She wanted to scream. And melt.

He pulled slightly back, then kissed her that way again. And again. And again.

She arched, yearning into him, silently demanding more. Still cradling her face, he leaned forward. His knee bent into the wall, trapping her with the heat of his thighs and stomach.

A moan ripped from her. He inhaled it. Then gave it back to her by slipping his tongue between her lips.

She jolted. He steadied her with the weight of his body, stroked his hand into her hair. He was kissing her. Cord Caldwell was kissing her the way she'd fantasized it a hundred times.

Her tongue tasted his. She wanted . . . she wanted to make him as wild as he was making her. Though she could feel his desire in every contact, she sensed, too, that he was holding most of himself back while making her burn.

Her head bit into the wall as he kissed her deeper, with a thoroughness that caused her to writhe. His palms pressed open-handed down her neck, over her shoulders, down her arms, until he'd found her hands. Their fingers laced and he drew her arms up, pinning the backs of her hands above her head. He leaned heavily against her and she felt the thrust of his arousal between her legs.

She was greedy for him, jealously anxious for more.

"I told myself one kiss," he murmured, drawing back. The sensation of his words caressed her flushed lips. One." With a groan, he found her mouth, kissed her again. Pulled away. "That's six already."

"Cord," she whispered, not knowing how else to vocalize the whirlwind of need within.

He swallowed, then released his weight from her hands, from her body, freeing her. "Even one was too many." He scowled, then swore under his breath.

Wren rested against the wall, needing its support. She watched him, waiting for him to look at her again. Instead he stalked from the room. She listened to his footfalls muffled by the rug, the squeal of the front door, then nothing.

She brought her fingers to her lips. Dazedly, she tested the heated fullness of them. She dipped her middle finger inside, touched it to her tongue. Then flattened her hands against her lips and closed her eyes.

With all her might she hugged the impressions into herself. The depth of her emotions, the crackling hunger of her body, the wonder.

Heaven help her, she longed for it to go on. Now that she'd tasted his searching kisses, she was famished to taste them again. She, who should know better and was spoken for by another.

Guilt turned in her gut like burning paper, curling in on itself. Sweet Edward, who was smart and loyal. Who trusted her.

But . . . But Cord.

Her gaze ran over the parlor. The sofa where he would lay his half-naked body and perhaps think of her.

She managed to push herself away from the wall. Her senses and her thoughts swimming, she padded into the foyer, looked up to reach for the banister—

And saw him.

Standing in the open doorway, on the outside. Framed by an inky darkness as deep and predatory as his eyes.

She couldn't move. Never in her life had she felt so weak. Willing to ransom everything she held dear, including her pride, for another kiss. To feel like *that* again.

He walked toward her.

She found just enough strength to move toward him. This time it was she who reached for his face, who grasped his cheeks in the instant that their mouths joined and tongues intertwined.

She strained into him, pushing him backward a few steps while they pawed madly at each other. His shoulders bumped against the entry wall. He wrapped his hands around her buttocks and lifted her against him. He was reaching to the depths of her, at once claiming her and submitting himself.

Yes, she thought. *Yes.* The word circled in her head. *This is what I wanted.* Yes. *For him to touch me like this. Ravenously.*

His hands ground her against his arousal.

She raked her fingernails into his hair. She pulled his head to her with all her strength, kissing him until her muscles grew feeble and nothing remained but redorange desire. Only when her lungs demanded more air, did she break away. Her temple rested against the hollow of his throat.

Gulping for air, she listened to the rapid thud of his heart. Her fingers brushed along the front of his shirt, two riding the scalding heat of his skin, two the coolness of the cloth.

She wanted to cry and to sing. To shout and to laugh. To blurt out something foolish like, *I love you.* To ask him if she was dreaming this.

Sufficiently recovered, she tilted her head back, hoping to throw herself headlong into another kiss.

But the eyes peering into hers were stormy. A furrow marred his forehead. "Seven kisses," he said. His breath hitched.

Please don't let him leave me again, she thought. For years, she'd been waiting to start living. These tumultuous gales of feeling, right or wrong, were undiluted living.

His hands slid away, mimicking the plummeting of her spirits. He was done with her.

Keeping her chin up so he wouldn't think her a child, she stepped back.

"Seven kisses," he said, as if he couldn't believe what he'd let himself do. One of his elegant savage's hands rubbed down his face. "I'll go."

She bit the side of her tongue. She could see, in the uncertain, turbulent depths of his eyes, in the tense lines of his face and body, that he was shaken. If he wasn't his usual controlled self, then she was in desperate trouble because she absolutely wasn't in *her* right mind. "There's no need," she replied quietly. "This is where you sleep. I'll go."

She wanted to say a good deal more, but nothing formed coherently enough to be articulated.

For safekeeping, she engraved the image of him onto her memory. Cord, next to a door open on a void of darkness, his shirt falling open, and his finger-tousled hair lifted by a wayward wind. Just seconds ago she'd been locked in his arms kissing him. The truth seemed outrageous.

Shoring every bit of her fragmenting resolve, she turned from his near-crushing desirability and mounted the stairway. In her room, she shut the door behind her. Her resolve ran out.

Countless moments came and went while she held the knob and rested her forehead against the door, her mind flying in a thousand different directions.

Her body had *never* behaved that way before. She hadn't even known it could, until just then. Cord had awakened in her the most glorious, frightening, over-whelming sensations—

Oh, Lordy, she'd shown him too much of her heart. Again.

Edward. Mildly frantic, she tried to summon the image of Edward's face. His intelligent eyes and thick blond hair seemed fuzzed, far less real than a midnight blue gaze and a jaw rugged enough that it had abraded the pads of her fingertips.

Dumbly, she stared at her fingertips.

Her skin pebbled, simply to imagine the bliss of being loved by Cord. Of marrying him and—

Who said anything about planning to marry? His words, as he'd spoken them mere minutes ago, echoed in her head, drowning out the din of her rushing thoughts.

"Ohhh," she moaned. She circled to the bed. "Ohhhh." She lowered her head between her knees like her mother told her to do when she felt nauseous. She set her hands on both temples and pushed, hoping to squeeze some sense into her brains.

Fool! For all her grand adult dreams, she was just a naive fool. Fool! To her, seven kisses with Cord Caldwell was a monumental, life-changing event. But what were seven kisses to him? Less than nothing. He'd looked at her tonight across a lamplit pine table and told her he'd never been in love. Yet if even half the rumors about him were true, he'd done more than kiss a great many women over the years. Without loving a single one. And certainly without proposing marriage.

She'd been fully cognizant of that, but had chosen to

overlook that knowledge. She'd been ready to sacrifice anything in the world to kiss him.

Groaning, she rolled onto her back on the mattress and locked her hands around her knees. Somehow she had to withstand the plunging, overpowering waves of wanting she felt for Cord. And not, under any circumstances, throw her heart away for the second time to a man who didn't, wouldn't, and couldn't want it.

Alexandra tucked their wedding-ring quilt under her arms and watched her husband strip off his suit jacket.

Robert rested it over the back of their honeymoon chair.

"Another late night," Alexandra said. She'd been in bed alone, trying to fall asleep without him when she'd heard him come in.

"Yes." The frame squeaked as he sat at the foot of the bed. She studied his back, wide at the top, tapering to a narrow waist.

Her heart burned with hurt. Robert had been hers. Totally. She'd been so sure of that, and too busy raising his children and running their home to consider that other women might be coveting him and making plans to steal him from her. But now . . . these last days since finding the note in his jacket pocket, she wondered how she could have been so trusting. And she wondered if he was still hers.

Her entire body braced against the fear that he wasn't. What if he didn't love her or want her anymore?

He sighed wearily.

"Burning the midnight oil at the office again?" she asked, trying to keep her tone light.

Nodding, he bent to take off his shoes.

"Doing . . . ?" She was bitterly ashamed that she felt the need for him to prove where he'd been.

"Work."

"Robert, I'd like it if you'd answer me with more than just 'work.' "

"It's dull, love." He turned, and gazed at her with an expression she'd long thought to be affection in his rich brown eyes. "Truly. I didn't want to bore you."

Oh, God, she wanted to shake him, to hurt him—anything to test his devotion and make him prove how much he loved her. "I'm not bored by it."

"I was doing some of Edward's accounting work. Whenever he's out, I take over a portion of his responsibilities."

"Oh." She wanted desperately to believe him but couldn't quite.

He straightened, and fitted his feet into his slippers.

"Where are you going?" she asked.

"To the study. I've a few bills to pay." He smiled apologetically at her. "Keep the bed warm for me," he whispered before closing the door with a gentle click.

Alexandra stared at the spot he'd just occupied, then threw aside the covers and followed him. "Robert," she said, when she reached the hallway.

He turned.

"What's happened to us?" she asked softly.

"Happened?"

"Yes, what's happened? We used to be closer than we are now. I used to see you more. We never used to go to bed separately, we'd always wait for each other."

"We're still close, Alex."

"Are we? If you have to tell me we are in order for me to believe it?" She set her hand against the molding surrounding her bedroom door and gazed at him painfully. Robert, separated from her by several feet of hallway. A stretch that suddenly seemed a chasm.

"This is a busy time for me," he said. "That's all."

"That's a lot when your family rarely sees you because of it. You're busy because you made choices to be. Do you think you can make choices to be with the children more, at least?"

"Alex," he said pleadingly. With his bleak expression he was telling her that he couldn't take this discussion tonight on top of everything else. As if she were the one being unreasonable.

She could see the tiredness in him, the weight of too many responsibilities. What she wondered was whether his mistress was one of them.

"Good night," she whispered coldly, emotions churning. *Stop it*, she told herself, as she slipped back into bed and pulled the chilled blankets over her. *Stop imagining things and overreacting.* Difficult for someone who'd always kept all the aspects of her life neatly stitched together and taken pride in that.

She'd simply force this problem with Robert to her will through hard work, just like she had other circumstances. Whatever was wrong with Robert and her, she could fix.

Couldn't she?

No, an evil little voice inside answered. If Robert has betrayed you, then everything, but everything, is ruined.

Chapter 10

Wren smoothed the napkin on her lap for the twen-
tieth time.

"Helmut, I think Mr. Caldwell needs more eggs," Aunt
Fanny called.

Helmut, tower of forbearance that we was, walked
from the kitchen into the dining room bearing a fresh
platter of fluffy eggs.

"Lovely!" Aunt Fanny beamed at her small-boned but-
ler cum cook, cum carriage-driver, cum handyman as he
slid the platter onto the table and took his seat opposite
her.

"Mr. Caldwell, don't you agree that breakfast is the
most important meal of the day?"

"I do."

"I swear it's true! Bird, please pass the bacon."

Aunt Fanny grasped the china plate Wren handed her
in dimpled ivory hands. "Wouldn't you like any more?"

"No, thank you." Since kissing Cord last night, she'd been unable even to consider sleeping or eating. In fact, she was barely managing to sit across from Cord and pretend to be unaffected.

Ordinarily in the morning, Cord blessed her and Aunt Fanny with easy smiles and lazy conversation. Today, he'd hardly looked in her direction and only answered Aunt Fanny when asked a pointed question.

His eyes were slightly bloodshot and his lips had a firm, tired cast to them. Otherwise, he appeared outwardly the same as every morning. His trail clothes were fresh and clean, and his hair was wet. Shiny and slick.

Exactly where did he wash, since he didn't have the privacy of a room? By the rain barrel beside the back porch, probably. Her mouth went dry. If she put her mind to it, she could watch. And that . . . him wetting his body . . . was something she urgently yearned to see.

"Mr. Caldwell, more coffee?" Aunt Fanny already held the spout of the pewter urn over his cup.

"Thank you."

"I know how you like your coffee," she cooed, as if indulging him beyond all measure. She poured happily, then moved to set aside the urn. "Of all the people I know, the person who cooks the best breakfasts is—" Her elbow knocked over her orange juice.

Cord's hand darted out, somehow catching the crystal goblet before it crashed. Orange juice sloshed over his hand and wrist, spilling onto the lacy white tablecloth. He was out of his seat before Wren could blink, pressing his napkin onto the stain.

"My goodness me," Aunt Fanny whispered, mesmerized.

Cord folded under the soiled portion of his napkin and soaked up the last of the juice.

"Your hand, and your sleeve, Mr. Caldwell." Aunt Fanny whisked a shockingly pink handkerchief from her pocket. "Allow me to dab away the moisture."

"That's not necessary." He lowered into his chair, used the last dry part of his napkin to wipe his hand, then rolled his plaid sleeve twice until the juice didn't show. "Good as new." He smiled at Aunt Fanny to reassure her.

His smile wasn't for her, and still, Wren nearly swooned at the sight of it. There was something irresistible about the flash of his white teeth, and the equally bright flash of his goodness showing through his fatigue.

Aunt Fanny reached over and patted Cord's forearm affectionately. "What I was going to say before Mr. Caldwell so gallantly corrected my blunder right before my eyes like a, why I swear, like a veritable Lancelot, was that Mrs. Morgana Morgenstern makes the best breakfasts I've ever had the pleasure of setting inside my mouth. You know Morgana, don't you, bird?"

Wren pursed her lips.

"Of course you do! She bobbed you upon her knee at the city fair when you were three years old." Aunt Fanny shook her head with frustration, rattling the two rashes of tight curls decorating each end of her forehead. "Helmut, you know Morgana."

He nodded, but didn't look up from his food.

"Her breakfasts are divine, I *swear*. Lovely buttermilk pancakes with blueberries. Blueberries, I tell you! And pats of butter as big as my hankie. With more fresh berries on top. And whipping cream drizzled over all."

Aunt Fanny smiled at each of them in turn, delighted with her tale.

"Sounds lovely," Wren remarked.

"The loveliest." Her aunt went to work on her helping of bacon.

Wren smoothed her napkin for the twenty-first time, to keep herself from fiddling with her necklace, her bodice, or her hair. She'd agonized over her looks this morning. The gown she wore, a sunny peach with a square neck and fitted three-quarters sleeves, had been the fourth she'd tried on. Ultimately she'd selected it because it brought color to her otherwise pale, sleep-deprived face.

She'd twisted, curled, and pinned her hair into almost every style she knew and still wasn't happy with the elaborately knotted braid she'd chosen.

"You'll be able to reacquaint yourself with Morgana at the ball she's hosting on the ninth." Aunt Fanny swept bacon crumbs off the black-organdy platform of her breasts. "Do not, under any circumstances, forget that we are to attend that."

"We won't," Wren answered.

"I'm positively brimming with anticipation! However good Morgana's breakfasts are, her gala balls are even better. The only hostess in town who can compare, is Mrs. Astonia Colleywell. You remember Assie, bird."

More pursing of lips, feigned thinking.

"Ass's affairs are . . ."

Ass? Wren listened to Aunt Fanny prattle for a few more moments, then took a sip of cold milky coffee.

Cord leaned back in his chair and met her eyes for a moment.

Her heart clawed up her throat.

He looked away.

That's it! She had to talk to him, to vent everything brewing between them. Her cup clattered against its saucer. She scooted back her chair. "Aunt Fanny, will you excuse Mr. Caldwell and me?"

"Certainly. Off for another of your defense lessons? I do say, you young people astonish me with your energy." She leaned across the table toward Wren. They embraced in the way Aunt Fanny was wont to do whenever they parted, sometimes when they parted no farther than the parlor to the kitchen.

Aunt Fanny extended her arms to Cord. He bent toward her, and she christened his cheek with a kiss.

When they reached the back door, Cord held it open for Wren. As she swept past, she caught scent of his soap. That rich, manly, leather-and-spices smell.

She bit her bottom lip against a stab of memories from last night. It was excrutiating to be around him after what they'd shared. More so, even, than she'd expected. As she led him into the tall grasses of the field, she relived the way she'd buried her nails in his hair, drawing his mouth closer and closer.

She halted and faced him. "Cord, I—"

He extended a bonnet to her. He must have taken it from the peg adjacent to the back door. It was one of her aunt's. Straw with a profusion of imitation apricots, strawberries, and plums sprouting from the brim. At least it matched.

"Thank you." She put it on. He donned his renegade hunter's Stetson.

He slung his hands into the pockets of a pair of denims. The crisp browns and greens of his shirt offset the white of the undershirt and the wary indigo of his eyes. Behind him chalky gray clouds hung in the sky, fat and unmoving.

She felt totally unprotected, here, in this place of their beloved lessons where he was supposed to be teaching her to defend herself. "I think we need to talk about what happened last night," she said.

"There's nothing to talk about."

"Of course there is."

"No. There's not." He shifted away from her, and she could almost feel the hostility rising like barricades around him. "If you want to learn, then let's practice."

"Cord." A frown tugged at her brow. "I think it was clear last night that—"

"Let it go."

"No, I can't—"

With a growl, he turned on his heel and walked away.

She gaped at his back. Anger rolled through her like a clap of thunder. After their kisses, he owed her his attention at the very least.

She dashed after him. "I think it only right that you extend me the courtesy of acknowledging what happened last night."

His jaw hardened. Kept walking.

"Or is this the routine?"

"What routine?"

"The one you use on all the women you kiss?"

His steps slashed to a stop. "Leave it," he warned, eyes narrow.

"I'm sorry, I can't. It's not in me."

He yanked his hat off one-handed and glared at her.

She glared back, angry and miserable and a little intimidated.

"What's the good in ripping it apart, Wren?"

"In this case, the good is my sanity."

"It won't happen again," he said, the muscles in his cheeks hardening. "How's that for your sanity?"

Her insides froze. This is how she'd rationally wanted him to respond. Even so, to hear him say it would never happen again with such assurance made her long to prove him wrong.

"That's exactly what I hoped you'd say, thank you very much." She drew herself up. "I think you were probably able to tell that I enjoyed . . . kissing you. But when I got to thinking about it afterward, I, too, realized how foolish we'd been."

"Foolish," he said. The word sounded dead to her.

"Yes. And I'm relieved that you agree. You're set in your ways. Extremely independent. There's your career." She waved a hand, indicating the endlessness of his unsuitability. "You certainly—understandably with your options—don't want to settle down with one woman. And there's your—your eyes."

"My eyes?"

"That color. No woman, in her right mind, could hope to have such eyes look only at her with love." What was she saying? She'd started off making sense, but had seriously lost her way. "Of course, I myself put little store in kisses. I'm practically engaged, as you know. And I've dreams to attend to before any man."

Silence.

"Finished?" he asked.

"Yes."

"Then let's start our lesson."

Her fingers played over the folds of her peach skirt. "I'd dearly like to know how you feel about everything I just said."

"I already told you. It shouldn't have happened, and I won't let it happen again." He settled his hat low on his head, in the way she was becoming familiar with. "Your father gave me an assignment, and I mean to honor him by the doing of it. No more, no less."

His characterization of his dutiful feelings toward her sounded dreadful. Hearing that was almost as awful as when he'd told her five years ago that he had no romantic feelings for her.

Cord watched Wren fidget. An impeccably dressed china doll standing in the middle of acres of Indian grass wearing an oversize hat. After she'd left him last night, he'd paced away the rest of the night. God, what he'd done had been so wrong it didn't have a name. The Colonel had gotten him his job as an agent, mentored him, taught him, promoted him. *Trusted* him.

For Christ's sake, he'd kissed her roughly, pawed at her. Women like her ought to be treated gently.

A frown stitched her brows as she averted her attention toward Austin. "What are you going to teach me today? I don't see a gun or a whip or a horse."

"I'm going to teach you how to break holds."

"What does that mean, exactly?"

Her refusal to meet his gaze irritated the hell out of him. "It means I'm going to show you how to fight off an attacker using your own strength and quickness."

She nodded, almost imperceptibly.

Obviously, his actions last night and this morning had intensely disappointed her. Well, he couldn't erase what he'd done, but he could sure as hell fix it from here on out. He'd detach himself from her as much as he could. To hell with her disappointment and sad eyes. It's what would be best for them both. "Okay, let's get to it."

Still, she didn't look at him. His already black mood worsened. "Look at me," he growled.

She finally did, hurt and ire smoldering in her expression.

Fine. At least he could use her ire. "If I come at you like this, straight on, with arms outstretched, do you have any idea what to do?" He halted, his tanned hands near her ivory throat.

"Uh . . ." Her pulse fluttered in her neck. "Knee you? Down . . . low."

He moved back. "That's what most women would think, and that's why it won't work. It's the first place your attacker will anticipate you striking, the first place he'll protect. Hand-to-hand defense is about moving counter to his anticipation, and about speed."

She scowled in that concerted way of hers.

"Better to kick him in the knee. Raise your leg and snap your foot outward. Try it."

She did a few times.

"Keep your balance. Harder. Harder, Wren."

She grunted a little with her kicks.

"Now, we'll go through this slow. When I come at you, kick toward me. Yes, like that. Now, grab my arm."

She halted. "Grab you?" Her tone was critical, her expression informing him in no uncertain terms that grabbing him was the last thing in the world she wanted to do.

"Expectation again. It's not what he'll expect. Because you're right-handed, you'll need that hand to strike. So use your left hand to grab my right wrist. Try."

She hesitated a moment, then reluctantly wrapped her fingers around his wrist, tight.

"Now pull me toward you with your left hand and at

the same time, drive the heel of your right hand up into my chin or nose."

They practiced the motion a few times slow. They were so close, just a whisper apart.

"Now the whole thing," he said stepping back, fighting the lust surging through him with his blood. "Kick, grab, drive."

"I've got it."

He came toward her faster. She kicked, deliberately missing just wide of his knee. Her hand wrapped around his wrist. She jerked him forward, and grunted softly as she extended her right arm hard and fast. He slanted his chin to the side and back. The flat of her hand rested along the plane of his jaw.

She held him fast. Silver fire snapped in her eyes, endlessly hot. Anger at Sackett, at her father, at Miles Fenner, at him. The steeliness beneath the porcelain exterior had flared to life.

Their breaths came in shallow unison. Her breasts strained against the low cut of her neckline.

His body roared, ravenous for her.

He forced himself to break the contact. "Good," he said, his voice hoarse.

They gazed at one another, the space between them crackling.

He could feel his defenses eroding, his body's hunger growing in tandem with his emotional hunger. Like putting a starving man in a bakery and telling him not to touch. Madness.

"Should I ever try to—" she made fists— "punch?"

"Yes. Look for openings. For instance, after you get him in the chin, bring your arm all the way back, make a fist, and explode forward." He demonstrated.

She made a fist the wrong way. He took her hand, and heard air suck between her teeth. Another shaft of lust arrowed through him. He cursed silently, and repositioned her thumb on the outside of her curled fingers. "You'll break your thumb the other way," he said harshly.

Pursing her lips, she nodded.

"He'll expect you to try to punch him in the face. Punch him here instead." He indicated his midsection, between the ribs. "You'll knock his breath out and stun him."

"Okay."

"I'm going to come at you from behind this time, wrap my arms around you like Sackett did."

Wariness stiffened her shoulders. "Is that necessary?"

"Did Sackett grab you that way or not?"

"He did."

"Then it's necessary. Turn around."

She turned, every muscle in her slender body braced. He thought bitterly of all the women who would welcome his touch, then banded his arms around her lower chest.

Her body lurched as if he'd whipped her. "I—I made a mistake. I don't want to practice this." Her voice wavered.

"This isn't a joke, Wren. I'm not trying to seduce you, I'm trying to teach you. Like you asked me to."

Wren closed her eyes. Lordy, at this moment she'd rather let any outlaw in America cart her off than feel the warm power of his arms around her. It was too hard to try to hate him while simultaneously being overwhelmingly attracted to him. How weak of her, that she couldn't conquer her body's desires, even moments after he'd told her he'd never kiss her again. When would she ever learn?

Desperate for something safe to cling to, she focused her attention on a distant tree, and prayed for strength. "You're right." Least of all, was she willing to humiliate herself by admitting to him how difficult this physical closeness was for her. "Continue."

"The first thing you want to do in this situation is use your feet." His voice was coming from close to her ear. A tendril of hair fluttered against her neck with every word. "You'd slam the heel of your shoe into my toes. Then you'd bring your fists up and ram your knuckles against my hands, just below my knuckles. The pain will cause your attacker to release his hold."

Her heart thundering, she practiced the moves a few times.

"He'll expect you to try to strain forward. Again, go against expectation and yank back, knocking the back of your head into his face."

She swallowed, unsure how much more she could take. His wrists were perilously close to her breasts, scalding the skin just beneath. The tugging inside her, the one that always reached for him, was gaining strength. Terrifying her. After putting his head-knocking advice into practice, he finally, mercifully, let her go.

"I've more to teach you," he said, "once we go over everything we've learned a few more times."

"I need just a moment," she whispered. Her back to him, she walked toward the closest shelter, a pecan tree. Her emotions rose. The pressure of them against the puny walls around her heart, pushed tears into her eyes.

Get a hold of yourself, Wren. Don't be a baby. He's doing this so you'll know how to defend yourself, something you dearly need to learn how to do. Yes, your body is a traitor toward him, but your will is powerful enough to withstand. Show him that you're as strong in your way as he is in his.

She sniffed hard, and some of the moisture abated.

If she kept avoiding looking at him, she might not have to see how devastatingly appealing he was. And maybe, he'd let her actually punch and kick him later. That'd be worth something. She'd love to punch him.

Wrapping her courage and dignity around her, she returned to him.

The clerk looked up later that day when the bell attached to the railroad office's front door jangled. "Good afternoon, Mr. Caldwell." James scurried to his feet.

"Good afternoon." Cord watched approvingly as James slid open the top drawer of his desk and extracted a file.

"I collected the information you asked for." He handed it over the wooden console.

Cord flipped open the front and scanned the neatly penned columns.

"The amount of money in the train's safe was unusually high on each occasion that the Sackett gang attempted a robbery." The clerk looked meaningfully at Cord from under his eyebrows. Light glared off the circular glass of his spectacles. "I found that very interesting, so I took the liberty of doing a bit more checking. In the case of each robbery, the amount aboard was the highest it had been in a span of weeks. Once as high as fifteen weeks."

Cord nodded. He'd suspected as much.

"You've good instincts, Mr. Caldwell."

Not good for whoever the snitch was. Someone, some railroad employee, had been leaking information to the Sacketts. Which meant he now had two men to track. Sackett and the snitch.

Cord took the papers from the file, folded them, and pressed them between the pages of his logbook.

"Anything else I can do for you?" James asked, looking childishly anxious to please.

"Yes. I need you to keep an eye on the amounts aboard trains traveling between here and Dallas. Is Wilkes working that route?"

"Yes, sir, he's the operative the Pinkerton Agency assigned. Usually rides the late train and Duncan rides the early."

"Fine. I want you to track the amounts on that route starting two weeks ago, then daily until you receive word from me otherwise."

The clerk nodded avidly.

"When a noticeably higher amount is to go out"— Cord tapped the empty file—"an amount as tempting as these were, then have a letter delivered to me immediately."

"Yes, sir. You can count on me, sir."

"We'll keep this between us. No reason to notify anyone yet."

"No, sir."

Cord scribbled Aunt Fanny's address on a piece of paper and pushed it across the desk.

James tucked it into the pocket of his silken vest. "If you don't mind me asking . . ." He pushed his spectacles up his nose with his pinky finger. "What is it you intend to do?"

"My job." Cord tipped his hat in thanks and exited the office.

He intended to sit back and let the railroad bait the hook for him. Then, if at all possible, to be aboard that train. He wanted like hell another crack at facing Sackett down.

* * *

Wren peeked around the corner of the alley alongside the railroad office. She watched Cord walk down the street away from her, trying to squelch the worry that had motivated her to follow him here. Instead, it intensified.

The cracked window alongside her alley hideout had enabled her to hear the bulk of the conversation between Cord and the railroad employee. Evidently, Sackett had a method of discovering when the amounts of money in the railroad safes would be high. How? Someone within the railroad was telling him? He was stealing the information?

Her brow knit. Cord's muscular form disappeared from view around the next corner. The only thing she understood for certain was that Cord was trying to anticipate where Sackett would strike next. Dare she hope he wanted to warn his fellow operatives who were still on the job?

She swallowed convulsively. No, Cord was arranging to confront Sackett himself. She *knew* it, in every fiber of her body. It would be just like him to go after Sackett alone.

Heavily, she leaned against the side of the building, feeling the abrasiveness of the brick through her sleeve. She loathed the thought of Cord holing up in a railroad car alone, waiting to do battle against an outlaw she'd kept him from catching the first time.

What could she do to help him? The most obvious choice, asking her father to help Cord, was the one thing she'd promised Cord she wouldn't do. Her hands were tied. And his life was at risk.

She felt sick inside. She didn't know whether she could bear to stand aside and do nothing.

Chapter 11

Wren stood smack in the center of female heaven. All around her, in a literal pack, in fact, stood men. Handsome, formally dressed, attentive, ball-attending men. All of them acting as if they were charmed by her.

Usually being at this kind of event, surrounded by an audience of appreciative men would have caused her to flourish. Tonight, the gaiety around her left her unmoved. She'd come only because her presence meant so much to Aunt Fanny.

"I've another one," she said, smiling in hopes that the physical act would lead to the emotional response. "On which side does a chicken have the most feathers?"

The gentlemen regarded her with baffled smiles.

"The outside." She winked.

They all guffawed.

"Your turn. Surely each of you has at least one joke suitable for polite company."

The man on her right gazed at her warmly. "If you insist. . . ." His thick black eyebrows lifted.

"I do."

"Well, it goes like this. Three men walked into a saloon. One was a . . ."

Wren continued looking at him with a pleasant expression, but her mind wandered from his words. In the week since the seven kisses with Cord, her mind had been wandering often. Every time, to a puzzle of a man with a square jaw and eyes that made her belly flip every time he leveled them at her.

Since they'd arrived at Morgana Morgenstern's ball an hour and a half ago, Cord had been sitting in the same place.

The side of the ballroom attached to the entry hall was comprised of a wide stairway. It bumped up five steps to a landing upon which clusters of chairs, low tables, and potted ferns had been arranged. Five more steps led to the entry hall. Cord was sitting in a chair upon the landing, one knee bent, one leg outstretched.

The gentlemen circling her laughed. She joined in, then transferred her attention to the next man in her circle. "Do you have a joke for us, sir?"

He dipped his chin and obliged.

Since the day after the kisses, when she'd been angry at Cord, her feelings toward him had been a confusing jumble. She was so attracted to the man that the air hummed whenever they were in the same room. She didn't want to desire him, yet was hurt that he didn't want to desire her. She admired him and simultaneously wanted to strangle him. She felt unsafe emotionally when he was close, and unsafe physically when he was parted from her farther than a yell.

When he'd told her he wouldn't let anything happen

between them again, he'd meant it. He'd been reserved, detached, courteous, but indifferent ever since. And it was driving her *mad*. In the past, if one of her friends or family members had been in the doldrums or somehow otherwise in a state she found disagreeable, she'd never rested until she'd lifted their spirits. She regarded that kind of thing as a personal challenge.

With Cord, because she knew his detachment was the best thing for them both, she'd had to bite her tongue and endure it.

More laughter from her ring of men, though less enthusiastic. The tall fellow with thinning hair must have told a dud.

"And you, sir," she said to the next.

Their defense lessons had continued, only, she suspected, because he'd made a deal with her and he was a man who kept his word. After the day he'd taught her to break holds, he'd accomplished the sessions with a minimum of touching.

Three more men told jokes and Wren made a better effort at listening. Once everyone had their turn, she executed a curtsy. "Thank you, gentlemen. You've inspired me. I think it best I excuse myself before I do something unwise like fall in love with all of you at once."

They chuckled and murmured polite protests as she eased away. She stepped into the line forming at the food table behind an elderly gentleman who looked like he'd be fortunate to live long enough to sample the oyster patties.

While she waited, she smoothed her gown into place. It was cherry-colored silk with a tight waist, snug sleeves, a fashionable bustle, and a low V-shaped neck.

The elderly gentleman's inching pace allowed her time to survey the spectacle of the ball. Morgana Morgenstern, maker of wonderful breakfasts, owned a mansion of a home. Chandeliers dripped from a soaring ceiling, spilling candlelight on the silvery wallpaper, the polished floor, and the swirling couples. Ebullient music wafted from the string quartet in the corner.

Wren spotted Aunt Fanny, deep in conversation with two ladies who also appeared to favor unorthodox hairstyles. Miles Fenner was also in attendance, speaking with characteristic drama to a small audience.

Today's voice lesson had been her last, thank you God. Her singing and acting instruction had continued side by side with her defense lessons. In the past two weeks she hadn't missed a single one of Mr. Fenner's classes, though she'd been more and more tempted to bury her head under a pillow and feign an illness.

Coward, she thought, as she picked up a creamy china plate from the head of the line. Regardless of his techniques, Mr. Fenner had helped her improve her voice. That's all that mattered. Especially because—a sizzle of excitement spiraled through her—the audition for the traveling troupe was tomorrow. She could hardly believe it, hardly wait to prove Mr. Fenner wrong.

She selected some olives and several squares of cheese. Leaning forward, she spotted chocolate downtable. Her mouth watered. She'd have to come back for that. Chocolate definitely deserved a fresh plate. She helped herself to a deviled egg.

As she waited for the elderly gentleman to wobble a wedge of tomato onto his plate, her gaze pulled inexorably to the platform halfway up the stairs. Cord looked away just as she looked up, giving her the impression that he'd been watching her. Her pulse stuttered. She waited for him to look at her again.

He didn't. His full attention returned to his conversation with the distinguished gentlemen sitting next to him.

Suddenly, Wren wasn't quite as hungry as she'd been. She helped the elderly gentleman snag two more tomatoes, then waded through the crowd toward the wall, hoping for some privacy.

As the chitchatting throng thinned, Wren noticed, to her dismay, that a huddle of young women already occupied the wall. They stood clustered together, partially hidden by a bank of ferns. There could be no mistaking what—or rather who—had captured their attention.

Every one of them was staring at Cord like a dehydrated longhorn peering at a river. They resembled herself so much at that age that it hurt to watch.

Embarrassed for them, she approached the nearest of the group, a girl with a fresh, perfectly round face.

The girl glanced at her, then back at Cord.

"May I ask what you're doing?" Wren said.

"Watching him," the girl whispered.

"Why?"

"*Why?* Look at him."

"I'm sure there are plenty of young gentlemen equally as handsome, gentlemen who'd value you as you deserve—"

"Just look at him," the girl interrupted, her patience beginning to fray.

Wren looked. She felt at once much older and wiser than the girl beside her and yet beneath the years and the lessons—exactly like her.

Of course these girls loved him. How could they not? In his dark, plainly cut suit, sitting in that insolent position, with those fiercely blue eyes, he was every girl's fantasy come to life. A fantasy who'd crush their illusions if they allowed him to.

Wren eyed the girl beside her. The dreamy wonder on her face, the eyes twinkling with fruitless hopes. She was so misguided, so inexperienced. Yet so earnest. Wren wondered with a shudder whether Cord might still see her as she saw the round-faced girl. Lordy, she hoped not. She didn't want to be anything like her.

Her gaze pulled back to where Cord sat, aloof.

This is probably how he liked it, to sit removed from everyone. He could flirt with ease, say the right words when the situation called. Just so long as he avoided the discomfort of having any of these girls profess their devotion right to his face. So long as he didn't have to touch or look at the woman he'd given seven kisses to.

Wren chewed on a cheese square. The thing tasted wooden, and when she swallowed it, it promptly lodged itself halfway down her throat, right next to her heart.

"He's an operative with the Pinkerton Detective Agency," the round-faced girl whispered in a voice tipped with awe. "He tracks and catches criminals."

"Is that so?"

"Yes. He's single-handedly arrested the Betton gang, Crazy Tim Timmler, the Boyds and all but one of the Sackett brothers."

"Hm." Wren sampled an olive, which tasted no better.

"Can't you just imagine him out there, on the range? Riding for miles." She shook her head in admiration. "Tracking outlaws against all odds. Drawing his guns and facing them down. Endangering himself—"

"Yes." She imagined Cord, riding in the safe car, a gun in both hands as he waited for Sackett to attack. Her chest tightened. "Very noble of him."

The girl turned her full attention to Wren. She studied her suspiciously. "You wouldn't be so blasé if you'd met him, like I have."

"You're likely right. Do you enjoy olives?"

"What?"

"Here." She handed her plate to the girl. "You've my permission to eat the rest."

"Miss, no, I don't like—"

Wren weaved through the crowd, searching for Aunt Fanny.

"Bird!"

Wren turned toward her aunt's voice, and spotted her sweeping toward her, pulling Cord in her wake.

Oh, no.

"I couldn't very well let our poor Mr. Caldwell here sit through the entire ball without dancing a single time, now could I? A travesty, I *swear*." Aunt Fanny used her lemon yellow handkerchief to fan her flushed face.

Wren stared at her aunt, dread and something that couldn't be anticipation winding through her. Cord's stiffness and silence spoke volumes.

"Imagine," Aunt Fanny said. "The two of you have spent nearly every minute of the last two weeks enjoying one another's company. And here you are at Morgana's ball and haven't taken advantage of a spin around this lovely floor together even once." She laughed heartily, the sound of merriment ending in a gasp followed by a hiccup. "What can account for that?"

"I asked Mr. Caldwell to strive hard to resist me tonight," Wren said hoping some levity would break the painful awkwardness of the situation.

"Well I'm sure he's tried, but what do you expect?" Aunt Fanny asked. "You're very pretty, bird." She patted

Cord's arm. "Give our Mr. Caldwell here a dance. What do you say?"

"If you insist."

"I do!"

The older woman bent Cord's arm and set Wren's hand into the crook of his elbow.

"Thank you for your help," Cord said sheepishly.

"You're welcome. Now hurry off, they're about to start a waltz." She gave them both a gentle push.

They reached the dance floor and the music started with a swelling flourish. Grudgingly, Cord took Wren into his arms and led the way into a waltz.

"Sorry about the way Aunt Fanny forced you into dancing with me back there."

"Not at all."

How she hated that courteous tone. In its own way, it struck her as the height of rudeness.

Wren moved within his arms, letting him turn her this way and that. He held her with incredible gentleness and at the same time held her as far removed from his own body as possible.

She was acutely aware of his hand splayed across her lower back, his other engulfing her fingers. The beat of her blood intensified. Her nerves strung tight, tighter.

Their stares clashed, then locked for an interminable time, several dizzying turns, before he averted his eyes.

She bit her bottom lip, foolishly disheartened. Irritably, she squeezed his hand to get his attention. "There is a group of girls behind the ferns who are quite enamored with you."

"I hadn't noticed."

"Truly? Well, I know they're there because I spoke with them. It might be nice if you could introduce your-self, say a few words. It would mean a lot to them."

His lips thinned.

"Don't worry. I don't think any of them have plans to lie in wait for you outside in the shadows."

He sighed. "Wren . . ."

"Never mind."

Their feet moved in unison as they whirled.

His jaw firmed, and he appeared on the verge of speaking, when Wren's shoe skidded and she lost her balance.

Cord caught her instantly, his expression sharp with concern. "Are you all right?"

"Yes." Other couples danced past them. "I think I slipped on something."

He released her hands and scanned the floor, then bent to pick up a lady's earbob. "This must have been what did it," he said.

"Yes." The last note of their waltz hovered on the air and died.

"Mr. Caldwell." An elegantly thin hand slid onto Cord's sleeve.

Cord dragged his gaze from Wren to the newcomer. It was Robin Wentworth. "Good evening."

The tall, stately blonde smiled beguilingly. "Good evening. Hello, Miss Bradley."

"Hello."

"I believe you found my earbob for me." Robin said to him, motioning to the piece of jewelry he held, then to her unadorned right lobe. "I can't thank you enough. I was terrified to think I'd lost it."

"My pleasure." Cord extended his palm to her. She plucked the bangle from it and fastened it to her ear.

"It's a treat to run into you somewhere other than outside Mr. Fenner's class," Robin said.

"Likewise."

"I wondered, if it wouldn't be too much trouble, if you'd care to dance with me."

Cord had absolutely no interest in doing so. "Certainly. That is, if you'll excuse us, Wren."

Wren's face blanched. "Of course," she said formally. Everything about her expression had hardened, except her eloquent eyes. Disappointment shone in their depths.

Every time he'd hurt her over the past week, he'd seen the evidence of it in those eyes. It never failed to spear him with pain.

Wren presented him with her back and walked away.

Irritation knifed through him. He could never have her. At the very least her dreams of the theater precluded it. She knew that as well as he did. So why couldn't she just leave him be? Wasn't it enough that he couldn't bear to let her out of his sight, even though being near her made him insane? Wasn't it enough that he couldn't sleep at night? That he existed in a constant state of semiarousal which escalated at the mere sound of her voice or the smell of her floral perfume?

"Shall we?" Robin asked.

As he led her onto the floor, Cord berated himself for wanting so bad to go to Wren and ask her forgiveness.

He caught Robin looking at him inquisitively. The dance had started. He gave her his stock apologetic smile. "I got lost in your beauty," he murmured. "Forgive me."

"Forgiven," she pronounced.

He offered up a false chuckle and pulled her snugly into his hold. Tonight, Robin was just what he needed. She was pretty and friendly and available. With her, he could remember all the women in the world other than the china doll.

"You dance well," she whispered.

"Thank you."

"I've been waiting for this all night," she confessed, a blush infusing her cheeks with rosettes of color. "I was hoping you'd ask . . ."

This was the problem with charm. It wasn't truth. None of the women he'd bedded had truly *known* him. No more, anyway, than they knew the snake oil they purchased from traveling salesmen really would cure measles.

So? What the hell did he care? They were adults, capable of making their own decisions.

As he circled the floor with Robin in his arms, he tried to rustle up some stirring of attraction toward her without success. Robin was much too perfect. She didn't look like a real person to him. Didn't have gray eyes. Probably had never in her life shot a gun or told a joke.

Damn it all! Could he not quit thinking of Wren for two minutes? He'd spent the entire evening slouched in a chair staring at her. He'd been unable to stop himself, even if the people sitting near him must have thought him a rabidly jealous idiot.

To be honest, that's how he felt. Snarling inside, like a dog. Seething with angers he couldn't define. Ready at the smallest provocation to palm his gun and shoot to death any of the men who'd smiled at Wren tonight. Who'd dared to touch her.

"You're h-holding me very snugly," Robin said.

"Am I?" he whispered near her ear.

A shiver of delight tremored down her spine, and he found himself wishing it were Wren shivering in his arms.

He smiled wolfishly, feeling a lack of pleasure so great he wanted to throw back his head and howl.

* * *

Darkness blanketed the carriage as it rumbled along the dirt ruts leading away from the lights of Austin. Aunt Fanny had left the party earlier in the night, insisting the "young folk" stay and waltz away the night.

After his dance with Robin, Cord had retreated to his chair on the platform and waited. Wren had used the additional hours to laugh, sip punch, chat, and dance with a torturous series of men. The fact that he'd not been fooled by her forced gaiety hadn't made it any easier to watch.

When Helmut had returned for them, Wren had climbed into the carriage without a word. They were sitting across from one another, almost to Aunt Fanny's now, and she'd still not spoken.

Cord leaned deeper into his seat. He'd been hard with wanting her for the entire ride. His hands were shaking, for Christ sake, with the restraint it was costing him to hold still.

Helmut pulled the carriage to a graceful stop in front of the house.

Cord moved to open the carriage door for Wren, but she brushed aside his arm and let herself out. He stepped down behind her. With a musical rattle of the harness, the horses pulled the carriage toward the stable.

Cord expected Wren to hurry to her room without speaking to him. But with her gloved palm resting on the front door handle, she paused.

He stopped behind her on the porch, scene of their truce that first night, and prayed she'd say something, anything, to him. He loathed her unnatural silence.

Slowly, she turned. "Seeing as how I seem to be a person you hold in very low regard, I have to ask . . ."

He grimaced and wished it was day so he could protect his face from her scrutiny with his hat.

"Does our deal still stand?"

An ugly suspicion occurred to him. "What, have you told your father about my wish to continue pursuing Sackett?"

"No." But the guilt in her eyes as she lowered her lashes and looked away told another story. Had she just thought about tattling on him, or had she done it? He held himself rigid.

"I'm sorry I asked," she murmured as she let herself in and closed the door, shutting him out of her life.

He walked numbly to the porch railing. What the hell had that been about? She knew something, that's what. She knew something she wasn't letting on. Surely, though, she hadn't told the Colonel. No, there's no way she'd risk their bargain and the advantages it afforded her goals. So why had she looked so damn guilty?

From the beginning, he should have played it straight with her. No truces. But he'd been blinded by his desire to catch Sackett and clear his own name. Now he feared she was going to make him pay.

He braced his hands against the railing. Mutely, he stared out at the prairie, looking for answers in the voiceless acres. What had happened to him? To his life? Where had he gone wrong?

He'd been hounding his destiny as a Pinkerton detective from the moment he'd decided as a boy that's what he wanted to do with his life. Once he'd become an operative, he'd worked harder and ever harder, redoubling his efforts, yet never feeling in his gut that he'd reached . . . it. That point when he would be fulfilled inside, when he'd have done enough. In the weeks since his suspension, his sense of incompleteness had worsened. And now this, his lowest point yet.

He felt lousy about Wren hating him, and lousier because the emotion proved a lesson his parents had burned into him. Making yourself vulnerable to another person's whims was the surest road to misery. For years he'd witnessed the devastation his father had endured for loving a woman who'd never loved him in return. Though Cord had blamed his mother for it at first, over time he blamed his father more. The man had failed at something important. He was the one who'd let his heart be stolen, who'd stood back as it was crushed before his eyes without ever having the pride or guts to demand it back.

That wasn't for Cord. Never would be. He'd seen too much, knew too well what it could cost a man to love a woman. He'd been six years old when he'd sworn never to allow the same to happen to him. He'd curled himself into a ball in the darkness of his armoire that night as his parents' vicious screams rang through the house. A thousand times more before he'd finally broken free and left for college, he'd had cause to renew his vow.

His boots crunched over dirt as he stalked from the porch and kept going, needing a small taste of freedom.

If he could just fulfill his promise to the Colonel and get his job back, then he could make up for all the time he'd wasted and he'd feel better. Whenever he caught one of the outlaws he'd been assigned to hunt, it filled a void inside of him. For that stretch of time, he could rest knowing he'd brought peace, fixed something, made things right for those the criminal had victimized and robbed.

Since the beginning it had been his goal to give up his work once he felt he'd accomplished enough, when he felt whole. Then he could retire to a plot of land and a house of his own.

Like he'd told Wren, he'd been saving for that, hanging his hopes on it. Yet the dream had never seemed less likely than at this moment.

The lamplight from Aunt Fanny's house, from Wren's room, dimmed as he trod deeper and deeper on a journey to nowhere. The spaces of accomplishment after every outlaw he caught were growing shorter instead of longer. The hole inside his chest wider instead of smaller.

He shoved his hands into his pockets. If he could just get his job back, things would be better. He needed back his job. He needed Sackett.

Chapter 12

The following morning, Wren stood at the end of Aunt Fanny's second-story hall, peering out the window. She'd risen ungodly early. So early she'd watched every golden detail of the changing from night to dawn.

She squinted through the crack between the gauzy curtain and the wall. From her vantage point she had a good clean view of the rain barrel out back. Cord hadn't emerged to wash yet, but she expected him to soon.

Today was truly the day.

November 11. Audition day.

A spark of anticipation mixed with disbelief trembled through her. Since the instant she'd spotted the advertisement, she'd known that today's opportunity had been fashioned just for her.

Her music folder was ready. Her song and Lady Isobel's monologue from *East Lynne* practiced to an embarrassing degree. The pink gown she'd brought expressly for the audition had been carefully pressed and was buttoned up her back.

It was the same pink bodice and skirt she'd been wearing the night Sackett had snatched her from City Hall's back alley. She figured if she could survive Lloyd Sackett in the outfit, she could most certainly win an audition in it. Already she'd accomplished a small victory simply by overcoming the memories that had haunted her when she'd donned the dress.

Imagine. To finally walk onstage for a *real* tryout with a *real* company. The path which had brought her to today had been a long one. All her life, to be exact. And the only obstacle remaining between her and the theater was Cord Caldwell.

When she'd asked him last night whether their deal not to interfere with one another still stood, his expression had told her unequivocally no. Though she didn't entirely believe that he could actually be so cruel as to forbid her from going, she didn't entirely believe he couldn't be. After all she'd been through for this chance, she could *not* risk the possibility that he might oppose it. She'd decided to sneak away. She wasn't certain she could do it. But she was a few degrees more certain of that than his cooperation if she confided in him.

Either way, oh, was he going to be *furious*.

Her hand moved to her heart-shaped locket. "Bumblebee bumblebee bumblebee bumblebee," she sang softly, "Bumblebee bumblebee bumblebee bumblebee."

The hinges of the back door whined as it opened. Wren dropped her necklace and hastily tucked herself against the wall.

Cord walked into the morning.

Her breath caught. Lordy. The man wanted nothing to do with her, he'd made that eminently clear. Yet she was still powerless to stop this fluttery, heated, restless craving she contracted whenever she looked at him.

He wore a fresh pair of denims, boots, and last night's shirt open down the front. Her view of his chest reminded her forcefully of the night they'd kissed. She wondered how many other women had the privilege of knowing that he slept in cotton drawers, then shrugged into his shirt upon rising? Directly afterward, she wondered whether it was wise to be proud of such knowledge.

He set aside the folded shirt he'd been carrying and opened a leather kit. As if through long habit, he propped up a small mirror, then mixed a bowl full of shaving foam. After smoothing the mixture onto his shadowed face, he started running the razor over his cheeks.

Warmth circled hungrily in her belly. It appeared, to her disgust, that her woman's body had absolutely no sense of justice or self-respect.

Once he'd finished shaving, Cord pulled off his shirt and tossed it over the nearby porch rail. In the sunshine, his upper body was tanned, as hard as granite, and yet stunningly sleek and beautiful.

Wren wet her lips, entranced by the intimate scene. She watched the graceful play of his muscles as he splashed water from the barrel over his chest and shivered. With moisture pooling above his collarbones and cascading over the mounds of his stomach, his attention appeared to catch on the far horizon.

In the rustle of the wind, he stood, gazing into the distance, and Wren knew in her gut that he was thinking of criminals still uncaught.

As quickly, the moment passed. He extracted a cake of

soap, lathered it, and began to wash. When he started unbuttoning his denim pants, she leapt back with a gasp.

Openmouthed, she blinked at the window curtains. *Good God.* She tried to remember why she'd not made a better effort to rise early and watch Cord bathe before now. She couldn't recall any reason she found satisfactory.

To compose herself, she smoothed the baby-fine hairs at her forehead, then pulled her bodice into place. If she dallied any longer, she'd risk her plan.

She hurried down the staircase to the foyer. Cord had only one weakness that she knew of. His ambition toward his work. She'd use that weakness against him now.

She knocked twice on the inside of the front door.

"I'll get it," she called, for Helmut's benefit. She'd heard the telltale rattling of kitchen pans long before Cord had emerged for his bath.

Wren opened the front door. "May I help you?" she asked the vacant air. Paused. "Certainly, I'd be happy to relay the message to Mr. Caldwell. Thank you."

She shut the door with an audibly loud click, then proceeded to her usual seat at the dining table.

Aunt Fanny breezed in moments later. "Was someone just at the door?"

"Yes, an employee of the railroad."

"I thought that's what I heard! I'm glad I'm not losing my mind." She giggled at herself as she took her seat at the table's head. "Whatever did he want at this early hour?"

"He asked that Mr. Caldwell visit him at their offices this morning."

Fanny tipped her head. "Well, our Mr. Caldwell is quite important, it would seem."

"Yes. Best that he answer their summons."

"Certainly best."

Just then Cord walked in. The light gushing through the room's double windows glinted in the blue of his eyes, and on his wet, neatly combed hair.

"Mr. Caldwell," Aunt Fanny said, before he'd had a chance to sit. "A gentleman from the railroad offices was just here."

His brows stitched together. He rested his elegant savage's hands on the back of his chair. "Here?"

"I *swear*," Aunt Fanny said.

Wren almost laughed. She'd anticipated having to fool Cord by herself. Aunt Fanny's unknowing involvement was more than perfect.

"They've requested your presence at their offices this morning," Aunt Fanny said. "You'd best go."

Cord glanced at Wren.

"Bird doesn't need your protection twenty-four hours a day!" Aunt Fanny scowled at him mightily. As abruptly, she laughed, gasped, hiccuped. "Though it's heartening to see the determination with which you pursue your assignments. *Very* heartening." She made a shooing motion. "Now get on with you."

Cord hesitated.

"We'll save your breakfast and have your coffee waiting when you return. Now git!"

"I'll be back in less than half an hour," Cord promised.

"I said git!" Aunt Fanny yelled, grinning broadly.

Wren listened to Cord's retreating footsteps. She could clearly imagine him putting on his renegade hunter's hat one-handed as he strode to the stables.

Some of the tightness cinching her chest loosened. She'd had no idea just how tense she'd been before . . .

before she'd triumphed over the Legend. Her smile started small, but was soon tugging across the whole of her mouth.

"Well, you're certainly happy this morning," her aunt said.

"Very."

Five minutes after claiming not to be hungry for breakfast, with Aunt Fanny's unbroken string of chatter to Helmut still wafting from the dining room, Wren slipped out the front door.

She rushed down the steps, imagining Cord's reaction when he found out she'd escaped. Maybe he'd be half as angry as she'd been last night when he'd taken Robin Wentworth onto the dance floor in front of her nose. A *quarter* as angry would suffice. No, even an eighth as angry, she thought as she scampered toward the stables. Even an eighth.

Cord pushed his way into Austin's railroad offices, jangling the bell.

James jerked upright behind his desk. "Mr. Caldwell."

"Why didn't you send a letter, like I told you?" Cord planted his hands on the high wooden console. "I expressly asked that you notify me by letter."

James peered at him, eyes round. His head extended forward, as if he hoped to understand Cord better by moving his brains closer. "Notify you?" he asked tentatively. "About the monetary amount aboard the trains between here and Dallas?"

"Yes."

"I was planning . . . to notify you. By letter, as we discussed. Later today."

Foreboding pricked Cord. "You didn't ride out to Fanny Fortengay's home this morning?"

The man shook his head, his expression fully perplexed. "No."

"Did you send anyone else?"

"No, but as it happens, I'm glad you're here." He pushed his spectacles up the bridge of his nose using his pinky finger. "I've just received word that I'm to place seven thousand dollars in the vault tomorrow on board the eight-ninety-five to Dallas. That's the highest amount in a month."

Cord heard him, but only with the small portion of his brain that wasn't turning over the facts, trying to figure out what in the hell had happened this morning.

"Sackett is likely to try and rob—"

"Let me be sure I'm clear," Cord said. "No one from the railroad visited Fanny Fortengay's house this morning?"

James shook his head. "No."

Worry pierced Cord, as surely and as deadly as a bullet burying itself in his heart. *Wren*. He shouldered through the door and ran to Aunt Fanny's dapple gray mount. He was in the saddle and galloping hard in seconds.

Jesus. His mouth went dry. If it hadn't been for Aunt Fanny's involvement, he'd have suspected one of Wren's tricks. Likely, so she could attend her audition. But she'd promised him there'd be no more escapes, and he'd told her outright he wouldn't interfere with her audition. Not only that, but Aunt Fanny wouldn't lie to him about his summons from the railroad. The only other option was that someone who wanted him out of the house had paid them a visit and lied about his identity.

He pressed his heels into his mount's flanks, increasing their speed. What if Sackett had found them? What if he was planning to hurt Wren somehow? Use her to get to him?

Fear sucked at his breath and whited his thoughts. If the bastard did anything to her. Harmed her. *Bruised* her in any way, he'd kill him. He'd goddamned kill him in cold blood.

Cord charged into Aunt Fanny's house, his heart pounding. Immediately, he heard Aunt Fanny's voice.

His mind whirred, shifted. He told himself to calm down. He hadn't returned to broken windows, to a deserted house, or to blood sinking into the carpet.

He stopped in the doorway of the dining room.

Aunt Fanny glanced up at him. "Good, you're back! We saved some coffee. . . ." Her smile wavered. "Is something wrong?"

"Nothing worth worrying about," he lied, deferring to years of training that had taught him never to alarm unnecessarily. "Is Wren here?"

"Upstairs."

"Did you speak with the gentleman from the railroad this morning?" Cord asked.

"Ah . . . no. Wren did."

"Did you see the man from the railroad?"

Looking befuddled, she shook her head. "No . . . why—"

"Excuse me a moment."

Aunt Fanny nodded, lips pursed.

Cord took the stairs two at a time. Damn it all. Aunt Fanny hadn't lied to him. Wren had lied to them all.

He threw aside her bedroom door, sure of what he'd find. The room was empty. She'd run from him. *Again.* Again, damn it.

Wasting no time, he turned on his heel and strode from the house toward the gray mare. He'd go to Austin's theater first. No doubt remained that this was the morning of the traveling troupe's audition. She'd run from him to attend it.

He arched his leg over the saddle and headed back into town the way he'd come.

Apparently, her assurance that she wouldn't flee again had buckled under her lack of trust in him. She'd feared he'd stand in the way of her all-important dream of the theater, so she'd deceived him. No one person was as important to her as walking across some godforsaken stage and spouting the dialogue of imaginary people.

This ravening sense of betrayal mixed with fear wasn't easing—and wouldn't—until he could see her.

The director of Markham's Traveling Troupe of Players, a small man with a head of white, bushy hair, consulted the sheaf of papers he clasped. "Miss Bradley?"

"Yes," Wren said, a strangled feeling in her throat. Thank goodness he'd finally called her. Over the past fifteen minutes, her nervousness about her upcoming performance had grown side by side with the worry that Cord would find her and stop her before she had a chance to audition.

The director inclined his head and motioned to the stage. The aspiring actor who'd just completed his monologue and his song took his seat, causing the feet of his chair to scrape against the wooden floor.

"Thank you," Wren murmured as those sitting next to her in the row angled their legs to the side so she could scoot past. "Thank you."

She began the long, lonely walk to the stage.

It all came down to this. All her choices, her parents hurt, the years of pining, the hours upon hours of practicing.

Ghastly. She heard Mr. Fenner's taunting voice, felt the tip of Sackett's gun against her temple, cold and deadly. Both hovering remembrances would have gleefully dragged her down if she'd let them. Instead, she stuck out her chin and used them to solidify her resolve. She'd prove them wrong.

She passed the director, passed the other actresses and actors who could quite well be more talented than she was, swallowed the vulnerability that came from wanting a thing so much, and climbed onto the platform.

Everyone hushed. The director raised a pencil over the notebook he held. From the hallway beyond the theater, rapid footsteps penetrated the quiet.

Wren's gaze centered on the open double doors at the back of Berryhill's Hall. *Oh, no. Not now, God. Please not now.*

Cord loomed in the opening.

Her hopes plummeted.

He caught sight of her immediately and stopped in his tracks. His cheeks were flushed, his hair windblown, and his hat missing. He stood with utter stillness, his forehead furrowed above troubled eyes. She could see the billowing of his chest beneath his shirt.

The director blinked at Wren, waiting. A few of the other hopefuls shot glances behind them to see what she was looking at. Mumblings arose from the gathering.

Would he dare walk up here and pull her from the stage? Possibly. He owed her nothing since she'd broken one of her stipulations. All deals were off. What had she been thinking? She should have trusted him earlier. It would be the worst thing she'd ever endured to come this close to her dream, only to have him snatch it away.

Let me do this, she begged Cord wordlessly. She put everything she was behind the entreaty. *Please, please let me.*

Cord stared at her, reading, she knew, the message in her eyes. His lips twisted into a narrow frown. He didn't move forward to snatch her, nor away.

Half-certain he'd storm to her and escort her from the building at any moment, she decided to at least begin and steal as many seconds of her one great chance as fate allowed. She cleared her throat, and spoke the first sentence of her monologue. The one minute he'd granted her became two.

Challenge and wonder flowed with her blood as she lost herself in the body, heart, and soul of her favorite character, English Lady Isobel from *East Lynne*. She felt a kernel deep inside, submerged, come sprouting upward. Slow at first, then faster. Drawing at her, calling her home with a sweet song. It was the little girl she'd once been, the child with the white dress and the blue sash who'd sat in a seat in a theater like this one and fallen in love. To be onstage again felt like sun after weeks of rain.

Cord stood at the back of the vast room in shadow, stunned.

She was . . . She was wonderful. His entire body stilled beneath the spell she was casting.

She fairly dazzled, as if someone were spotlighting her with a beam that blossomed from the inside out. There was no mistaking her distinctive lemon-and-butter hair or the whimsical smile. Those were pure Wren. But the rest of her had been transformed. Her movements were fluid, her expressions heartrending, her words seeming to spring from her lips for the first time in history. She *was* her character. Awe filtered through his anger and apprehension.

Cord couldn't take his eyes off her. He tried, but found it impossible *not* to stare, humbled as he was by the magnificence of her talent.

Again, he discovered he'd misjudged her. In his own mind, he'd belittled her dreams of the theater since he'd first learned of them. He'd thought her impractical, her aspirations foolhardy, her talents minimal.

He'd been gravely wrong. Wren belonged on stage. He'd never been more sure of anything. The china doll had found her rightful place in the world.

Pride expanded in him, maturing his feelings toward her in a way that was bittersweet. There had been times, since he'd found her in that prairie, that he'd entertained impossible fantasies of what it would be like to love her and be loved by her. He closed the door on the last of those fantasies now. Wren was going to win a position in this company, and spend her life performing for adoring audiences.

She'd been right when she'd told her father that she didn't belong to anyone anymore. She belonged to the theater, and had, he suspected, for some time. That was as it should be. His beautiful Wren deserved her dream come true.

In that moment, he became her champion.

Chapter 13

All the hopefuls had performed. The director had adjourned to his office to make his selection.

Wren sat rigidly in her seat, waiting for him to return. She was trying hard to appear calm, assured, worldly. How she imagined the ideal candidate for Markham's Traveling Troupe might appear. Unfortunately, when her turn at the front had ended, the bulk of her confidence had gone with it.

Knowing that Cord was sitting at the back only made her every sentiment more extreme. He'd taken the last seat in the last row after she'd finished her song. She'd been too afraid to look at him since, but she could still feel his attention on her, steady and measuring. If she failed, him witnessing it would make it far worse. If— please, please, please—she succeeded . . . she didn't know how she'd feel having him here. Her emotions toward him were all mixed up. She'd been prepared to dislike him after last night, and then he'd gone and let her audition this morning, even though her father might extend his suspension, or punish him in some other way, if he found out.

The rustling of paper heralded the director's return. He strode onto the stage, list in hand.

Wren's heart skipped a beat, then found a rushed rhythm. *Oh. My. Lord.* Her tongue darted out to lick her lips. She was so very close now, peering at her dream full in the face, with only seconds separating her from it.

The director halted before them, his hair floating in an artistic cloud around his head. "Thank you, all of you, for coming. I was impressed by each of your performances, appreciative of your time and various talents. However," he smiled regretfully, "as you know, I've only the funds to hire three of you. So. I've selected the three who I felt had the most refined abilities and the most sterling potential."

Yes, Wren thought. She didn't want him to compromise. Other than herself, just the black-haired fellow and the gentleman with the deep voice.

"Without further ado," the director said, "I'd like to welcome the following individuals to Markham's Traveling Troupe of Players."

Yearning stabbed though her. She twined her fingers together and held her breath.

"Mr. David Wagner," he said.

She loved acting more than anyone here. That would pull her name from his lips next. It *must.*

"Mr. Christopher Thurston."

Fear scratched at her. One more. Hers. Hers, God. *Hers.*

"Miss Wren Bradley."

Her heart lifted and expanded with a forceful billow of joy and excitement. Goose bumps streamed over her skin in waves. Only vaguely was she aware of her hands rising to cover her lips. He'd called her name. She'd made it!

And then she was standing and the other hopefuls were smiling bravely, shaking her hand, wishing her well. Then her two fellow cast members surrounded her, asking questions. She answered by rote, hardly able to pay them any attention because her brain was spinning around the ceiling doing dives and flips. She'd really done it! Lordy, she had. She truly was good at this, like she'd desperately hoped all those nights, lying in bed alone and thinking about her future.

She couldn't quit grinning. She'd get to wear costumes made just for her, and rehearse like she'd watched the Dallas company do so often, and act in front of an audience like the ones she'd sat in countless times. She wouldn't spend the rest of her life as the Colonel's daughter, or Alexandra's younger sister, or Edward's wife.

"David, Christopher, Wren." The director beckoned them to where he stood leaning against the front of the stage. They gathered round him.

"Congratulations," he said, crossing his arms over his papers. "And welcome to Markham's Traveling Troupe. Each of you showed me something in your auditions that I found extraordinary. That's not to say we won't work together in the future to improve your craft." He raised his bushy brows. The brown eyes beneath glittered with warmth. "Only that I saw in you talent of a very high caliber."

Wren viewed him with even more admiration than she had moments before. Her gaze wandered to the two actors beside her. The black-haired fellow and the gentleman with the deep voice, just as she'd hoped. She couldn't believe she was so privileged as to be a part of this elite circle with them.

"Now to the particulars," the director was saying. "The troupe is currently on a vacation, which will last ten more days. At which time we'll all be meeting here in Austin to begin rehearsals for our next production."

Wren nodded avidly.

"As I'm certain you're all aware, the life of a cast member is an arduous one. It doesn't pay well, particularly at your level. However, and luckily for you," again the glint in his eyes, "the company will cover your travel and living expenses. You'll have just about enough left over to afford whatever other necessities you might need. Which reminds me, pack very few of your own personal belongings. Only what you yourself can carry."

Wren kept catching herself smiling idiotically. She attempted a more professional expression.

"All of the actors assist," he continued, "with advertising, scenery, costumes, and props in every city we visit. We work hard and we're a close-knit group because of it."

He looked at each of them, seeming to test whether they were understanding everything. "Once we complete rehearsals we'll be on the road for a year without returning."

A year? A slice of reality split into Wren's euphoria. That was far longer than she'd anticipated.

"So, by all means, enjoy the next ten days. Take advantage of the time to conclude any business matters that need tending and to spend time with your family. You won't be seeing them again for quite a while."

Wren blinked at him. One whole year. She'd never been apart from her loved ones for longer than a few weeks. Not that she couldn't. Consciously, she pushed aside her concerns. She wanted this too much to let anything bother her.

"Wren?" the director broke into her thoughts. "How does everything I've said sound to you?"

"Excellent."

"Very good. Now I'll need each of you to tell me where you might be reached in the coming days via the telegram. That way, I can communicate with you should anything pertinent to your situation arise."

Wren told him where she could be reached in Dallas.

"See you back here on the twenty-first," he said, as he ambled away.

The black-haired fellow turned to her. "I heard you say you'd be in Dallas over the next little while. So will I. My cousin lives there, and she's the nearest relative I have in these parts. I was thinking you and I might want to travel together to Dallas and back."

"Thank you, that's a lovely offer," Wren replied. "But I already have a traveling companion." She pointed to the back of the theater.

Cord, object of a thousand infatuations, was still sitting in the last seat of the last row. He was watching her as carefully as before, his elbows now resting on his parted knees, his fingers dangling between. Longing curled within her. The flush of her victory waned another few notches.

"If you'll excuse me," Wren murmured, then made her way to where Cord sat.

He rose as she approached.

They stood a few feet from one another. "Thank you," she said, wanting very much to like him again and have him like her despite the hurt lingering underneath the surface. "You did one of the most precious things anyone's ever done for me when you let me audition."

His nodded slowly.

"I did it." The glory of it washed over her. "I actually did it, Cord."

"Frankly, I'd have thought the director a raving idiot if he hadn't chosen you."

"You thought I was good?"

"Better than good."

She smiled her gratitude. That he'd been here to witness this momentous occasion, that he'd thought her good, bound him to her as nothing else had before. Arching onto her tiptoes, she pressed a kiss to his cheek.

He didn't flinch, at least.

They walked from the theater side by side, the distance between their bodies carefully polite. "Dare I hope," Wren asked, "that you've forgiven me for tricking you this morning?"

"That might be taking it a little too far."

"I was afraid so."

They emerged onto the bustling street, and Cord squinted against the sun. He'd left his hat behind somewhere, just as he had the night Sackett had kidnapped her. She supposed he did that whenever he was in a panic. They started toward their horses.

"I realize I told you there wouldn't be any more escapes, Cord." She stole glances at him. "I *profusely* apologize. It's just that you'd been disliking me so actively for so many days. I worried you'd not let me audition."

"I know what you worried." He kept his gaze focused ahead.

She could see suddenly that she'd hurt him. Before now she'd no idea she even had that power. It made her dizzy. "You showed me by your actions that I should have trusted you."

They reached the mount that Wren had been riding, its reins looped over the post. He helped her up.

Wren regarded him from beneath the thin shade of her pink hat. "Under no circumstances do I expect you to give me a lesson today, seeing as how I broke the faith of our bargain."

He handed her her horse's reins. "Good, because you're not getting one." His half smile blunted his words.

"I'll accept that decision, even though I treasure our lessons. Even though I'd be prostrate with grief over missing one. Even though you're such a marvelous teacher—"

"You're not getting one," he said as he swung into his saddle. He was smiling outright.

Seeing that gratified her entirely too much.

He led her through town in the direction of Aunt Fanny's house at a trot.

Wren sat tall within the sidesaddle, daydreaming about reporting for rehearsals, the roles she might receive, their opening night, the raucous applause.

Well out of Austin, she slowed her horse's progress. "Cord, would you mind if we stopped for a while? I feel as if I need to . . . I don't know"—her gaze scanned the sky and the trees alongside them—"commemorate what's happened before going back to Aunt Fanny's and on with my life."

"That's fine."

Their horses plodded from the road and threaded through a stand of trees until even the view of the city vanished. A tiny, sun-filled clearing opened in front of them.

Cord dismounted and held her horse's bridle until she'd slipped from her horse.

Wren strolled through the meadow. Lordy, what a wonderful day. She enjoyed the nip of chill in the wind, the clear autumn sunlight, the enormous drifting clouds, the man walking beside her.

At the far end of the meadow, just past the line of shade, she spotted a stretch of ground that curled upward. "Sit with me?" She lowered to the ground and leaned against the backrest the earth had formed.

Cord followed her down. Again, a courteous distance away. He crossed his powerfully muscled legs at the boots.

The blades of grass encircling them rustled, leaning in on themselves. Idly, he picked up a strand and set it between his lips.

She'd always thought friends were most necessary in times of pain. But having Cord—if she could call him a friend—with her at this point of achievement seemed far more critical just now.

Gazing out at the meadow, she let her mind drift to all that had led up to today. The years of wanting, the hours upon hours of work, the times she'd been certain she'd fail. She even let herself reminisce openly about the man who'd broken her heart and driven her to the theater to find solace. The memories brought deep humility to the surface. And with that humility came tears.

At the first sniffle, Cord's brow darkened. He threw aside his blade of grass. "Crying?"

She placed a gloved fist beneath her nose and nodded.

He pulled her onto his lap just like that, as effortlessly as he'd don his Stetson. The initial shock almost instantly gave way to delicious warmth and comfort that was better than a hearth-heated blanket.

"This is supposed to be a celebration," he said gently, pressing her head against his chest.

"It is." She was crying in earnest now. She leaned heavily against him. "I . . . do this s-sometimes . . . when I'm h-happy."

"Hm." Cord held her snugly, occasionally wiping a tuft of hair to the side, rubbing her back, rocking. He never spoke, not once. No silly words about how she should get ahold of herself. Just compassionate silence while she gave vent to her feelings.

For all that today represented a shimmering beginning for her, it represented an ending, too. She cried for the girl she'd been, for how much her parents had loved that girl, for the way she'd miss her family during the year she was gone, for Cord, for dreams that had come true and dreams that hadn't.

At length, the tears abated somewhat. She let new thoughts come, used them to test her composure. They whiffed like mist through a heart that felt raw and light and somehow clearer.

She noticed that her reticule was still fastened around her wrist—its contents squished against her belly. She groped for it and pulled out a fresh hankie. It smelled of the breeze that had dried it, and of soap. She used it to mop her cheeks and chin, then blew her nose.

She plunked her head back against Cord's damp shoulder. Maybe she'd rest here a moment more. She listened to the reassuring thump of his heartbeat, feeling safer than she had since Sackett.

"What?" Cord asked. "Are you done?" He grimaced with mock-disapproval. "Is that the best you've got?"

A laugh bubbled up her throat. "I cried plenty. Look at your shirt."

He glanced at the dark, wet patch and shrugged. "Hell, I've seen better than that from a three-year-old who didn't know the first thing about crying." His grin was unspeakably kind, a blatant attempt to restore her good humor.

She smiled back. "I'll attempt to do better next time."

"Maybe I need to give you lessons."

"Add that to the list, detective." Her giggle softened to quiet. Lordy, she was close to him. Closer than she'd been since they'd kissed.

Awareness sent awkwardness tripping though her. When she moved to scoot off of him, he let her. She eased onto the ground next to his legs, not wanting to part from him any farther than that. Her knees drew up beneath her skirts. One more pass over her face with the embroidered handkerchief, then she folded the square and hid it away.

"Want to hear a joke?" Cord asked, breaking the quiet. "You know, to commemorate the occasion?"

She smiled, ever surprised by the layers of him she kept uncovering. "Please."

"At what time of day was Adam created?"

"I don't know."

"A little before Eve."

She laughed through her sore chest and gritty eyes, which only made the pleasure that much sweeter. "Okay, I've got one for you."

"Shoot."

"Two boll weevils traveled from the country to the city. One became rich and famous. What did the other become?"

"What?"

"The lesser of two weevils."

He groaned, and awarded her that melting I-can-strip-your-drawers-off-with-my-teeth smile.

Her belly did a slow, delicious flip.

She studied his ocean blue eyes, the relaxed set of his jaw, the dark hair tousled by wind. He'd been awfully good to her today, this man who wasn't her fiancé, who'd never marry anyone, who belonged only to the criminals he chased. "I'm not sure, Cord, what my new career will mean for you and me. That is, for your assignment as it pertains to me."

His face sobered. "As far as I'm concerned, my duties to you are finished. You're capable of taking care of yourself and making your own choices."

She'd been waiting months for someone to say that to her. So how come his words brought a rush of bottomless sadness? Pathetic reaction. Ludicrous. A few weeks ago, she'd have paid him all she had to set her free.

"I'll tell your father as much," he said, "but I can't predict how he'll respond."

"You'll stay with me until you speak with my father?"

"Yes.

She nodded thoughtfully. "I need to go back home, to mend rifts and spend what time I have left with my family."

"We'll leave tomorrow then," he said. "I'll put you on the early train to Dallas, then follow on the eight-ninety-five."

"You won't be riding with me?"

"There's some business I need to attend to here."

She recalled the discussion she'd overheard between him and the railroad clerk. Evidently, Cord had reason to suspect that Sackett would attempt to rob the eight-ninety-five, and he didn't want her anywhere near that train because of it. That's the only explanation she could figure.

"I can wait until you finish your business and take the later train with you," she said, already suspecting how he'd respond.

"No. You're going on the early train."

That adamant light in his eyes absolutely meant trouble. Fear slithered down the nape of her neck. "Very well," she said, in the same instant she decided, irrevocably, that if she had to move heaven and hell, she was going to get herself on the eight-ninety-five with him. Aspiring actresses weren't the only ones who needed friends and protectors. The two of them would stick together.

Chapter 14

Phillip Bradley looked up at the knock on his study door. When he'd come home from the office this afternoon, he'd asked Cook what they were having for dinner, and she'd told him "hmrph." Perhaps she was coming to amend her 'hmrph' to venison, gravy, potatoes, and broccoli. One could always hope.

He opened the door to find his future son-in-law standing on the threshold.

"Hello, sir."

"Edward! Hello." He clasped Edward's hand in a firm shake. It had been too long since he'd seen the boy. Months, in fact. Wren would be so very pleased that he'd returned. Immediately after the thought, he had to remind himself that Wren had gone. *She'll be back*. He assured himself of that, as he'd been doing since her abrupt departure. "Good to see you, son."

"The same to you, the same to you." Edward thumped him on the back.

Edward's face was free of the usual residue of travel, his hazel eyes clear, his cheeks freshly shaved, comb tracks showing in his blond hair. Even his sterling gray frock coat was immaculate. "You look good."

"Thank you, sir."

"Come in." Phillip waved him into the masculine environs of his study. They sat in matching armchairs on either side of the window, facing one another. "Glad to be home?" Phillip asked.

"Very glad."

"When did you arrive?"

"Midday. Just enough time to change clothes, visit my parents, and come here. When Cook let me in she mentioned that Wren is away."

"Yes, and she'll be sorry she missed your return." Phillip's pride prevented him from elaborating more than that. He'd never been one to confide in others, or to air family difficulties. "I regret that you'll have to wait to see her, as I'm sure you're anxious."

"Yessir."

"She's in Austin, visiting my sister and, from what my sister tells me, taking singing lessons."

"Singing lessons?" Edward's sandy brows lifted.

"Yes. I'm hoping, sincerely, that this trip will have satisfied her theatrical aspirations."

"That makes two of us."

"While you were away, she gave us a scare. So much so, I assigned Cord Caldwell to her as protection."

Edward's face blanched. "Cord Caldwell, did you say?"

"Yes."

The younger man fidgeted slightly. Then again, crossing his legs. "Do you," he cleared his throat. "Do you think such a measure was necessary?"

Phillip understood his upset. No man liked to hear their intended was in the company of another man. "I wouldn't have done it if I didn't think it necessary."

"Of course." Consternation settled in the line of Edward's jaw, but he inclined his head anyway, deferring to his judgment just as Phillip had known he would.

"Can I pour you a drink?" Phillip asked.

"Certainly."

Phillip moved to the cabinet where he stored his decanters. It was good to have Edward home. His arrival was a sign that things were returning to normal.

He'd known Edward's parents half his life and Edward since his first squalling breath. He'd been on assignment with the agency, when he'd first met the Cliftons. He'd never forget what the Dexter gang had done to the couple's home—first looting it, then burning the remains. He'd found the Cliftons picking through the rubble, that icy day, searching for their family heirlooms.

Phillip had caught the gang, but had been unable to recover their belongings. He'd returned to the Cliftons anyway, unable to forget their plight. When he'd offered Timothy, Edward's father, work, the man had immediately accepted. They'd been friends ever since. Timothy had assisted him in Raleigh, St.Louis, and here, where both men and now Edward were employed by the Southern Atlantic.

He handed a glass to Edward, who sipped it before setting it aside. "Sir, I'd like to ask you a question."

"Go right ahead."

"I'd like to ask your blessing, truthfully. I'd like to ask for Wren's hand in marriage."

Phillip smiled at the young man, eminently pleased. More evidence that things would be as they should be again soon. His hopes for Wren hadn't been dashed, only postponed.

Phillip placed his hand on Edward's shoulder. "Yes, son." He squeezed. "You have my blessing."

Across the city of Dallas, Alexandra sat in Robert's study, surrounded by his things. Books, masculine-looking artwork in shades of forest green and brown and steel gray. A desk large enough to sleep under. The chair that engulfed her fashioned of aged leather.

She stared at each item in the room in turn, as if the inanimate objects could talk and assure her that her husband was still faithful to her.

Ironically, the one item that burned at her thoughts was an item she couldn't see. Not that she didn't know where it was or couldn't visualize it there. Her husband's bank-book rested in the desk's narrow middle drawer. It would be surrounded by the fountain pen she'd given him one Christmas and a scattering of mints.

Her lips twisted at the ludicrousness of what she was doing. Suspecting Robert, but avoiding all possibility of confirming her suspicion. Every time she even imagined confronting him, following him in secret, or rifling through his bankbook, her heart solidified to stone. If she asked, he might tell her to her face he loved someone else. If she followed him, she might see them kissing. If she opened his bankbook, she might find that he'd spent money on someone other than her children and her household. Those possibilities opened like a black and yawning abyss before her, waiting to plunge her into a nightmare she didn't think she could survive.

She crossed her trembling arms on the desk's surface and laid her forehead on top. She was so fearful, so weak. She'd always thought herself the strongest of the sisters. Wren would be stunned to see her now.

Dear God. Her children. Their marriage. Their home. Everything would be ripped apart and irrevocably changed if she found evidence against him. She didn't think she could live with Robert for the rest of her life after something so destroying. Nor could she contemplate the stigma, the abject aloneness of divorcing and raising her children single-handedly.

She rolled her head to the side and dragged a blank sheet of paper and a pencil toward her. She started to draw. The raspy noise of the lead scratching across the paper comforted her.

She sketched a roof, then marked it evenly with three dormer windows. Vertical lines depicted walls made of stone. Elegant molding framed the front door and a patio encircled the entire lower floor.

She paused, frowning at the picture. Her home looked large enough to shelter a brood of ten. And whyever not? She smiled sadly. May as well dream big dreams.

For years, she'd been a scribbler. And for as far back as she could remember, she'd taken pleasure in drafting her dream home in all its various incarnations. As a child it had been a gingerbread house, heavily encrusted with edible candy fixtures. Nowadays it looked about like this.

Her drawing hand faltered, then stopped.

Never had her imaginary home seemed more out of reach than this one did at this moment. Even the candy house, she'd believed in more.

She fisted the paper with a crackle and dumped it into the wastebasket at the desk's edge.

The child sitting in the train seat behind Wren leaned forward and hit her squarely in the head.

"Abraham!" his mother hissed. "Do not hit the pretty lady. Apologize at once."

"Sorry, miss," the little beast mumbled.

Wren ground her teeth. Abraham had been poking, kicking, and otherwise abusing her for the entire seven hours of the train ride to Dallas thus far. His numerous mother-induced apologies no longer even implied remorse.

She tilted her head and gazed out the window at the passing Texas landscape. Squat hills, scattered trees, a small lake tucked into a trough of earth near a homestead. Whenever they rounded a curve in the track—like now— Wren was able to glimpse Cord's rail car. The passenger car she rode in was near the front, while the car containing the railroad's safe was located in the final third of the train's length. For a conveyance that afforded its occupants amusements like smoking and joke telling, the safe car appeared ominous to her. No windows and no lettering upon it—just thick planks of wood comprising its sides.

She wondered if Cord was enjoying himself inside it. Probably. She wondered how he'd react if he knew she was on this train with him. He'd have an absolute fit, that's what.

Before dawn this morning, she'd parted from Aunt Fanny with much hugging. Cord had then taken her directly to the early train and put her on it. She'd sat obediently in her seat until the last possible second. Then she'd scurried to the door between the cars and leapt out the side opposite the depot platform. The body of the train had shielded her from Cord's view as she'd trotted across the strip of land and into the neighborhood beyond. She'd spent the morning calling on one of Aunt Fanny's elderly friends who lived in the area. They'd had dandelion tea and sweet buns.

When the second train had pulled into Austin, Cord had almost immediately boarded the Pinkerton car. She'd purchased her ticket and hurried onto this passenger car unnoticed.

Wren reached into her bag and pulled out the slab of Helmut's apple bread Aunt Fanny had sent with her. She wasn't hungry in the least, but she was beginning to get desperate for any diversion that might fend off the disturbing memories of Sackett that had haunted her quiet moments since the ride began. She broke off bites of it and ate, her stomach a tense ball.

Sackett likely wasn't even coming, she told herself, watching the woods slip past. Surely, he'd have attempted to rob them by now if he was going to do so.

She went over her plan in her mind. If and when he did attack, she'd stay here in the passenger car and assist Cord by firing out one of the windows. Maybe some of these other passengers would lend their gunfire to the cause. Her anxious gaze took in a car filled mostly with women, a trio of elderly gentleman, and the overly scrubbed face of a young man wearing a too-small suit.

The trip would pass in peace. She dearly hoped so anyway, for Cord's sake.

"Another hand?"

Cord sighed. "No, thanks." He pushed his cards across the table toward the Pinkerton operative named Wilkes and an employee of the Southern Atlantic named Cummings.

Interlacing his hands behind his head, Cord leaned back in his seat and swiveled to face the interior length of the car. He shouldn't have played the hands he had. Might as well have given his money away, for all he'd been able to concentrate.

The memory of Wren's tears yesterday filled his mind accompanied by a surge of protectiveness. The way she'd looked up at him afterward with little droplets on her lashes . . .

He was humbled by the goodness in Wren that had risen to meet his awkward attempts at comforting her in the meadow. He didn't have a lot of experience dealing with women who cried for happiness.

He sighed, let his eyes drift closed.

Without doubt, he'd been right to pull away from Wren when he had. But when she'd needed someone yesterday to share her success, his logical decisions hadn't been worth crap. His will was slipping. He could feel it. Sliding away from his ability to catch it back.

It didn't matter now, anyway. Their time together was over. Regardless of what happened with Sackett today, he'd see her maybe one more time when he visited her home to speak with her father on her behalf.

Loss and soul-deep loneliness stirred inside him.

With his thumbs, he rubbed the base of his neck. Days ago, he remembered thinking her father foolish to call her precious. Now, he could see the man's point. Wren had a way of making a man crave to please her because the rewards were so great. To watch her laugh, to illuminate her eyes with surprise, to feel affection in her touch—

Think about something else, man! Damn it all. He wasn't the one for her or for anyone. Even if he had been, she had the theater to follow, and he'd never stand between her and it.

"Whaddya think, Cord?" Cummings asked. "Sackett not going to show?"

Upon his joining them in Austin, both men had followed Cord's authority without question, regardless of his status with the agency. They'd proved loyal to their friendship for him, his superior experience, his reputation.

"I don't know," he answered. He'd expected the outlaw to strike before now, but his hunches were still telling him that Sackett would hit this train. Sackett had ridden south from Dallas, most likely biding his time in this territory, between Dallas and Austin. That made this route a logical target. The snitch in the railroad would have informed him how much they were carrying, and Sackett would be needing, right about now, some fresh cash. That made this train a profitable target.

Critically, he eyed the car. The only furniture in the place was the table and chairs at the front end where they were sitting, next to the safe. At the far end of the rectangle, toward the caboose, stood two reinforced wooden barricades, both slanted slightly so that pockets of space had been created in the back corners. Those pockets would protect both them and their stash of weaponry during an attack.

"I don't think Sackett's coming," Cummings said. "It's getting late—"

Suddenly, brakes howled. Everything within the compartment hurtled forward. The cards, cups, coins, and cigars sailed headlong as Cord leapt to his feet, his shoulder catching the brunt of his weight as he was thrown against the front wall. The other men banged against the wall next to him.

Clanging and shrieking brakes filled the air as the unwieldy train struggled to halt before colliding with whatever obstruction Sackett had no doubt placed over the tracks.

This was goddamned *it*. He was going to get Sackett here and end this thing. Adrenaline coursed through him in streaks.

With a dying scream, the train heaved to a stop.

The operative, Wilkes, looked to him.

"Get your guns ready."

Weapons in hand, they moved to the side of the car with the massive door set into it and peered through a narrow opening between the wooden slats.

Cord couldn't see anyone yet. He stepped farther to the side, angling his gaze. Six heavily armed riders charged from the woods into view. The first was Lloyd Sackett. Despite the brown bandanna encasing Sackett's face, Cord instantly recognized his wiry frame, the look of his horse, and his stance in the saddle.

"Is one of them Sackett?" Wilkes asked, his voice tight.

"The one in the brown duster."

The outlaws galloped nearer, aiming at the windows of the passenger cars to discourage hostile fire. Thank God Wren wasn't on this train.

He scanned the land fringing the tracks. The nearest cover was across a swath of prairie, a half mile distant.

Sackett and his gang came to a lunging halt in front of their car. Cord watched them free pouches of black powder from their saddles.

"If possible, I want Sackett alive," Cord said. He looked to the two men, confirming they'd heard his instruction.

"Yes, sir," Cummings replied, too quickly and too loudly.

All three of them lined up behind the barricade nearest the door. They'd feel the explosion least from here. "Shield your ears," Cord said.

Seconds slipped past. Cord counted them all. Beyond the protection of his wrists against his ears, he could make out Cummings's harsh breathing. The only sound from outside was a faint rustling. Seemingly harmless, actually deadly. Sackett was fixing to blast down the doors. Soon now.

Reflexively, Cord relaxed and tightened his grip on his guns. The rasp of his breath mingled with the thrum of his pulse. Relaxed, tightened, relaxed, tightened.

The door exploded with an earsplitting roar. Shards of wood hurtled across the interior on a rolling blast of smoke.

The force of it slammed into Cord, crushing him against the wall. He braced, felt pain sting his upper arm. As rapidly, the pressure lessened. All around him, a hail of debris pattered to the floor.

Through the suffocating haze, Cord dived behind the adjacent barricade. He coughed and checked his arm. His shirt was ripped, his bicep bloody where a spike of wood had sheared off a layer of flesh. It was nothing.

His eyes stinging, he assessed the damage to the car. Breeze swept through the ragged opening where the door had been, shifting the dense cloud.

Sackett must have used twice as much powder as usual, because the detonation had also ripped off a section of the car in the wall opposite the door, leaving a hole where the splintered boards peeled outward.

Cord looked to his companions. Wilkes had already sighted his guns on the door. The railroad man was coughing hard, dust shaking from his hair.

"Cummings, aim at the hole across from the doors." Cord jerked his head in the direction.

Cummings hacked to clear his throat and complied.

The noise of someone approaching the wrecked door penetrated the ringing in Cord's ears. He squinted burning eyes and raised his guns.

He caught a glimpse of Sackett before gunfire erupted, spraying close. Cord ducked behind the barricade, heard the bullets ping off its wood and metal front. Without killing Sackett, Cord was damned restricted as to what part of the man he could shoot.

The firing paused. "That you, Caldwell?" Sackett's voice reverberated through the eerily silent car.

"It's me."

"Hot damn, this is my lucky day." Sackett's shadow shifted, disappeared.

From the hole opposite the door, Cord heard footsteps, grass crunching. He checked the view. Nothing, until the wind lifted a curl of emerald fabric and a tendril of blond hair into the opening. His body jerked against a torturous lash of recognition.

Cummings aimed at the newcomer, squeezing the trigger.

"Don't shoot!" Cord screamed.

The railroad man pulled back at the last instant, his bullet whizzing into the ceiling.

The outlaw's gunshots bellowed, some of their shooting now directed toward the hole. A pair of gray eyes peeked around a splintered piece of wood, then away. A slender hand holding a gun appeared and fired.

Terror mauled Cord. He lunged from his position, unloading both six-guns at the outlaws. Sackett and his men ducked. Cummings and Wilkes joined in, covering him as he ran to the hole.

Cord leapt through it, landing with a roll on the rocky ground outside the train. Wren yelped, swung her pistol, and pointed it at his heart. He froze until he saw she'd recognized him.

"He went through the hole," Sackett yelled. "You there, ride around the backside of the train!"

A bullet whined between Cord and Wren. He leapt to his feet, pressing against the car on the other side of the hole from her. He couldn't breathe, couldn't believe she was here, that she'd endangered herself like this.

"Are you all right?" she asked, her voice breaking, her face white.

Bullets ricocheted within the car, spewing through the opening between them. He stepped farther from her, out of range. "Get back to your car," he yelled over the rash of noise.

She blanched. "You're hurt."

"I'm goddamned serious, Wren!" Jesus, if anything happened to her. "Go!"

She blinked at him.

"Go!"

With the back of her gun hand, she pushed away the sweat on her brow. Never taking her eyes off him, she shook her head.

Cord swore. The shooting lapsed, and he hurtled across the opening and swept her into his arms. Protecting her with his back and body he ran toward the nearest passenger car. He'd not crossed a quarter of the distance, when he glanced over his shoulder and saw two of Sackett's men galloping around the caboose toward them.

He looked to the passenger car. It was too far. They'd be within shooting distance of the outlaws before he could get her to cover.

"God damn it!" Desperation closed in on him, black and fast. Hating his choices, he grabbed the only one open to him and sprinted back from where they'd come.

From his arms, Wren shot at their mounted attackers.

They reached the edge of the hole. He swung her to her feet. "Stay behind me."

She answered by twining the fingers of her free hand around the back edge of his trousers.

One of Sackett's men was firing from the edge of the blasted door. Cord raised his Remington and shot. The man lurched backward at the impact of the bullet connecting with his chest, then toppled from sight.

Cord barged into the car and rushed Wren behind the barricade. Cummings's body lay there, twisted onto its side. Cord pressed Wren's head against his chest and covered her eyes with his forearm. He used his other arm to turn Cummings. The man had been shot through the head.

"Damn it," Cord breathed. He rolled him against the wall, away from where Wren might glimpse his head wound. "Wilkes!"

The operative knelt behind the adjoining barricade. Grit from the explosion coated his face and clothing, but his hands and his gaze were steady. "Sackett got him, but I managed to hit Sackett in the thigh."

Cord nodded. He held Wren immobile, tight against him. "There are two at the back."

"And three left at the door."

Cord bit his tongue, unwilling to let loose a string of cusses that would terrify Wren. If not for her, he'd have holed up and faced them. As it was, he refused to keep her here. "I've got to get the girl out." He flicked open his gun chambers and punched bullets expertly into place.

"The money—"

"I'll take care of the goddamned money." If he left Wilkes here alone with the cash he'd be signing the man's death certificate and giving the railroad's money—money Pinkertons had sworn to guard—to Sackett. No, he'd not do it. "Cover the three at the door—"

Gunfire screamed through the car. They hunched lower.

"I'll handle the two at the back while I empty the safe," he yelled. "Meet me at . . ." His mind spun, attempting to approximate their location, and decide what town he and Wren could make. Somewhere with a sheriff who'd help him, a sheriff he could trust. "Waxahachie tomorrow afternoon. The sheriff there will help you round up reinforcements." Again, godforsaken choices. But under pressure, this was the best bet for them all. He had faith in his tracking ability. He could evade Sackett, he was sure of it. He could get Wren safely to Waxahachie.

"I'll be there," Wilkes said.

"Hold them off long enough for us to get a decent head start. I'll leave the door to the safe ajar. When you have to, shoot it open. They'll see that the money's gone and abandon you to come after me."

Wilkes nodded.

"Ride directly to Waxahachie. If you stay with the train you might get stranded here." He had no idea how severe the damage to the tracks might be. The train could easily be stalled for a day or more. Cord gazed at Wilkes, eye to eye so there'd be no mistaking. "If anything happens to me, forget about the money. Protect the girl. Do you hear me?"

"Yes."

"Cord," Wren whispered, anguish in her voice. He knew how frightened she was of Sackett.

"I'll be right back for you," he promised, unable to bear looking at her face. "Shoot at anything that moves—except me."

Wilkes and Wren let loose a barrage of defensive fire and Cord launched from behind the barricade. He kicked the table off its legs and used its surface for a shield as he crouched in front of the safe.

He spun the lock, praying that he could get Wren out of this. He stopped at the first number of the combination and spun the other direction. Wilkes was good, but Cord didn't trust him to protect her. He revolved the lock the other way, as fast as he could.

Behind him, he heard Wilkes's fire veer toward the hole. An outlaw screamed.

The safe popped open.

Cord shoveled the seven stacks of hundred-dollar bills into his shirt, then shot his way back to the barricade. "Let's go," he said, tucking Wren against him and propelling her to the inside of the hole. Cord raised his guns and, in lightning succession, shot both outlaws guarding the exit.

He heard Wren's ragged intake of breath and cursed himself for not hiding her eyes. Together, they jumped to the ground outside the car.

"*Run*," he growled, pulling her toward the horses belonging to the outlaws he'd just shot. The animals were standing still, obeying their training.

Metal hissed against leather as he sheathed one of his guns. "Mount up."

In tandem, they climbed into their saddles and spurred their horses into a ferocious gallop toward the open prairie.

Chapter 15

Together, they flew. Over the field, beyond the reach of Sackett, and still Cord didn't bid her stop.

Wren rode like she'd never ridden before. She bent over her animal's straining neck with her green skirts draped to her knees. Her traveling hat tugged skyward and flipped from her head, unleashing a torrent of blond hair.

So many thoughts and feelings pressed in on her, that she finally had to let go of them all. Couldn't consider any of them just then. She focused solely on the horse beneath her and the man before her.

Cord galloped just ahead, his gray shirt torn open across a gash in his upper arm. His profile was tense and granite hard against the wind, his renegade hunter's hat firmly in place. She watched as, one by one, he pulled the stacks of money from his shirt and secured them in the outlaw's saddlebags.

Lordy, he was a hero. Her hero. After what she'd just seen, she knew positively that he had courage enough to stand at the gates of hell and face down the devil himself. He'd killed three outlaws . . . her brain worked through its daze to try and reconcile the man she knew with the man who'd done that. She'd always sensed the steeliness, the utter and unbending bravery in him. But she'd never witnessed it, never truly seen it until today.

Her throat closed. Whatever Cord had done, he'd done on the side of right. He deserved to be a legend.

Her gaze returned to the cut on his arm. She had no way of knowing how bad the wound was, if it was costing him agony, if a bullet had buried itself in his flesh—fear racked her, causing her muscles to shake uncontrollably. Let him not be shot. Oh, let it not be that. There was just her, no doctor to help him.

She wished he'd slow down. Been wishing it for at least three miles. She urgently needed to tend the wound and reassure herself that he was well.

Cord glanced at their back trail. Wren checked it, too. Their flight had taken them up ever-rising stretches of earth, until the hill they were cresting displayed a view of the train, sitting in a ribbon of land surrounded by trees of green, gold, and orange.

Cord reined his mount to a trot.

"Have they set out after us yet?" Wren asked, slowing her horse.

"No. The gunfire stopped five minutes ago, which means they only just realized the money's gone. Also, Sackett's been shot. It'll cost them more time to see to his injury."

"So we're safe for a few minutes?"

"You're safe, period. Sackett's a decent train robber,

but he's no tracker. He'll catch up to us only when I want him to." His indigo gaze bored into her, growing more intense as their horses halted. "Correct me if I'm wrong," he said, "but I distinctly remember putting you on a different train this morning."

"You're not wrong."

He bit off a curse. "I put you there for your own protection, Wren."

She tested a smile on him. "Do you think I'm so silly, so undependable that I must be protected every moment?"

His lips tightened.

She'd asked the question lightly, but could tell by his response that that's exactly what he thought—that she was so silly she needed protecting every moment.

When he moved to dismount, a mixture of alarm and anger pricked her. She eased from her saddle and their horses ambled away to munch grass, leaving them facing each other without barriers.

"I'm not a child anymore, to be sat in a seat and told to stay," she said, as calmly and firmly as she could.

"It was for your own good—"

"What about *your* good?" She scowled. "What about that? Does our relationship only work one way? You protecting me like a hawk, but me sitting primly in another train while Sackett closes in on you? While he shoots you to death?" Her heart sprinted, fueled by indignation and the terror she'd felt for him when she'd watched Sackett's gang gallop from the woods.

"Yes," he answered.

"I *couldn't*." She whipped her hair out of her eyes. "I'd do almost anything you asked of me, except that. Except turn my back on you when I thought you needed me."

His chest lifted on a breath. He looked away, then slowly back. "You give me too little credit. Situations like that are my job. I expected him, Wren. But then, you must have known that. Didn't you?"

"Yes."

"What? You followed me to the railroad office? Eavesdropped?"

She nodded, ashamed and righeous both. "I'd intended just to shoot from the passenger car. But I couldn't get a clear shot. There were so many men with Sackett, Cord. I knew you were outnumbered." She shuddered to think of him holed up in that ruined train car, slowly overpowered. His life meant more to her than catching a criminal, more even than restoring his honor.

She could tell by his glower that he didn't feel the same. That truth squeezed the air from her lungs. "You were the one risking yourself today, not me," she said. "I can't feel sorry for doing what you trained me to do, or that in saving my life you saved your own."

"I'd never have taught you to shoot if I'd known you'd do what you did today."

His words cut.

"Promise me you'll not do something like that again," he said.

"I can't." How could he expect her to value him less than he valued her? "I can't promise any such thing."

He waited, brows lowered, for her to recant. She stood at her tallest under his unvoiced pressure, her fisted hands concealed by the folds of her skirt.

"You're a stubborn woman," he said.

"You're a foolish man."

"Really?" The muscles in his cheeks flecked. "I didn't used to be, before you."

"Well, I've always been stubborn. But I haven't been known to engage in gun battles with outlaws, until you."

Quiet, filled with the noise of the horses chomping grass, intervened between them.

"Wren," he sighed. For the first time his mask of fury slipped, and she saw the fear beneath.

With a single throb, her heart softened. She went to him, stopping a mere whisper away.

He hauled her into his arms and embraced her fiercely tight. His head buried against her shoulder.

Shock gave way to a rush of bliss that flooded past everything else. The suppressed fears and the ire broke free. She started to cry because he was alive and she was alive. And he wasn't so angry over what she'd done that he wouldn't hug her.

Her toes dangled off the ground as he clasped her body intimately against his.

"Are you hurt?" His words were hoarse against her windblown hair.

"No."

"God." He rocked her.

She cried.

"I was afraid they'd hurt you," he rasped.

"No, but they did hurt you."

"I'm sorry you had to see me kill those men."

"Don't be sorry. You did what you had to."

She leaned back so that she could run her hands over his cheeks, his neck. Her fingers brushed through the hair at his temples beneath his hat. She sniffed. "You must think I'm crazy. To be so angry, to cry so much."

"You laugh more than you cry," he said.

"I show too much of myself."

"No. You make me realize I've only ever half lived." Staring into her soul, he cradled the back of her head and kissed her. It was slow and tender. Nothing between them but breath, and her tears. She couldn't get enough of him. Their tongues touched, parted, lips brushed, parted. The contact promised her she was real and safe again. Her sanity returned in hot, arousing, healing strips.

She pressed her hands over his shoulders, then around to the corded muscles of his back. When she reached for his hand, he squeezed back, the pressure warm and loving, a silent communication that told her not to worry.

"How did it happen?" she asked, nodding at his wound.

He stared at her, and she sensed that their relationship had changed yet again. He was looking at her starkly, no veils in front of his eyes. It was as if the rawness of their embrace had stripped away his defenses.

An answering rightness filled her heart.

"When the doors exploded, a splinter caught me," he answered.

The splinters she was acquainted with were tiny, grimace-while-you-plucked-it-out affairs. After disengaging her hand, she peeled back the ripped flaps of his sleeve, to reveal a nasty-looking gash.

She rolled her lips inward.

"Don't look like that," he whispered, his voice persuasive. "I've had worse from a bee sting." He smiled encouragingly. "It's not deep." He released the button at his cuff and pushed his sleeve all the way to his shoulder to prove it.

She gently probed the outer edges of the injury. He was right. It was wide, but not deep. "Here." In her father's stories about his adventures, making bandages, slings, and other essentials out of petticoats had often figured. She pulled up the front of her skirt. "I can use my petticoat as a bandage."

He shook his head. "I don't want to ruin your things."

"Do you really think my petticoat means more to me than you do? Where might I find a knife?"

He read her determined expression, then freed a knife from the saddle of the horse he'd been riding.

"Thank you," she murmured as she took it from him. Blade flashing, she sliced out a band of white. With gentle efficiency she wrapped the bandage around his injury.

"Satisfied?" he asked, so close to her nape that the fine hairs there stood on end.

"Very, thank you." She stepped away. "Have you forgiven me for trying to save you?"

"Instead of asking me that every time you do something to make me mad, how about not doing anything to make me mad in the first place?"

"Just like a man. Simply tell me you forgive me and we'll go on."

"Are you asking for my forgiveness, doll?"

"No."

He dredged up a smile. "Then I guess I haven't forgiven you yet."

She smiled, too, that airy smile he treasured. Arching onto her tiptoes, she gave him a quick kiss.

It was such a natural gesture. Like a kiss she would give him if she were his. He memorized every detail of it. He could only imagine being able to kiss her like that whenever he wanted, holding her hand as they strolled down a city street, watching her expressions as they sat beside each other in a dark theater, meeting her gaze across a roomful of people and knowing that she belonged to him.

To have the right to those small things would mean that he had the right to something grand. Her heart.

He swept her into his arms because he didn't want her to see the longing in his eyes, and set her atop her horse. Her hair tumbled across her shoulders. God, it was incredible down like that. Butter and lemon, shiny, and so long it brushed her waist. From the decorative tassel on her saddle, he yanked free a strand of leather and handed it to her. "For your hair."

"Thank you." She beamed at him as if he'd handed her a bar of chocolate.

He threw his leg over his horse's back and checked the distance. The outlaws' horses were still standing alongside the train.

He reached into his shirt pocket and extracted his compass. If they headed north-northeast they should arrive in Waxahachie by midday tomorrow. He stashed the compass and discovered Wren studying him, faith in her gaze. "I won't let anything happen to you, Wren. Land like this has been my home for almost a decade. They're on my territory now."

"I know. I trust you, Cord."

His heart constricted. "Do you still have that gun?"

She motioned to her skirt pocket. "Yes."

"Where'd you get it?"

"I paid Helmut for it last night."

Cord shook his head. "Just keep it close."

"I will."

With that assurance, he led her down the far side of the hill at a brisk trot. *I trust you, Cord.* Her words rang in his head, twining with the memory of kissing her. He'd kissed a lot of women in his time, but never like that. That hadn't been a kiss between a seducer and the seduced, or between a man who wore charm as a disguise and a girl who believed it to be true, or between a guardian and his charge. That had been honest. Man to woman. It had made him want, like he wanted food or air or water, to strip her naked and make love to her.

I trust you, Cord.

While he'd give his life to protect her from Sackett, he wasn't at all sure that he could protect her from himself.

"Colonel!"

Phillip Bradley turned to see his future son-in-law weaving through the lamplit throng of people waiting at Dallas's train depot for the eight-ninety-five from Austin. "Edward!" he called, lifting a hand.

Edward hurried up to them, exchanged greetings with Ruth, Alexandra, Robert, and the children. "I was at the office," he said, "trying to catch up and must have lost track of time."

"No matter," Phillip replied. "Her train's late." They'd received a telegram from Cord this morning, informing them that Wren would be arriving on the early train. A few hours later, they'd received another from Wren telling them she'd be on the eight-ninety-five. Alexandra had insisted they all gather at the station this evening to meet her.

He watched the dark horizon for signs of steam from her train, and saw none.

To his way of thinking, it was about time Wren came to her senses and returned home. It didn't matter much to him whether she'd run out of money or grown homesick.

Either way, she'd learned a critical lesson about independence. He hoped she'd better appreciate from now on the roof he provided for her and the plans he'd laid for her future.

He glanced at Alexandra, who was standing a good two feet away from Robert, her face drawn. Robert was holding small Robbie's hand, and Elizabeth was straightening her brother's collar for him. Alexandra seemed separate from the conversation between Robert and their children. She was standing with her arms wrapped around herself, peering sightlessly into the distance.

Phillip moved to her. "Something bothering you?" he asked quietly.

She smiled without her usual luster. "I think I'm just tired."

He remembered Wren giving him the exact same answer to the exact same question the night she'd climbed from her window and been abducted by Sackett.

"Pa, look," she said, gesturing to the depot building. "The stationmaster."

Phillip turned to see the portly gentleman climb onto a crate beneath one of the platform's lamps "Ladies and gentlemen!" he called. "Ladies and gentlemen, may I have your attention!"

All those waiting, turned en masse. Conversations subsided.

"I regret to inform you," the station master said, "that the eight-ninety-five en route from Austin was ambushed and attacked."

Phillip felt the blood leach from his face. Instinctively, he reached for Ruth's hand, which was already reaching for his. Their fingers gripped hard.

"All of the passengers are safe," the man said.

Phillip's worry eased slightly.

"The track, however, is ruined. They're still sixty miles south of here. It happened about five o'clock, but it took this long for one of the employees to walk to the nearest working telegraph station and send us the news. Even working through the night, our man doesn't anticipate they can fix the track until midmorning. The train will get under way shortly afterward and be here round about one o'clock in the afternoon, at the earliest."

"Who robbed them?" one of the men called out.

"Lloyd Sackett and his boys."

Phillip's heart froze. *Oh, my God.* He prayed that Cord, and thus his daughter, wasn't involved in this.

"Did they get the money?" someone else asked.

"Our employee didn't think so. The money's gone, to be sure, but a Pinkerton man and an unidentified woman rode from the train shortly after the ambush. We have reason to think they have the money and are protecting it."

No.

Mumbling traveled over the cluster of people before someone asked, "What Pinkerton was it?"

"It was Cord Caldwell."

From behind him, Phillip heard Edward make a sound of distress low in his throat. In juxtaposition to Phillip's own sentiments, excitement swirled audibly through the crowd.

"Caldwell will get the bastard," a man whispered.

"Sackett's as good as dead."

"Isn't that just like Cord Caldwell to guard the money in such a way? Imagine the bravery . . ."

Phillip tried to swallow, and couldn't. Ruth was holding his hand deathly hard. What in God's name had Cord been thinking, letting Wren anywhere near Sackett? Taking her from the train with Sackett on their heels?

Please, let nothing have happened to my baby. Anything, anything on earth, but that. Suddenly, the problems between him and Wren seemed inconsequential. Certainly not important enough for them to have parted angrily.

"Phillip?" Moisture glistened in Ruth's eyes. "Is there anything you can do?"

"I could if I knew where Cord was going." Numbly, he rubbed his forehead. "I've no idea where he'd take her. Besides, they're so far away. By horse it would take two days to reach the wreck. . . . The train will be here before then. Maybe there will be another operative on board who'll have information." He tried to appear calm in front of his wife, daughter, and grandchildren, who were all depending on him.

Robert met Edward's eyes, his expression grave. Edward looked sick to his stomach.

"Mommy?" Alexandra's son Robbie looked up at her, his chin trembling.

Alexandra went to him, smoothing his hair to the side of his forehead. "Don't worry, sweetheart," she murmured. "Aunty Wren will be home soon."

"Not today?"

"No, probably not today," she replied, only a small tremor audible in her voice. "Mr. Caldwell will bring her back to us. You'll see. He'll take care of our Wren."

Phillip hoped to God she was right. He was no longer so sure.

Chapter 16

〜ⵋⵋⵋ⌒⌒〜

Wren gripped the saddle horn with both gloved
hands. Her gaze probed the impenetrable darkness for any shifting shadow that might possibly belong
to Lloyd Sackett. Problem was, every eerie shadow
looked like it belonged to Lloyd Sackett so far from
nowhere this late at night.

She rolled her head from one shoulder to the other, trying to loosen the rigid muscles in her neck and shoulders.
Her back ached as if she'd been transporting wooden
beams or some such, when she'd done nothing more tax-
ing than hold the near-weightless reins. The tip of her
nose had turned scratchy with cold and her derriere bones
had long since gone numb. Worst of all, she wore a brown
woolen coat which Cord had freed from the ties at the
back of her saddle. It afforded her a measure of warmth,
but for heaven's sake, it belonged to one of the men Cord
had killed. That alone was spooky enough. She certainly

didn't relish the smells of whiskey and smoke that wafted from the garment every so often.

This is adventure, she told herself. Not quite in the form she'd longed for all her life, but thrilling nonetheless. Oddly enough, she recalled specifically asking Cord five years ago to take her with him on the trail. Now here she was, thinking what a strange way wishes had of coming true. She reached for her locket and twisted fast.

She moved her attention upward and decided to hold tight to the familiarity of the stars. But even her precious, glittering points of light appeared strange from the swaying back of a dead outlaw's horse. Always before, she'd wished upon stars from the safety of her roof at home, or from some other equally secure spot.

Come to think of it, there had been few times in the whole of her life when she'd been insecure. Her parents and sister had insulated her from anything scary or dangerous or sad. No longer.

For his part, Cord appeared totally confident out here in the far reaches of the wilderness. During the dying afternoon and the aging night, she'd watched him read animal tracks, check his compass, scan the skyline, and assess the back trail.

Not once had she sensed indecision in him, or worry or fear. Thank goodness for that, because since riding away from the stranded train, he'd served as her touchstone of calm. If he ever whispered, "Oh God no," or "Shoo, deadly snake," Wren knew she'd likely die of heart failure in the next instant.

She, who'd always deceived herself into thinking she was brave.

The howl of an animal rent the night.

Wren jumped, a gasp sucking through her lips.

"Coyote," Cord said, his voice disembodied in the darkness.

Another coyote, then another, yapped in high-pitched answer. Underneath their calls she could hear the wail of a creature in distress. Chills trembled down her neck and arms.

"It's all right," Cord assured her. "They'll not bother us."

"I'm not worried," Wren lied. "I think coyotes are . . . charming."

He chuckled, and she dearly wished she could see him better. "Do you?"

"Indeed. Want to hear a joke?"

She could almost make out the white of his smile. "From you, always."

"What holds the moon in place?"

"Don't know."

"Its beams."

A pause, then, "Not bad."

"I thought you'd learned to laugh at my jokes."

"I thought we were beyond false laughter, you and I."

"Fine. I'll just," she reached over her shoulder, "pat my own back here." She gave her shoulder a few thumps.

This time he did laugh. Answering heat and satisfaction blossomed in her abdomen, proving him right. True laughter between them *was* better than false.

From close by, she heard critter feet scuttling through invisible vegetation. She frowned and strained to see what manner of animal had ventured so near. "Does the prairie always sound like this?" she asked.

"Yes."

"So noisy?"

"Yes."

"How do you sleep?"

"I guess you just get used to it. It's inside, in the quiet, that I get touchy."

She entertained a sudden vision of him, snoring soundly on the bedroll beside her while she stared, wide-eyed, into the dangers of the night. Just how much protection would a blanket afford a person against rabid coyotes?

"I don't expect you to sleep outside tonight," he said, "if that's what you're thinking."

"Hadn't even crossed my mind."

"Yes, it had." Again, she spotted the pale shine of his smile. "There's a house up ahead."

"Really?" The most she could discern around them were the vague contours of a clearing.

"It's just there."

No. She still couldn't see it.

"You'll be able to sleep for a few hours," he said.

"What about Sackett?"

She heard his saddle creak. "It's hard to follow tracks with so little moon. Taking into consideration all the times I laid down false prints, or erased our own, I'd say he's at least six hours back."

Wren bit her lip, worried that he might be endangering himself for her sake by stopping.

"I studied the valley behind us at the last ridge," he said. "They weren't in sight. I wouldn't stop here if I wasn't positive we'd be safe."

As if by magic, the outline of a small frame house materialized before Wren, mere yards away. She dismounted and followed Cord to the murky door.

"Are you acquainted with these people?" Wren asked in hushed tones.

"No."

"You think they'll mind being awoken in the dead of night by strangers?"

He considered her for a heartbeat. "They're not here."

"How do you know?"

"Lack of smoke from the chimney. But mostly lack of horses. The residents probably left temporarily to visit the city or family. Either way, they're gone." He tried the front door and found it locked.

"Oh." *Gone*? They were going to let themselves in anyway?

He pulled his leather book from his trouser pocket and flipped it open. From inside the flap on the inner back cover, he extracted a couple of delicate metal tools. He inserted one into the keyhole and worked it deftly back and forth.

Apparently they *were* going to let themselves in anyway. Doggone if he wasn't picking the lock.

Cord paused. Slotted the second instrument into the hole.

It occurred to her that what he was doing was most likely against the rules. The laws of the United States applied to Pinkerton operatives, didn't they? She wondered if he did things like this often, if this sort of daring was what had landed him in his current trouble. "What was it you were suspended for, anyway?"

"Funny you should ask that now."

"Funny?" she whispered frantically. "Why funny?"

He spared her a grin both reckless and kind. "I was suspended for raiding a house."

"What!"

The lock clicked free.

While he moved around the interior, she stood immobile in the dimness, trying to assimilate what he'd just told her. "What do you mean, breaking into a house?"

"Just that." A match sizzled to life, its flame catching the wick of a lamp. Cord placed the glass hurricane around it and turned the flame down as low as possible. Nevertheless, for the first time in hours, she was given the gift of seeing him clearly.

His beige hat was dusty, his cheeks reddened by wind, his trousers wrinkled. He wore a long black coat, yet another item borrowed from the outlaws. All in all, he looked rumpled and fierce and so beautiful to her that her eyes misted.

"We can't afford to start a fire, unfortunately," he said.

"Sackett might spot the smoke?"

He nodded and moved to the chest at the end of the bed. Within he found three blankets. He hung the first blanket over the window, notching the fabric into the top of the frame. She covered the second window in the same manner, while he took care of the third.

That done, he turned up the lamp, and the room glowed with honeyed light.

"I'll see to the horses," he said as he ducked out.

Wren glanced uncertainly at the rustic wooden walls that framed the one-room space. The living area corner, composed of the hearth and two chairs, gave way to the box-bed corner, which melded into the table-and-chairs corner, which merged with the shelves of the kitchen corner.

It looked to Wren as if a married couple lived here together. She liked the way the wife had added dashes of color and personality, with the red-and-navy-blue quilt, the collection of milk pitchers on the mantel, and the bunches of herbs tied with twine ribbons hanging on pegs in the kitchen.

She wiped her hands on the front of her dirty traveling skirts and wondered what she could do to help. More light. She didn't see any other lamps, but they likely had candles stored somewhere.

She located the candles in the cabinet, lit them, and distributed them to every spare niche in the room. In the box next to the hearth, she found two more quilts. Unwilling to lie in their host's bed, but knowing they'd need somewhere to rest, she spread the blankets in a double layer on the planked flooring. Then she unbuttoned the high neck of her traveling costume and lost herself gazing at the licking flames of all the candles. The room looked like a fairyland now.

Behind her, she heard Cord return. He'd collected the outlaw's saddlebags. He doffed his hat and jacket, then hunted through the first bag's contents. "How does smoked bacon, crackers, and cold beans sound?"

"Like exactly what I was hungry for. How'd you know?"

"Mind reader, I guess." He scowled at the assortment of food he'd unearthed. "There might be vegetables or fruit stored in the house somewhere."

"I'll look." Wren opened cupboards until she discovered the stash left over from harvest months. She chose a jar of peaches.

Cord heaped her plate with more than she could eat of everything before doling out his own portion. As they sat across from each other at the rustic table, she thought how good it was to be sheltered from the wind and protected from howling coyotes.

They ate in companionable quiet, the smells of beeswax candles and dried rosemary encircling them.

Sitting across from Cord like this, close and friendly but not touching, she grew worried that he wasn't going to take her in his arms again, like he had this afternoon. She dreaded the next hours if they meant wanting him this badly and waiting for a caress that wouldn't come.

"Finished?" Cord asked.

She nodded, and he carried the remains of their meal to the kitchen.

"Need help?" she asked.

"No."

Unsure what to do next, she padded toward the hearth, then curled up on one of the chairs. She'd have dearly loved to stretch out on the blankets, but didn't feel comfortable doing so in front of Cord.

Finally, Cord returned. He sat in the remaining armchair with one boot resting on the opposite knee. His gaze didn't meet hers.

"You were telling me, earlier, about breaking into that other house," Wren said, needing conversation from him.

"Was I?"

"I was hoping you were."

"Wren . . ."

"Please, tell me."

He considered her in that all-seeing detective's way he had. His hair was mussed from his hat, his eyes endlessly blue. "I don't want you to think less of me, tonight," he said.

"Nothing you say could make me think less of you."

A sad, devastatingly handsome smile curved his lips. "A month ago I tracked Sackett to Little Rock. I had evidence that suggested he'd holed up inside the home of a local judge."

Wren wrapped her hands around her knees, wishing instead that she could wrap her hands around him.

"Little Rock's sheriff was dead set against raiding the home of a citizen as prestigious as the judge. But I'd suspected the judge of having dealings with Sackett for some time. I convinced the sheriff to back me up, forced his hand some, and he followed me in when I broke down the judge's front door."

"And?"

"The judge was in the process of undressing for bed. We didn't find Sackett."

"Do you think they'd been warned?"

"Maybe. It's likely the judge had an ally within the sheriff's office. Either that, or they got wind of us and were quick about hiding. I still believe he was there, or had been moments before. I received a tip from a reliable source, and I had other evidence. Unfortunately, Lloyd Sackett is the only one who can confirm his whereabouts that night."

"You think he will, if we catch him?"

"If *I* catch Sackett," he corrected her, "I know he'll cooperate. Men like him would turn state's witness against their own brothers to save their hide."

"I'm guessing that the judge wasn't too happy to have you break into his home."

"No. He sent a heated letter to the agency."

"And the agency suspended you."

"They did."

"I'm sorry."

He transferred his gaze to the candles she'd placed on the hearth's mantel.

Her heart swelled. He'd not been willing to tell her about his suspension when she'd asked him all those days ago. He had enough faith in her to do so now.

Gauging by the determination in his profile, she'd no doubt that he'd capture Lloyd Sackett. That his suspension would be tossed to the wind. And that he'd ride out on countless future mornings to track those who dared disregard the law.

A wide lock of hair slipped free of the leather tie and drifted in front of her eye. She attempted to rake it back into place, only to have her fingers snag in the tangled mass of her hair.

Cord stood immediately. He rifled through the saddlebags in the kitchen, then strode out the door.

Wonderful. She'd called attention to the ruins of her hair and he'd fled. She probably looked like one of those mean stray cats with ratty fur.

What remained of her vanity knotted into a miserable clump. She was on the blankets, reaching into the chest in search of a mirror, when the hinges squeaked.

Cord stood in the doorway holding a small black comb. "I went outside to wash it for you."

Everything within her stilled.

He grinned a lazy, sensual, consoling grin. A grin that dared her spirits to rise.

She loved him.

She *loved* him. Again. The truth of it splashed all through her, joy and sorrow combined, so positively true it resonated like the pealing of a bell in her soul. How could she not love a man who reunited lost children with their mothers, who'd taught her how to shoot, who fed her chocolate, who fetched her a comb and washed it for her? How could she not?

He handed her the comb. She simply stared at it, overcome.

"Well, that's one way to do it, I guess." He gave her a quizzical look. "But it might be faster if you actually touched the teeth to your hair. Here." He lowered himself to the floor, freed the tie that bound her hair, and lifted the comb from her slack fingers. Then, with the gentlest imaginable pressure, he began to comb out the snarls.

Wren closed her eyes and seriously considered crying. Oh, Edward. She was sorry. For him and for herself. Loving Cord Caldwell would surely bring her misery. She only had a handful of days before she left—not enough time to make him love her. He wouldn't give up his work, she couldn't give up hers for a man who could promise her nothing. It was doomed—*doomed*—and yet, she was powerless to stop herself from loving him any longer.

The pressure on her scalp eased as the tangled weight of her hair lessened. The strands grew softer until she could feel their downiness whispering over her ears and along the back of her neck.

When he finished, they sat in silence for a suspended moment. She turned, and they gazed at each other. Understanding and acknowledgment of needs too-long suppressed passed between them.

She lifted onto her knees before him and slowly sank her hands into his hair. Her fingers delved through the dark brown strands, curling into them, feeling his heat. She pressed her face against the softness of his hair and placed a fervent kiss there.

Mine! she wanted to say. *Cord Caldwell, you're mine from this moment until the end of time. Only mine.*

His face lifted revealing eyes not drowsy, but stormy and sharply hungry. "Do you know how beautiful you are to me?"

Oh, God. How badly she wanted to believe he'd never said those words to anyone but her.

"I lie awake nights, thinking of you." His face was lined with pain.

"Cord," she breathed.

He took her in arms corded with strength, then turned and lowered her until her back rested on the quilts. He was above her, one muscled thigh covering her legs, taking her mouth in a searing kiss.

She kissed him back, madly and deeply and hot. It wasn't enough. She wanted—wanted to tell him she loved him. To kiss it into his face and along the line of his jaw. But if she scared him, she thought dazedly, if he stopped because of it, if she drove him away again, she'd never forgive herself. So she tried to show him with her touch. She wrapped her hands around the back of his neck and pulled him closer. *I love you.* She writhed against him. *I love you.*

Cord was fragmenting inside, the world dimming through the haze of his vision. As he kissed her, he worked urgently at the buttons down the front of her bodice. When he'd released the last, he parted the garment and rose onto his elbow to look at her.

She was spread beneath him. Her lips were parted, her eyes clear and unshuttered. Her necklace glittered, rising with the quick pulse of her breath. The rose tips of her breasts arched against the thinness of her chemise.

His body clenched with desire. Slowly, he pulled down the cloth covering her breasts and gazed at her nudity.

He had to close his eyes. His need of her had gone unsatisfied too long. It beat in his blood now. Pounding. He shouldn't be doing this, had gone too far already—

He opened his eyes and slid his thumb under the bottom swells of her breasts, then across the nipples, which strained at his touch. She was perfect. He measured one round breast with his palm.

She moaned his name. *His* name.

His gut burned and clawed. She should be afraid of him—God knows he was of himself. If she knew the extent of his need, and how little control he had left to battle it, she'd be terrified.

He bent and licked at her nipple. Then sucked. At the first taste of her, he knew. No matter how he wanted to claim her by thrusting himself inside her—if he came in his trousers, if he lay awake all night in rigid agony—she was too fine to be taken by a man who wasn't her husband—who'd never be her husband. This was no experienced whore or worldly widow. This was Wren, the Colonel's precious daughter, the china doll. Too fine, too fine for someone else's shack, for a man who'd vowed never to give his heart to a woman.

He moved to her other breast. She moaned, the sound like the ripping of satin.

He couldn't take her virginity. Not when every taste and touch and glance reminded him of her value. If he'd been a better man, he'd have had the willpower to stop everything now. But he wasn't, and he didn't.

He smoothed feather kisses down the center of her belly until he came to the waistline of her skirt. He paused.

Rapture had heavied Wren's body, her senses. Cord appeared slightly fuzzed. A legend backlit with weaving candlelight. He . . . oh, he *couldn't* stop. She was only just sampling heaven for the first time. She wanted to luxuriate in it forever, feast on it.

Impatiently, she planted her hands on his chest and pressed him hard onto his back. Her fingers, at once clumsy and tingling with sensation, succeeded in freeing the buttons down his shirt. She stripped the garment, and his undershirt, from him.

Her inhale hissed between her teeth. He was broad and ridged with muscle, every inch of him unforgivingly taut. The white bandage encircling his upper arm cut stark contrast to the tan of his skin. He was lying back, unmoving, gazing up at her with unabashed, masculine lust. Hers to do with as she would.

She glided her fingers down his chest. His skin was hot and smooth, scarred in places by wounds too old to hurt. The exploration halted at his trousers. She glanced at him. He blinked, slow, his attention never leaving her face.

She wasn't ignorant of men. Her sister had told her about their bodies and what they liked, though she'd never seen. . . . Modesty didn't exist in this place they'd created. Here, with her dress falling open and her breasts uncovered, she could abandon herself.

With a flick, she unhooked his trousers.

He swore silently.

She parted the flap, unsatisfied until he was exposed as fully as she. He let her stare at him, never flinching, while she drank in the sight of him for silent moments. Curiosity and admiration drowned the weak voices of caution and propriety Wren knew she ought to be hearing. This part of him . . . Lordy, this part of him was as majestic as the rest of his body, as virile and strong.

Hesitantly, without daring a peek at his face, she stroked up the back of his shaft.

He groaned.

He was hard and pulsing beneath her touch. She caressed him more boldly, wrapping both hands around him, running her joined palms up and down the length of him. Cord held himself strictly still, until she bent to flick her tongue—

His elegant savage's hand shot out to cover hers.

His head was flung back, his breath coarse.

She waited. Squeezed.

"Stop," he said, his voice husky.

"Why?"

"I'm losing control."

His admission thrilled her. She—*she*—had the power to make him writhe. She needed to push him to the edge and over, to see ecstasy on his face, to feel it between her hands, and know what it was to make him convulse. "I want you to," she said hoarsely. "I want to watch you lose control."

His gaze found hers.

Her body answered his look with an arousal that strained between her legs, drawing at the essence of her. She pushed his hand aside and saw that a shining drop of fluid had gathered on the tip. She bent and darted her tongue over it.

He thrust upward and she took him into her mouth, swirling her tongue over him, glorying in the taste and the naked intimacy of it.

When she again straightened to stroke her hands over his arousal, he was slick. Her caresses quickened. She felt each change in him—the swelling.

"Wren," he rasped.

He was looking at her with those eyes that she loved.

"Wren."

She gripped him more tightly, moved faster, willing him forward.

He hurtled over the edge. She held him as he throbbed, trapping his moisture in her hands.

She had given him this. There could be no greater satisfaction.

In the hush afterward, he lay before her, breathing deep and gazing into her heart. The moment was timeless, perfect. She wanted to throw back her head and scream with victory, to plant her palms on his chest and laugh.

He handed her his discarded shirt to clean with. When she had, he pulled her on top of him, fitting her against the planes of his body. Her face was above his, her hair curtaining to the floor.

He kissed her. Leisurely and mind-numbingly deep.

"I'm sorry," he whispered into her open lips.

"Why?"

"It wasn't supposed to happen like that."

"I loved it like that."

"It was selfish."

"Only on my part."

They kissed again, and his hand found her naked breast. He rubbed her, teasing her nipple to pining fullness, effectively sucking away her temporary lucidity and replacing it with fever again.

He buttoned his trousers most of the way, then rolled her onto her back. Slowly, one crooked finger at a time, he pulled her skirts up her legs. Once he'd looked his full, he nudged her knees apart. Wider and wider. He left her exposed that way while they kissed.

Vaguely, Wren wanted to control him again, yet sensed that she'd become the controlled. He paused sometimes simply to look at her, always leaving her legs open and untouched when he did.

"Cord."

"Wren?" His lips curled with wicked amusement.

She strained against him. "Hm." It was a protest.

"Hmmmm?" It was a challenge. His fingers blazed an unhurried trail along her inner leg. Through the cloth of her drawers, she felt his touch profoundly. Her nerves crackled with it, her body tensed and quivered with it. When he stopped halfway above her knee, she almost sobbed.

"Higher," she groaned, aching for him there.

"Higher?"

"Yes!" He was enjoying torturing her far too much.

He swept gradually higher.

"*Oh*," she whispered.

"Oh," he said, nodding.

The teasing light drained from his face and he concentrated on her with deep intensity, reading every nuance of her expression as he separated the slit in the fabric. Another unbearable pause, heavy with anticipation. And then his fingers slid against her most private folds.

She bolted at the first splintering contact. Air compressed from her lungs and she couldn't get it back, it was so good. His lips found hers in a kiss, as his fingers spread her, circled, delved. She'd not known. She gripped his arm, holding to him like a buoy. She'd not known anything could feel like *this*.

And still he continued. The world tinted with rich colors of flame and wood, with smells of man and sex. It felt like heaven burning. Sensations lapped at her, claiming everything until nothing existed but Cord and the way he was touching her. The lapping turned to needs that thrashed and roiled and demanded.

"Yes," she moaned, twisting and arching into his hand to deepen the touch. "Don't stop."

He kissed her again in answer. She breathed his breath, mouth to mouth. The pressure and pace of his fingers increased in time with her drumming heart.

Her body coiled tighter. The rapture climbed steeply, pushing her toward something that was red and plush and unknown and wanted. So wanted. "Don't stop. Oh. Don't stop."

"I won't," he murmured against her lips.

The feelings expanded again and again until bursting, until there could possibly exist no greater pleasure, until her skin flushed, until—she threw back her head, and blissful convulsions consumed her. Her body shook, racked with ecstasy, grasped with tremors that went beyond herself, spun away her thoughts, threw to the wind everything she'd thought to understand before.

When the last pulse subsided, she rested on the blankets, groggy and sated. Whatever Alexandra had told her hadn't prepared her for *that*. The absolute, blinding surrender of it.

She was dazedly aware of Cord, righting her clothing, pressing kisses to her earlobe, her throat, the heart of her palm.

She reached up and cradled the side of his jaw in her hand, to still his motion. "I don't know what to say."

"You don't need to say anything."

"It was . . . miraculous. I want to say that."

He settled her onto her side against him, resting her head on his shoulder. Wren could not believe the wonder of what had just happened to her. Could not believe she should be living this outrageous dream. It was more than one person deserved.

"Rest now," he whispered.

"Yes," she agreed, sleepy and as satisfied as a child after Thanksgiving dinner.

He kissed her forehead. So many kisses, she thought, too many to treasure them all as they ought to be treasured. Maybe he'd kiss her more tomorrow and she'd be able to cherish them better.

A tendril of unease curved beneath her thoughts. Tomorrow . . . Distantly, she remembered Sackett and piles of money and gunfire and riding so very fast. Her last thought before sleep was that tomorrow was a day to be feared.

Chapter 17

Cord knelt beside Wren, one elbow propped on his knee, one hand lingering close to her face. He'd stayed up all night, doing what he was doing right now— staring at her.

After what had happened between them he knew she'd expect too much of him this morning. He, then, should withdraw from her now to save them both future pain. A strange kind of madness, this. To realize clearly that he was digging a grave for himself by letting things go too far, by allowing his heart to care for her too much. And at the same time, being totally unwilling to stop.

Jesus. He was like a man savoring every bite of a poisonous fruit, even knowing it would kill him.

Wren was curled on her side, her hair a tumbled blond banner around her face. The quilt covering her coasted over the curve of her slender hip.

A sense of dread filtered through his admiration of her,

tainting the pleasure of watching her sleep. They were running out of time, he and Wren.

He shook his head. No sense in delaying the inevitable. He ran his fingers through her hair, easing the shiny strands away from her temple. "Wren."

She stirred, murmured.

"Wren," he said again.

This time she cracked open her eyes and stared up at him drowsily. In the next moment, remembrances dawned across her expression and she grabbed the shirt he'd found in the saddlebags and pulled him to her for a kiss.

He kissed her back, too harshly probably. She tasted ungodly sweet. That she would come to him like this, with such eagerness, stunned and humbled him. It awakened yet another dangerous yearning inside him, just as did all her affectionate ways, her smiles, her caresses lately. Yearnings that were uncovering a depth of need so great, he couldn't see its end. He pulled away.

A line of worry bisected her brows, even as she smiled at him. Wrapping the quilt around her, she gave their surroundings a cursory check. "Is it time to go?" she asked, her voice rough with the slumber.

"Yes."

"You blew out all the candles."

"I packed everything up."

"It's still dark out."

"I know." He rose and handed her the cup of water he'd already poured. "I don't feel comfortable giving Sackett any more time to catch up."

"How far away is he?"

"A couple hours, I'd guess."

He passed her a cloth-wrapped bundle. "Breakfast. To eat when you're hungry."

She nodded and took a sip of water. "You bathed."

"Yes." A smile coaxed its way across his mouth. It pleased him that she'd noticed.

"You always do that first thing in the morning," she pointed out.

"I guess I do."

"You do," she confirmed. "Every time I've ever seen you in the morning your hair's been wet. The only thing that's missing is your usual cup of coffee."

"You're right. I couldn't chance a fire." He winked and slung their saddlebags over his shoulder.

She looked mildly startled. "Are the horses readied?"

"We're waiting only on you."

"Oh!" She took a gargantuan gulp and simultaneously tossed aside the quilt.

Outside, Cord waited in the chilly darkness, which was punctuated by little but the mist of the horse's breath.

When he'd given her enough time to see to her personal needs, he walked back in and found her peering at a tiny looking glass, which she'd propped precariously against the bed's footboard. Her lips clamped the edge of her tongue as she attempted to weave her hair into an elaborate bun at her nape.

That she should feel the need to improve on her appearance pricked his heart.

She frowned at her reflection. "It's really not fair that I should be paired with a man more beautiful than I am." She dropped her hands and studied her lopsided hairstyle. "It's an indignity, I tell you." She glanced up at him. "An indignity."

Despite himself, he chuckled. The woman was god-damned irresistible. He wanted to . . . The mix of things he wanted to do dazzled him. Comfort and cuddle her, protect her, reassure her, trap her in bed, naked, and make love to her for days.

She stashed the mirror in the chest. He noticed that she'd already folded away the quilts and washed her cup.

He handed her the outlaw's woolen coat she'd worn the night before. While she buttoned her small frame into it, Cord scrawled a note of explanation to the homeowners.

Outdoors, he donned his hat and moved to lift Wren onto her mount. She stopped him before he could walk away by running her fingers into the hair at his nape. "I enjoyed my time with you, here." Her caress was feather-soft against his neck. "I wanted you to know that."

He smiled, and turned to his horse. His restraint cost him. He ached to put his hands all over her, lay her down, part her clothing, and bring her to orgasm again.

There were reasons—good reasons—why he couldn't. As the horses trotted from the clearing, he forced himself to relive unwanted memories. He never wasted a moment of thought on his childhood these days, categorically refused to give his parents any more hold on his life. And yet, today, he needed to remember why loving a woman was the one thing he'd promised himself he'd never do.

He grimaced. The eastern horizon was alight with the first stretchings of dawn to guide him. He could hear the hiss of an opossum, the whickering of raccoons.

Beyond the noises and the sights, the memories came, filtering in through the crack in his emotions that Wren had hammered free.

He'd been six years old, lying in a child's bed that night so long ago. He'd heard his parents' carriage return from their evening out, listened as they'd dismissed his nanny for the night. He'd been eager to see them, so he'd kicked aside his warm blankets and padded down the hall.

"How dare you laugh at me in front of our friends?" he heard his mother hiss. "How dare you, William?"

"Enough. I'm too tired to talk about this tonight."

Cord stopped in the darkness of the hallway. They sounded angry again. His mouth went dry with worry. Carefully, he plastered his body against the wall so they wouldn't be able to see him.

"You know something?" his mother asked, her voice hard and cold. "I don't care if you're tired. I'm not letting you shove me aside this time. We talk now."

He could hear his father hanging up his coat and hat. "Give me your coat, Alicia."

"My coat?" her voice rose shrilly. "You want my coat?"

Cord peeked around the door that led to the massive, marbled foyer. He saw his mother rip the expensive garment from her shoulders and throw it at his father's feet. Her hat followed, then her gloves. She looked scary, with her eyes so mad and her hair falling down. He licked his lips. Please, no.

His father's face reddened.

"If you're angry with me again" his mother said, "then tell me directly." Her pale hands curled into fists.

"I don't know what you're talking about."

"Yes, you do. You haven't forgiven me. That's what this is about. It's been a year since Michael, and you haven't forgiven me. But you're not man enough to tell me to my face, so you snipe at me, make me look foolish, belittle me before those I respect."

His father's face blanched. "I've told you before *never* to mention that man's name."

Cord felt his chest tighten beneath his pajamas.

"Why not?" she demanded. "You're the cruelest, least intelligent man I know if you think that keeping silent about him and"—she flung out a hand—"demeaning me is going to win back my devotion to you."

"Shut up, Alicia. Just shut the hell up."

"No!" She stomped her foot. "I refuse to let you keep punishing me day after day."

"When have you ever been punished by anything I did?" His voice rose and his eyes blazed. "I'm the one who was faithful to you, who loved you, who gave you everything I had. I built this house for you, for Christ sake!"

"I never wanted this mausoleum of a house."

"Maybe you'll appreciate it a hell of a lot more if I throw you out."

"Do it then!" she screamed with sudden, shrieking force. "I don't think you have the guts, you bastard."

"No?" He stalked to the entry table. "No?" he yelled, snatching up a vase with small pink roses painted on it.

"Don't!" she gasped, even as he hurled it.

It shattered against the front door, landing in a pile of sharp pieces. The silence following was awful. It sounded to Cord like death. He sank to the floor, huddling behind the protection of his knees, and started to cry.

His mother walked over to her ruined vase. Stared at it for a long moment, then knelt and began to gather it up.

"That was my mother's," she uttered in a frightening voice Cord didn't recognize.

"I'm glad I broke it," his father spat, his breath coming fast. "I'm glad you had to watch something you treasured destroyed."

His mother looked up, slowly, her eyes filled with loathing. Then she rushed at him, one bleeding hand cradling pieces of the vase. With a grunt, she ripped the pocket watch from his vest.

"Alicia!" he bellowed, making a grab for the watch too late.

She threw it to the floor, where it landed with a sickening crash, then skidded. Cord sobbed. That watch had been his daddy's granddaddy's.

She chased it, raised her foot, and drove her heel into the glass face. Her expression contorted as she faced her husband, who stood frozen with rage. "I'll ruin you," she whispered. "If you ruin me, I'll ruin you, William. I swear to it, I will."

"Try it," her father growled. "There's no disgrace you can do me you've not already done."

"You've no idea how much I hate you."

Cord turned and ran and ran and ran, until he was cowering on the floor of his armoire. Their voices wouldn't go away, though. He heard every word as they screamed and broke things and hated each other. Using bunches of his shirt, he tried to cover his ears. Didn't help. Couldn't stop crying.

He promised himself he'd never love or marry anybody. And that next time he'd run farther. But he'd never been able to run far enough.

"How far is Waxahachie?" Wren asked.

Cord started. The memories fell away like mosaic pieces clattering away from his eyes. A strangling feeling, part despair and part plea remained. That battle between his parents had occurred decades ago. And still, it had the power to jerk him back. As did all the other fights, every word of which was emblazoned on his memory.

He cleared his throat. "About seven hours, I'd guess."

She nodded.

He stared at her, Wren with the fragile morning light painting her hair platinum and casting her skin porcelain. Already her eyes sparkled with a color as stormy as the clouds, but as clear and refreshing as rain. She was outright, impossibly beautiful. What had he thought about her, that first night on the prairie? That she was a raving beauty. He'd been right, though he hadn't known the half of it then. She was doubly, triply gorgeous to him now.

He saw her as she'd been last night, her bodice open and her breasts naked for him, their nipples pink and tight. The feel of her beneath his mouth and fingers. Like molten honey, hot and responsive and so unashamed.

It gave him an erection, just thinking about it. He ached for her, ached with a ferocity that made him mistrust the attraction between them even more. It was deceiving, a wanting this powerful. It held the capacity to make a man forget.

Things between his parents must have started just this way, all sweet and rosy and full of promise. So strong an illusion, that they'd made the ultimate mistake of marrying one another, then done the unforgivable by bearing a child between them.

He resettled his hat, sloping it low across his forehead.

* * *

Alexandra knew her parents were expecting her at the house, to huddle together with them for support and comfort, just as they'd done until late last night. Still, she lingered.

She leaned against the doorframe of Robert's study. What pretense was left? she asked herself bitterly. What reason not to know the truth? The dire situation with Wren only highlighted what was important in this one, singular life. Those whom you loved and those who loved you back.

Knowing whether Robert still fell into the latter category would be better than not knowing. Up until this situation, she'd been the type of person who walked forward and discovered, when most of her friends contented themselves with whispered wonderings.

So what was stopping her? She'd just open his bankbook. Simple. Look for proof of his infidelity.

"Mommy!" Elizabeth called from down the hall. "Time to go, yet?"

"In just a moment," Alexandra answered.

She stepped into his study, her stomach twisting, and shut the door behind her. Quickly, before she could lose her nerve and disappoint herself with her cowardice, she strode to the desk and pulled open the thin, topmost drawer. The bankbook rested exactly where she'd known it would.

Heaven, her marriage. Her perfect marriage. Her fingers, poised above the book, started to shake. She had the right to know, didn't she, if her marriage wasn't perfect?

Yes. She gritted her teeth. She had the right, and the nerve, to know.

She lowered into his chair, lifted the book onto the desk's surface, and flipped to the most recent entry. Heart knocking, she skimmed backward from there, having practiced this countless times in her head.

Every expense was an ordinary, household expense. Nothing out of order—until she arrived at the most recent deposit of funds.

Her brow furrowed. She pointed her index finger at the sum, and tried to understand. The number was too low. Too low by a full third. Robert earned far more money than that.

All her muscles braced. She looked back through the last several deposits. They were low, all the way back . . . she flipped madly, the finely lettered transactions blurring.

June. The deposits were low all the way back to June. Five months. For five months, he'd been spending a third of their money elsewhere. That was the only explanation for it. Her father would have told her if Robert had been demoted, or his salary reduced.

What had happened in June? She racked her brain, but couldn't think of anything unusual. They'd been making love as often then, been as affectionate as always.

She stared at the desk top, but didn't see it. All she saw was a man who had been taking money from their home, from her and her children, and spending it on someone else for *five months*. To keep herself whole, she wrapped her arms around her chest and tried not to smell his scent hanging in the air—both tart with lemon and sensual with cloves.

She'd dreaded finding mysterious disbursements, in small amounts here and there. This was worse. It showed he'd planned this thing. It proved he was spending far more money than she'd ever dreamed on another woman.

"Mommy?" A small fist knocked politely on the door.

Feeling like a criminal, she hurriedly returned the bankbook to its place. "Come in."

Elizabeth poked her dark head into the room. "Ready now?"

"Ready." She pushed to her feet and pretended to occupy herself brushing lint off her skirt, so that her daughter wouldn't see her expression.

"What were you doing in here?"

"Just checking on something for Daddy."

"Oh." Elizabeth joined her in brushing away imaginary lint, crouching to sweep her palms along the burgundy fabric near Alexandra's hem.

It almost broke her mother's heart to watch her.

"Daddy's here. Should I fetch him for you?"

Her breath caught. "Daddy's here?"

"He just came home. He said he wants to go with us to Grandma and Grandpa's."

Praying she'd not left anything amiss that might incur Robert's suspicion, she wrapped Elizabeth's hand in hers and led her toward the front of the house. Violent emotions churned beneath her placid exterior, and her instincts begged her to lock herself in her room and scream and break things and hide under the covers until she'd made Robert sorry for what he'd done to her. So sorry, he'd get on his knees and grovel.

Little Robbie was waiting by the door. He'd donned his coat, apparently having buttoned it himself because the top hole had been missed, as had one halfway down. He looked up at her with trusting eyes.

She was a woman and a mother, no longer a child to scream and throw things and manipulate people's apologies. She handed Elizabeth her coat. Though she was shattering apart inside, she smiled at her children. "Put on your coat, Elizabeth. Robbie, we'll leave in just a moment."

Robert's voice was coming from the adjacent parlor, where she found him speaking with Nanny in low tones.

He looked up when she stopped in the doorway. "There you are." He smiled.

"May I speak with you a moment?" Alexandra asked, her tone brittle.

"Of course." He followed her into the privacy of their bedroom and leaned his lanky, handsome frame against the dresser. His black hair was neatly combed, his suit showing just the faintest of creases at the inner elbows.

"You came home in order to go with us to my parents'?" she asked.

"I know you told me it wasn't necessary that I spend the day with you all, but when I got to work I didn't feel right about not being there to lend my support."

"So you decided to join us." It was all she could do to maintain her frayed composure.

"Do you . . ." He studied her expression. "Do you not want me to be there with you?"

No, she longed to scream. *No! I don't want you anywhere near me, with your pat sympathy, when I've just seen with my own eyes the evidence that you're spending a third of your income on someone else*. It was impossible even to consider having to pass this already awful day in his company. She couldn't do it. "I'm thinking of Mother," Alexandra lied.

Guilt curled within her, which made her angry. That she should feel guilt over a tiny lie, when he'd obviously been feeding her lies for months. "In your presence, I fear that Mother feels compelled to act strong, when what she really needs is an environment where she can show how she's truly feeling. She'll do that if it's just me."

"Oh. I understand." She didn't trust the concern and hurt in his eyes. It looked false to her. "I hadn't thought of that."

"I know you hadn't."

Silence encompassed them. Alexandra watched him, wondering if she dared confront him with what she'd discovered. Beneath her betrayal and hurt, terror squeezed. What if he told her, right now, here in their bedroom, that she was right? That he didn't love her. Could she survive it?

"Mommy?" Robbie called, impatience vibrating in his young voice.

"The children are waiting," she said stiffly. "We'd best be going."

At his nod, she left their room and him.

Nanny handed her her coat as she steered the children out the front door. "Come, then. Let's get on with our day." She'd think about Robert when she was sure she could handle it. Later. Just . . . later.

Chapter 18

Waxahachie's town square would not be winning any awards in Wren's mind or heart.

Among other establishments, her wary gaze cataloged a bank, a general store, a boardinghouse, a hotel, a livery, and what only marginally resembled a sheriff's office. As in most Texas towns, the storefronts formed a square around a central courthouse.

This town was perfectly acceptable, she scolded herself. No need to be so critical of it. If only Cord wasn't going to confront Lloyd Sackett here across the barrels of drawn guns, she might even come to like it. As it was, their arrival was making her even more sick to her stomach than she'd been all day. She forced down a queasy swallow.

She'd consumed the breakfast Cord had packed to make him happy. Now it weighted her tummy like an immense, lead bread ball, and none of the reassurances she'd been giving herself had lightened it.

What if he died? That was the reality of today, wasn't it? The commonsensical part of her personality warned her not to take these thoughts farther, not to torment herself. But she couldn't help it. What if Cord died?

A chill of purest, numbing fear iced through her.

She could only barely imagine looking at him dead, identifying him, staring full into his slack, handsome face and the unmistakable proof that he was gone. All life drained from his powerful body. All life ripped from her heart.

Already, she felt cold to the soul. She peered at Cord's back and darted her tongue over her lips.

The closer they'd drawn to Waxahachie, the more tempted she'd been to blurt out her concerns. It would have helped to cut open the sore of her worry and let it bleed and be medicated by his assurances. She'd yearned to make him swear to be careful, or to talk him out of catching Sackett. Anything.

And yet she plain refused to be like the other women over the years who had doubtless begged him to give up the dangers of chasing criminals. Women who had, in doing so, belittled his abilities.

Under no circumstances would *she* be like *them*.

Tracking wanted men was what Cord did. To love him meant accepting his work.

Like she'd been doing all day, she ran her fingers over the front brim of his hat. He'd insisted she wear it shortly after sunrise to protect her from the sun, and thank God he had, because the comfort of wearing something of his was the sole thing that settled her.

She pressed her palm against the top of the crown. The sun-warmed felt permeated her bloodless fingers with heat.

She dropped her hands when Cord looked in her direction, not wanting to be caught fondling his renegade hunter's hat. She needn't have bothered. His gaze swept past her. He kept to the almost unbroken silence he'd offered all morning.

A sigh eased from her. At the very least she'd be beside him, available to back him up if things got bad.

Cord halted their journey in front of the sheriff's office. He tended to the horses while Wren tottered around on clumsy legs, hoping to walk off the effects of long hours in the saddle.

"Stiff?" Cord asked, looking concerned.

"Only a little."

Cord shouldered the saddlebags from their saddles, then reached out and stilled her hand, which, without her knowing it, had been at her neck, twisting her locket. "It's going to be fine," he said softly.

She nodded. They gazed at each other for a prolonged space in time, before Cord broke the spell by leading her to the door. He held it open for her and she preceded him into the office.

Within, three men rose to their feet. The first, a stocky man with dark thinning hair, she immediately recognized as the one Cord had called "Wilkes" in the train car. The graying, seasoned-looking gentleman, she assumed to be the sheriff, and the third man his deputy.

"Thank God," Wilkes said, slapping Cord on the back. "I've been hoping like hell I'd see you here."

"Same here," Cord answered. "I had a bad feeling about leaving you back at the train to fend off Sackett and his boys alone."

"Well, yeah." He smiled knowingly. "It was hairy there for a while. But you were right. Once I shot the safe open and they noticed there wasn't any money in it, their enthusiasm cooled fast."

"Glad to hear it." Cord looked to the sheriff. "Hello, Amos."

"Hello, Cord." They shook hands. "Always good to see you. Especially this time, since it looks as if you've brought a pretty lady with you."

"Gentleman, this is Miss Wren Bradley."

Wren snapped her gaze away from the two jail cells looming behind the dusty front office. She inclined her head in greeting and tried to act as if she visited sheriff's headquarters and jail cells often.

"And this is my deputy, Matt Tucker." The sheriff motioned to the man standing alongside him. The gangly deputy looked to Wren to be a few years younger than she was.

"Would you mind taking these, Matt?" Cord asked, extending the saddlebags to him.

"Not at all, sir." The deputy hoisted them over his shoulder.

"There's seven thousand dollars in there. Take it straight to the bank and deposit it."

The deputy wrapped a protective arm around the leather satchels. "You can count on me."

"Once you've done that, send a telegram to Colonel Phillip Bradley, Southern Atlantic Railroad offices, Dallas. Inform him where we are and that his daughter's safe. Tell him we've cornered Sackett and that I'll have his daughter to him by tomorrow."

"You want me to ask him to send more operatives?" the deputy asked.

"No. If Waxahachie was nearer the railroad line, they'd have a chance of making it here in time. As it is . . . How far are we from the nearest station, Amos?"

"A good four-, five-hour ride."

"Sackett will be here long before anyone from Dallas could make it," Cord confirmed. "We're on our own."

"Yes, sir," the deputy said. "Is there anything else?"

"That's all."

The deputy rushed from the office.

"Did you manage to round up some men?" Cord asked Wilkes.

"I did," Wilkes answered. "The sheriff here was kind enough to help me rustle up a posse of cowboys."

"Excellent," Wren replied, her interest peaking. "What's our plan?"

Wilkes and the sheriff regarded her in baffled silence.

Oh, Lordy. Had she said that *out loud*?

Tentatively, she peeked at Cord, ready to be confronted with a frown.

Unexpectedly, he grinned. The sunshine pouring in the front window burrowed into the dark blue of his gaze and caught there, lending fire to his eyes.

Butterflies with velvet-hot wings spiraled in her belly.

"You really are something," he murmured. "You know that?"

"I try."

"To begin with," Cord said to her, "my plan is to put you under the protection of the sheriff. The two of you will watch from a safe position and serve as lookouts."

Wren glanced at the sheriff, smiled, then turned her attention back to Cord. "May I have a private word with you?"

"Certainly." He followed her to the room's corner. "Yes?" he asked, in a tone that informed her he already knew exactly what she was about to say.

"Cord, I'll feel a whole lot better about things if I can stay closer to you. Do you have enough faith in me to let me do that?"

"This isn't about faith," he said, his expression turning deeply serious. "This is about a promise I made to your father. I vowed to him that I'd protect you at any cost."

"That was before you taught me to protect myself. Now I'm capable—"

"You've had two weeks of experience with a six-shooter, doll. Two weeks." The muscles in his jaw firmed. "I saw you at the train, I know how brave you are. I also know that you're new to this, but believe yourself to be experienced. That's a dangerous combination."

"I may be new, but I'm not completely helpless—"

"No, you're not. In fact, you're the least helpless woman I've ever met. I don't doubt for an instant that you'd run into the fray to help me. That's part of the problem." He crossed his arms over his chest. "The other part is that Sackett has seen us together. If he gets ahold of you, he won't hesitate to use you as leverage against me." He shook his head, absolutely refusing to allow that possibility. "I'm going to be right in the middle of things. That's no place for you. Not only for your safety, but for mine. Arresting Sackett is going to demand all my attention. If I'm distracted by worries about you, I could make a mistake."

He was, of course, right. She was an actress, not an accomplished gunfighter. Her inexperience could plunge Cord and the rest of them into trouble.

"Do you understand?" he asked.

"I do," she answered reluctantly.

"You'll stay with Amos no matter how bad things might get?"

Her anxiousness increased sharply. "How bad might they get?"

"I hope not bad at all, but I always try to plan for every outcome. I need to know you'll stay with Amos, Wren."

At least he'd involved her in some way. A week ago, even two days ago, he'd probably have shut her out of the situation entirely. She'd do well to be grateful for her role as lookout. "I'll stay with Amos."

"Thank you." Cord took her hand and led her back to the men. They gathered round the sheriff's desk. "Here's how it's going to work," Cord said.

Cord shouldered through the doors of the Gold Dollar Hotel thirty minutes later. The bright, well-kept interior of the downstairs restaurant and bar welcomed him. All the wooden surfaces had been buffed, the green brocade curtains looked new, and not a single age spot marred the mirror hanging behind the line of alcohol bottles.

There were few occupants at this early hour. A whiskered drunk lounged at one of the tables, staring at a bottle of rum, and a vagabond crouched on the floor in the corner, gnawing on a chunk of bread. Cord ignored them both as he walked to the bar, where a dark-skinned, dark-eyed woman chatted with the barkeep. Their conversation trailed off as he approached.

"Is there a room available upstairs?" Cord asked.

"The one you've stayed in before is vacant, Mr. Caldwell," the barkeep answered.

"That'll do." He paid the fee up front, as was his habit.

"I'll escort you," the woman said, sliding sinuously from her stool.

Cord ascended the narrow stairway behind her, the hem of her loose white-linen dress lapping at his knees. On the upper floor, she opened the door to the third and last room, then waved him in.

Cord ducked his head as he passed beneath the doorway. The woman studied him as he lowered the saddlebags onto the bed.

"Thank you," he said.

"Do you need . . . anything . . . else?"

"No."

She curled her tongue into her cheek, paused a moment more, then clicked closed the door behind her.

Mentally, Cord ran through his responsibilities. He'd hidden his horse and Wren's behind the saloon. He'd done a good job of it, but not so good that Sackett wouldn't find them. The woman and the barkeep both knew where he was, and that he had satchels with him. The two would doubtless relay that information to Sackett when he came calling.

From the saddlebags, he pulled blankets and towels. He raked away the bedsheets, shaped the linens into a mass that somewhat resembled a body, and tucked the sheets back around it. His work wasn't convincing, but he didn't need convincing. He needed a second or two of doubt. He rested the bags at the foot of the bed, then made a show of moving around the room. Below, his actions would sound like those of a man preparing for a premature night's sleep.

He halted, waited dragging minutes without moving, then crept soundlessly from his chamber and entered the first of the rooms, at the head of the hall. It contained a windowless storage space, crammed with broken lamps, headboards, and chairs. Cord lowered his body onto the floor with a sigh. He checked his guns, rested his back against the door, and settled in to wait.

The hotel stairs groaned under the weight of men's footsteps.

"It's about damn time," Cord murmured. He'd been waiting for a couple hours. He turned and dropped to his hands, slanting a look through the sliver of space between the bottom of the door and the floor. He counted the boots as they moved past. Three men.

As he'd expected, Sackett had brought protection. He'd send his henchman in first.

"Ready?" Cord recognized the whispered voice as Sackett's.

He rolled onto the balls of his feet, wrapped one hand around the doorknob, his other around his Remington. His heartbeat picked out a rhythm of impatience and vengeance too-long checked.

"Go," Sackett hissed.

In the same instant that Cord heard the third door crash open, he lunged into the hallway. Sackett was standing with his back toward him. Cord threw himself at the outlaw, whipping his arm around Sackett's neck before his quarry could turn to confront the surprise threat. Gunshots erupted from within the third room, where Sackett's boys were apparently falling for the body in the bed.

Cord rammed the barrel of his six-shooter beneath Sackett's chin. "Drop your gun."

"Goddamn!" Sackett snarled, trying to rip free.

Cord held him fast. Nudged the hammer back.

Sackett twisted his own pistol, trying to point it over his shoulder toward Cord. Cord caught Sackett's wrist in his gun hand.

Wheezing, cussing, Sackett fought for control of his weapon. Cord slammed Sackett's wrist against the wall with grunting force, until the weapon dropped from the outlaw's grip.

Inside the third bedroom, the gunfire abated. Cord heard Sackett's cronies move toward the doorway. "Lloyd, he's not in here—"

Their eyes rounded at the sight of their leader trapped and Cord's gun unswervingly fixed on them. Sackett coughed and wrapped both weakening hands around Cord's forearm.

"Lower your guns," Cord said to Sackett's boys.

A wicked, rusty blade glinted at the periphery of Cord's vision, then bit into the collar of his shirt. "Lower *your* gun," a feminine voice spat. She poised the knife's edge against the skin of his neck.

The dark-haired woman, *damm it*.

Sackett's cronies took advantage of the opportunity and bolted backward. Cord held his fire to placate the woman as the henchmen shattered through the room's window, and landed with a crash below.

Against the backdrop of the garbled gunfire and yelling that resulted outside, Cord pitched his voice low. "I'm not letting Sackett go."

"It's that or lose your head," she answered, her erratic breath panting against his neck. "Don't give up, baby," she crooned to Sackett. "I'll get you out of this."

Like hell. He wasn't letting Sackett go this time.

Suddenly, the pressure of her knife against his neck jerked away. Cord turned to see the vagabond from downstairs forcing the woman's arms behind her back. Quick as a jackrabbit, he stripped the blade from her fingers and bound her wrists with a length of rope.

Cord released his hold on Sackett's neck. The man bent double, sucking air. None too gently, Cord forced one of Sackett's arms up his back. "I can't fault your timing, Wilkes."

"Thanks, boss." The operative swept crumbs from his filthy, tattered vagabond's shirt and grinned. "Did you think the crust of bread was a nice touch?"

"Damn nice."

Based on the noise floating through the broken window, Cord could tell that the cowboy posse the sheriff had assembled had swarmed from their locations in the adjacent buildings. Clearly, Wilkes had signaled them as instructed before joining him upstairs.

The woman writhed against Wilkes's restraint, attempting to kick and bite. Tsking, the operative bent her gently but firmly to the floor, then used his hand as a temporary ankle shackle. Grimacing, Wilkes raised her knife. A whistle coasted between his lips. "Did you see this thing?"

"Yes."

"She didn't cut you with it did she?"

Cord tested his neck. He shook his head. The knife had grazed, but not broken, his skin.

Wilkes whistled again as he carefully slid the knife into an open loop on his gun belt. "Guess she was keeping it beneath her skirt. I'm glad Wren suspected her, because I sure didn't."

Cord stilled. "Wren?" he asked, unwilling to believe he'd heard correctly. He'd stationed her in the attic of a building four storefronts away, for Christ sake.

Wilkes winced at his slip, then nodded sheepishly.

"Wren?" Cord growled. He waited, watching the mouth of the hallway. "Wren?" he called again, louder and more demanding.

From the stairway landing, she peeked into the hall. Then, looking guilty as sin, eased the rest of the way out. Strands of pale blond hair curved against the open neck of her green bodice. Breath-stealing silver eyes regarded him from beneath the brim of his hat.

Seeing her in his Stetson sent possessiveness surging through him—hot, fierce, primal.

"In my own defense," she said, "let me take this opportunity to point out how well I was succeeding at staying out of the fray."

Wilkes tried to hide a chuckle behind his wrist.

"You told me you'd stay with Amos," Cord said.

"I did. He's right here."

Amos walked around the edge of the landing. "She did like you asked, Cord. We watched the woman meet Sackett behind the saloon. When the first shots were fired, Miss Bradley here saw the woman race back inside. Miss Bradley guessed she was coming to help Sackett and insisted we tell Wilkes. I agreed." The sheriff took in the scene in the hallway—both Sackett and the woman captured. "Nice work. If you don't mind, I'll go on outside to see how my boys are doing with the rest of the gang."

"Thanks for your help," Cord said.

"Pleasure," the sheriff said with a smile for Wren. Then he tipped his hat and ambled off.

"I'll just"—Wren gestured toward the landing—"scoot back over here. I can see you have your hands full. Continue arresting criminals, et cetera." She vanished behind the wall.

Confounding woman.

Cord glanced at Sackett's bowed head, at the oily coppery locks. Inside himself, he recognized the stirrings of victory—an emotion as old as the first lion who'd roared over the carcass of its kill. This was a moment he'd waited a long time to experience.

"Ready to take these two in?" Wilkes asked.

"Ready."

Wilkes hauled the woman to her feet and preceded Cord down the hall. Wren was waiting for him on the landing next to the banister. "Just follow me."

"Okay," she said. "I'll be right behind—"

Sackett drove the bootheel of his good leg into Cord's shin. Pain sliced up to Cord's knee. Sackett bolted toward Wren. Cord felt the sickening sensation of the outlaw's wrist slipping from his hold. He lifted his gun, aiming as he flung out his arm in a desperate grab. Fingers buried in cloth and he was able to yank Sackett back, just a yard before he'd have reached her.

Cord jammed Sackett's arm up his back until the outlaw groaned in pain.

Wren had pressed herself flush against the stair rail, one hand splayed across her skirt pocket as if she'd been reaching for something. Her pulse thrummed fast in her neck.

Cord felt none too stable himself. Had his grab missed, he would have killed Sackett without a moment's hesitation. His reputation, his career, his honor be damned. To hell with evidence and justice. He'd have killed him outright. He'd have killed him merely to keep him from laying so much as a dirty finger on her skin. "Are you okay?"

"Yes," she answered, peeling herself away from the banister.

Nostrils flaring on a deep inhale, he hauled his gaze to the scene below. Earlier, the restaurant had been near vacant. Suppertime brought a crowd, however, and the downstairs had been bustling with turmoil moments ago. Now everyone in it was staring at him, agape. He spotted some members of his cowboy posse lingering inside the door. "I need four of you up here."

The group separated from the crowd and bounded up the stairs. Carefully, Cord transferred Sackett to them.

"Wait," Wren said, just as the men were about to drag him downstairs. "I'm glad I was here to see you get what you deserve," Wren said to Sackett.

The outlaw's eyes slitted.

She walked to Sackett, a shiver of revulsion trembling her shoulders. Cord could practically taste her determination not to cower. "You hurt me that night. I wanted you to know that, just as I want you to know that I helped bring you down because of it."

It was then that Cord realized how far she'd come since the night Sackett had kidnapped her. Between then and now she'd developed the guts to stare down the baddest outlaw in the West, and he was damned, *damned*, proud of her.

"No one can get away with making victims of people for long," she said to Sackett.

His thin lips curled into a snarl. "You damned—"

"Speak rudely to her, and you'll pay for it," Cord interrupted.

Sackett's sneer cut toward him.

Cord motioned to the cowboys. "You can take him to his cell in the sheriff's office."

Once the men had escorted Sackett to the bottom of the stairs, Cord placed a hand on Wren's waist and guided her in the opposite direction. The room he'd rented at the end of the hall seemed as good a place as any to talk to her in private. They'd not be missed for a couple of minutes.

He closed them in and lit the lamp against the waning sunlight. In a room full of broken, bullet-punctured furnishings and walls, the lamp was in the minority for having survived.

Wren looked calmer, but not wholly recovered. Her eyes, usually clear as a pool and sparking with emotion, still had clouds in them. "You certain you're okay?" he asked.

"I am. Thanks for saving me."

"It was nothing." He slid his hands into his pockets, still idiotically unsteady because of her close call. It was one thing for him to be in danger, quite another when she was threatened. "What were you reaching for when Sackett came after you?"

"Oh." She pulled a butter knife from her pocket. "Amos took my gun from me. He said he'd feel a lot better about protecting me, knowing I didn't have the power to draw a gun on him to make him change his mind. This was the only weapon I could get my hands on."

"Too bad Sackett didn't see it. Would have put the fear of God in him."

"That's what I thought." She laughed, and the spark in her eyes returned. God bless that spark. He started toward her, drawn by it, by her affection and humor and courage.

Color lit her cheeks as she read the look in his eyes.

He tipped the hat back and pressed a kiss onto the sensitive skin below her ear.

She fingered his shirt away from his neck, where the woman's knife had cut through. Delicately, she pressed her lips to the reddened skin there.

His body clenched with wanting.

Their lips found each other, tongues intertwining in a feverish rush. He burrowed one hand into the hair at her nape, used the other to draw her hips flush against his and the evidence of his desire. Insistent desire. God, he'd never wanted a woman like this.

Wren's arms were a place of comfort unlike any he'd ever known. There was solace here. Real and warm. Healing. He'd been starving to kiss her for what seemed like weeks, but it had only been hours.

Their noses brushed, then he set his forehead against hers and traced her jaw with his thumb, trying like hell to rein in the lust that was pounding through him. He shouldn't be doing this here. Someone would come looking for him any minute.

Her breath feathered over his chin. Graceful hands rose between their bodies and she began unfastening her bodice. One button, two. Deliberately exposing herself to him. God, he groaned inwardly. He couldn't get any harder.

She tilted back her chin slightly, regarding him through dipped lashes, parted lips. She'd never been shy. But this . . .

His gaze devoured the erotic sight of pale fingers revealing chest, chemise, then breasts as she pulled down the fabric shielding them. He went to his knee, wrapped an arm behind her hips, and pulled her to him.

She arched forward with a mewl of impatience. He covered one breast with his palm as he sucked on the other nipple. She moaned. The suction he gave her was soft, but gaining in pressure—

"Cord?" Wilkes's voice drifted through the door.

Cursing under his breath, he pushed to his feet and crossed the distance to the door. He braced a hand against it to ensure that Wilkes wouldn't open it and catch a glimpse of Wren. "Yes?" he answered, shaking his head over the scratchiness of his voice.

"We've got Sackett and his boys in custody at the sheriff's office," Wilkes said. "You want to question them tonight?"

"I'll be there in a minute."

"Sure." Wilkes's footfalls grew quieter as he walked away.

Wren was buttoning up her dress. "Go," she whispered, shooting him a sheepish smile. "You've got a job to do."

"Remind me to quit the damn thing."

She chuckled. "Just for that, I'll give you your hat back."

He took it from her and settled it low on his brow. He admired the hell out of the way she looked with mussed, mostly unbound hair—as if he'd just finished tumbling her as thoroughly as he wanted to. "Do you know how precious you are to me?" He'd meant for the question to come out light. It hadn't.

Her eyes moved over his features, seeming to test him. "I'm not sure."

He didn't want her scrutinizing him too closely. "Things could get ugly while I'm interrogating Sackett," he said, changing the subject as deftly as he knew how. "I won't bar you from it, though, if you want to be there."

"Thank you," she said quietly. "But I've had my fill of Sackett for one day, for one life."

"Amos invited us to stay the night at his home. Want me to walk you over?"

"I think I'll spend a few more minutes here if you don't mind."

"I don't mind. I'll send Amos's deputy over in a while." He ducked his head under the doorframe and glanced back. "Here's hoping I can keep Sackett in jail longer than you stayed in that attic."

Wren was sitting on the boardwalk a few storefronts down from the sheriff's office, where Cord was still interrogating Sackett and had been for three hours. When she heard a door bang, she glanced up in time to see Cord walk from the building.

His steps faltered when he spotted her across the darkness.

He was a legend through and through, she thought, from the tip of his faded beige Stetson, to the woman-killing indigo eyes, the roughly masculine hands, the untucked shirt and dusty trousers.

Relief tumbled within Wren. Small at first and then growing outward as it unfurled. Racing now, expanding. The showdown was finally and completely over, and Cord had won.

His collar was shredded and stained with rust. Tiredness marked his features. But he had emerged quite gloriously—thank you, God—quite obviously *alive* at the end of the day.

"I thought you'd gone to Amos's house," he said.

"I decided I'd rather wait here. I didn't want to leave you."

"It didn't bother you being out here?"

He was asking her if her memories of Sackett had haunted her. He'd seen the fear that sneaked up on her in dark, quiet places more than once. "No, it didn't bother me." She'd reflected on that herself. Confronting Sackett earlier today seemed to have loosened his hold on her. It had been the final step, she supposed, in proving to her own heart that she wasn't his victim anymore.

"I'm glad." He extended his hand. She grasped it, and he pulled her to her feet.

"Did Sackett clear your name like you'd hoped?" she asked.

"Yeah," he said slowly. "He did."

"Tell me about it tomorrow?"

"Tomorrow," he confirmed. "If you'll wait here for another second, I'll get our horses."

"I'm not going anywhere."

"I hope not." He squeezed her hand before walking away.

Sadness caught in her chest. The farther he walked, the duller and blacker the feeling grew. He was an operative, on the verge of regaining his job and his power. She was an actress who'd won a part in a traveling troupe set to leave soon and not return for months on end. Neither of them had uttered a word about the future of the fragile feelings growing between them, and this was why. What hope did they have of a future? None.

The thought was so wholly glum, she tried to shrug it off. She'd have Cord a little longer yet.

He disappeared behind the Gold Dollar Hotel. Gut-deep dread constricted round and round her, tightening like an enormous, venomous snake.

The first time, five years ago, had nearly destroyed her. She had no idea how she'd live through watching Cord walk away from her again.

Chapter 19

~~~~∽◯◯∽~~~~

The next afternoon, Cord halted their progress a few miles outside of Dallas. He'd reined in his horse in the middle of a wide, grassy valley with the excuse that they needed an afternoon snack. What crap. He'd stopped for himself only, wanting, like some lovesick dimwit, to sit on a blanket beside Wren and look at her. Just as he'd convinced her to ride to Dallas instead of taking the train, so that he could have her to himself a little longer.

He was now sitting on a blanket, leaning against a tree trunk, one knee drawn up, doing just what he'd stopped to do. Looking. "Apple?" he asked, handing one to her.

"Thank you." Wren shined it against her bodice.

Cord glanced at the food she'd spread across the ground between them atop a faded red napkin. Amos's wife was the best sort of grandmotherly variety—the kind that always sent more food than could be eaten. Fruit, bread, jerky, and sweets were left over from the lunch they'd shared. He snagged two sugar cookies.

Last night, Amos's wife had fussed over them, filling their bellies with stew and pie, stoking the stove to overflowing so they'd be warm enough, fetching water so they could bathe.

Wren's bath, in particular, had been torture for him. He'd sat chatting with their hosts, actually able to hear the swishing of her bathwater in the next room. Vivid images of her naked with hot water swirling around her rosy skin had flooded his mind. All night after that, he'd lain rigid on his borrowed bed, obsessed with fantasies of her.

He ate the first cookie in a single bite.

"Windy today," Wren said, her apple poised in midair, half-marred by dainty bites.

"Yep."

She surveyed the blustery white and steel gray sky. "Think it'll rain on us?"

Her emerald traveling outfit, the one she'd been wearing for three days, looked better on her every hour. The top buttons were open, exposing her throat and a vee of chest above where her bodice pulled snug across her breasts. Breasts he had weighed in his palm—

"Cord?" She regarded him quizzically.

"No, it won't rain on us." The brewing storm had been blowing gusts flush against them all day. The air held a bite of cold, but no wetness yet.

She eyed him skeptically a moment more, then started back in on her apple. A bead of juice slid onto her supple bottom lip, but she licked it away before it could run down her chin.

She was the sweetest poison he'd ever sampled. She felt sweet, looked it, tasted it. His heart ran with a melting kind of heat—affection and attraction combined.

He ate his second cookie and listened to the small feminine sounds she made—a faint sigh, the whisper of her skirt's fabric, the jingle of her necklace.

She'd been reserved all day, not once asking what had happened with Sackett last night. He figured she wanted him to tell it to her without her having to pry. She deserved that, and more, from him. He resettled his hat. "Sackett admitted he was hiding at the judge's house that night in Little Rock."

She turned to him, eyes instantly alert. "So he *was* there, just like you thought."

"Yep. Someone tipped him off that we were coming."

"This means you'll be reinstated."

"I hope so."

"Of course you will," she said, her proud expression tinted with a sorrow he didn't understand. "Where in the judge's house was Sackett hiding that you weren't able to find him?" he asked.

"In bed with the judge's wife."

Her brows lifted.

"I saw her in that bed, just assumed she was a sizable woman. Didn't want to look too close."

Wren laughed. "Were she and Sackett . . . amorous?"

"No, just crafty at hiding him in the one place I was too gentlemanly to study in detail."

She lowered her apple, leaving a portion uneaten. "What are you going to do next?"

"I'm going to hunt down Sackett's informant."

"He wouldn't confess who that person was?"

"Sackett insists he doesn't know the man's identity."

"You believe him?"

"Yes. Sackett has no loyalty. He'd be more than willing to turn the man over to me for a lesser sentence. Evidently, the informant communicated with Sackett only through letters."

"No return address, I suppose."

"No. He didn't use the post at all. The informant needed a faster form of communication, and more private."

"What? Did he hire a rider to deliver the letters?"

He grinned appreciatively. "You ought to be a detective."

"I think I'd make a fine detective, now that you mention it. Is there much demand for theatrical operatives?" Her smile was wry, without her usual whimsy.

"There is from me." He tucked a tendril of her hair behind her ear. "I don't need a return address, anyway, to know where the informant is."

"Where?"

"Dallas."

"Dallas?"

"All Sackett's big-money train robberies have taken place west of Little Rock. The Southern Atlantic headquarters for that region, the central region, are in Dallas, which means load information on the trains Sackett targeted would have passed across the desk of someone in that office."

"That's my father's office, though. I know everyone who works there."

"And one of them is robbing the company." He flipped a letter from the inside pocket of the black duster he'd been wearing. "I found this in Sackett's saddlebag."

Wren read it, eyes wide, before handing it back.

Cord skimmed the contents of the letter. The informant's words to Sackett were spare. He'd detailed only the departure time, route, and number of the train he and Wren had been riding.

"The penmanship is purposely squared so that it'll be impossible to match with someone's normal handwriting," Wren mused. "But what about the stationery? It's excellent quality, heavy vellum with that distinctive navy sailboat embossed on the top. Could you search the railroad offices looking for it?"

"I'll do that. But I doubt our informant would keep this stationery in his desk."

"Right. So what are you going to do?"

"If nothing comes out of this letter, I'll start combing through records at the bank, the courthouse, anywhere. It's tough to hide as much money as his cut of the robberies must have amounted to."

The wind whisked past them, freeing the tendril of her hair again and sending three of their food wrappings tumbling.

Wren snatched them up before they could blow out of reach.

"Just one more thing before we go," Cord said.

She cocked her head as he reached into the pocket of his duster again and brought out a foil-covered square.

"*Chocolate*." Her silvery eyes danced. "I insist you have some this time."

"Nope. All yours," he said, unwrapping it. He fed it to her.

"I shouldn't," she murmured.

"You should," he said softly, watching her. Treasuring every second. A man like him, a man in his profession, never had moments like this with a woman like this. Surprises and teasing were luxuries of intimate friendships.

"Courtesy of Amos's wife," Cord said.

She swallowed, grinned with drowsy pleasure. "That woman was so sweet on you, I'm surprised she didn't strap you to your dinner chair and refuse to let you leave."

"She must have been one of those *few* women who like me."

"Can't say I blame her." They stared at each other, their smiles drifting away until there was nothing left but to pack up their supplies.

Things couldn't ever be the same for them when they reached Dallas, and they both knew it. Their time together was over.

"Remember when we rode home together that first night?" Wren asked. "After Sackett snatched me?" The evening had recently darkened from the bronze of sunset to the brown haze of a young night. Their horses were plodding onto her street, and she was feeling nostalgic.

"Yep."

"You were bringing me home from a rescue then, too." She swiveled in the saddle and watched the street's night shadows, every one of them familiar to her, slip over Cord's face.

"It was nothing," he said with a smile that told her he knew the comment would rile her.

"You're right," she answered, playing along. "It *was* nothing."

"In that case, you're welcome." He dipped the front of his hat with an elegant savage's hand.

It had been *so* much more than nothing that she couldn't even think how to express herself. Uneasily, she eyed the red brick of her approaching home. She'd asked him to bring her here. Now that he had, she didn't want their journey together to end.

But it was ending, and fast. Wren licked her lips. She wanted, frantically so, to say something grand to him, something that would make him understand how much this—he—meant to her. "Cord."

He studied her with those dark, attentive eyes.

She took a breath. "I—"

"Wren!" Her mother's voice cut through the stillness.

No, Wren thought. She needed a moment more with him. Only a moment more. She stared helplessly at Cord, fighting the urge to wrap her arms around him in order to keep him just as he was at this moment—always.

"Wren!" her mother cried again.

She looked to her home. Mother was silhouetted by the open front door, which spilled a beam of cheery light onto the walkway and yard.

"It's Wren!" her mother exclaimed to the interior.

Their horses came to a stop on the street. Wren watched in amazement as Mother, Alexandra, Robbie, Elizabeth, and Cook poured down the steps. Pa's outline filled the threshold. A grin plucked at Wren's lips, then grew. She'd been concerned that her parents might still be disappointed with her, that her homecoming would be stifled by awkwardness. Apparently not.

Of course, they didn't know yet that she'd joined a traveling troupe. That revelation could wait until morning. She slipped from her horse, oddly shy.

She met her family halfway, exchanging hugs with Mother, Alexandra, the children, and Cook.

Just as she turned toward the house, her father walked down the final step. He stood with his hands hanging at his sides, spine ramrod straight. For the first time in memory, her father looked vulnerable to her. The contrast between his frozen stance and the warmth in his eyes revealed his longing, and his ineptitude in the face of it.

She rolled her lips together and felt tears prick the backs of her eyes. He was a good man, susceptible to mistakes just like the rest of them. But good. Understanding that her father needed her to initiate affection between them, Wren crossed the distance and wrapped her arms around his middle. "Pa."

"So glad you're safe, Precious," he said gruffly.

Precious. "I am, too."

He smoothed a hand over her hair, patted her back stiffly. For him, those were extreme gestures of adoration. He was telling her without words that she was more important to him than their differences. That was true of how she felt about him, too.

As she pulled away, she pressed a quick kiss to his bearded cheek. A kiss that said, *I know, Pa. I feel the same*.

Cord squinted into the light emerging from the house, feeling blinded by it. He'd watched Wren's shadow run into the arms of her family, the tendril of blond hair he'd caressed a few hours ago floating behind her.

He dismounted and stood in the street alone, like the outsider he was.

The Colonel's wife separated from the group and approached. "Thank you for bringing Wren safely home, Cord."

"The pleasure was mine," he replied truthfully. Despite his initial reticence or the fact that Wren had maddened him, scared him, and kept him in a state of semiarousal for days. In the end, it had been his honor to watch over her.

Wren's mother beckoned to a boy who was standing on the edge of the festivity. "He'll take care of the horses."

"Much obliged," Cord said, passing over the reins.

"Come on inside." She placed a hand on his arm and led him up the walk. "We were relieved to receive your telegram yesterday."

"Yes, ma'am. I sent it as soon as I could."

Cord craned his neck to get a glimpse of Wren as they all piled into the front hall. He spotted the top of her blond head.

The Colonel's wife parted from him with a smile and hurried to the front of the gathering. He doffed his Stetson and set it on the hat rack.

Wren's mother raised her arms and smiled. "Silence, everyone! Silence!"

The talk mumbled off.

"We've a surprise for you, darling," Wren's mother said.

"A surprise?" Wren asked.

"Yes! A delicious surprise."

"Hrmph," Cook said.

Alexandra winked at Wren.

Mrs. Bradley walked down the hall, stopping beside the door leading into the dining room and, looking like a cat who'd just eaten a canary, reached in and ushered out a man.

Cord's entire body clenched. His vision dimmed, and for a torturous length he was aware of nothing but the man's face and the hollow thud of his own heart.

Everyone looked at Wren in a mass expectant hush.

"Edward," she squeaked.

"Wren," he said, coming toward her with arms outstretched.

Cord sized Edward up in one glance, as he would any other enemy. Average size, fit, blond, young. He hated him on sight.

Edward enfolded Wren in his arms. "I've missed you." He squeezed her, then laughed as he spun her into the air.

Black fury surged through Cord. She wasn't Edward's to touch. Wren belonged to him. Only him. He watched the other man's fingers bite into her cloth-covered back. He was holding her too tight.

Cord saw Wren looking up from Edward's shoulder. He sensed that she was trying to find him in the crowd.

He was on the verge of elbowing through the gathering and yanking Wren from his arms when Edward whirled her into the parlor. The group followed the couple. Cord stood rooted to the spot.

His hands were on his guns. He dropped them.

"My God." In the privacy of the vacant hall, he hunched over, bracing his hands on his knees. His chest was ungodly tight, his muscles straining against the force of the pain. He blinked, trying to clear his head. From the other room, the sounds of celebration and laughter taunted him.

Wren was his. She'd cried happy tears into his shoulder. She'd relied on him, god damn it, when she'd been afraid. She'd lain before him on a pile of blankets and let him touch her. She trusted him.

He wanted to announce that to everyone. To acknowledge what they'd shared and to be recognized as the man she loved.

He straightened. Stumbled heavily against the wall. Tried to focus on the tall clock standing in the corridor.

He needed to get ahold of himself. He'd go to her, that's what he'd do. He'd go to her, pull her aside, and demand that she break Edward's heart for him. Wren would do it if he asked her to.

Would she? a sinister voice within him responded. Has she ever told you she loves you? Has she made you any promises? What do you have to offer her that's better than what the theater has promised?

He had no answers to those questions. Without answers, he had no right asking her for anything, he realized with a cold stab to the center of his chest. But, God, he needed at least to be near her.

He walked into the parlor.

He'd not felt so raw and defenseless in decades. Not since he was a kid, and he'd sworn never to let that happen again. Ruthlessly shuttering his expression, he swept a glass of punch off the table so that he'd fit in in some rudimentary way. Then he positioned himself in the most secluded corner of the room.

Without glancing up, he knew Wren was watching him, trying to catch his attention. He didn't give it to her. He drank the punch in a single swallow and waited for her to turn away so he'd be free to stare at her.

With every passing moment, he felt meaner, like a bear with its paw caught in a rusty trap. Betrayed. It took all his strength to suppress his ugly urges, to keep from making a fool of himself over her.

Various family members drifted over to chat with him. He answered their questions by rote. It was near impossible to be civil while cataloging Edward's every movement. He saw him clasp Wren's shoulder. He saw him looking at her with adoration and hunger. He saw him laugh heartily at her jokes, jokes Cord had thought were meant only for him.

He tested Wren, too, analyzed every look and gesture she gave to Edward. Was the affection on her face more or less than she afforded him? She smiled, and he ravaged himself with worry that her smiles for Edward held more joy than her smiles for him.

Edward leaned in close to tell her something and set his hand on her lower back. When Cord realized he wanted to kill Edward for that—not wanted to—was willing, physically and mentally to do so, he abruptly excused himself from a conversation with Alexandra and stalked to the front door. He needed out.

"Cord!"

Cord stilled with his hand on the front doorknob. The Colonel. Had the voice belonged to anyone else, anyone he respected just a fraction less, he'd have kept walking. He turned.

"Will you come into the study for a moment?" the Colonel asked, though it was more an order than a voluntary invitation.

Cord followed him into the study and took the same seat he'd taken when the Colonel had given him this assignment. He forced himself to remain utterly motionless while his boss shut them in, then lowered into his desk chair.

"I'd like to hear what happened with Lloyd Sackett." The Colonel reclined into his chair with a squeak of leather. His fingers interlaced atop his belly, a gesture deceptively relaxed. It clashed with the grave intensity in his eyes.

Cord related the details in a matter-of-fact sequence, finishing with his plans to apprehend the informant.

The Colonel didn't waste either of their time denying that a criminal could be hiding in his railroad office. They'd both seen too many criminals in too many forms to be surprised.

"How was it that Wren came to be anywhere near Lloyd Sackett during the train robbery?"

"Because I suspected Sackett might ambush the late train to Dallas," Cord answered, "I expressly put your daughter on the earlier train. Without my knowledge, she disembarked and bought passage on the eight-ninety-five. She embroiled herself in the altercation with the Sackett gang."

The Colonel smoothed a hand over his graying beard, shook his head over his daughter's actions. "I can't say I'm surprised. Once I got to thinking about the telegram we received from her changing her travel plans, I became suspicious."

"I tried to return her to the passenger car. But in the end the best I could do was remove her from the scene."

"Under the circumstances, you did fine. She's here now, and alive."

Cord nodded.

"As of this moment, I'm personally reinstating you to the agency," the Colonel said. "I'll handle the necessary explanations."

"Thank you." Cord felt nothing inside, didn't care.

"Don't hesitate to inform me if there is anything I can do to assist you in your search for the informant."

"Yes, sir."

"Now then." He leaned forward, resting his forearms on his desk. "About my daughter. I seem to recall telling you that you'd only need to guard her for a few weeks, until Edward returned. I'm glad Edward hasn't made a liar out of me." He reached into a desk drawer. "Edward's assured me that he'll be glad to look after Wren and curb all her little foibles in the future."

Cord scowled. "Your daughter doesn't have any little foibles."

The Colonel tipped his head, clearly perplexed by Cord's response. "I'm certain Edward will be happy to watch over her regardless." He set a banknote on the tidy surface of his desk. "As such, I'm releasing you from your responsibilities to Wren." He busied himself unstopping his ink.

Cord sat very still. Freezing-cold logic cracked through the scarlet fire of his emotions. He was being cut off from her.

"Cord, I'm going to pay you for the time you've spent with Wren. It's the least I can do—"

Cord rose and placed his hand on top of the banknote, stopping the Colonel before he'd set pen to paper. The thought of taking money for his time with Wren sickened him.

"Cord." The Colonel glanced from his hand to his face. "I insist."

"And I refuse."

"I want to do this. I *want* to reimburse you the wages you'd have made with the agency if—"

"With all due respect, if you give me that piece of paper, I'll tear it to shreds."

The Colonel's eyebrows climbed. "Very well," he said slowly. "As you wish."

Cord straightened, crossed his arms, and regarded the man who had done so much for him over the years. "There's one more thing."

The Colonel searched his face, then settled back into his chair to listen.

"The reason your daughter traveled to Austin was so that she could audition for a traveling troupe of actors. I could have stopped her from doing so. I didn't. The truth is that I'm glad I didn't."

The Colonel greeted his words with unrelenting silence.

Self-destruction was hounding him hard tonight. Even if it hadn't been, he'd have told the Colonel everything, he'd have spoken up for Wren. "I realize you expected differently of me, sir. However, I won't apologize for doing what I felt was right. She's worked hard, and she deserves the place she won in the troupe."

"She won a place?" the Colonel said, his voice low and hoarse.

"Yes. I'm sure she'd have rather told you in her own time, but in good conscience I had to inform you of the role I played in it. I'll bear whatever penalty you see fit."

The Colonel's head dropped against the back of his chair. He gazed unseeing at the ceiling.

"It's going to be a difficult life," Cord said. "She knows that. She's willing to pay the price for it."

When the Colonel didn't move, Cord walked toward the door. Halfway there, he turned. "You said earlier that Edward would be happy to watch over your daughter. You spoke as if she needed to be passed into the care of another. Sir, I think you're wrong. She doesn't need me or anyone else to watch over her any longer."

The Colonel released a painful breath. He stood, lips tight. "I can't say that I approve of your actions in regard to the audition. Nor that I agree with your assessment of

Wren's maturity. Still," he approached, "you accomplished the most important thing I hired you to do. You protected my daughter's life. In that, you've done me a great service. There will be no penalties."

"Thank you."

They shook hands, then Cord walked from the study, passed the parlor doorway without a glance, jerked his hat from the rack, and stormed into the night.

He was an idiot, the worst kind of fool for having drunk Wren's poison and for having enjoyed it—even though he'd known, he'd *known* god damn it—that he was digging himself a grave.

Well, he'd completed his digging, and the grave he'd sentenced himself to was rotting his heart.

Chapter 20

T he next morning Wren spent triple the usual amount of time on her appearance. Cord had seen her look far too homely far too many days in a row.

She settled on the lavender bodice with the frothy white neckline, cut in the square shape she favored. The matching skirt was decorated with a flounce of lace that peeped out from under the hem.

Studying her reflection critically, she held a sassy little purple hat aloft over her artfully woven hair. Excellent. No sense mussing the carefully draped and pinned curls yet. She'd carry the hat with her downstairs and put it on after he'd arrived.

Cord would come for her this morning, of course. He was still assigned to her, even if his attention would be divided by his hunt for the informant. She had hopes that he'd allow her to assist in his search. They'd become a team in Waxahachie.

Very deliberately, she avoided thinking about how soon she'd need to return to Austin. They'd be together here in Dallas for a stretch of time yet, and she didn't want to squander it worrying about their future. She'd live the time she had left with him the best she could and deal with the pain later.

She liberally dabbed her skin with floral perfume, even flipping up her skirts to pat some onto her upper thighs.

Downstairs, she glimpsed dawn creeping over the horizon through the parlor window. Not a soul was up yet, evidently. Not even Cook. Lordy, she must have arisen in the middle of the night, she'd missed him so horribly, been so eager to see him again. After days of sleeping together in the same house, she wasn't able to rest without Cord nearby anymore.

Once she'd lit the downstairs lamps and put a kettle on, she settled onto the fourth stair step. From here she faced the door directly, and would be able to answer Cord's knock in the absolute quickest amount of time.

She set her hat beside her and mounded her hands in her lap. Distant worries stirred beneath her decided optimism. Last night she'd felt pulled a hundred different ways by everyone's expectations. Her family had fussed over her and expected her to answer their welcome with her usual enthusiasm. Edward, whose arrival had completely broadsided her, had expected her to react with rapture. All she'd felt for him was an uneasy mixture of affection, guilt, and compassion. Cord . . . she didn't know what he'd expected of her, only that she'd not accomplished it. She'd kept searching out his gaze, and he'd kept ignoring her in the short span of time before he'd departed.

When he came for her this morning she'd have an opportunity to set things right. She gazed at the door and daydreamed of a broad-shouldered Legend, sauntering across a sunlit field toward her, a renegade hunter's hat in his hand and a sensual gleam in his eye.

A knock sounded on the front door at ten in the morning. Wren's emotions instantly tangled with her thoughts, plunging her into a giddy, nervous state.

She bolted from her step. Then paused, reminding herself not to scold him for keeping her waiting so long. He'd probably wanted to allow her time to sleep late.

"Wren?" Mother's voice drifted from the parlor.

"I've got it." She set what she hoped was an irresistible expression on her face and opened the door with a *whoosh*.

"Morning," Edward said. He extended a bouquet of pale pink roses to her.

She stared at him, all her heady anticipation dissipating like snow beneath a warm, disappointing rain.

"What's the matter?" he asked, eyes crinkling with humor. "Cat got your tongue?"

"No." She rattled her head to clear the silliness and took the flowers from him. "Sorry, come in." It was good he'd come. She'd postponed telling her parents about her position with the theater because she thought it right to settle her relationship with Edward first. It wouldn't be fair for him to hear about her decisions from her father.

Edward swept off his gray top hat and hung it on the rack.

"Thank you for the roses," she said as she led him into the parlor. "They're beautiful."

"Not nearly as beautiful as you."

She smiled politely.

Her mother set aside her stitching when she spotted them. "Oh!" She pressed to her feet. "Good morning, Edward."

"Good morning, ma'am."

"If you'll excuse me." Her mother's gaze darted back and forth between them with such enthusiasm that Wren wondered what was the matter with her. "I've some chores to attend to," she murmured as she bustled from the room.

Wren fetched a vase from the cabinet and arranged the roses on the marble-topped table. Pink roses had always been her favorite. Except . . . Except what? She fingered a satiny petal. Except, like the rest of her old life, they no longer suited her. Purple roses. Now, those she'd adore. Or maybe midnight blue roses, like Cord's eyes.

"Will you sit with me?" Edward asked, breaking into her reverie.

She glanced up. He patted the spot next to him on the sofa.

Though cringing inwardly, she sat beside him. She tried to concentrate fully on Edward, as he deserved.

"Wren, I . . ." She noticed that he was trembling slightly.

Foreboding pricked her.

He extended his hands, palms up, and she obediently placed her hands in them.

He took a breath. "Wren, I love you."

The pricking turned to distress. It spiraled through her, forming a lump in her stomach. Oh, please do not let him propose.

"We've known each other for a long time," he said, his face earnest. "We make each other happy. We never argue. Our two families couldn't be closer." He released one of her hands. From his pocket, he extracted a small dark green-velvet box.

Her mouth dried. Her heart beat painfully and loud.

With his thumb, he flicked open the lid. An enormous diamond set in platinum rested in the box's folds.

"Wren Bradley"—he took a deep breath—"I'm asking you to marry me."

She looked into his boyishly handsome face. The cheeks that had always had a tendency to turn rosy in chilly weather. Hazel eyes, with long pale lashes. And proper, neatly trimmed hair so blond it was almost white.

She envisioned him as he'd been at other times. A round faced six-year-old. An unusually small and spare ten-year-old. A fourteen-year-old who'd been gangly because he'd sprouted so fast.

Trouble was . . . she couldn't envision him in the future, except as a longtime friend with towheaded children of his own and a quiet wife as appropriate as he was.

Certainly, she couldn't imagine him in her bed, caressing her like Cord had. Nor as the father of her own, dark-haired, sapphire-eyed babies.

"I was going to ask you later," he said to fill the uncomfortable silence. "In a more romantic setting. But I couldn't wait."

She carefully lifted the velvet box from his hand. "It's astounding, Edward. The most incredible ring I've ever seen, without a doubt." She set it aside, unable to imagine how long he must have saved to afford such a piece of jewelry. "And your offer. I'm speechless."

He smiled. But the longer she gazed at him, the more his smile edged downward.

She gathered her courage. "I can't accept, Edward."

He flinched.

"I'm so sorry," she said quickly, "but I don't think, any longer, that you and I are meant to be husband and wife. You need someone who can love you as you deserve to be loved. Unreservedly."

His expression turned defensive. "And you can't?"

Filled with sadness, she shook her head.

"Why?" he asked, almost angrily. "What changed?"

"I grew up."

"Does this . . ." He searched her face, shards of anger and accusation in his gaze. "Does this have anything to do with Cord Caldwell?"

Her heart was thumping in her ears again. Lordy, this was awful. "Yes and no. Yes, I realized what I've just told you during the time he was guarding me. And no, because I'd have realized it without his presence eventually."

"Wren." His tongue tsked, once, and his head pulled back on his shoulders. He looked for all the world like a disapproving parent. "Don't tell me you're enamored with him. *Please* don't tell me that you fancy yourself to be the one woman in a decade of women that Cord Caldwell will settle for. You're smarter than that."

She bristled at his words, hating them especially for the truth embedded in them. She was all too aware of her proven penchant for loving Cord too recklessly.

In a single agitated motion, she pushed to her feet.

"I won't justify your comments about Mr. Caldwell with a response, Edward." She walked almost to the table bearing the roses before turning. "I auditioned for a part in a traveling troupe while I was in Austin."

His smooth brow furrowed.

"I won a spot." She paused long enough to let the pronouncement sink in. "For the next year, I'll be performing with the troupe across the country. I'm sorry to inform you of all of this at once, I realize it's a great deal to absorb. It's just that I thought it best to be completely honest."

Edward snapped the ring box shut and buried it in his pocket. "I'll save it," he said, "for when you come to your senses."

She gritted her teeth.

He pushed to his feet, paced restlessly toward the door, faced her. "*Think*. Think logically. Ever since your father gave our family a fresh start, I've worked hard to be worthy of his support. I've saved money for our future. I can support you like you need to be supported. I can give you things—"

"I don't want things."

"Of course you do. Look at you." He gestured toward her clothing.

Regardless of her gracious intentions, frustration with him jangled through her. Yes, she enjoyed fineries. Certainly she did. But for years she'd lived in this house in splendid comfort and longed to feel *alive*. She'd been the most alive of her life wearing dusty clothing and sleeping on a floor of blankets.

"Your tastes are as they should be," he continued. "You're a Bradley, and you're meant to be my wife. You ought to look as valuable as you are."

"You're talking about me as if I'm a trophy."

"No, I'm not."

"Yes. Yes, you are." For the first time in a long time, Wren looked at Edward and really *saw* him.

Because of his humble beginnings, he still couldn't accept, down deep emotionally, that no one cared about his family's past except him. In everyone else's eyes, his family and hers were already equals, and had been long past. "Oh, Edward," she murmured. "I don't want to be one of my husband's valuables. I want to *be* valued, for all the things about me that have nothing to do with money, or my family's prestige, or whatever outward beauty I might possess."

His jaw set into a forceful line. "I'll call on you tomorrow. We'll discuss this more then."

"We can discuss it all you like, but I've already made my decision."

He turned on his heel. Wren followed him to the door, handed him his hat.

"I'm not giving up on you, Wren."

"I'm sorry to hear that because I'm not changing my mind, Edward."

"As I said, I'll call tomorrow." He walked with immaculate posture to his horse.

Feeling battered, Wren closed the door and headed for the kitchen. She found her mother and Cook leaning over a scattering of recipes.

"Well?" Mother asked, her gaze darting to Wren's left hand. Mother had known of Edward's plans, evidently. It only made sense, Wren supposed. As circumspect as Edward was, he'd surely asked her father for her hand already.

"Nothing to report," Wren answered. "When do you expect Pa home?"

"He told me he'd be here around noon, to eat with us before returning to the office."

"I've something I'd like to discuss with you then."

"Of course, darling."

"So I accepted the position the troupe offered me," Wren said to her parents, as they sat around the dining table. "I'll be returning to Austin in six days, then I'll be gone for a year."

Mother set down her fork. Blinked. "My." She fussed over a tendril of gray-blond hair that had come loose, smoothing it into her hair, giving Wren a smile that didn't illuminate her eyes. "My. You won't be able to visit over Christmas? You won't be coming home at all?"

"I'm afraid not." It seemed an incredibly long time to Wren, also. The idea of carrying her one bag across the country for a year without ever once seeing anyone who loved her caused her to quail. Dreams demanded sacrifices, however. She couldn't in good conscience quibble with a gift as tremendous as her first chance at a real acting job.

"What did Edward have to say about this?" Mother asked.

"Edward." She glanced at her father. He wasn't scowling at her, just watching her seriously. She took that as a positive sign. "Edward asked me to marry him this morning, and I declined."

"Oh, darling. Are you sure you want to turn him down?" Lines of consternation marred her mother's milky skin. "He's such a fine man. He'd make you a good husband."

"However fine he may be, I don't love him. Almost needless to say, after my response to his proposal he wasn't terribly pleased to hear about the acting troupe."

A heavy pause followed. Three untouched plates of

food sat before them, cooling. She met her father's gaze directly. After what she'd been through in the past few weeks, it no longer made her quake to confront him. Every day her woman's steps grew more sure.

"I'm not going to become everything you hoped I might," she said plainly. "I know that must be hard for you both. I *know* that. If you could find it within yourself to accept this decision of mine, however, I'd be grateful."

Her father smiled at her, warmth and sadness in his dark brown eyes. "I'm not a man accustomed to changing my ways. I think with you, Wren, I've assuredly changed too little too late." He fiddled with his napkin, seemingly gathering his words. "Last night I came to realize that it's not my part to make choices for you anymore or to refuse to accept the choices you make. I still don't think the profession of actress is worthy of you, but from now on I'll keep my opinions to myself unless you ask for them. They're sound opinions, mind you. You'd do well to ask for them now and again." He winked wryly.

She laughed with relief and gratitude.

"Go and do as you will, Precious. You've my blessing. So long as you're happy and safe, I'm satisfied."

"As am I," Mother said. "My. Well, it seems congratulations are in order. To our Wren, actress extraordinaire." She raised her water goblet.

Wren lifted her own glass and all three of their goblets met in the middle of the table. "Thank you."

"You're welcome, darling." Her mother reached for her abandoned fork.

Pa flipped open the napkin covering the bread basket. He transferred a slice of bread to his plate. "When were you planning to tell me about Cord's part in letting you audition?"

"What?" Cord had already told him?

"Just that. He informed me he could have stopped you from it and didn't. Furthermore, he said he was glad he didn't. Something about you deserving this chance to perform."

"He said all that?" she whispered, staggered. For her? Why was she surprised? She remembered, all at once, how he'd taken her home that first night and told the truth despite knowing it could jeopardize his career. He was uncompromising about that sort of thing. Still . . . that he'd stood for her in the face of his respect for her father was an important thing. "You—you didn't punish him for that, did you?"

"No. I revoked his suspension and released him from his assignment to you. He'll be concentrating on closing the Sackett file from now on."

Her heart bumped her chest. "Released him?"

"I thought you'd be glad. You're free."

The final tie—an important one—binding her and Cord had just been severed. "Of course. Yes, I'm glad to be free." She looked dully at her lap.

The man who'd begun a burden to her had become a treasure. She'd counted on his responsibilities toward her lasting a little longer. Mostly because . . . she swallowed hard. Fear gripped her. Because she wasn't sure his feelings for her alone were strong enough to bring him back to her.

Last night couldn't have been it. He'd not even said good-bye. After all that had passed between them, he'd come to see her with or without the constraints of duty. He couldn't *not* come, knowing how deeply that would hurt her. No, no, no. Cord wouldn't do that to her. He'd not stay away after everything they'd shared. She had to believe that.

Once she'd finished lunch, she'd return to her stair step to wait.

Cord sat at a table filled with documents staring at the wall and thinking of Wren.

"Mr. Caldwell?"

He looked up at Dallas's very thin, very tall records keeper.

"Is there anything else I can do for you?" the man asked.

"Not at the moment, thank you."

"I'll be at my desk if you need me." He extended a bony finger toward the large, central console of City Hall's records room, and shuffled away.

Since leaving Wren last night Cord had slept too little, eaten too little, and thought too damn much. Usually, burying himself in his work assuaged whatever personal troubles he might be having. Not this time.

He'd searched the railroad offices until the wee hours to no avail. First thing this morning, he'd met with the Colonel in order to determine exactly which employees had been privy to the monetary details the informant had divulged to Sackett. Namely, five men in the Dallas office. The Colonel and his secretary. Wren's brother-in-law, Robert, who handled scheduling. Edward, who served as the office accountant. A man named Honeywell, who handled correspondence by forwarding orders to the branch stations via telegram, post, or special delivery.

Cord's list of suspects was damn awkward, seeing as how half of them were the Colonel's sons-in-laws. He envisioned Edward's fingers digging into Wren's back last night as he'd swung her, and bile rose up his throat.

He raked his hand through his hair. Concentrate on the work. Difficult, because without Wren the work seemed utterly meaningless. Without her, he barely even felt human.

Cord had spent most of the day so far poring over bank records, and now property deeds belonging to his suspects. Nothing. No evidence of where the informant had stashed his stolen money. No one who appeared to be living above his means. No clues to be had from any of the local riders the informant might have hired to deliver the letters to Sackett.

The man Cord was looking for was smart and damn good at covering his tracks.

He'd still find him.

Cord scrunched shut his eyes, opened them, and tried hard to focus on the piles of land deeds before him. A thief had to *put* his stolen money somewhere. Land purchase was an option. He hunched over the table and resigned himself to going through the deeds one more time.

It was best that he leave things where they stood between him and Wren. What more was there to say? She had her dreams, and he wanted her to reach them. His throat closed. It would only worsen things to have to talk to her again. It would only make things messier than they already were.

Chapter 21

On the evening of the third day after her homecoming, Wren was still sitting on her step waiting for Cord. Her gown was just as pretty, hair as carefully fashioned, heart breaking with Cord's abandonment.

Still, she waited.

She couldn't bring herself to stop waiting, because ending her vigil meant giving up on Cord. And her fallible, destructive, impossibly stubborn heart wouldn't quit hoping. Hoping for what exactly? she asked herself, leaning heavily against the banister, stare fixed on the unmoving door.

Hoping that he missed her. That he thought of her sometimes. That perhaps he'd still come—

"Chocolate?" Her mother extended the telltale china saucer to her. Three whole squares of chocolate luxuriated upon it.

You have a crumb . . . Recollections of the times Cord

had fed chocolate to her with those beautiful hands of his hit her so forcefully, she physically ached. "I shouldn't."

Mother smiled and waited.

"I really shouldn't."

"Hm?" Her mother's brows lowered.

"No, thank you," she murmured.

"Truly?" Mother whispered, looking shocked.

Wren nodded.

Her mother shuffled away, staring uncomprehendingly at her saucer.

Moments later, the front door sailed open and her sister bundled into the foyer, bringing with her a whiff of chimney smoke, a slicing glance of nighttime sky, and a wind that was cool, but not biting.

Alexandra halted, her hands stilling on the buttons of her coat. "That's it," she declared. She whipped off her coat and hung it. "You've done quite enough waiting. C'mon. Up with you."

Alexandra slid a hand under her arm and lifted her. They marched upstairs to Wren's room side by side. Wren sank into the pink armchair and Alexandra pulled over the wooden chair from the vanity.

"This is about Cord Caldwell, isn't it?" Alexandra asked.

Wren sighed. She didn't want to cry, but she could feel the tears rising. She nodded.

"Oh, *Wren*." Alexandra squeezed her hand. "You're not alone. We've all got a sweet spot for him. How could you not fall a little in love with a man like that?"

"Not a little," Wren said. "And not for the first time."

Her sister studied her gravely. "What do you mean, not for the first time?"

Wren found she suddenly, direly, needed to tell her sister. Maybe if she spoke everything with Cord out loud it would authenticate what had happened. She'd never told a living soul about the things she'd said to Cord Caldwell five years ago. She revealed every last detail to her sister now, who listened without once interrupting.

"I see," Alex said at last. "And now you love him again."

Wren groaned, wrapped her arms around her upraised knees and dropped her forehead on them. "Yes."

"What are you going to do about loving him this time?"

"Do?"

"Well, sitting on a stair step isn't exactly a renowned way to catch a man's heart."

She lifted her head. "I was waiting."

"I think you've spent enough misery on him sitting around here waiting. If you love him and want him, tell him so."

She'd thought of doing just that a thousand times. But the prospect of exposing her feelings to him made Wren shudder to her soul. She didn't think she could bear to do it again. The hurt last time was too destroying, her fear of failure too deep. "What good would it do anyway?" Wren asked. "He never wants to marry anyone, and I'm committed to the troupe for at least a year. I'm leaving in four days."

"Are you? Is acting more important to you than he is?"

"I want this, Alexandra. I've worked hard for it."

"I know you have. We all have choices to make, though, Wren. None of us can have our cake and eat it, too."

"You have."

Wren saw pain slash across her sister's eyes before Alexandra rose from her chair. She stood staring out the window for a long time, arms crossed. "You're right," she said finally. "Why *would* you want to hang your hopes on a man like I did? You should leave Cord behind, follow your dreams, and come to depend only on yourself."

Wren couldn't have been more surprised. "Alexandra?" she said tentatively.

Her elder sister sighed, but didn't reply.

Wren framed her words before speaking. "The reason I didn't come to you with all of this about Cord sooner was that it's difficult for me, occasionally, to confide my problems to someone so perfect. It'd be a kindness to me, a service really, if, should you be experiencing a hardship, you were to tell me about it." Wren held her breath.

"Do you have any idea how weary I am of being perfect?" Alexandra asked. She pushed the curtains wider and surveyed the stars. "Perfection is just an illusion that some people are better at projecting than others. I've always admired you for your openness. I think it would make life easier. Me?" She smiled unhappily. "I've been so successful for so long at projecting a certain image that I began to believe it."

Without a word, Wren went to her sister.

"Robert is having an affair," Alexandra said.

Wren's heart dropped. "Do you know for sure?" she whispered.

"No." Alexandra moved to Wren's dresser, began picking up and resituating the porcelain figurines.

"I've found some evidence, though," Alexandra said. "It's looking more certain day by day." She proceeded to explain about a letter she'd found, Robert's late nights at the office, his unexplained use of a third of their money.

"Lordy," Wren breathed. She resisted hugging her sister or making a fuss, knowing Alexandra wouldn't want pity or even sympathy. She simply wanted someone to hear her, same as Wren. "I don't know how you've held up through all of this."

"Me either." Alexandra released a pent breath. "Heavens, I'm glad I told you. It was getting to be too much for just me."

"Of course. I understand completely." Alexandra had never shared a single weakness with her before. Wren had thought all along it was because Alexandra didn't have any weaknesses. In actuality, Alexandra had been locked behind the responsibilities of the older sister to the younger. Now they were just women. Friends. Neither of their lives without flaws.

"Next time I get tired of being too perfect you'll be hearing from me," Alexandra said.

"You'll be hearing from me before then, I'm sure. As soon as I get tired of being too imperfect."

An almost tangible closeness and trust drifted between them, bringing comfort.

"We're a fine pair, aren't we?" Alexandra murmured.

"Very fine," Wren answered.

Alexandra studied her sister. With her stunningly lovely face and her true heart, she wondered how any man could *not* love Wren? Certainly her sister was more beautiful than she. And braver. "Is Cord even in town anymore?" she asked.

"Yes. Pa would have told me if Cord had found Sackett's informant."

"Sackett had an informant?"

Wren nodded. "Someone within the Southern Atlantic was telling him which trains to rob."

Something black and instinctive pierced Alexandra.

"I saw one of the informant's letters," Wren continued. "The handwriting was squared off, the stationery a distinctive ivory vellum with a blue sailboat embossed on the top. Cord didn't think it would help much with his investigation. That's all I know."

Nausea roiled in Alexandra's stomach. One birthday— she couldn't remember how long ago—did it matter? She'd given Robert a set of stationery. Ivory vellum with a sailboat embossed in blue.

It had to be a coincidence. Robert wasn't a thief. Wasn't capable of that.

Do you really know what Robert's capable of anymore? a voice within her immediately responded. *Do you?*

The doubts began to creep in. No, surely not. Surely Robert hadn't been in league with Lloyd Sackett.

Surely. How many times had she said that word to herself in the past weeks? When nothing about her husband seemed sure anymore. Still, she refused to believe he was so greedy, so deceitful that he had been orchestrating train robberies. What were her motives, though, in refusing to believe? Was she defending him in her own mind because he deserved to be defended? Or because she couldn't stand to face the truth?

"Are you all right?" Wren asked, touching her arm.

"Mm-hm. Just tired." Her voice sounded stale even to her. "I'd best be going."

Wren couldn't sleep.

Irritably, she threw aside the tangled blankets and

padded to her armoire. She slid on her shoes, not bothering with the laces. Since Alexandra's departure hours before, she'd been thinking. She'd thought while taking a bath, thought while dressing for bed, thought while lying in bed staring forlornly at the patterns of moonlight on the wall.

No longer. She flung her black cloak around her shoulders and coasted to the window. All that thinking hadn't eased the throbbing hurt within.

The hinges squeaked satisfactorily as she pressed open the window. She balanced her palms on the sill and leaned out, testing the night. The neighbors were all sound asleep, nary a light in view. No surprise there.

Above, the stars were masked by clouds that slid past in fuming pale gray strips, illuminated from behind by the hidden moon. Fine. She didn't feel young or naive enough to wish upon stars tonight.

Tonight, she simply needed to get outside this room, this house. Wind on her face would help vent some of this awful anger and some of this restless misery.

In the old days, she'd have climbed out her window. Instead, she walked straight out her door and down the stairs. When she caught sight of the parlor, her progress faltered. He'd sat on that chair waiting for her that first morning, logbook in hand, eyes measuring.

She *missed* him. The loss of Cord hit her like this sometimes recently, so powerful strong she had to stop and take some breaths.

Pathetic. Here come the tears again. She swallowed them back. At the rear door, she freed the locks and let herself out. She dashed moisture from her eyes and hurried toward the gate.

"Going somewhere?" Cord's voice slid through the night.

She froze. Her heart kicked, then thundered furiously fast. It was the same thing he'd said to her all those nights before when she'd tried to escape out her window.

She turned, the silence stretching with tension.

Inky darkness cloaked the powerful lines of his body, rendering him little more than a shadow. She could just make him out, leaning against the wall of her mother's greenhouse.

"Did he ask you to marry him?" he asked without inflection.

He . . . he was speaking to her of Edward? Hysteria nudged her. Didn't he have any idea how much she loved him? Had he failed to recognize the look on her face? Now? All the times before when she'd told him with her eyes?

With hands that shook from the rushing of her blood, she slipped her hood off her face and onto her shoulders, so he could see the proof of her emotions.

"Did he?" he asked.

"Yes."

"And you accepted him."

"No."

His shadow shifted as he pushed away from the greenhouse. Stopped. He was still far removed from her. Moonshine glinted in his eyes now, planed across one side of his stubbled jaw. "Do you love him?"

At the ridiculous question, all the hours she'd spent on the step rolled together with her bitterness. She narrowed her eyes and advanced on him. "That's none of your business."

"Do you love him?" he asked harshly.

She ran the last few steps, planted her hands on his chest, and shoved.

Lordy, she could smell him. Leather and spice. She pushed him again. He trapped her fingers against his chest. In the next instant, one of his hands circled both her wrists.

"Let me go!"

"Do you really want me to?"

She searched his eyes, saw the passion and the fury there, and knew that his mood was every bit as ferocious as hers. She struggled against his hold, which was as unbreakable as it was gentle.

"Do you?" He swiveled with her until he'd pinned her against the greenhouse wall and lifted her arms overhead.

Her chest burned. Erotic fire spread across her thighs and belly, opening within her, ravenous.

"Do you?" he growled.

"No," she said, and his lips lowered onto hers. She kissed him angrily, her teeth tightly locked, wanting to punish him. He pulled back, scowling.

"You didn't come," she hissed. "I've been waiting for you for three days, and you didn't come."

"I thought it would be best."

"How could you possibly?"

"I have no claim to you anymore, Wren."

"You were angry with me because of Edward," she accused. "You were trying to hurt me by withdrawing."

"The hell I was." He cursed under his breath as he pressed closer, fitting his arousal against her abdomen. His face slanted down, lips near her ear "I've thought of nothing but you," he said, his voice hoarse. "I can't get you out of my mind."

Longing struck Wren with the force of a whip's lash. Unwilling to allow herself to speak pleas she'd later regret, she arched her breasts against his chest.

Air rasped through his teeth. He kissed her, and she

opened for him this time, taking his tongue into her mouth. They both moaned. He reached beneath the folds of her cloak and ran the back of his hand along the tips of her unbound breasts while they devoured each other.

At length, she ripped her mouth from his, needing air. "Cord."

He released her wrists. She tried to rend open his clothing, but he was faster. He swept her into his arms, freeing the ties of her cape as he carried her into the greenhouse.

Smells of verdant soil and roses encompassed her. The door clicked closed, cutting off the wind, leaving them in a cocoon of earth and sky and glass. He tossed her cloak onto the floor, then set her on her feet upon it. She felt him wedge off her shoes and then her nightgown came whistling upward over hips, waist, breasts. She was left naked before him, doused in moonlight.

Cord's gaze devoured her for long moments.

She held herself tall before him, at once burning with desire, quivering with modesty, and wildly proud to show herself to him this way.

He reached out, touching her with nothing more than his fingertips. His caress skated over her face, coasted along her shoulder. Worshipfully, he covered her breasts, traced his way down her ribs, scratched with exquisite lightness up her spine. At last, his fingers dipped to the vee between her legs, testing her there.

Her restraint crumbled and she grabbed for him. With a ragged groan, he embraced her nude body against his, lifting her as they kissed. She wrapped her hands around his neck, her legs around his hips, and writhed against the fabric of his clothing.

Oh, so good. Goose bumps shivered her flesh, tightening her nipples. She raked her fingers through the hair at his nape, trailed fervent kisses down his jaw and neck to reassure herself that it was him. That he'd truly stepped from her fantasies into reality.

Cord. Her eyes misted and the tears she'd held back for days slipped down her cheeks. Beautiful tears. Joy.

"Wren." He looked at her, blue eyes piercing her. "Am I hurting you?"

"No."

"I'm afraid I will."

"I won't break."

"God," he pressed his lips against her neck. "You're so damn fine."

"*You* are," she whispered, reaching between their bodies, dying with urgency to feel him.

He turned her, resting her bottom against the cool surface of the planting table. She released the top button of his pants, and then his fingers tangled with hers, opening his fly to free him.

She took the hot length of him in her palm. In answer, he lifted her breasts and took their tips into his mouth.

She stroked him, fast and faster still, his mouth mimicking her cadence until they were both breathless. She couldn't slow down. Her body was driving her forward, empty without him. Craving him. More than before.

She guided his arousal toward the center of her. He pulled his hips strongly back.

"No." She wrapped her hands around his hips, tried to draw him to her.

He lifted her from the table, tight in his arms. Her chest and belly fit snug against his. She felt him reaching beneath her, and then he was stroking her between her legs. Her body strained, reaching for release, already snared in rhythmic rising pleasure.

His face was drawn with desire. He was staring into her soul with smoky eyes. A tempest of love so overwhelming it could be matched only by the sensations he was summoning, roared within her.

She wanted everything with him. She wanted to join their bodies, nothing held back.

She slid her hand between them and wrapped her fingers around his erection. Lowered—

"Wren." He raised her, separating them.

She reached for him again.

He slid his finger across her slick folds, attempting to satisfy her with his touch alone. She pushed his hand away. She'd not allow him to refuse her what he had given to other women. She had to know him as intimately as she could. He *must* give her that. "Make love to me."

"You don't know what you're saying."

"I do. Look into my face." His gaze clashed with hers, both of them matched in ferocity and will. "I do," she insisted.

He parted her.

"I do," she murmured again.

He guided his erection to her opening.

"Yes," she said.

He stared into her eyes.

"Yes," she said, fervently.

And he entered her body with one sure thrust.

Wren gasped at the pain that mixed with the pleasure. Her body arched, muscles tightening.

His hand splayed across her lower back as he waited, still. Only when she'd adjusted to him did he begin moving. Slowly up and down in a motion so sweet, the pain faded in the face of thrumming need. She started to move in his arms with his rhythm, up and down. Wrapping her arms around his neck, hearing his breath, sinking her teeth into his shoulder. Up and down. Her nakedness rubbing against his clothing.

He knelt and her back came to rest against the cloak-covered earth. Then he was on top of her, penetrating to her center, overriding everything with the overwhelming feel of him there.

She held on to his biceps, looked into his turbulent eyes. This was so right. To express her feelings for him eloquently without words. To couple her emotions with his, to surrender to him and watch him surrender to her in the same moment. She loved him, wanted him to the very depths of who he was.

Her body. Oh, Lordy her body was tugging at her with a sweetness so piquant it consumed everything— thoughts and hopes—until there was nothing but silken ecstasy. It grew, intensified by the feel of him filling her. It surged over her heated flesh, wrapping around her even as it lay her open. He was driving into her. And then her whole body was gripped with shattering release.

He followed in the next instant, completing her.

They stayed that way, struggling for breath, until the last convulsion ebbed away. He lowered on top of her, briefly resting his head on her shoulder, then rolled onto his back. With one arm, he held her snug against his side. His other wrist rested against his forehead.

Muted wind whistled past their sanctuary. Overhead,

she saw that the clouds had skittered away, leaving a sky laden with stars. Their silvery eyes winked at her.

Wren knew she probably wasn't in her right mind. Yet, she wasn't so addled that she couldn't recognize their lovemaking as the most exciting, honest, and satisfying experience of her life.

Wren rested her hand on Cord's chest, because she could. Because what they'd shared had given her this small ownership of him. Her fingers flicked open the first two buttons of his cotton shirt and she dipped her hand inside, resting her palm against his warm skin. Feeling replete and slumberous, she indulged herself by staring at his profile.

Her body had been yearning for rest, and for the first time since he'd left her she felt safe and comfortable enough to sleep. She smiled at her folly. As if she'd doze now, during this waking dream, every second of which was too precious to waste.

She circled her palm, cherishing the hard contours of him. *I love you.* The words waited on her lips, only as far as the next breath. She longed to say them, and yet she held them back. If he were ever going to speak those words to her, she sensed that he'd need to say them first. "What were you doing in the garden tonight?" she asked quietly.

"I've—" he cleared his throat. "I've been here every night since I brought you home."

Her hand stilled. "Why?"

"I can't stop wanting to protect you," he said, his voice husky. "I kept telling myself not to come here, and I kept coming anyway." He ran his middle finger across her bottom lip.

She shivered, as much from her inner delight as from the chill seeping through the cloak.

"Cold?" he asked.

"No," she replied, mostly because she didn't want him to move and break their bubble of happiness.

He sat up anyway. "Here." He shouldered out of his coat and stripped his shirt over his head.

The sight of his bare upper body, paired with trousers unbuttoned part of the way, made her wonder just how soon was too soon to insist on lovemaking again.

Wren propped up on her elbow, took the shirt from him, and looked for her nightgown. She spotted it beneath the planting table, mashed into the floor. She grinned. Three days—three days!—she'd dressed to perfection for him. The first time she'd left the house looking plain and rumpled, he'd seen her.

She donned his shirt and the smell of him enveloped her. He proffered his brown canvas coat.

"You keep it, Cord."

"Nope, all yours."

She accepted it and was instantly, deliciously dwarfed by the coat's size and sheer maleness. "Thank you." She fastened a couple of the buttons.

He'd changed the bandage around his arm, she noticed. It was smaller now, no longer made of petticoat. Who had fastened it for him? Jealousy needled her. For heaven's sake, he'd probably fastened his own bandage. No need to lose her head. . . .

Too late. She'd lost her head over him long ago. Where this one man was concerned, all logic deserted her. She curled her bare toes into the fabric of his trousers.

Cord was staring at her intensely. She wasn't very

experienced in these matters, but she hoped that look meant he found her arousing. She wanted to lie back down with him, kiss hungrily, make love again and again.

"I'm sorry," he said.

She waited for him to qualify his statement, for the grimness edging his jaw to lessen. When neither happened, she knotted her fingers in the wrinkles of her cloak, needing its support. "Sorry for what just happened between us?" she asked, praying she'd mistaken his meaning.

He nodded, one curt jerk of the chin.

Dread burgeoned, stitching her brows together, robbing her mouth of moisture.

"It shouldn't have happened," he said. "I shouldn't have let it happen."

What? Did he . . . did he not remember who had pushed aside his attempts to keep her chaste? Of course he must remember. Did he think, then, that she had no right to make the decision for herself? "Cord, I was the one—"

"And I was the one who should have been able to control myself. You deserved better—"

"Please, stop! Stop talking like that."

He pushed to his feet in one vicious movement. Once he'd fastened his pants, he paced to the end of the greenhouse, rounded.

She rose unsteadily. It was important, somehow, that she at least stand up to him as an equal.

He paced away, circled again. Faced her. "Marry me."

Hope lifted within her like champagne bubbles fizzing to the surface.

"I want to make this right," he said. "Marry me."

The bubbles stilled, then cascaded down down down.

Something vital ripped open inside her. Cord Caldwell, ever the savior. Ever willing to fix things that were broken. Earnest and honorable. So intent on rescuing her, he'd marry her.

She looked down and slowly began unfastening the buttons on his coat. In her world of dreams and other intangibles, she'd invested too much hope in him. He, who'd never promised her anything, who'd told her outright he'd never been in love and never wanted to marry. Had he truly thought she'd settle for trapping him into a union he didn't want? That she'd be desperate enough to marry a man who didn't love her?

Her eyes sank briefly closed. She didn't need him to rescue her. She needed him to cherish her. Throat burning, she freed the last button, slipped his coat from her shoulders, and extended it to him.

He ignored it. "Marry me," he said again, waiting intently for her answer.

"No."

It was a short word, no, but the pain of it slid into Cord's chest like a foot-long dagger. He'd thought— hoped—she'd actually want to be married to him. God help him, when he'd said the words he'd expected her to accept.

"No," she repeated, impaling him again. "I don't need or want you to save me."

Cord didn't understand. Couldn't she see what he saw? She'd deserved better than what he'd given her on a floor of dirt. She should have had candlelight, chocolate, and silk sheets.

The wrongness of what he'd done crushed down on him, condemning him more surely than any judge or jury.

He'd taken her virginity, for Christ sake. He started to shake, inside and out. Look what he'd done. His Wren. God. She had tears in her eyes.

She'd deserved so much more.

"I insist," he said, his voice cracking, "that you marry me."

Very deliberately, she folded his coat and placed it on the cleanest edge of the table. Still wearing his shirt, she gathered her filthy cloak, nightdress, and shoes.

She was leaving him. Just like that. He rushed forward, slamming his hand against the door just before she tried to open it. "I insist."

Her attention swung to him. "Have you ever wondered why you do this, Cord? Why you always try to make things neat and pretty?"

He waited, chest hitching, a coward because he didn't want to hear what she was about to say. Those silver eyes of hers had insight into him and he'd never wanted to allow her, or anyone, that.

"You're still trying to heal what was broken between your parents," she said. "Trying to make up for what you felt was your fault. Even your job. It's what you do for a living, for goodness sake." Tears shimmered along her lashes, but didn't fall. "Well, I'm not going to let you fix this so that you can feel better about yourself. Some things are just plain awful. There's nothing that can be said or done to make them okay again. There are no shortcuts or substitutes."

She was wrong. Denials rushed to armor him against her words, to save him from a wound that had sunk too deep.

"Let me out," she said, voice flat.

He dropped his hand, and she slipped from the greenhouse.

He stood, stripped of his clothes and every other layer of protection. He watched her move farther and farther away from him.

He'd asked her to marry him, and she'd refused.

His skin pebbled. He couldn't move.

She closed the back door behind her. When she reached her room, she drew the curtains and extinguished the light, leaving him more alone than he'd ever been in a life of aloneness.

Chapter 22

C ord sat on his bed, his chest bare beneath his coat, his head in his hands. The woodstove in the corner of the boardinghouse room slept in gloom, unused. The lamp rested on the beside table, unlit.

His muscles quaked. God. His fingertips dug into his scalp. He'd never stolen any woman's virginity. How *could* he have done so to Wren, whom he . . . what? Whom he loved?

Instinctively, he recoiled at the possibility that he might feel something infinitely deeper for Wren than he had toward anyone else. His heart fled to its familiar hiding place behind old memories, and old fears, and even older pain.

Instead of abating, his misery intensified. The hiding place he'd relied upon for so long wasn't good enough anymore. Just as the hole inside him had grown too big to be ignored. Wren had done this. She'd walked into his life and by her light illuminated the darkness in him. Her passion had shown him his lack. Their relationship had taken him to a plane too high. He couldn't retreat now to the half-life he'd had before and be content with it. She'd left him stranded between what he'd been and what he still had to become.

Ruthlessly, he drug his emotions from behind their dark walls. He scavenged through them, trying hard to be rational in the face of so many aged and twisted belief systems about women and marriage and love.

Did he even know what it meant to be in love? What it felt like? No. He'd no connection with the feeling and few examples of it he trusted.

Snippets of his parents' hatred cracked through his thoughts. The remembrances crooked bony fingers at him, enticing him to hide again. To run. Safer that way. Safer. Safer. Always safer.

Was that the truest test of a man? To be safe?

Cord snarled and pushed to his feet. He pulled his log-book from his saddlebag. The leather-bound volume contoured to his hand, its weight as customary as his own skin.

He carried it to the room's only chair, which rested beside the window. His hands stiff with cold, he lit the lamp on the bedside table and in its light studied the outer edges of the book. Letters wedged the space between the pages and the back binding. He'd purposely avoided noticing how many before. Now he saw that their width made up half the thickness of the book, even though much of the stationery had been flattened wafer-thin with the passage of time.

He pulled free the stack of letters. The first, small and lavender-colored, was dated 1865, the year he'd left for

Harvard. It was addressed to him in the dormitory, his mother's neat scrawl faded by years. He turned it over. The seal she'd affixed still held it tightly closed.

He wished, violently wished, that he were anywhere else but here, doing anything else but this. He didn't even know why he'd kept the damned letters.

Yes he did. Honesty about his past was coming hard.

He'd not read them because he'd refused to be trapped by his mother's and father's bitterness a moment longer. After a childhood of their influence, it was the last thing he'd wanted as a man. Not reading them had been a way of proving to himself how little he needed them and how much he disdained them. So why had he kept the letters at all? He'd kept them because they mattered to him, despite everything.

With a slash of his thumb, he rent the delicate envelope. He needed, at this point in his life, to concentrate on Wren without his parents' legacy polluting his thoughts, and he couldn't do that with all these unread pages carrying reminders in their coal red depths.

Cord let the last letter, written by his father two months ago, slip from his fingers. His chair groaned as he leaned back. He propped his elbow on the windowsill, covered his mouth and chin with his hand, and watched dawn creep over Dallas's main street.

All that he'd read seeped into him, absorbing gradually.

You're still trying to heal what was broken between your parents. Well, I'm not going to let you fix this so that you can feel better about yourself. What Wren had seen in him had been exactly right.

My God. He'd been using his father's devastation as an example of what might happen to him, avoiding any kind of commitment to a woman, and trying through his job to mend things because he'd failed so miserably at mending what was torn between his parents.

He couldn't bear that Wren had refused him, that she'd robbed him of the chance to make things right. It was fundamental to him that he repair what had happened between them. And his past was why. He rubbed at his temple, pressed at the tension around his eyes.

More than a decade's worth of envelopes and stationery littered the floor around him. His gaze swept across it. In all these years his mother and father hadn't changed. Most of their letters held pleas to write or to visit. Some held declarations of love for him, some held inconsequential details about friends and family, several held offers to send him money. *Every* letter held their hatred for one another.

His father had scathingly reported on his mother's alleged affairs. His mother had accused his father of verbal abuse. Evidently they'd separated two years ago and still, his mother was belittling his father at every opportunity and his father was blaming his mother for ruining his life.

Their screams of condemnation, always directed at the other one, had risen in his ears with every word he read. Enough. He closed his eyes and consciously released it. All of it—the past, his guilt, his woundedness.

Their howling immediately stopped, leaving him immersed in silence.

His lids opened, and he looked through gritty, tired eyes at the street beyond his window. His parents were cowards, more willing to wallow in suffering than to change anything about themselves.

"Never again," he whispered. Like them, he'd stayed exactly the same all these years and refused to change. "Never again."

Did he love Wren? He asked himself the question carefully.

Did he love her?

He remembered kneeling over her that first night on the prairie, the way she'd rested her hand against him. He saw her standing behind Aunt Fanny's house with his gun in her hands, smiling at him with triumph. He relived the fulfillment he'd found in comforting her the day he'd taken her from the audition and held her in his lap. He recalled how she'd fought for him at the train and bared herself to him last night.

The depths of her delighted him. Her passion, her intelligence, her humor, her determination, her sadness, her hopefulness. He didn't want any man but him to make love to her, to be the father of her children, to grow old holding her hand.

Wren lived every moment, basking in whatever emotion it brought her. She made him feel as if he'd forever been waiting. Waiting . . .

For her.

Did he love her?

God, yes. If not being able to breathe without her, if caring for her more than for himself, if being willing to risk any pain for the joy of a few days of being adored by her was love, then he loved her completely.

And none of that changed that Wren Bradley had told him no. He'd have gone to her and mounted a full-scale courtship anyway, if it wasn't for the knowledge that in asking her to stay with him he'd be asking her to give up her dream.

He rose, planted his hands on the windowsill, and leaned his forehead against the glass. The smell of dew and wet grass emanated from the chilly surface.

Better than anyone, he knew how hard she'd fought for her dream and her freedom. He'd watched her confront her father, heard her practice for endless hours, seen with his own eyes just how brilliant an actress she was. She desperately wanted to succeed in her career, and she richly deserved to. He'd rather live every day of the rest of his life alone than take that from her.

He couldn't protect her, or make her laugh, or talk with her, or touch her anymore. But there was one thing he could still do for her, one way he could love her from afar. And he knew suddenly, exactly, what that was.

Alexandra sat alone in the buggy, drumming her gloved fingers against her knee. What was keeping him?

She shouldn't have agreed to let Robert drop her by her parents' house. She hadn't wanted to ride with him and could have already been there by now on her own. He'd insisted, however, and she'd acquiesced because she didn't want him to look too close and see the shifting doubts behind her eyes.

She squinted through the unseasonably warm and breezy afternoon toward the front door of her home. Since her discussion with Wren night before last, she'd decided she must talk to Robert. It's just that. . . . What if—and it sickened her that she'd even think it—he *was* Sackett's informant? How far would he go to keep his secret safe and her silent? It was that fear that had kept her from confronting him yet.

Robert strode from the house, thrusting an arm through the second sleeve of his suit jacket as he approached. The sun gilded his ebony hair as he flashed a matched set of dimples at her.

Cheater, she thought. *Heavens possibly a thief, too*.

The buggy dipped when he climbed in.

Alexandra tried to sidle away from him without gaining his notice.

He paused, grinned at her. He seemed filled from the inside out with energy this afternoon. She resented that, had been trying to avoid him for precisely this reason since mother had fetched the children earlier today.

They traveled with no sound between them but the sound of the horses and of wheels clattering over road. Alexandra kept her gaze firmly averted.

When they arrived at the turn to her parent's house, Alex leaned into it, only to have the vehicle continue forward. "Where are we going?"

"I'm taking you on a ride."

She watched her parent's street slip past. "I don't want to go for a ride today, Robert. Wren's expecting me."

"She can wait for a few minutes, can't she?"

"No, we've plans."

"Well." His raven brows lifted. "I've plans, too."

Anxiety flickered. No cause to worry. She told herself that repeatedly as they gained speed. With a queasy feeling in her stomach, Alexandra watched the neighborhoods thin and the countryside approach. She gripped the chair rail and made herself swallow. "Please take me back, Robert."

"Not on your life." He leaned forward, the wind whipping his hair.

Oh, heaven, she'd been a fool to get in the buggy with him. Had he found out that she knew about the stationery? Could he be planning to hurt her, way out here where no one could hear her scream? No. Yes. What should she do? The ground rushed by now, the horses at a full gallop. Should she leap? No, that was too ridiculous. She needed to stop thinking so insanely. He'd not given her cause to jump.

Still, her grip on the chair rail tightened further, and her muscles bunched—at the ready. She hadn't taken this road out of town in years. It led to nowhere, the ruts thinning into tall grass. "Where are you taking me?"

"It's a surprise."

"I demand to know," she said, her voice shrill.

His quizzical look questioned the vehemence of her reaction. "All right, then," he murmured. The horses lunged from their hectic pace into a quick trot. "Look," he said, smiling, tilting his head forward.

She turned in the direction he'd indicated just as they topped a small rise. Before them. . . .

Oh, my Lord.

Before them sat a house. The horses slowed to a walk, and then the buggy stopped with a gentle rock. Not just any house. *Her house.* The house of her dreams.

"Surprise," Robert whispered.

Trancelike, she stumbled from her seat onto the ground. The home was almost exactly, no, *exactly* as she'd imagined it. Three dormer windows pressed outward from the roof. Stone walls, marked with oversize, gleaming windows comprised the sides.

She walked toward it, not believing what she was seeing. The shiny green shutters matched the front door, which was framed by elegant ivory molding. A porch encircled the entire structure, and wooden furniture already sat upon it in cozy companionship with wispy ferns she vaguely recognized from her mother's greenhouse.

She pressed her hands to her cheeks as she walked up the two steps onto the porch. Her heart swelled to thrice its size with amazement, and confusion, and an astonishment so thorough it made her feel as if she'd just staggered off an hour-long ride on a carousel.

Her fingertips stroked over the brass door knocker and door handle. She glanced to Robert, who'd followed her. He was beaming.

"Can I go in?" she asked.

"Of course. It's yours."

She entered to a collage of impressions. A generous entry hall. Lamps shedding warm, gold light. Wooden floors so highly polished, she could see her reflection in them. Airy rooms waiting for her to enliven them with decoration. It was so incredibly grand. Tasteful, inviting, and generously sized. Precisely her style.

Her jaw had dropped at some point. She closed it and turned to regard Robert, who stood with his arms crossed, looking smugly pleased with himself.

"I don't understand. How did you . . ."

"Like this." He moved past her into the hallway, and gestured to an enormous grouping of framed artwork.

She drew even with the first picture in line, and her heart fired. Her own artwork. The scribble she'd drawn of this house just days ago in Robert's office, still bearing the wrinkles from when she'd crumpled it.

"I changed the front doorknob because of that one." He chuckled.

Robert had used her recent sketches as blueprints. Every detail, down to the doorknob of this house, was a precise replica of her latest drawings. "I'm astonished," she breathed, making her way down the hall. Pictures she'd thought she'd thrown away. Pictures she'd drawn when she and Elizabeth had been coloring together. Pictures on scraps of paper, on stationery, one on fabric. Pictures her mother must have saved from her childhood without her knowing. A whole wall, commemorating the development of her dream.

A lopsided gingerbread house was last in line. Along the bottom her mother had written, "Alexandra, age 6."

"I considered adding the candy-cane fence," Robert said. "But I worried about ants."

She faced him. "How on earth can we afford this place?"

"I've been saving a bit here and there since I first learned this was something you wanted." He stroked her cheek. "Since we began building, I've been spending a third of my income on it."

She was afraid to hope that he hadn't been cheating on her all these months, that he hadn't built this home with money stolen from the railroad. She had to be honest with him before there would be any clean room inside her for gratitude. "Oh, Robert. You've no idea what's been going through my mind these past weeks."

"Overseeing the building of this place demanded a lot of my time, I know. I'm sorry about that."

"I've been concerned about much more than your absence, I'm afraid." She pooled her resolve and told him everything, from Theodora to the sailboat stationery.

When she'd finished, he regarded her without speaking for a few moments. His Adam's apple bobbed. "Theo— Theodora is the woman who sewed these curtains for me." He gestured toward the draperies visible in the parlor across the hall. "She's seventy, I'll introduce you. As for the bankbook . . . the secret account was for the house. I wanted to surprise you."

"I never dreamed you were building me a house," Alex answered. "There was never a single hint."

"I was careful." His brow darkened with anger.

"What about the sailboat stationery?" she asked, desperately hoping he could refute the evidence.

"I can't explain that one away, Alex. Except to say that I had noticed a month or so ago that my supply of that stationery seemed lower than it should have been. I shrugged it off." He shook his head, lips thin. "I'm not robbing trains, and I certainly didn't use that stationery to send letters to Lloyd Sackett. How could you even believe that of me?"

"We'd grown distant . . . I worried I might not know you anymore."

"But adultery?" His dark eyes flashed with pain. "Stealing from the Southern Atlantic, for God's sake?"

"The evidence kept stacking up."

"Then *why* didn't you say anything to me?"

"I was afraid to."

"You've never been fearful."

"I was about this." With her expression, she begged him to understand. "I was afraid to find out that you might not love me anymore."

"Alex." His tone was ripe with frustration. "We should have talked about this right at the beginning."

"I agree. I—I thought I'd pushed the doubts aside, but instead I'd pushed them down. They just kept piling up inside, and the more afraid I grew, the more real they seemed."

"I can account for every penny I spent on this house," Robert said. "Every one of them was earned legitimately—"

"Sh." She pressed her fingers against his lips, stilling his defense of himself. It hurt too much to hear it anymore. The truth of his innocence was in his eyes, as plain and clear as water. She ran her fingertip along his cheek and chin. "I believe you." And she did.

Visibly, his anxiety drained away.

"I'm sorry, Robert, for mistrusting you. I'm the one at fault."

He grabbed her hand, cushioned it between his. "I don't want you *ever* to think I don't love you. You're the most precious person to me in the world."

Tears clogged her throat. "Can you forgive me for suspecting such awful things about you?"

He nodded. "Yes, but talk to me the next time."

"I will."

"Can you forgive me for neglecting you to the point you suspected me a thief and cheater?"

She laughed with pure relief. "Yes." Her husband was still the man she'd fallen in love with, and he'd pardoned her for doubting that. His humor proved it.

"I'm never surprising you again," Robert murmured, teasing in his tone. "Too damaging to the marriage." He kissed the tip of each of her fingers.

Desire burgeoned in rippling hot ribbons within her. *This is mine*, she thought, looking at him, peering at the house around her with new eyes now that her worries had been banished. A storm of revelation and joy tumbled within her. "Thank you, Robert, for this. I know 'thank you' isn't enough, but thank you."

"It is enough." He wrapped his arms around her waist. "All our marriage, I've longed to do this for you."

They kissed softly, with the miracle of rediscovery that came sometimes even after years of marriage and two children.

"Here," he said, leaning toward the back door. "There's something else." He twisted the knob and pushed the door open.

Beyond, a ribald cheer arose.

Delighted shivers coasted down her arms. "Who's here?"

"Everyone. We had a devil of a time hiding their carriages."

She walked onto the back porch and grinned like a fool at the crowd assembled there. Her mother and father, holding Elizabeth and Robbie. Wren. Nanny, Cook, Edward, and a host of other friends.

Alexandra didn't have words to capture the soaring of her spirit. She and Robert descended toward the gathering. Both her children raced forward, meeting them halfway.

Robbie squealed, hugging her hard, then extending his chubby arms toward his father. Robert swept him up.

"Isn't it beautiful?" Elizabeth asked her.

"It's so beautiful, sweetest." She embraced her daughter. "The most beautiful house in the world."

"I know!" Elizabeth replied. "It's ours."

"Imagine that." Appreciation for all she'd been given brimmed inside her.

"Can we go play?" Robbie asked.

"Sure," Robert answered. "I'll take you over to the other children." As they wandered off, her parents and Wren approached. Edward followed close behind Wren.

"Did you know about this?" Alexandra asked them, brows raised, smile disbelieving.

"Mother and Pa have known for months," Wren answered, "as they informed me this morning on the way here. No one, apparently, felt I could keep the secret." Wren smiled, for Alexandra's benefit. Her sister was luminous. She was incredibly glad Alexandra's suspicions had been unfounded and that things had ended so wondrously well for her.

"I find this spot to be the prettiest in Dallas," Edward said near her ear. "Don't you agree?"

"Wholeheartedly."

"I'd like to build you a splendid house here one day."

"That's a very kind offer," Wren replied.

"We could travel to New Orleans to shop for furniture. Wouldn't that be nice?"

Since she'd declined his proposal, Edward had visited her every day. The man's relentless pursuit had become downright annoying.

Her attention strayed to the children playing tag. Her niece and nephew ran to join them as Robert moved to the tables to shake hands with some of the men from the railroad. Wren watched without really seeing as Edward's voice mingled with those of her family. She wondered what Cord was doing at this very moment. At least she knew he was still in Dallas hunting the railroad's mole. Pa had promised he'd tell her when Cord left. She dreaded that news, though she didn't know why. His departure could hardly make things worse than they already were. The hours since their lovemaking, a terrible string of them that amounted to a day and a half now, had been the most agonizing of her life.

". . . have news of your own," Alexandra was saying.

"Wren?" Edward said after a slight pause. "You sister just asked you a question."

"Oh." Her gaze jerked to her sister.

"When Mother dropped by to pick up the children this morning," Alexandra said, "she mentioned that you have had news of your own."

"Yes, a telegram from the director of the traveling troupe."

Edward abruptly turned on his heel and stalked away. Mother looked after him with a troubled frown, but Wren was relieved. The only thing she could count on to drive him off lately was his intolerance for anything to do with her profession.

"Do you have it with you?" Alexandra asked. "I'd love to see."

Wren appreciated what Alexandra was trying to do— deflect some of the attention and excitement to her. Maybe she should pull Alexandra aside later and whisper that she needn't bother. She preferred to be alone and unnoticed in her current, miserable state. She reached into her pocket and handed over the perplexing telegram she'd received this morning.

Wren had memorized every word Alexandra was reading. It seemed that someone had given a large sum of money to the troupe—for her. The director had written to tell her that not only would she be able to afford hotel rooms, better-class train passage, and a porter to carry as many trunks of luggage as she wished, but that the entire troupe had been endowed with money enough for new costumes and better sets.

Alexandra whistled as she handed the paper back. "Who do you suppose gave the money on your behalf?"

"Aunt Fanny. She's the only one Mother and Pa and I could think of."

"Probably so. Aunt Fanny has always been a great supporter of your acting. Not to mention that she has more money than she knows how to spend." Alexandra reached for her hand and clasped her fingers warmly. "That's wonderful, Wren. I'm thrilled that you'll be able to travel in such comfort."

"Thank you."

"Isn't that excellent news?" Alexandra asked their parents.

"Yes, very good," Pa replied.

Mother nodded. "Delightful—"

Just then a howl sliced the air. Wren located the source of it immediately—a skinny little girl of about four had fallen to the ground. It was Mabel, the friend of Elizabeth's they'd picked up this morning and brought in their buggy. Her mother wasn't here.

Wren picked up her skirts and charged across the expanse of grass. She hadn't been the closest, but by far she'd been the quickest to reach the girl. She scooped the child up. Mabel, red-faced and openmouthed with sobbing, pointed to her knee.

Alexandra rushed over. "Is she all right?"

"Only a scrape," Wren murmured. "I've got her." Wren wove through the throng of curiously staring children, her heated bundle nestled in her arms. She took Mabel around the far side of the house, and out of sight. Then she examined the cut, rocked her, and continuously reassured the enormous brown eyes that everything would be okay.

The girl wrapped her arms around Wren's neck and

laid her cheek against her heart. Her crying became snuffles as her breathing evened out.

After a few minutes, Wren peeked down at her. "Ready to go back and play?"

The girl nodded, and Wren set her carefully on her feet.

"Thank you, Miss Wren, for saving me." She smiled, then ran with a darling, stiff-legged gait around the corner.

Wren's heart contracted. She hadn't thought . . . she'd just acted . . . she'd done exactly what Cord would have done had he been here. A month ago, she'd have turned toward the girl's crying, frowned, been concerned, doubtless started toward the child too late. Today, she'd registered the cry and simply raced to help.

"Oh," she breathed. "Oh." She leaned heavily against the side of the house. It was her turn to bleed and cry. Scalding tears tumbled over her lashes.

Cord had inspired her to be better. How could he do this to her? She mopped heedlessly at her tears with the backs of her hands. Why couldn't he allow her to hate him? Must he be so good? Wasn't it enough that she'd given him everything freely, and he hadn't loved her? Was it necessary that he care for lost children and mop up orange juice with his sleeves?

How *could* he have left her alone to do his job for him? It was his job to do these things. Not hers. Not *hers*. Her heartache rattled her shoulders uncontrollably.

Maybe she'd been filled with unforgivable pride to have refused him. Maybe she should have accepted his marriage proposal. It was certainly more than he offered most women. But then what would she have done? Given up her dream of acting so she could sit at home darning his socks, waiting for him to come back to her from one of his extended assignments, and regretting that she'd forced him to marry her out of pity?

Her lungs ached with her weeping. At least this way she had standards and could hold her head up in public. She was lonely and wretched without him, would probably spend the rest of her life dashing to help people in honor of a man who didn't love her, but she had her standards.

She abhorred her standards.

Chapter 23

❧

Cord stood on the threshold to Edward's bedroom. He'd already searched the rest of the house to no avail. This was the final room. The party the Colonel had mentioned to him, the one celebrating Alexandra's new home, would surely keep Edward away another hour.

Ordinarily, he solved his cases before the need for picking the locks and breaking into suspects' houses became necessary. But he'd been working hard on this case, and still nothing. He'd already searched the home of the Colonel's secretary for clues, without success. If he found nothing here, he'd move on to Robert Todd's house, then Honeywell's.

He was getting desperate to find the informant so he could get the hell out of this city. It was driving him mad to be here. On the streets he couldn't look left or right without searching for a beautiful blond slip of a woman wearing a jewel-toned dress, a heart-shaped locket, and a fashionable hat.

Soundlessly, he made his way into the bedroom to the rolltop desk. Drawer after drawer, compartment after compartment, he checked for something he'd recognize when he saw it. Some clue, some piece of evidence he could use.

He abandoned the desk and moved to the bed. Nothing underneath it. His hands ran over the covers and beneath the pillows, searching for anything hidden. Nothing was amiss. He worked his way through both bedside tables and the dresser.

Everything in the room, just like everything in the rest of the house was orderly, clean, and perfectly respectable. He struggled to keep his personal dislike of the man from influencing his suspicions.

The doors of the armoire slid open noiselessly. Cord frowned at the array of suits hanging within. He checked the labels, noting that they'd all been tailored. Excellent quality. Once he'd worked his way through the garments' pockets without success, he searched the shoes lined along the bottom. They rested on a precisely cut rectangular piece of carpeting.

He pulled a corner of the carpeting back an inch, then farther. The shoes tumbled together. A seam in the wood revealed itself.

For the first time in quite a while, Cord's interest in the case surged. With a heave, he cleared the carpet and the shoes. Beneath, a square piece of wood rested flush against the armoire's false bottom. It was cleverly constructed. From the front, the added depth of the secret chamber was concealed by scrolling woodwork.

Cord lifted out the square of wood, hoping he'd find all manner of damning evidence within. He found a thin stack of stationery, ivory with a sailboat embossed in blue. And a green velvet box.

"Well, I'll be damned," he whispered. He'd solved the case. The stationery was circumstantial—not enough to arrest or convict Edward as Sackett's informant. Still, whenever Cord found an important piece of the puzzle, like this, he always knew he'd solved the case. It was only a matter of time before the other pieces slotted into place.

Damn if Edward Clifton hadn't been stealing money from the railroad his future father-in-law protected. That slimy, shiny-faced bastard.

He thumbed open the lid of the velvet box. A platinum-and-diamond ring nestled within. Wren's ring, he realized. Jealousy and frustration hovered at the edge of his thoughts.

The diamond was huge. He lifted the ring from its bed, walked to the window, and held it to the sunlight. The color was clear as glass, without a single imperfection visible to the naked eye. His instincts stirred, speeding his heartbeat and raising the small hairs on the back of his neck.

Not a single one of his suspects had done anything to reveal that he possessed a fortune in railroad money. Until now. The ring was a slip. He'd worked a few cases in the past dealing with stolen jewelry, and recognized this diamond as something only an oil baron could afford. Edward's salary as an accountant was substantial, but not in the same league as this ring.

He turned the velvet ring box over. The words, "Maxwell's, Atlanta, Georgia," were emblazoned in genteel silver script on the bottom.

He didn't want to tip Edward off until he had evidence in hand, so Cord went through the motions of replacing the ring and the ring box, aligning the stationery, and righting the armoire. His mind clicked over his next course of action. One of his Pinkerton operative buddies was based in Atlanta. He'd send him a telegram immediately and have him visit Maxwell's to find out just how much Edward had paid for his gem.

Cord heard back from his friend in Atlanta the following morning. He read the contents of the message as soon as he received it, standing in the telegrapher's office.

Edward had paid for the ring at Maxwell's with a draft from a local bank account. Cord's Pinkerton friend had used his operative's authority to discover that the account contained five thousand dollars.

Cord looked up from the paper. The tapping of the instruments punctuated the realization that he had just secured his evidence. He was glad to wash his hands of this godforsaken assignment, gravely satisfied that he'd caught Edward, and yet sorry for the hurt Edward's betrayal would cause Wren and the rest of the Colonel's family.

Wren. A physical pain clenched him.

The telegram went on to say that Edward had left forwarding information with his Atlanta bankers, pointing to another account at another bank should he need to transfer his funds quickly. The Pinkerton man had found another five thousand at the second account. All told, he'd followed the trail, one bank account at a time, until he'd uncovered a twenty-five-thousand-dollar fortune.

Cord pocketed the telegram and shouldered from the building.

Cord found the Colonel and Robert sitting across from one another inside the older man's office at the Southern Atlantic.

The Colonel waved him in. "I'm glad you're here, Cord. Robert was just telling me about the stationery the informant used. White with a blue sailboat on it."

"It belongs to me," Robert said. He turned in his chair to frown up at Cord. "I didn't write the letter to Sack-ett—"

"I know. Edward did. In case any of the letters were discovered, he was probably trying to cast suspicion on you."

Cord's words seemed to swirl through the stunned quiet that followed.

"Edward?" Grooves delved into Robert's forehead.

Cord nodded. "Edward bought an expensive engagement ring from a jewelry store called Maxwell's in Atlanta. I had an agency man check the account that paid for the ring." He withdrew the telegram and set in on the Colonel's desk.

Robert walked behind his father-in-law to read the contents over his shoulder.

Once they'd finished reading, Robert regarded him gravely. The Colonel rubbed his hand slowly down his face, then shook his head at what Cord knew must seem to him like a colossal waste of potential and promise.

As little as Cord liked Edward, the pain the man's guilt was causing the Colonel gave him no pleasure. "I'm sorry, sir."

"So am I. More than I can say."

A knock sounded. They looked up to see Edward standing on the other side of the door's glass panel.

"Enter," the Colonel said after a few beats. He pushed to his feet so that they were all standing as Edward let himself inside.

"I came to bring you the report I . . ." His gaze moved cautiously around the circle of men, pausing noticeably upon Cord. "What's wrong?"

The Colonel sighed wearily. "Cord is going to have to hold you for questioning, Edward."

"Why?"

"Because we've discovered evidence that implicates you as Lloyd Sackett's informant."

"That's preposterous!"

Cord watched Edward for signs of guilt. The man gave few away, yet. He was cool, he was smart, and he was a thief in businessmen's clothes.

"What possible proof do you have to support these allegations?" Edward asked Cord, his hazel eyes fiery with indignation.

"Bank accounts in your name spread across the country," Cord answered. "All told, they contain a little more than twenty-five-thousand dollars."

Moisture beaded on Edward's pale upper lip.

"Are you going to try and tell us that money doesn't belong to the Southern Atlantic?" the Colonel asked.

Edward looked to the Colonel. His navy vest expanded and contracted with suddenly shallow breaths. His attention shot back to Cord, shifted again to the Colonel. Cord could almost see the cage lowering over the man.

Sadness, but no pity or understanding showed on the Colonel's face. "What do you have to say for yourself?"

Edward dashed from the office.

Cord was after him instantly. He chased Edward down the hallway and into the office's central room, filled with milling secretaries and rows of desks. The occupants let out a gasp as Edward and Cord barreled through their space.

Edward skirted a desk, threw a chair into Cord's path. Cord leapt it easily. He sprinted down the aisle, gaining, until he drew close and snagged a handful of Edward's jacket.

Cord skidded, viciously jerking Edward to a halt.

Edward hurled an arm upward as he turned toward Cord, glancing an elbow off Cord's chin. Cord sucked at the pain, relishing it compared to the pain he'd been living with since losing Wren. He threw his muscle behind an uppercut that sent Edward sprawling onto the floor.

Amid the muffled retreat of the secretaries, Cord saw the Colonel and Robert stream into the room.

Edward staggered to his knees, testing his jaw with shaking fingers.

"Don't get up unless you want more," Cord said, his breath coming hard.

Edward's hair was rumpled, his trousers filmed with dust from the wood floor. He growled, and tried to stand once again, but the Colonel planted a hand on Edward's shoulder, keeping him down.

"I wouldn't if I were you," the Colonel said. He looked to the secretary standing nearest. "Fetch the sheriff."

"Yes, sir."

"I'm not such an old detective that I don't still carry a pair of cuffs," the Colonel said as he pulled some from beneath his suit coat. His gaze darkened with betrayal. "I knew of your ambition and admired you for it. I trusted you."

Edward looked at him beseechingly. "You have to let me explain."

The Colonel's lips twisted as he snapped the cuffs onto the younger man's wrists. "I know the truth when I see it. You had every chance in life, and you threw them away for money you'll never spend."

Edward's face reddened. Beneath his customary control, Cord recognized raw resentment and fury. "What the hell do you know about what chance I had?" Edward demanded.

"Everything I need to know," the Colonel answered quietly.

Wren was sitting on the floor of her room, packing her trunks that evening when she heard her father let himself into the house.

At the sound, her heart started to thud. He brought bad news, she just knew it.

After a brief conversation with Mother in the foyer, his footfalls could be heard on the stairs.

She set aside the paisley shawl she'd been folding and waited. He knocked, precisely as she'd expected him to.

"Come in."

He made his way a few feet into her room, but stopped at the edge of her folded piles. "Evening, Precious." He smiled tiredly.

"Evening."

His attention traveled over the open trunks. "So you really are leaving us tomorrow morning?"

"Yes, I guess I really am."

He nodded slowly, thoughtfully.

Using her arms, she pulled herself up so that she was sitting on her bed. "Is something the matter?"

"It's Edward. He was the one sending Sackett information about our trains."

So Cord had found his man. Edward. Surprise and sorrow trickled through her, but neither emotion went deep. She'd wondered over the past days if Edward could be capable of such a thing. Worried, truthfully, that he might be after the wretchedly insecure side of himself he'd revealed the day he'd proposed. "I'm so sorry, Pa."

Edward's poor parents. And hers, too. They'd known Edward and liked him all his life.

"I was more concerned about you," Pa responded.

She didn't feel up to explaining how insignificant was her disappointment over Edward compared to her anguish over Cord. So she answered simply, "Thank you for that. I'm fine."

"Very well." He walked to the door, paused holding onto the outside knob. "You asked me to tell you when Mr. Caldwell left town."

Her muscles tensed. "Yes."

"He left today."

"Today?" she asked weakly.

"This afternoon, as soon as Edward was in the sheriff's custody and Cord was certain we had all the information we needed to prosecute."

"Oh."

"He was needed in Houston."

The despair coursing through her was so black and complete that she couldn't speak. The second her father closed the door, she huddled facedown on her bed and sobbed. Scalding tears that had no end melted into the familiar pink-and-yellow quilt of her childhood.

He'd truly gone. Oh God. He'd left her when she loved him so.

Chapter 24

Wren waved to her family one last time and climbed the steps leading into her train car. Her chest felt unbearably tight with the effort it was costing her not to make a scene. Her mother and sister were painfully upset as it was to be saying good-bye. A brave, cheerful facade from her was imperative.

She carried her bag in front as she made her way down the aisle to her seat. Once she'd settled in, she gazed out her window and confirmed that her family had kept their promise. They were already walking down the depot platform away from her. She'd asked them to do so. Her departure was hard enough without prolonging it, staring at them through a window for long minutes, then having to watch as they slipped from view with tear-stained faces.

No, they'd had a lovely breakfast. They'd brought her to the depot, and at the very first call for passengers to

Austin, Wren had hugged them and quickly boarded.

Of course, now that she was sitting all alone, strangers milling about her, she second-guessed her choice. Maybe she should have clung to them for as long as possible.

Happy day, she told herself. *This is a happy day. You're traveling to become an actress, just what you've always wanted.* Her spirits sank lower. Steam from the engine floated by her window in curling wisps. The conductor strode past, one arm bent smartly behind his back, the other clasping his pocket watch.

Whatever you do, don't search for Cord, she thought. She watched a mother herd her children down the platform. Saw a man unloading cargo from a cart into his wagon. More people bustled into her car, finding seats.

Inexorably, her gaze began to search for the one man she most wanted to be present, the one who wasn't and wouldn't be. *Stop it*, she told herself. *He's not here. He's in Houston.* But as she'd been doing since her arrival at the station, she hunted for him anyway. She'd never felt so pitiful or desperate in her life as she did now, sitting here, frantically seeking something so hopeless. But she couldn't stop herself.

Her eyes strained, trying to find him near a lamppost, beneath the station's overhang, loitering in the alcove of an arched brick doorway—

She gasped. A hat, a stained beige Stetson, jerked from view beneath a distant alcove. She leaned forward, pressing her palm and the tip of her nose to the glass. *Cord.* It had to be him. That Stetson had looked for all the world like his renegade hunter's hat.

Her pulse thundered in her ears. She'd never concentrated as ferociously as she concentrated her sight, her will, and her heart on that brick archway.

Nothing. The hat didn't reappear. The conductor walked past again, checking his watch.

Wren sprang to her feet. "Excuse me." She shuffled past the gentleman who'd just lowered into the seat beside her.

"Ma'am, your bag," he said.

Wren ignored him, murmuring a string of rushed "excuse me's" as she wove in and out of the people crowding the car. Anxiety mounted. She had to get *out*. There'd be no living with herself if she didn't go to check, to make certain it wasn't him. *It was him*, though, a tiny, calm voice whispered. *It* was *him*.

It wasn't. She was insane, she knew it. This was the low point of her existence. Bunching her indigo skirts in one hand and elevating them enough so she could run, she leapt onto the platform and hurried toward the red brick arch. The longing that had tugged at her every time she'd ever laid eyes on Cord Caldwell pulled at her now, drew her recklessly, faster, forward. Let it be him. Let it be him.

When she was five yards from the alcove, he stepped into the opening. Her eyes met his in a shriek of sparks that sounded to her like the clash of metal on metal. Her Legend in the flesh. Cord. Everything about him was blessedly familiar; the way his hands were buried in his pockets, the brown canvas coat, eyes the color of the ocean, the ruggedly square jaw.

Her feet cut to a halt. *You see*, the soft voice whispered. *It's him. He came . . . for you.*

She could do nothing but gape.

The sight of Wren, so close, struck Cord bodily. He froze, his skin pebbling.

She was gorgeous, with her gown of blue, the wisps of fine blond hair at her forehead, the cheeks that he knew stood out when she smiled, the eyes that were gray in this moment like a sparkling sky after a thunderstorm. Even her hands, the hollow of her throat, the necklace she wore. All pieces that made up who she was. Wren, the woman he'd fantasized about a thousand times since he'd seen her last.

"I thought you'd gone," she said.

"I wanted to," he said, finding it hard to speak. "I couldn't."

She walked past him into the brick alcove beyond. He followed. The square of space inside housed an unused door, so it was quiet and private.

"What are you doing here?" she asked.

"I can't explain it." He doffed his hat with one hand, used his other to rake through his hair. God, he'd not wanted her to see him. So why did he feel like kneeling at her feet because she had? Everything in him trembled to beg her to stay, to love him even half as much as he loved her. Ruthlessly, for her own good, he tamped the words back. He'd never forgive himself if she didn't get on that train as she was destined to. "I wanted to honor you, I guess, by being here."

"Honor me?"

"It was my way of paying my respects to you and your dream."

"All aboard!" the conductor called, his booming voice rolling through their alcove.

Wren flinched.

Cord ground his jaw. "You'd best be going." It cost him a year of his life to utter the words.

"You," Wren whispered. Her gaze roved down the entire length of him, then back to his face. "You're the one that gave all that money to the troupe on my behalf.

So that I could bring trunks of clothing and stay in hotels and eat good meals. It was you, wasn't it?"

"No."

"Yes, it was," she said. Because it had been a wild, secret hope of hers since she'd received the telegram from the director, a hope she suddenly suspected to be true. There was only one person who championed her dream more than Aunt Fanny, and it was Cord.

Tears pricked her eyes. "You spent the money you'd been saving all these years for your ranch. On me. Is that what you did?" If he'd only give her a little something, some sign, some hint to trust in. Anything that would show her he returned her feelings.

He looked toward the train, anguish clear on his profile.

And she knew then that was exactly what he'd done. He'd sacrificed his dream to make hers sweeter. With that knowledge came more—he'd not speak first because he refused to ruin her chance with the traveling troupe. Which meant if she wanted him, she'd have to tell him.

Her mouth went completely dry, and for a moment she felt dizzy with terror. She heard his words from five years before. *While I like you as a person, very much, my feelings toward you aren't romantic.* She saw him take Robin Wentworth in his arms and dance away from her. She saw him standing half-naked in her mother's greenhouse insisting she marry him for the wrong reason. She couldn't do it again. She simply *couldn't* set herself up for devastation one more time.

"All aboard!" the conductor called.

She couldn't possibly. But for Cord, for him, she somehow would. For her love of him she'd strip her heart bare this one last time and risk all.

"Go," he said softly. "It's what you want, Wren."

"Yes. I want that. Acting is part of who I am, and I'll never be able to give it up. I also know that there will be more opportunities for me than just this one." She discovered she was twisting her necklace. She dropped it, fisted her hands. "You see, what I've always wanted most of all was to become a woman and to make my own choices. And at this moment, there's only one thing in the world I want more than to be a member of that traveling troupe." She took a breath. "And it's you."

His gaze searched her face, and in his expression she recognized a longing he couldn't quite cover. It gave her courage.

"I love you madly," she said. "And I pray you love me, too."

He looked as if he didn't dare believe her. For all the women who'd adored him, no one, including his parents had ever truly loved him, and he looked afraid to trust that she might. "Will you have me?" she asked, her voice breaking.

Cord prayed a crazy backward prayer of thanks so gut deep he could barely find the words. She was everything in the world to him. In one step he had her in his arms. He cradled both his hands behind her head. Their lips met, tongues intertwined. Warmth passed from her into him, filling him, uncurling into his hollow places, bringing him life. He walked her back, until her shoulders came up against the wall, and still he kissed her. His thumbs rubbed across her cheeks. He tasted her, loved her, worshiped her.

In the distance, the whistle blew and the train chugged forward, away from the station.

Their kiss turned into a string of softer, lustier kisses, interspersed with rubbing of noses, nuzzling, nipping of lips, and tasting of tongues.

Wren pressed her fingertips to his cheek, absorbing the heat there, reassuring herself that he was real.

He looked her straight in the eyes. "I love you, Wren."

She inhaled sharply, savoring the rush of joy his declaration brought. So much to hold within this one inadequate body.

His hands coasted down to her waist. "Marry me," he murmured.

"Say it again."

"Be my wife."

Lordy, he looked intense.

"Please, have me. I can't live without you."

She brought him to her for another kiss. Oh, to smell him again, the scents of leather and wind, was unspeakably good. Against his lips she whispered, "I would adore, more than anything else in life, to marry you."

"Yes?" he asked, pulling back just enough to study her face.

"A hundred times yes."

Cord gave her the thousand-degree, I-know-what-you-look-like-naked smile.

Her tummy did a slow, complete flip.

There was a happiness in his eyes that surpassed anything she'd ever seen in them before. There was no greater glory than this, to own the love of a sapphire-eyed, squared-jawed cowboy with a heart of gold. "Do you think there's time to get your money back from the troupe and buy some property for the two of us?" she asked.

"Hell, yes." Cord winked and shifted against her so sensually, her insides sizzled into flames. "I'll leave them some for their costumes and sets, just to soften the blow of losing you."

"It'll be a terrible blow to them, I'm sure." She smiled.

"Would have been fatal for me." He kissed her earlobe, her neck. "The rest of the money will be just for us."

"A place of our own."

"Maybe a theater, too."

"Yes, a theater, too." She trapped his face between her hands. "Cord, of all my dreams *you* are the only one I cannot live without."

"And you are the only dream I've ever known." He pulled her flush against him and captured her mouth in a kiss ripe with a yearning that stretched backward in time and forward to a future brighter than the sun.

Epilogue

Spring, 1879

Cord sat in the middle of the darkened theater, his seven-month-old daughter asleep in the crook of his arm. Though little Madeline was an angel and a beauty, he only had eyes for her mother at the moment.

Wren moved across the stage holding his heart in her hand and the enthralled attention of every member of the audience. The opening night of the first production of the small, local troupe they'd formed was an enormous success. He didn't need to hear the applause or the comments from the audience to know it. The performance had been a bloody masterpiece. In his wife, Dallas had just discovered a star. He'd need to take her to Broadway soon.

She was speaking the last lines of dialogue. He knew

the play by heart, had spent hours practicing with her at home in the evenings.

The final word held on the air, then drifted away. For a long moment, a hush covered the gathering. Then the curtain began to sweep closed and the clapping began.

Cord was the first one on his feet, grinning, and slapping his thigh because he had his daughter in his other arm. God, he was happy for Wren. And so damn proud.

Madeline jerked awake, and peered up at him, eyes wide. He smiled down at her, kissed her on her nose. Delighted, she squeezed her shoulders toward her chin and awarded him with a baby grin. "Your mother's a genius," he whispered.

Wren's entire family cheered from their seats alongside him, each face lit with delight.

The curtain swept open, and the minor actors and actresses took their bows. Last of all, it was Wren's turn. She walked regally to the center of the stage, fairly shining, and took her first bow. Cord whooped, and slapped his thigh harder.

Wren spotted Cord in the crowd immediately. He was smiling broadly, cradling their daughter in his muscled arm, standing beside her parents and Alexandra's family. She loved him so entirely, was bursting with such happiness, that the world around him seemed to be spinning. Only he was constant.

She swept out her arms and bent into another low and graceful bow. When she rose, her eyes were watering. Here they came again, happy tears. No matter. She could still see Cord through them. And as soon as she finished bowing, he'd hold her and kiss them away, and once they got home tonight he'd make slow, sweet love to her until morning. Lordy, but she was the luckiest woman in all the world.

The audience was still cheering. She glanced side to side at her fellow cast members, nodded once, and they all bowed again in unison.

She remembered standing in a flower bed years ago thinking her happy ending was just seconds away. Her gaze met Cord's as she straightened.

"I love you," he mouthed.

"I love you," she said back, over the uproarious applause. Her happy ending had taken longer than she'd supposed, followed a path she'd never expected.

But, *oh*. It had been worth the wait.

**Take a break from the holiday hustle
and bustle with Avon Romance.
Two fantastic love stories . . . by two
unforgettable authors.**

She's the Rita Award-winning author who is
also known as Ruth Wind . . .

Don't miss **Barbara Samuel's**

NIGHT OF FIRE

Imagine Cassandra St. Ives' surprise when she discovers her secret admirer is no proper gentleman . . . but a virile stranger who knows her heart's desires.

She's been called "a superior writer" by
Romantic Times . . .

Don't miss **Margaret Evans Porter's**

IMPROPER ADVANCES

Darius thinks the stunning widow Oriana Julian is a scheming adventuress . . . but she stirs in him an undeniable passion he is powerless to resist.

Avon Romances—
the best in exceptional authors and unforgettable novels!